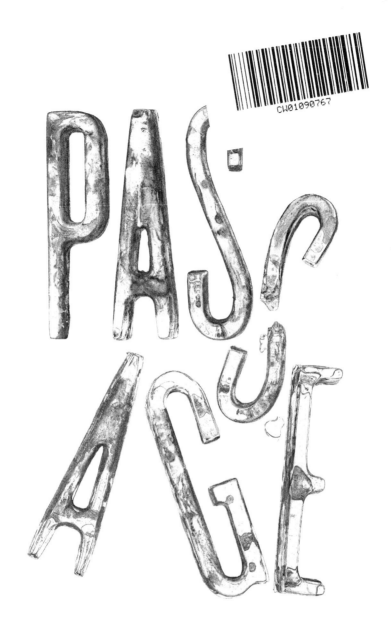

Passage

Angus Wardlaw

Daredevil Books

Daredevil Books
'Dangerously Good Reads'

DAREDEVIL

This Daredevil Books edition first published in 2023

A catalogue record for this book is available from the British Library

Hardback ISBN: 978-1-7393932-2-9
Paperback ISBN: 978-1-7393932-3-6

Typeset in Adobe Garamond Pro by Jill Sawyer

At Daredevil Books we are committed to improving environmental
performance by driving down CO_2 emissions and reducing, reusing and
recycling waste. We support sustainable forest management and ensure
that no paper is sourced from endangered old growth forests, forests of
exceptional conservation value, or the Amazon Basin.

www.daredevilbooks.co.uk

For Barney.
Best son in the world and descendant of
Captain F. R. M. Crozier, RN.

Unfortunately, too much of this story is true. However, most of it is made up because many of the facts about Sir John Franklin and his search for the Northwest Passage have been forgotten, lost or assumed – often incorrectly. And whilst it is impossible to know what happened to Sir John Franklin's men with any certainty, it is safe to assume that they would have endured the most dreadful privations during their passage through one of the harshest environments on earth. This novel is an attempt to bring their journey to life using the frustratingly scant, incoherent evidence that Franklin and his men splayed across the western coast of King William Island all those years ago. Any references to real people, events, establishments, organisations, or places are intended solely to provide a sense of authenticity and are used fictitiously. Any other characters, and all incidents and dialogue are drawn from the author's imagination, and it would be ill-advised to assume anything to be fact.

In Memoriam

O ye frost and cold,
O ye ice and snow,
bless ye the Lord:
praise him and magnify Him for ever.

Franklin memorial,
Westminster Abbey
(Daniel, 3:69)

Crew lists

HMS *Erebus*[1]

Officers

Sir J. Franklin Kt. K.C.H.	Commodore
James Fitzjames	Commander
Graham Gore	Lieutenant
H. T. D. Le Vesconte	Lieutenant
J. W. Fairholme	Lieutenant
Robert O. Sergeant	Mate
Charles F. Des Vœux	Mate
Edward Couch	Mate
James Reid	Master (Acting)
Stephen S. Stanley	Surgeon
Charles H. Osmer	Paymaster & Purser
Harry D. S. Goodsir	Surgeon (Acting)
Henry F. Collins	Second Master
Thomas Terry	Boatswain, 3rd Class
John Weekes	Carpenter, 2nd Class
John Gregory	Engineer, 1st Class

---

1   Crew lists from National Maritime Museum, 1845.

Petty Officers		**Age**	**From**
Samuel Brown	Boatswain's Mate	27	Hull, Yorkshire
Richard Wall	Ship's Cook	45	Hull, Yorkshire
Robert Sinclair	Captain of the Foretop	25	Kirkwall, Orkney
Joseph Andrews	Captain of the Hold	35	Edmonton, Middlesex
William Fowler	Purser's Steward	26	Bristol, Somerset
James W. Brown	Caulker	28	Deptford, Kent
John Cowie	Stoker	32	Bermondsey, Surrey
John Sullivan	Captain of the Maintop	24	Gillingham, Kent
Phillip Reddington	Captain of Forecastle	28	Brompton, Kent
John Murray	Sailmaker	43	Glasgow, Scotland
John Bridgens	Sub Officers' Steward	26	Woolwich, Kent
Thomas Watson	Carpenter's Mate	40	Gt. Yarmouth, Norfolk
Thomas Plater	Stoker	27	Westminster, Middlesex
William Smith	Blacksmith	28	Tibenham, Norfolk
Francis Dunn	Caulker's Mate	25	Llanelli, Wales
Edmund Hoar	Captain's Steward	23	Portsea, Hampshire
Daniel Arthur	Quartermaster	35	Aberdeen, Scotland
William Bell	Quartermaster	36	Dundee, Scotland
John Downing	2nd Quartermaster	34	Plymouth, Devon
James Hart	Leading Stoker	33	Hampstead, Middlesex
Richard Aylmore	Gunroom Steward	24	Southampton, Hampshire

James Rigden	Captain's Coxswain	32	Upper Deal, Kent

Able Seamen

George Thompson	AB	27	Staines, Berkshire
John Hartnell	AB	25	Brompton, Kent
John Stickland	AB	24	Portsmouth, Hampshire
Thomas Hartnell	AB	23	Chatham, Kent
William Orren	AB	34	Chatham, Kent
William Clossan	AB	25	Shetland, Scotland
Charles Coombs	AB	28	Greenwich, Kent
John Morfin	AB	25	Gainsborough, Lincolnshire
Charles Best	AB	23	Fareham, Hampshire
Thomas Mc. Convey	AB	24	Liverpool, Lancashire
Henry Lloyd	AB	26	Kristiansand, Norway
Thomas Work	AB	41	Kirkwall, Scotland
Robert Ferrier	AB	29	Perth, Scotland
Josephus Geater	AB	32	London, Middlesex
George Williams	AB	35	Holyhead, Wales
Thomas Tadman	AB	28	Brompton, Kent
Abraham Seeley	AB	34	Gravesend, Kent
Francis Pocock	AB	24	Upnor, Kent
Robert Johns	AB	24	Penryn, Cornwall
William Mark	AB	24	Holyhead, Wales

Royal Marines

Daniel Bryant	Sergeant	31	Shepton Montague, Somerset
Alexander Paterson	Corporal	30	Inverness, Scotland
Robert Hopcraft	Private	38	Nottingham, Nottinghamshire
William Pilkington	Private	28	Kilrush, Ireland
William Braine	Private	31	Oakhill, Somerset
Joseph Healey	Private	29	Manchester, Lancashire
William Reed	Private	28	Bristol, Somerset

Boys

George Chambers	Boy, 1st Class	18	Woolwich, Kent
David Young	Boy, 1st Class	18	Sheerness, Kent

HMS *Terror*

Officers

F. R. M. Crozier	Captain
Edward Little	Lieutenant
George H. Hodgson	Lieutenant
John Irving	Lieutenant
Frederick Hornby	Mate
Robert Thomas	Mate
Thomas Blanky	Master (Acting)
John S. Peddie	Surgeon (Acting)
Alexander McDonald	Assistant Surgeon
G. A. MacBean	Second Master
E. J. H. Helpman	Clerk in Charge
Thomas Honey	Carpenter, 3rd Class
John Lane	Boatswain, 3rd Class
James Thompson	Engineer, 1st Class

Petty Officers

		Age	From
John Diggle	Ship's Cook	36	Westminster, London
Henry Peglar	Captain of the Foretop	37	London, Middlesex
William Gibson	Sub Officers' Steward	22	London, Middlesex
Cornelius Hickey	Caulker's Mate	24	Limerick, Ireland
William Goddard	Captain of the Hold	29	Gt. Yarmouth, Norfolk
Reuben Male	Captain of the Forecastle	27	Woolwich, Kent

Alexander Wilson	Carpenter's Mate	27	Lindisfarne, Northum.
John Wilson	Captain's Coxswain	33	Portsea, Hampshire
Thomas Darlington	Caulker	29	Plymouth, Devon
William Johnson	Stoker	45	Kiston-Lindsey, Lincs.
Thomas R. Farr	Captain of the Maintop	32	Deptford, Kent
Luke Smith	Stoker	27	London, Middlesex
David McDonald	Quartermaster	46	Peterhead, Scotland
John Kenley	Quartermaster	44	Fifeshire, Scotland
William Rhodes	Quartermaster	31	Redingstreet, Kent
Thomas Johnson	Boatswain's Mate	28	Wisbeach, Cambridge
Thomas Armitage	Gunroom Steward	40	Chatham, Kent
Samuel Honey	Blacksmith	22	Plymouth, Devon
Thomas Jopson	Captain's Steward	27	Marylebone, London
Edward Genge	Paymaster's Steward	21	Gosport, Hampshire
John Torrington	Leading Stoker	19	Manchester, Lancashire

Able Seamen

George J. Cann	AB	23	Battersea, London
William Strong	AB	22	Portsmouth, Hampshire
Henry Sims	AB	24	Gedney, Lincolnshire
John Bailey	AB	21	Leyton, Essex
William Jerry	AB	29	Pembroke, Wales
Henry Sait	AB	23	Bognor, Sussex
Alexander Berry	AB	32	Fifeshire, Scotland
John Handford	AB	28	Sunderland, Northum.

John Bates	AB	24	London, Middlesex
Samuel Crispe	AB	24	King's Lynn, Norfolk
Charles Johnson	AB	28	Halifax, Nova Scotia
William Shanks	AB	29	Dundee, Scotland
David Leys	AB	37	Montrose, Scotland
William Sinclair	AB	30	Galloway, Scotland
George Kinnaird	AB	23	Hastings, Sussex
Ed. Lawrence	AB	30	London, Middlesex
Magnus Manson	AB	28	Shetland, Scotland
James Walker	AB	29	S. Shields, Co. Durham
William Wentzall	AB	33	London, Middlesex

Royal Marines

Solomon Tozer	Sergeant	34	Axbridge, Somerset
William Hedges	Corporal	30	Bradford on Avon, Wilts.
William Heather	Private	35	Battersea, Surrey
Henry Wilkes	Private	28	Leicester, East Midlands
John Hammond	Private	32	Bradford, Yorkshire
James Daly	Private	30	Tubberclaire, Ireland

Boys

| Robert Golding | Boy | 19 | Deptford, Kent |
| Thomas Evans | Boy | 18 | Deptford, Kent |

Barrow Inlet, Adelaide Peninsula, 29 May 1854

SNOWSTORM, BLIZZARD, SQUALL – FOR those who have ever been caught in an Arctic whiteout, they will truly know what darkness is. In such circumstances, they may even start to wonder why it is that black has come to represent fear and misery and not white. Black is the colour of absorption; perhaps the colour of self-absorption; a fear of the unknown. If anyone should fear black, then they have only themselves to blame. White, however, is the polar opposite. It reflects and scatters everything: colour, light, sound, warmth – even a sense of locomotion may be suspended within its milky cataract.

Unlike darkness, succour will not be granted with the rising of the sun, or the pulling back of one's eyelids, or the comfort of striking of a light. Any sense of distance, movement, space or time will be smothered – life held in limbo as nature's cold, heartless shroud descends.

It was just such a weather state in which Aglooka had dismounted his sledge to assist one of the other sledge drivers. His runners had barely come to a standstill on the snow as he stepped off onto what he hoped was the ice. Ahead, the leading *qamutik* lay in turmoil: the dogs were amok as they began to tear at each other with rapidly escalating ferocity. For whatever reason they were fighting, Aglooka knew that if any of their animals became injured it could tip the fine balance of his search party's survival into that of disaster. Out on the Arctic sea ice, every piece of gear had to work perfectly, without flaw, and every man and beast had to be relied upon to pull far more than just their own weight.

So now, bounding through the white nothingness towards the whirling frenzy, Aglooka waded into the fray to help separate the other driver's tangled traces as he and his young companion were already laying into their animals.

Inuit treat their dogs with the same respect they reserve for tools, and they have no qualms when it comes to making them bend to their demands. But when any of their *qimmit* fight, only a fool would forget what these 'tools' could instantly transform into: maniacal four-legged muscles with a hinged arcade filled with flesh-ripping teeth. No doubt bitterly learnt, the Inuit had kept alive a very simple technique of their prehistoric forebears whereby any frenzied dogs could be made to unclamp themselves from each other by dragging them off by their hind legs like chattering, gnashing wheelbarrows.

Removing several of the dogs in this manner, Aglooka could now just about make out what they had been fighting over. Could it be that after nearly ten years of fruitless searches a dog had finally found what they had come all this way for – all this way as part of the largest, most costly maritime search ever mounted? That possible discovery now lay among the drifting snow and crumbling schist in the form of a skeletal hand – still partially clad with taut, brown, leathery skin and, tattooed crudely into the crook of its thumb and forefinger, a barn swallow in flight.

The Advance

✵

The Admiralty Boardroom, 7 February 1845

'A NAME, GENTLEMEN… WE NEED a name.'

The four Sea Lords, seated round the long Sheraton table, all appeared to be wracking their silver heads for someone to lead the Royal Navy's best-equipped discovery expedition ever to put to sea. Hanging over them in its oak niche was the somewhat effete portrait of King William IV. His pose lent the unfortunate effect of making him look utterly disinterested as he gazed dreamily out of the casements over a blustery Whitehall.

Sitting beneath the *Sailor King* was Thomas, 9th Earl of Haddington. As First Sea Lord, he was the political head of the Royal Navy. He had faithfully promised his new Queen that her sailors would, for once and for all, be the first to finally conquer the Northwest Passage and thus impose her sovereignty over the waters there. He also faithfully promised that with its discovery, there would be no more blood, treasure or time lost in rounding the Cape or the Horn as her gilded vessels returned with spoils from the Colonies. Thereafter, her great expansion of the British Empire would be afforded a beeline to the untold riches that could be extracted from the Orient. But, in order to achieve all of this, they just needed to establish where exactly the Passage was.

On paper it all seemed tantalisingly straightforward: just the last few inches of fuzzy lines inked on a chart, but the reality was an entirely different kettle of fish. For this to be achieved, the Sea Lords needed to assemble the Royal Navy's finest men and

install them in ships bristling with the greatest innovations of
the age. Crew and equipment at unlimited expense wasn't such a
problem though, as the Navy had, over the course of nearly four
hundred years, become incredibly well versed at polar exploration. The only difficulty lay in persuading the right man to lead
it all. A man who had to be preternaturally capable, be imbued
with astonishing amounts of good luck and, far more crucially,
be socially palatable.

Sir John Barrow, as Second Secretary to the Admiralty, might
have been referred to as a civil servant, but despite what his aris-
tocratic and political masters might have believed, this quiet,
unassuming Cumbrian was anything but a servant. He was a
captain steering his vessel towards his own destiny, along the
channel of his own quite considerable ambitions and everyone
else on his deck was merely cluttering up his line of sight.

Barrow coughed delicately into his fist. 'Um… well, if it pleases
my Lords, might I air a thought?' Lord Haddington, from his
big chair under the *Sailor King*, frowned as he twiddled the stem
of his sherry glass. 'Yes, please do, Second Secretary.'

'I would like to propose Sir John Franklin, my Lord.'

Haddington stared at Barrow and took a sip of his sherry.

'Hmm…' It was unclear whether he was savouring his amon-
tillado or Barrow's proposal. 'The man who ate his shoes…
Doesn't entirely fill me with optimism, Second Secretary,' he said,
as he raised his eyes towards the other end of the great table.

Sir George Cockburn, sitting to Haddington's right, rapped
lightly at the table's green leather. 'Second Secretary, have you
finally taken leave of your senses? The man is a buffoon. If we
put Franklin in charge, I'll wager he'll have his ships form the
nucleus of an iceberg within the bat of an eye.'

Haddington raised his brow to Barrow at the far end of the
great table. He trusted Barrow's instincts implicitly and was

often quite happy to get lost a little en route, but in this instance, he was more than a little stumped.

'It's a valid point, Second Secretary. Isn't Franklin rather old?'

Barrow didn't need to refer to the closed journal in front of him but spread out his hand over the cover, as if to somehow suck up its secrets – or keep them there.

'Um, no, I don't think so. I gather he's only fifty-nine, my Lord.'

Admiral Cockburn sniffed as he unnecessarily straightened one of the gold buttons on his sleeve.

'Well, it certainly sounds like he's getting on a bit to me, Second Secretary – far too old to be waddling about on the ice.'

All four septuagenarians lowered their eyes again towards the various names on the shortlists they had before them. Admiral Gage, the other fighting man sitting at the First Lord's left, took a good pinch of snuff off the crook of his hand. As he did so, the wind indicator device above the fireplace happened to sweep round its broad face. Gage noted how the long, slender arrow was indicating that a southeaster was blowing – perfect for a run on the moody North Sea for Greenland. 'Yes, it's definitely a young man's game, and that is why my money would have to be on Fitzjames.'

Barrow involuntarily blinked rather more than he would have preferred to before Admiral Cockburn properly showed his true colours.

'Entirely! We need a younger man. Someone strong, who can represent a modern navy.'

Barrow pulled a slightly pained smile of diplomacy. 'Indeed, my lords, this is no task for the fainthearted. I also have it on good authority that Commander Fitzjames is a strong advocate for a new navy powered by steam.'

Haddington pursed his lips. 'Well, I must confess, that certainly gives him an edge in my mind, gentlemen.'

Cockburn, whose own mind seemed thoroughly made up,

was building Fitzjames's case. 'Yes, splendid fellow. I heard he once jumped into the Mersey River to save a drowning man – whippersnapper wasn't even drunk, by all accounts.'

Barrow rested his forefingers on the corners of his journal: the mosaic of his scheme was beginning to form its overall picture. He hoped it would grant Fitzjames enough satisfaction to hear about the praise that these wise mandarins, these still potent heads of Her Majesty's Navy, were now heaping upon him.

Barrow had been somewhat staggered at just how far the young man's ambition had got him. Fitzjames actually had the gall to ask to lead the entire shebang after Barrow had first proposed the expedition (how he came to hear of it so early on he could only guess), but the two somewhat vital qualifications Fitzjames lacked would make it indefensible to anyone outside of the Admiralty's oak-panelled microcosm: the first was that James Fitzjames had never actually captained a ship before, and the second was that he'd never journeyed further north than Hertfordshire (with the exception of Liverpool… perhaps). That said, Fitzjames had been everywhere else though – including a Singaporean brothel with the Second Secretary's son George, where an unmentionable indiscretion had occurred. It would have been an out-and-out scandal had Fitzjames not saved the day with suspiciously quick thinking and some magically gathered cash that he'd used to grease all the right palms in order to nip things in the bud. Fitzjames had sworn to Sir John 'upon his honour' that the story of what went on in Singapore would be taken to the grave with him regardless. But for Barrow, Fitzjames's intimation had been crystal clear: he would need to find a plum job for the upstart in order to maintain complete discretion on behalf of the Barrow dynasty. Or, perhaps even better than a plum job, a perilously heroic one?

Barrow, being something of a diligent researcher, had made the discovery that Fitzjames was the illegitimate child of a senior diplomat, and he thought this revealed rather a lot about the minerals of the man. Whether through the erasure of his past or the attempts at writing his future, Barrow could see plainly how the young man would stop at nothing – with inexplicable promotions, almost theatrical demonstrations of bravery in front of those who could make it count, shameless social climbing… These were all seemingly concocted for one thing, and one thing only: making his name.

For Fitzjames's continued discretion, Barrow knew that the glory of being present at the conquering of the fabled Northwest Passage would prove utterly irresistible. But therein, Barrow now found himself in a straits of his own making: on one shore, he needed Fitzjames's silence to be assured, but on the other, Barrow genuinely craved the final taking of the Northwest Passage. After all, this would be his lasting legacy before his impending retirement from public service.

He knew Haddington would never give the nod to Fitzjames as the leader, but it did amuse him to note how the admirals were starting to get somewhat carried away – especially Gage, who had seen in Fitzjames an archetypical leader for a new Royal Navy propelled by screws and steam and all steered by the unswayable optimism of entitled young Englishmen: the mainstay of the British Empire.

Gage continued his defence of Fitzjames with almost reckless abandon. 'I heard he also led the charge at Zhenjiang during the Opium Wars…'

Haddington frowned, 'Yes, well – regarding his bravery, there's the rub, is it not, Admiral Gage? Perhaps the last thing this expedition needs is a leader who is filled with derring-do. Perhaps we need a leader who will just derring-well do as he's told, eh?'

The Sea Lords took another sip of their sherries. Gage peered into the depths of his glass as he smacked his lips doubtfully. 'Hmm, I'm loath to ask, but is having another stab at James Ross completely out of the realms of possibility, then? He and Crozier always seemed to have had splendid successes together.'

Barrow pursed his thin lips with genuinely heartfelt regret. 'It would indeed be a match made in heaven, my lord, but unfortunately Ross's wife has just presented him with a new baby boy.'

The old men looked askance at Barrow: puzzled as to why this would present any difficulties.

He explained. 'She is most reluctant to let him go north, gentlemen… or indeed in any other direction at this juncture.'

Cockburn frowned.

'Oh, that *is* a pity…'

A look of mischief appeared on the admiral's face as another thought occurred to him. 'Unlike Franklin's better half, eh? Evidently, she's literally shooing him out the door like a Cullercoats fishwife.'

The First Sea Lord also had difficulties containing his mirth. 'Ah, yes – Lady Franklin. D'you know, all of a sudden she's become like a sister to Lady Haddington – putting all sorts of notions into her dear little head.'

Gage sniffed. 'Perhaps she's trying to salvage his name for him regarding the Hobart, er, *issues*? And wasn't it ten men he lost up there on his overland expedition?'

Barrow cleared his throat softly. 'No, eleven, my Lord.'

Haddington changed the subject. 'So, if not Ross, then, who is our next most experienced Arctic dreadnought?'

Cockburn brightened as he swivelled his head towards Barrow. 'Crozier, surely, Second Secretary?'

'Indeed, my Lord, I believe his tally is eight polar expeditions, north *and* south, with a total of fifteen years spent on the ice…' The Second Secretary paused as he nodded and smiled – as if his head was filled with pleasant nostalgic thoughts – before continuing, 'Yes, Crozier – he would be the most experienced polar officer we have on the List today, gentlemen…' The way in which Barrow left both his words and a sigh hanging meant that the Sea Lords were in no doubt that a *but* was coming on.

'… but, like Ross, he tells me he wants to have nothing more to do with the Polar Regions. Their last expedition to Antarctica lasted for four years and was a complete success, but, er, it seems to have taken its toll on both their nerves – not to mention their livers.'

Gage seemed particularly disappointed. 'Blast it all – can't we promote him or something? Every man has a price. What would he want?'

Barrow smiled so briefly that it was almost a twitch. 'The question isn't a *what*, my Lord, but a *whom*.'

Every man around the table could guess what was afoot before Barrow continued.

'It appears Captain Crozier is lovesick, my Lords.'

The old men collectively dipped their heads as if Barrow had just held up his arms and said, 'Let us pray.'

Cockburn's frustration was beginning to show. 'All right then – dare I suggest James's uncle? He's had more experience up north than one could shake a stick at, and he's probably forgotten more than we'll ever know about sailing under steam.'

Haddington, even from the far end of the table, could sense Barrow's discomfort so intervened on his behalf. 'Ah, I very much doubt we would be able to afford Sir John Ross on a number of levels, and besides, given his formidable imagination when it comes to drawing charts… It might very well make him an amusing asset within the fiction section of any library, but I would imagine the Second Secretary would, er' – he paused to order his next words carefully – 'be keen to avoid the *difficulties* we had with him in '34.'

Barrow's small bow of gratitude to the First Sea Lord hid the gamut of horror and relief as the blood started to return to the white ends of his tightly knitted fingers. The men all sat in silence as they thought hard, before Gage had an occurrence.

'What about George Back – did he not find himself very close to the heart of the Arctic?'

Cockburn shook his head. 'Hmm, probably closer to the

appendix, if I know him… Anyway, he's not interested since he received his knighthood. Shame really, as the man doesn't need a compass: the world always appears to revolve around him.'

This seemed to lift the men's moods a little before Barrow put a finger to his lips and leaned in conspiratorially. 'I believe, my Lords, based on all the distinguished names we've mentioned, that the answer is already staring us in the face.' Barrow looked up enigmatically towards the Boardroom's impressive lozenge-moulded ceiling.

Gage only just managed to resist the temptation to follow the Second Secretary's gaze heavenwards, as if the answer might have been thoughtfully carved there for them all to see.

Barrow continued. 'Forgive my obstinacy, my Lords, but if we could return to the Crozier question for a moment. I believe that his inclusion on the expedition could still be something of a cornerstone – my feeling is that if it were indeed possible to persuade Captain Crozier to join us in our great enterprise, then his presence would grant us more than a little latitude regarding the capabilities of the overall leader. So, for example – and purely as an example – were we to elect, say, Sir John Franklin to lead, then it would be prudent to enlist someone of Crozier's, er… capabilities as his second-in-command, would it not, gentlemen?'

The two admirals asked the same question in almost perfect unison.

'How?'

Cockburn added, 'Wouldn't there still be the question of his, er, *lovesickness*, as you call it?'

Barrow smiled. 'Well, indeed, my Lords, but I understand that the *whom* in the question of Crozier happens to be the niece of Sir John…'

The Second Secretary left the last words dangling in the air until the two admirals' wattles began to wobble over their gorgets as their heads twitched back and forth in search of the still fugitive answer. Barrow then upturned his palm graciously towards Haddington. The First Sea Lord shifted uncomfortably before taking his cue almost seamlessly.

'Ah, yes, well, Lady Franklin, in her inimitable style, has let it be known to Lady Haddington, in no uncertain terms, that should Captain Crozier need any encouragement to join the expedition, then she may be able to assist us greatly in that quarter.'

Both Admirals seemed even more confused, so Barrow stepped in to assist. 'Gentlemen, allow me to expand: the cause of Crozier's romantic complaint is the Franklins' niece… a very comely young lady by all accounts, whom they dote upon and have raised as their own since she was a child. I have it on good authority that Captain Crozier is smitten and has asked for the hand of this girl, um, twice, actually. However, in the likelihood that her suitor is about to make a third attempt, their niece will agree to marry him – but with certain terms that her aunt assures us, will guarantee the participation of the good captain regarding any of her uncle's efforts towards finding a Northwest Passage beforehand.'

Cockburn shifted uncomfortably as the treachery of the scheme dawned upon him. 'And this young, er…'

'Miss Sophia Cracroft, my Lord.'

'This Miss Cracroft has agreed to be part of all this, has she?'

'In principle, yes, my Lord – evidently any prospect of an engagement would have to be deferred until Sir John's commitments to the Service over the next three years or so are made clearer.'

The Sea Lords, with wide eyes, took another sip of their sherries. Barrow, whose glass had remained resolutely untouched throughout proceedings, cleared his throat and slid his glass towards himself.

'My Lords, I propose this to be Franklin's expedition with Crozier as his second-in-command.'

Admiral Gage's face took on the pained expression of one

bracing before having a tooth pulled. 'But what about Fitzjames? Seems a shame that he should miss out, surely?'

Quite innocently, Admiral Cockburn then neatly proceeded to slot the last piece of Barrow's mosaic into place for him. 'We could always put him in *Erebus* as Franklin's captain?'

It was all the Second Secretary could do to refrain from clasping his hands in delight.

With his work now complete, Barrow nodded to Cockburn and finally picked up his sherry glass. 'I believe that would be a most elegant touch indeed, my Lord, and with the addition of Commander Fitzjames as Franklin's captain, their triumvirate will, I am certain, assure the expedition's complete success.'

Haddington sat back hesitantly as he eyed his Second Secretary. 'And Sir John would be happy with that?'

Barrow tried his best to hide a smirk. 'Well, if he's anything less than delighted, my Lord, he could always consider the prospect of spending the rest of his days with his chilblained feet up by the fire – next to his dear lady wife… and Miss Cracroft.'

At this imagery, the Lords' cheeks took on a little colour as their shoulders began to shake with mirth. As the decanter made its way round the table again, Cockburn, ever the wag, added, 'Perhaps we should call this endeavour the Lady Jane Franklin expedition?'

The Sea Lords thumped the table and laughed loudly at the not unreasonable suggestion.

With Franklin as the expedition's titular head and Fitzjames as his strong, younger legs, then Crozier was the badly needed shoulder for them both. Barrow, quietly pleased with himself, sniffed at his sherry and wrinkled his nose a little.

With everyone evidently in agreement, Lord Haddington seemed greatly relieved and tapped his glass. 'So, gentlemen, I take it we're all agreed then – the name we have for the Royal Navy's fifty-eighth polar voyage is *Sir John Franklin*.'

He raised his glass and proposed a toast: 'Gentlemen – the

Sir John Franklin's British Naval Northwest Passage expedition!'

Barrow took a token sip of his sherry before gently opening his ledger at the ribbon. He smiled at the heading already written there in his meticulous hand: *Instruction addressed to Sir John Franklin, KCH...*

Sir John Barrow's swansong was *officially* commissioned.

Instruction addressed to

> *Captain Sir John Franklin, K.C.H., Her Majesty's Ship 'Erebus,' dated 5th May 1845, By the Commissioners for executing the office of Lord High Admiral of the United Kingdom of Great Britain and Ireland.*

> *1. Her Majesty's Government having deemed it expedient that further attempt should be made for the accomplishment of a north-west passage by sea from the Atlantic to the Pacific Ocean, of which passage small portion only remains to be completed, we have thought proper to appoint you to the command of the expedition to be fitted out for that service, consisting of Her Majesty's Ships 'Erebus,' under your command, taking with you Her Majesty's ship 'Terror,' her Captain (Crozier), having been placed by us under your orders, taking also with you the 'Barretto Junior' transport, which has been directed to be put at your disposal for the purpose of carrying out portions of your provisions, clothing and other stores.*

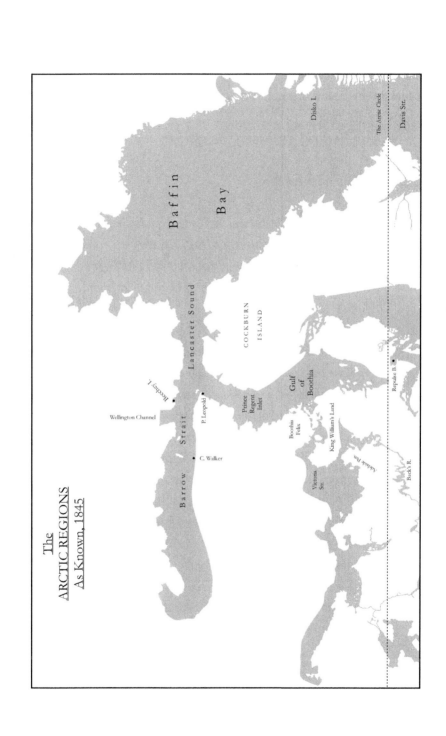

The
ARCTIC REGIONS
As Known, 1845

Baffin

Bay

Lancaster Sound

COCKBURN
ISLAND

Barrow Strait

Wellington Channel

Beechey I.

P. Leopold

C. Walker

Prince
Regent
Inlet

Gulf
of
Boothia

Boothia
Felix

King William's Land

Victoria
Str.

Adelaide Pen.

Buck's R.

Repulse B.

Disko I.

The Arctic Circle

Davis Str.

Greenhithe, 19 May 1845

THE WHITE DOVE PERCHED ON the main topgallant spar. The Hecla and Vesuvius-class vessels beneath the bird were Her Majesty's Ships *Erebus* and *Terror* respectively. On the dock, the band of the Royal Marines played some incidental music. Dignitaries, families and the day-trippers clambered excitedly up the gangway with all the decorum their top hats, bonnets and flat caps could foster. Sir John Franklin waved his own 'fore-and-aft' hat with elation at the sight of the white bird that had settled on his masts.

Swarmed by an eager gaggle of journalists, the commodore was in his element. 'Y'see that, gentlemen! How can we fail?' Leaping onto a small water cask as energetically as his rheumatoid knees would allow, some of the ship's crew also cheered once they understood what he had been looking at. Franklin hopped down again – with a wee twinge – and led the throng over towards a board covered with a Union flag. Standing either side of it were his two captains.

'Gentlemen, allow me to present Commander James Fitzjames: the captain of my own ship, HMS *Erebus*…'

The dashing younger man saluted smartly before the commodore turned to a more solid man of considerably less elegance.

'And the expedition's second-in-command: Captain Francis Crozier.'

Crozier touched the peak of his cap briefly and his attempt at a smile came across more as a grimace. Turning to the flag covering the board, the commodore flicked it away with a flourish to reveal a perfectly chalked chart of the Arctic Regions. Franklin seemed to be carried there instantly by the chart's meticulous lines that wriggled and writhed into the blurred edges of the unknown. He placed his palm in the centre as if to touch its cold heart. After a moment he remembered where he really was again and returned to the crowd.

'Now, the Admiralty Board has tasked me to investigate and complete the charting of a navigable route through this series of inlets here…'

He waved his hand over the chart of the entire top of the North American continent from east to west.

'The High Arctic, gentlemen! Welcome to the Frozen Bosom of the North: the most miserable place on the entire planet.'

As if to support his point, Sir John deftly took out his hand-kerchief and sneezed into it. Someone from the crowd heckled good-naturedly.

'Bless you, Sir John… So why on earth are you going back?'

Sir John still had his nose cradled in his handkerchief as he said, 'Ah, thank you – an excellent question!'

The audience laughed politely.

'I jest with you, of course, gentlemen – I'm going back in order to finish my business up there. I've personally mapped a thousand miles of the North-Western Territory and I've gone to great, great inconvenience in doing so. You know, I am sure, that no service is nearer to my heart than to complete England's survey of the north coast of America and the accomplishment of a Northwest Passage.'

Sir John swirled his hand over the middle of the chart as he continued. 'Temperatures in this part of the world can freeze the mercury of any modern thermometer, and every soul on my ships will be at the mercy of continuous ice floes – even in summer. But, if we are successful and can find the existence of a route through it all, we will have halved the sailing from London to Shanghai, gentlemen… halved! We will have discovered what I would like to call the White Silk Road.'

As journalists scribbled furiously in their notebooks someone shouted from the back. 'But what about the French idea for a canal, sir?'

Sir John looked askance before cupping a hand to his ear. 'Eh! What's that? French? Speak up, sir! I'm as deaf as a post – the guns on the *Billy Ruffian* were very loud at Trafalgar.'

His audience laughed at his dismissal of the French along with the affectionate reminder of HMS *Bellerophon*'s nickname. Feeling encouraged, Sir John continued his raking, 'Ha! Yes, only little Frogs would think to scrape out a hare-brained intestine through a desert.'

The commodore looked at the map again and pressed his finger through the neat chalking… through the Straits of Gibraltar… across the Mediterranean… through Egypt and onwards… towards the Red Sea. He then blinked at the crowd in order to try and see the whites of the Gallophile's eyes who dared to ask such an impudent question.

'Yes, well – perhaps not in my lifetime, young man. To whom do I have the honour, sir?'

A small, stooped man stepped forward and tried to straighten up as much as he could. 'Douglas Jerrold, *Punch Magazine*, sir.'

Sir John scanned the rest of the crowd wryly.

Douglas repeated himself somewhat louder. 'Er, *Punch Magazine*, Sir John!'

'Yes, yes – no need to repeat yourself, young man. I'm just a little surprised that you people at Punch aren't too busy drawing *cartoons* of Mr Peel or some such.'

As they all laughed jeeringly, a doubtful-looking journalist held up a pencil. 'Herbert Ingram, *Illustrated London News*… Sir, we know specially reinforced hulls and armour plating protect your ships, but how do you propose to actually get through ice tens of feet thick?'

'Ah, the *Illustrated London News* – welcome to you! Yes, well, as I've always said, "If we can't find a way, we'll make one," so, the metalwork at our bows will certainly go a long way to helping us achieve just that, eh?' Franklin, somewhat harried a little by his cold, gave some further attention to his handkerchief. He waggled his fingers and nodded to Commander Fitzjames as he did so.

'Please, James – would you?'

'Absolutely, sir.' Fitzjames stepped forward and put a hand on his hip, perhaps a little too commandingly. 'So, gentlemen, both *Erebus* and *Terror* are literally loaded to the gunnels with the latest innovations of our age – including transversely mounted Planet and Samson type auxiliary engines respectively.'

Most of the journalists' hands shot up again as they shouted questions at the same time, but Fitzjames quelled them with raised hands as he continued, 'These twenty-five-horsepower "rockets" of Robert Stephenson & Co will smash us through the ice as and when required using specially designed retractable propellers: another first for any wooden-hulled warships and we also have desalinators for fresh drinking water, um, on tap, as it were.' He looked around the throng to let his joke sink in. While it awkwardly took its time in doing so, he picked out a wide-eyed young Irish reporter waggling his pencil in the air.

'Er, any other delights aboard, Commander?' Nearly forgetting himself, he added, 'Oh, William Russell, *The Times*, sir.'

'Well, yes – absolutely – both ships are furnished with their own extensive libraries: from the Holy Bible to *Nicholas Nickleby* – a copy of the latter donated and signed by none other than Mr Dickens himself and a very dear friend of the Franklins.'

A fat, sweating newsman from deep within the bustle seemed far more determined to hear more from the commodore. 'George Reynolds, *The London Journal*. Sir John, your Coppermine Expedition ran out of food and you had to eat your own footwear—'

Sir John rolled his eyes deprecatingly as he poked his spotty handkerchief into his pocket. 'Ah, yes – that old chestnut.'

'Sir, how will you safeguard against the same measures occurring this time?'

Aghast, his fellow reporters' pencils hovered at the portly correspondent's effrontery for bringing up such an indelicate matter.

'No, no – it is an excellent question indeed, Mr, er, Reynolds, is it? Yes, the Coppermine – it is true that we couldn't find anything to eat so we drank tea and ate some of our shoes for supper.'

The delighted reporters' pencils wriggled away again as they jotted down their quote of the day. Captain Crozier fished out his pocket watch for a fairly subtle glare at the time, but, if the river was about to ebb, the commodore was now in full flow.

'No, gentlemen, I do not recommend eating any form of sole, other than perhaps the *Dover* variety. However, this time I've made sure that my ships have been victualled with enough preserved stores for five years that could, with care, even spin out to seven.'

He found evidence to hand in the form of a chunky red canister on a nearby pallet. He grabbed it and held it aloft. 'And, just delivered in person this very morning – sixteen tons of *long-promised* tins of Goldner's Patent Meats! No, sir, while I was forced to eat my own footwear in my last expedition, my men will probably be forced to let out their belts on their return from this one – isn't that right, Mr Goldner?'

Sir John held out an outstretched hand of welcome to two men who had been quietly making their way towards the gangway. They both seemed somewhat uneasy with the unanticipated attention. Mr Goldner rallied seamlessly to return Sir John an ostentatious bow.

'Ah-ha, ha – indeed, sir! Er, every morsel manna from heaven, sir!' This seemed to strike joy into the heart of Sir John and he began applause for the two men.

'Ladies and gentlemen, I give you Mr Stephen Goldner and

his agent, Mr Samuel Richie. Together they have, in no small part, made this expedition's success far more assured. Welcome, gentlemen – welcome! Without Mr Goldner's contribution we wouldn't have been able to contemplate the amount of time we shall need to spend on the ice – so I thank you, dear sirs! Thank you from the bottom of my heart.'

With a bashfulness that was genuine, the pair smiled and bowed but as they did so, Richie ventriloquised at Goldner through his clenched smile.

'Manna from heaven! What the bloody hell are you talking about, Goldner? Is *manna* Hungarian for *donkey guts?*'

Goldner hissed back, 'Shut mouth, stupid – or we'll both be in soup!'

'Christ, I hope it's not our soup?' drawled Richie.

Goldner didn't like cats at the best of times and when he looked down to see an overweight tabby rubbing against his spatterdashes and sniffing suspiciously, he shooed it away. '*Menj a picsába!*'

Sir John, raising his eyes to the dove, returned the red tin to the top of the pallet before chopping his palms against each other to get the dust off. 'And, what is more, the heavens have sent down a sign of our prospective good fortune with a white dove! Ha, good people, this… omen makes me most sanguine indeed. With God's assistance we are *ready to conquer!*'

Raising his hat by way of punctuating the proceedings, the crowd cheered, and the band struck up. The commodore replaced his headdress and rubbed his hands together excitedly.

'Right, how are we doing, Captain Crozier?'

Crozier laconically glanced overboard at the river. 'Slack water, ten minutes, sir.'

'Perfect. Would you start clearing the decks, please, Francis?'

Crozier touched his peak again and turned to the press pack

as it still cawed for more answers. 'Thank you, gentlemen, please follow me to the gangway.'

The reporters attempted to keep up with Crozier like oxpeckers on a buffalo's back. He ignored all their questions until finally, standing at the top of the gangway he folded his arms.

'Right then, thank you, gents – off you pop, now.'

The sound of a thousand final questions all at the same time was almost overwhelming and Crozier held up his hands in surrender. 'If God is willing, we'll bring you back some fine stories, but if He's not, I'm sure you'll be able to make up some of your own, eh, lads?'

In the meantime, the crews of *Erebus* and *Terror* went about the business of making their ships ready for the sea. Aloft, topmen ran up ratlines and stepped onto Flemish horses with the deftness of trapeze artists, whilst down on the deck, muscles bulged and rippled as every soul pulled together on lines with such synchrony that the hemp in their hands almost appeared to turn elastic.

Aft, on the quarterdeck, the officers of *Erebus* took it in turns to slip away from their duties for a moment or two to have their portraits taken by a meticulous little man with a daguerreotype camera. All were trying, with mixed degrees of success, to show a cool indifference to their moment in the sunshine – as if having their likenesses conjured onto plates of polished silver from within a cherrywood box-o-tricks was the sort of thing that happened to them every day.

Whilst Sir John had been attending to the gentlemen of the press, Charles Des Vœux, one of the more cocksure lieutenants, had struck a pose that verged on fresh when he undid a couple of his waistcoat buttons and shoved his hand to his breast à la Nelson. He even uttered the admiral's last words as he stared off into the distance wistfully whilst trying not to laugh, 'Kiss me… Hardy'. Once his picture was done, the rugby-playing Graham Gore tweaked the ear of 'Nelson' till he slid himself away yelping from the chair. Once seated, Gore elected to fold his arms hero-ically and ask his brother officers if it made his chest look even bigger. In sharp contrast, Harry Goodsir, the self-conscious ship's surgeon, just sat there awkwardly before the photographer made a suggestion. 'Er, perhaps try a more *scientific* air, doctor?' The gangly young Scotsman looked lost for a moment or two before striking a somewhat ill-conceived pose that involved touch-ing his temple with his forefinger – to gales of rebuke from his brother officers.

Even Sir John, returning from the journalists with his two senior officers, wasn't above affectation; taking his hat off to reveal his pale, delicate pate emerging from the tangle of a damp raven's nest. Sensing disappointment from the photographer, some of his confidence left him for a moment so he sought his expert opin-ion: 'Well, what do you say, Mr Beard – hat on, or hat off?'

Mr Beard tilted his head in order to exude deep artistic con-sideration. 'Oh, such a marvellous hat, sir! Er, hat on, I feel.'

After lots of fussing around with correctly hanging stars, medals and epaulette tassels, Franklin extended his telescope and struck a pose that he hoped was authoritative benevolence per-sonified. But, when combined with his flu, the net effect merely gave him the overall bearing of a constipated tortoise with his chins pressed into his starched white collars. Once his portrait was taken, he blew his nose once more and wandered off towards the gangway to search out his wife.

Having almost shoved the last reporter off the ship, it was then Crozier's turn. He sat down very heavily and glared at the photographer in a most unsettling manner. Mr Beard began to make another artistic suggestion, but wisely thought better of it. As soon as the shot was taken, Crozier strode off towards his own ship as he grumbled something unrepeatable about adrift tea and sugar from Fortnum & Mason. Last, but by no means least, was Commander Fitzjames, who, on seeing the potentially masterful merits of the telescope as a substitute sceptre, decided to strike the same pose as Sir John. Once his image was taken, he stood up and tugged at his waistcoat.

'Right. That'll do, Mr Beard. Clear away, please.'

Mr Beard, clearly not finished, squawked, 'Eh? But what about the officers of HMS *Terror*?'

Fitzjames looked about him to see the disappointed faces of the other officers and seemed to concede begrudgingly with a sigh. 'Pusser! Where is the pusser?'

As if by magic, the ever vexed-looking paymaster, Charles Osmer, appeared at Fitzjames's shoulder.

'Ah, there you are, Pusser! Would you make sure Mr Beard leaves his contraption with us, please? The handsome devils of *Terror* will just have to wait until we're under way.'

On the dock, various members of the ships' companies said their farewells to loved ones in their own very different ways: coy young men with their blubbing parents; a fishwife chasing her good-for-nuffin bleeder for some housekeeping money out of his fresh Arctic duties advance. Some children wuffled the thick fur of an enormous black dog that was being led aboard by a burly marine sergeant before two regulator crushers unceremoniously dragged a pair of paralytic tars up the gangway. On the brow, the petty officers saluted the ship before handing over the defaulters to a distinctly unimpressed ship's corporal. As they bounced back down gangway, the crushers threw up another salute towards the commodore, who was now with his wife on the dock.

At the dockside Sir John and Lady Franklin were trying their best to say their goodbyes without interruptions – off the ship, and on terra firma. The Franklins were looking anywhere but into each other's eyes as they both tried to find the inevitable words.

Lady Franklin was the first to break the silence. 'Now, darling, did you let that expensive photography person get on with his business?'

Franklin was at a loss. 'Photography?'

Jane frowned as she rested her palm on his hot cheek. 'Yes, dear – photography – the funny little chap with his big wooden box.'

'Ah, yes, darling. Seemed to know what he's doing. Hope that's the case… I want his likeness of me to keep you company.'

She looked down at her fingers as they fiddled absentmind-edly with her handkerchief. 'Oh, I don't need some silly picture to keep me company.' She clutched her handkerchief to her heart as her voice betrayed her emotions for once. 'You're here, always – here in my heart.' She quickly rallied by looking about the dock so that the infectious carnival atmosphere swept her away from some of her grief. 'Look at this… look at the ships – onwards, towards something great – something that has never been done before. All led by my lion. I must confess, I would do anything to be going with you, my love.'

Her husband smiled regretfully. 'Ah, if only, Jane… I shall be quite lost without you.' At this, the two began to laugh together at such a thought.

'I do hope that's not the case, you silly, darling man!'

Franklin embraced his wife and rested his cheek on her bonnet. 'It's funny, but all I wish for now is the day when I am able to say hello to you again, my love.'

He lifted her chin with his finger and thumb so that he could look into her big, steel-blue eyes that had always beguiled him but were now brimming with tears.

'You have faith in me, don't you, my love?'

'John, how could you ever doubt such a thing!'

He kept staring into her eyes, as if the truth was written there. He smiled warmly. 'I want you to promise me something, Jane.'

'Of course, anything, my love.'

'All I ask is for three years.' She looked at him questioningly, but he already had the reply. 'I want people to have a little faith in me… as I know you do, Jane. The results of this expedition will be my legacy. This will allow me to be remembered not as the fool who ate his shoes, but the man who did what the Royal Navy couldn't achieve in over three hundred years of trying: Sir John Franklin – the man who linked the Atlantic to the Pacific… finally conquered the Northwest Passage. So, I don't want anyone giving up on me – all I need is three years. Within that time, we will be perfectly fit, happy and self-sufficient, and if we should want for anything, then I'm certain Our Lord will provide. But will you at least give me three years of your faith, my love?'

The tears began to fall from his wife's eyes. 'You ask so much, John, but yes, I will yearn for you for three years and, mark my words, come three years to this day if there is no word from you then, by God, I swear I will send out a hundred ships and ten thousand men to find you.'

Sir John couldn't help himself. He buried his face in her breast. 'Ah, goodbye, dearest kitten. I've travelled the globe to find uncharted continents, lost rivers and gold, but the greatest discovery I ever made was so much closer to home.'

She looked into his big damp eyes and dabbed at their corners with her lilac handkerchief before scrunching it up and holding it to her heart again. 'Keep warm, My Lord!'

He tried his level best to steel himself, but he couldn't help but hiccup through his attempt at optimism for his wife. 'Be of good cheer, my dear Jane.'

Jane turned away and began her own leaden walk back to her waiting brougham. Behind her she could hear various orders being given and repeated back as the ships were being made ready to be towed clear by the two steam aids *Rattler* and *Monkey*.

As she approached her little black carriage the door was flung open from within. Sophia Cracroft had been waiting for as long as her patience would bear and clambered out.

'Oh, dearest Aunt – how was it?'

'Ah, you know, all rather wretched, really. Poor Johnny, I do hope he manages to keep himself warm. He does hate the cold so… His poor toes never quite recovered from the last time he went north and he's already sniffling terribly.'

'And did you see Captain Crozier? How did he seem?'

Jane stared hard at Sophia before attempting a consolatory smile. 'Yes, I did – he seemed fine, Sophia. Very gruff with every-one, but very self-possessed, I would say – exactly what should be expected of a man of his station.'

Jane, seeing Sophia's troubled face searching for some further reassurance, tried her best to put her at her ease.

'He's fine, Sophy, I promise you. They will all be fine. And it's in no small part, down to you, darling one. It would be a most vexing time indeed if it wasn't for Captain Crozier's presence.'

Sophia looked out towards the ships. 'Ah, poor Frankie. I think my turning him down for the second time broke his heart.' She turned back to her aunt and her eyes began to fill again. 'He was quite serious you know.'

Sophia fumbled around her neck and produced a chain with a ring on it. She held the ring between her thumb and forefinger. It was a beautiful thing surmounted by a large opal cabochon that sparkled with all the hope of a rainbow sprinkled onto water and frozen. She smiled at the ring as another tear trickled off her cheek. 'He'd tried to give it to me once before in Hobarton. He said this time I was to just keep it as a token of…'

As Sophia started fossicking in her sleeve for her handkerchief, Lady Jane touched her arm. 'We appreciate the huge sacrifice you've made, Sophy, we really do.'

'Well, if it means Uncle Johnny has more of a chance of suc-ceeding then it will have all been worth it, won't it? I just hope it doesn't get Captain Crozier down too much in the meantime – he's quite a delicate soul, really.'

Lady Jane took her niece's hands and looked into her big

melting, topaz eyes. 'They will come back as heroes and you will marry yours, my dear. What are a few years of longing, against a lifetime of having? We must both be patient and let time go about its business.'

Black smoke began to belch from the funnels of *Rattler* and *Monkey* as they strained and tugged at the ships' towlines. As the two bomb ships and their support vessels began to shrink away from the dockside the *let go* hawsers slithered off the dock and into the river after their masters.

From their vantage on the dock, Sophia could see Crozier standing next to the wheel as he calmly issued measured orders to the quartermaster. He spotted Sophia waving and, after what seemed like an eternity, solemnly touched his peak before returning his attention to the running of his ship. As the crowds on the dock and in their little boats on the water gave three cheers to *Erebus* and *Terror*, both Jane and Sophia's eyes bleared as Franklin's Arctic Squadron, with its steam-driven support vessels and the flotilla of waterborne well-wishers, bent to the east upon a thick, tea-coloured Thames.

The Long Forties, 24 May 1845

THE SQUADRON'S SAILING UP THE North Sea had been far from plain. The veering northwester that had brought *Erebus* and *Terror* out of the Thames had now picked up to a nine on the Beaufort Scale and was pushing them over a two-knot current to give them a gruelling point of sail as they were towed by their tugs. Their hawsers had snapped twice under the strain and Sir John, in his frustration, had ordered them to be let go as full sail to be put out in order to make up for the lost time spent fiddling about with towing lines. But as the gales strengthened Crozier had feared for their upper works. He ordered *Terror's* officer of the watch, Edward Little, to signal to *Erebus* that they were reducing sail and advised her to follow suit. Fitzjames had done so willingly once Sir John had retired for the evening – that way he could apologise in the morning rather than dice with the uncertainty of asking permission. So now, as the ships sailed with little more than teacloths put out, the decks were cleared in anticipation of a very uncomfortable night.

Apart from drinking with the man, there wasn't one jack aboard either ship who would have anything less than complete and utter faith in anything that Crozier would say or do. But then who would blame them? The man was a legend and the stories abounded – such as the time on Sir James Ross's expedition of '42 when Ross and Crozier had taken their men further south than anyone else on earth had ever been before.

After departing Hobarton for the Falkland Islands they had

been caught in a squall that was so fierce that it broke up the ice pack and sent colossal icebergs cavorting around the Southern Ocean. Tossing around in the pitch-black seas, one such beast, which was reckoned to be the size of Westminster Abbey, loomed out of nowhere in front of *Erebus*. Ross, a brilliant sailor with superb instincts, could only turn away sharply – but straight into *Terror* which had every stitch of sail out and was on a good run under Crozier's hand. The appalling crunch of *Erebus*'s bowsprit, entire foretop and half a dozen spars against *Terror* left the two ships entangled in a deadly game of seesaw as the massive swell rose and fell between the ships.

At one point, *Terror* was tossed-up so high that the crew of *Erebus* could only gaze up in horror at the sight of her keel looming out of the water above them like a breaching triple-plated leviathan. The next action would normally have seen the ship crash down on *Erebus* with existential implications but miraculously the ships' rigging released its tangled grip so that *Terror* could bear away.

But now it was Crozier's turn to dice with the colossal hulk of ice now looming before him. As soon as the catheads slammed down into the seething water once more Crozier headed for a dark fissure he had spotted in the middle of the iceberg that now threatened to smash the two ships to pieces. Could it possibly be a gap as the iceberg was breaking up? Not in their wildest dreams would most captains even think of steering a fully laden 325-ton warship with a beam of twenty-seven feet into such a dire strait. If it was easier to get a camel through the eye of a needle than a rich man to get into heaven, then Crozier must have been feeling wealthier than Croesus at that precise moment. On his crisp orders, the men flew to the lines as he steered the ship through the impossibly narrow passageway to their icy mausoleum. With the sheer white opalescent cliffs rising at least two hundred feet into the air on either side, the men could do nothing but hold their breaths in a heart-stopping grimace of panic.

Terror, running so close to the iceberg's sides sent the spray from the ship's bone lashing back and freezing onto the decks as if King Croesus himself were rolling diamonds teasingly across her fir timbers. One seaman, in a fit of horror and quite convinced that he had found better odds, was only just caught by a mate as he attempted to leap over the taffrail. All around, hardened hands began to sob uncontrollably with a few men even calling for their mammies. Throughout all the mayhem, the ship's captain was observed to have remained perfectly composed as he soothingly issued commands as if some sweet sonnet was playing through his mind. His total authority and perfectly measured actions left those around him open-mouthed in awe and admiration.

Once clear, Crozier immediately ordered the blue lights to be lit as a beacon for *Erebus* to follow them through next. When asked about his actions afterwards, Crozier said he had no recollection of most of it. On retelling the tale time and time again, the quartermaster said that Crozier had the air of a contentedly luncheoned father taking his family around a leafy ait on the upper reaches of the Thames in June.

Stromness, 31 May 1845

FOR ANY VESSELS HEADING 'NORTH about,' the Orkneys was their last touch at civilisation. Stromness, the main port, could be expensively depended upon for anything 'overlooked, overbooked or overboard', and the greatest contingent of this route's traffic was usually made up of whalers or the ships of the Hudson's Bay Company. Fur was the HBC's chief stock-in-trade, which, dictated by the fashion of the day, had become a vital part of the British economy and, accordingly, an exceedingly profitable one for the HBC.

The climate of the Orkneys was also incredibly dependable in two ways: the first was that the weather was influenced by the phenomenon of the North Atlantic Drift, which kept the temperatures at a consistently gothic measure so that winter and summer seamlessly melded into one. Rainfall was more or less evenly distributed generously throughout both. The second far more notable characteristic of the Orcadian climate was the wind. If it ever dipped below a four on the Beaufort Scale it would be something locals would remark upon in conversation with wide eyes and conspiratorial whispers. Nowhere else in the British Isles could one bank so faithfully on a good squall, gust or howl: it was an aeolian carnival.

From across Salthouse Bay, the Hall of Clestrain stood sentinel-like over any shipping that put into Stromness Harbour. Whether it was a flagship or a coracle, no vessel could fail to be observed through the house's rattling panes, and now, from behind them,

the laird pulled at his pink whiskers as he glassed the two heavily
laden bomb ships and the rest of Franklin's Arctic Squadron as
they strained to reach their way into Stromness.

By the time the ships' hawsers were on the quays' bollards, John
Rae Senior was there to welcome Sir John and his men. As the
agent of the Hudson's Bay Company, it was his duty to make them
feel welcome – as well as make sure the squadron had all that it
needed for the unpredictable journey that lay ahead. Rae also had
a particular personal interest in their journey as his favourite son
had been making his living in the Arctic Circle for nearly ten years.

Resolutely steadfast among the emerald, windswept blur of
Orkney stood Clestrain. This ancient stone edifice was a house,
hewn from blocks of stone that gave the appearance of the last
remnants of a grim ancient fortress, which, over aeons of stormy
sieges and bombardment, had somehow been reduced to nothing
but its single, most stoic turret. Architecturally, Clestrain's only
concession to homeliness had been the somewhat flamboyant
inclusion of a pediment in the Palladian style over the doorway,
but the Calvinistic weather fronts had swept it all away during
the Night of the Great Wind in '39. This then was the perfectly
apt ancestral home of one of the greatest Arctic explorers of his
day: Dr John Rae.

Perhaps due to an Orcadian upbringing that had seen the boy
Rae scale spume-lashed cliffs for eggs, sail his small dinghy in
mountainous seas just for the devilment, or whistle hymns as he
walked for days on end in the most perilous of weather events,
the Orcadian lad was made for the Arctic.

John Rae Junior was the fourth son of a family of ten and, as
arranged by his father, he had enlisted as a junior ship's surgeon
for the HBC immediately upon coming up from Edinburgh's
Royal College of Surgeons. It was only meant to be a summer
job, but during the passage his ship was beset in the ice and

the crew and passengers had to endure a very long and difficult winter. However, the young Orcadian thrived on the depravations and showed his mettle when he defended his passengers from the onset of scurvy by finding a drift-covered bush full of vitamin-loaded berries. This was the beginning of the nineteen-year-old's life-long attachment to the Arctic.

Rae quickly became indispensable at the HBC, mapping thousands of miles of North America as well as achieving the somewhat eccentric title of the 'most accomplished snowshoe-er of his time'. Rae's stamina and indifference to any hardship had passed into lore and his love and respect for the Arctic and its inhabitants had, without doubt, made him the foremost European authority on Arctic survival skills.

He found his Inuit friends to be a clever, kind people who were as gentle and loyal to strangers as they were to their own, and his adoption of their snowshoes, literally and physically, demonstrated just how far one could go with a little local knowledge. The locals soon came to recognise his approaching silhouette across the ice from afar; affectionately calling him Aglooka, or Long Strides, in allusion to his gait as he thundered across the ice on his ingenious footwear.

Over the ten years of his employment with the HBC, Dr Rae lived like the locals and eventually eschewed the traditional British ways of dragging everything they owned with them across the ice. Instead, he opted for lightweight sledges and dogs so that he could happily live off the land almost indefinitely using the ways of the Inuit. With his integrated approach, Rae managed to map out thousands of miles of coastline, rivers and routes to help carve out the vital commercial domain of the Hudson's Bay Company. This 'domain' was, in effect, a vast private estate owned by the HBC under a Royal Charter granted by King Charles II, and the extent of this colossal tract of Canada was five times the size of France, scooping up the Rockies, the Arctic Circle and the prairies within its purview.

At Clestrain's baronial table, John Rae Senior muttered grace after a murky broth was ladled out by a homely young local woman. Punctuated by their amens, Sir John and his two senior officers found themselves listening to the wind with a polite indifference as it howled dirges outside the house. It was *Erebus's* captain who tired of the howling first.

'Gosh, it didn't feel this windy even when we were out on the bay.'

John Rae grunted as he reached for his glass of wine and drained it in one.

Crozier thought he'd go in on different tack. 'So, Mr Rae, sir – how is your son?'

The Orcadian stared hard at Crozier for a moment before cracking into a few seldom used creases of affability. 'The lad's braw, thanks fae askin'… Has his heart set on mapping the Gulf of Boothia at the noo. Quite a large undertaking by all accounts.'

Sir John, encouraged, sallied forth. 'Lord, yes – he'll be breaking new ground there all right. Hope he saves something for us – we don't want any civilians beating the Royal Navy to the prize, do we, Mr Rae?'

Mr Rae raised his glass briefly. 'Well, good luck with that, Sir John.'

The commodore raised his glass in response. 'Here's to the Rae family… wherever they might find themselves in the world.'

As the men settled down to their supper, Fitzjames rubbed his spoon on his napkin somewhat unnecessarily before skimming it daintily across his steaming soup's lumpy surface as he said, 'So, Mr Rae, do you have any clue as to what has brought your son such success on the ice? I hear the doctor once covered over a hundred miles in one day – just to treat an injured Esquimau?'

'Well. I'm sure he would have done it for anyone who needed his attention, Commander.'

'Absolutely, sir, but it does seem an awfully long way to go, merely to treat one of the *Children of the North*, does it not?'

'Hmm, well – are we not all God's children, Commander Fitzjames?'

Mr Rae let the sound of the wind regale them once more as the cracks of his affability began to fade. After what seemed like an eternity, Rae nodded towards a heavily burled wooden bread-board in the middle of the table. On it, a pile of rugged-looking small loaves looked like they would lend themselves exception-ally well as material for dry-stone wall repairs.

'Bannocks.'

Fitzjames almost sprayed his soup as he squawked, 'Beg pardon, sir?'

'Bannocks – for yer broth, man.' Mr Rae slid the breadboard closer to him.

'Butter's a wee bit hard but I'm sure it'll soften with yer soup.' Rae drew back his moustaches with his thumb and forefinger before inserting his spoon into the general area of an unseen mouth. Fitzjames blinked uneasily at the more practical man's lack of finesse. In turn, Rae was also beginning to tire of the pompous Englishmen so began to stare at the quiet Irishman as he continued slurping.

'Captain Crozier, I've seen you here before, have I not?'

'Aye, sir – the *Cove* in '36.'

'Ah, yes, under James Ross, no?'

'Aye, sir.'

Rae laid his udder-like hands down on the table and straight-ened his arms as he pushed out his heavy chair noisily across the flagstones. 'Damn fine sailor.' He made a point of eyeing the com-modore as he stood up – as if he was assaying Sir John Franklin against the qualities of Sir James Ross. Rae then smacked his lips as he turned towards a grotesquely carved court cupboard.

Perhaps more out of his own defensiveness, Sir John's face coloured a little at what he suspected was some sort of back-handed comment regarding competency. Crozier quickly sallied the conversation.

'We were up here for the *Viewforth*.'

'The *Viewforth*, eh?'

Rae returned from the cupboard with a decanter of whisky. He cocked a severe eye over the contents by swilling the cut glass a little in the light of the candles before filling his and Crozier's glass. Almost as an afterthought, he slid it over to Sir John and nodded his head once. Sir John waggled a pudgy finger. 'Ah, no hard liquor for me, thank you, Mr Rae. Temperance is the ship that fairs far better in a storm.' Sir John slid the whisky straight past himself and onwards to Fitzjames, who at once seemed enthusiastic, but soon felt it prudent to also abstain. Rae shook his head before turning to Crozier to raise a toast.

'*Sláinte*.'

'*Sláinte mhaith*.'

As Crozier let the malty Highland Park thicken warmly under his tongue, Fitzjames attempted to get to the bottom of Rae and Crozier's Celtic bond. 'The *Viewforth*?'

Crozier swallowed his whiskey. 'Kirkcaldy whaler. The other nine ships in the fleet managed to get away from the pack ice in the spring, but the *Viewforth*… well, she was too far in.' He reached for a cobble-like hunk of bread and proceeded to break it up in his hands. 'They'd lost fourteen souls to scurvy by the time we'd got to them… remaining thirty were pretty much gonners.'

Sir John knitted his fingers as if to pray. 'Poor souls, how long were they caught for, Francis?'

'Oh, only a winter, sir – but they weren't provisioned well enough.'

Mr Rae chipped in between more slurps. 'But what they did have was plenty of blubber that was nae made off – could have saved them all if they'd used the bloody stuff to eat.'

Fitzjames seemed even more confused. 'So why didn't they use the whale, Francis?'

Crozier cut off a slab of butter and laid it on top of his bread like a lump of cheese. 'The captain refused to allow the men to use the whale skin and blubber for food. He thought it was only fit for the savages.'

Rae shook his head dismissively. 'Aye – strange, the man who puts manners before survival, eh?'

Sir John, who had been having no trouble with the soup, pushed his plate away and dabbed at the corners of his mouth briefly. 'Well, I'm not so sure, actually, Mr Rae. What would you have us all do? Make friends with the Esquimaux? Invite them round for supper?'

'Aye, well, that would probably nae do – I ken those folks don't like their food cooked in any instance, Commodore.'

Fitzjames caught the eye of Sir John with just the hint of a conspiratorial smirk pulling at the corner of his mouth.

'Good Lord, how uncouth.'

Sir John smiled at Fitzjames's quip as Rae started his ruminating again.

'Yes, well – eating your own footwear is far more civilised, I suppose?'

Sir John shrugged it off. 'Touché, Mr Rae, but at least it was a fine Northampton shoe… *Tricker's*, actually – good, thick leather… or cloth meat as the men came to refer to it with what I recall was a distinct lack of affection.'

The Orcadian now traversed his twitching glower towards Sir John. An awkward silence followed, but then, just as Fitzjames was dabbing at his mouth before attempting to defuse the situation, Crozier dissolved into a rare fit of laughter. Eventually, the others joined him so loudly that the wind was very nearly drowned out by their mirth.

The Whalefish Islands, 8 July 1845

Instruction addressed to Sir John Franklin (cont'd)…

2. On putting to sea, you are to proceed, in the first place, by such a route as from the wind and weather, you may deem to be the most suitable for despatch, to Davis' Strait, taking the transport with you to such a distance up the Strait as you may be able to proceed without impediment from ice, being careful not to risk the vessel by allowing her to beset in the ice, or exposed to any violent contact with it; you will then avail yourself of the earliest opportunity of clearing the transport of the provisions and stores with which she is charged for the use of the expedition, and you are then to send her back to England, giving to the agent or master such directions for his guidance as may appear to you most proper, and reporting by that opportunity your proceedings to our secretary, for our information.

3. You will then proceed in the execution of your orders into Baffin's Bay, and get as soon as possible to the western side of the Strait, provided it should appear to you that the ice chiefly prevails on the eastern side, or near the middle; but as no specific directions can be given, owning to the position of the ice varying from year to year, you will, of course, be

*guided by your own observations as to the course most
eligible to be taken, in order to ensure a speedy arrival
in the Sound above mentioned […]*

Erebus led the Squadron's passage through the Davis Strait and
into the eastern side of Baffin Bay as they hugged the coast of
Greenland. They had been searching all day for the relative protection of a wretched little cluster of black rocks in the middle of
Disko Bay called the Whalefish Islands. It was here that they were
to take on fresh water and tranship their stores so that they could
finally send *Barretto* back to London. As they had searched for the
Whalefishes, Commander Fitzjames had become frustrated with
Mr Reid, who had been there many times before with his whalers but had become quite befuddled. He had missed sighting the
islands that had been obscured by the early morning haar, but by
the time the fog had cleared again, the currents, along with the
distractions of weaving around huge bergy bits, had taken them to
an almost identical set of islands thirty miles to the S.S.W.

Terror and *Rattler* followed dutifully behind all day until
Crozier sent a timely signal asking if all was well as he was
beginning to suspect that *Erebus* had become 'navigationally
embarrassed'. Feeling the pressure, Fitzjames thought it prudent to stand off and have Lieutenant Des Vœux rowed out
in a gig to see if he could determine more precisely where they
were. Eventually, five Disko Inuit joined him with their kayaks
to pilot them to their correct anchorage. As soon as *Erebus*'s best
bower anchor caught, Fitzjames went aboard *Terror* with a bottle
of whisky by way of an apology. In the Great Cabin, he found
Crozier at his desk, drinking tea and writing letters.

As the commander knocked and entered, Crozier didn't lift
his head from his papers as he said, 'Ah, James! You managed to
find your way over from *Erebus* then?'

There was no friendliness in Crozier's chide but Fitzjames
managed to brush it off quite casually. 'Yes, imagine that, Francis!'

Fitzjames clung to the bottle of whisky awkwardly.

'I'm sorry about today. I, er, brought you something in the hope of making amends.'

Crozier scratched his signature into the end of his letter and slowly wiped the nib of his pen. He smiled wryly at Fitzjames's peace offering but said nothing so that Fitzjames felt the need to continue. 'Yes, unfortunately we were under the guidance of Mr Reid and…'

Crozier interrupted. His somewhat indifferent air began to transform. 'Mr Reid?'

'Yes, he…'

'He's *Erebus*'s captain now, is he?'

Fitzjames was starting to tire of being made to feel as though he was being carpeted by a particularly bitter headmaster.

'Well, no – obviously not, Francis, but he assured me he has been here many times before on his whaling runs and…'

Crozier interrupted once more as he spooned two sugar lumps into his tea. 'Hmm, it's a fine kettle of fish when a captain blames his people for his shortcomings, is it not?'

'Please, Francis, that's a little strong…' Fitzjames's eyes narrowed as it dawned on him what Crozier was doing. 'So, you knew where we were all the time, did you? And yet you did nothing to help remedy the situation sooner?'

Crozier considered Fitzjames blankly as he waggled his spoon in his tea as if it were a little bell used for summoning servants. 'Well, who am I to stand in the way of progress, eh?'

'Good Lord, how magnanimous of you, Francis. We wasted a whole day and you did nothing to help?'

'Are you blaming me now, Commander? I merely thought you and Sir John had changed your minds – decided on somewhere else to anchor, perhaps?'

'You did no such thing, Francis! You knew we were, er…'

'*Lost*. Is that the word you're looking for, James?' It was always uncomfortable for a leader to admit to being lost, and so Fitzjames shuffled uncomfortably as he tried to find his feet again.

'Lost? All right… yes – as ever, you're absolutely right, Francis.'

Crozier took a sip of his tea and winced a little before adding another lump of sugar.

'Ugh, wish I could find my tea from Fortnum's – useless idiots have obviously got our two ships very confused. Keep an eye out for me, won't you, James?'

Fitzjames shook his head as he decided to take his leave. 'Yes, well, we might very well have been lost today, but not as lost as you appear to be now. Enjoy the whisky, Francis… Oh, and, er, do try not to drink it all at once, won't you?'

As Fitzjames climbed down *Terror*'s ladder to his awaiting gig he was fairly sure he heard the sound of bone china being smashed from the direction of *Terror*'s Great Cabin.

Ahead of the *Barretto* transport being sent back to England there was much last-minute toing and froing of stores and equipment. It was back-breaking work for the men but during one of their six days there, Fitzjames, Fairholme and Le Vesconte managed to persuade their Inuit pilots to let them try out their kayaks, which, to the British sailors' eyes, seemed absolutely toy-like – something betwixt a kite and a coracle. They were astonished to find that they could be easily lifted with one hand and were made entirely of whalebones lashed together with gut, and all perfectly wrapped in stretched sealskins.

Lieutenant Fairholme, who was a burly man by any measure, found that the only feasible arrangement for him was to slide his legs into two of the tiny vessels and then gingerly paddle himself round the rocks of the bay. Whereas Fitzjames discovered that he could just about squeeze himself into the cockpit of a kayak by removing his trousers – only to immediately capsize and remain there flapping around until he was rescued.

On *Terror*'s deck, Crozier had his knuckles on his hips. He was furious at how much room Mr Stephenson's 'black devils' and the coal had taken up in his precious hold and wished dearly that both the engine and its engineer were still chugging to and fro on the London & Birmingham Railway. Both ships were sitting very heavily in the water at sixteen feet, so any item he deemed to be 'an unnecessary burden on the displacement' was offloaded onto *Barretto Junior*. Crozier found himself begrudgingly sacrificing two anchors and their cables along with the larger of the ship's cutters and the heavy iron davits from the waist. In exchange, he was able to swap them for as many of the provisions that they could possibly cram aboard including extra pemmican and salt junk. Even his Great Cabin had become home to fifty sacks of potatoes.

Also, the ten fresh heads of cattle that had come up with the transport from Stromness had been slaughtered, butchered and duly handed over as a very fitting exchange for the three hangdog matelots who were solemnly led aboard *Barretto*. They had been caught red-handed stealing spirit of wine by the ever-vigilant Pusser Osmer. There were many taboos in the Royal Navy – but to steal from another man's allowance? Well, that was quite beyond the pale. Sir John, after listening to the men's patent lies, decided to have the men punished by God's Will. He wanted no hand in the humiliating sea punishments normally meted out to sailors, which he regarded as cruel and unchristian. Instead he was sending them back home in disgrace, so that they would be regarded as the fools who were bound for glory but missed the boat – and all for the sake of a couple of quarts of alcohol. For the rest of the defaulters' lives home would be a prison of their own making: a place where punishment for their crimes would be far more effectively given by unspoken doubt from a loved one, or the sideways glances from fellow drinkers down their local, or even a innocent question from a child. Having already singled out the men as perfectly useless since the Orkneys, Crozier was pleased to see the backs of them anyway as they could well do with the space. For this, the ships' lists were adjusted accordingly with some of the hands being jockeyed between the two vessels in order to make up the numbers.

As HMS *Rattler* and the paddle frigate HMS *Blazer* had already turned back south whilst sixty miles out of Stromness, the transport ship *Barretto Junior* prepared to steam off after them from Disko but before their lines were let go, one of Crozier's young lieutenants handed *Barretto*'s purser a hastily penned letter.

'So sorry, Pusser – might I, er, trouble you with one last letter for the bag, please?'

'Of course you can, Mister Irving.'

'Thank you, um… letter to my sister. She'll worry so, otherwise.'

'It's a pleasure, sir – I'll see that it finds its way to her. Well, the best of British to you all.'

Barretto's crew gave three cheers from every shroud as they clattered off over a mirror-like bay – her keel pushing out an expanding 'V' in her wake. As the last vestiges of the steamer's pall disappeared over the horizon, the deafening peace seemed to fanfare their newfound solitude. That evening, Sir John invited the senior officers from both ships to join him for supper. Even at their best, such occasions had made intolerable demands on Crozier's patience during the all-too-frequent displays of Sir John's bonhomie – often surprising himself at the sight of his own knuckles turning white around his glass as he sat through the toadying and the same hackneyed stories being trotted out time and time again.

Fitzjames's charm had evidently worked wonders for him personally, as it had transpired that the selection of most officers of the expedition had all been good friends of Fitzjames's at some

point: Des Vœux and Le Vesconte had both served with him
in the South China seas, whilst even Crozier's own Lieutenant
Hodgson had been a pal of Fitzjames since their days on the
Cornwallis. All were cocksure, brave and ambitious young men,
and so, as Crozier saw it, their potential for calamity was limitless. Any acceleration in these bucks' careers had allowed them to
side-step experience with an astounding confidence. But Crozier
also saw that as long as his POs and other ranks knew what they
were doing, any folly on the part of their officers could be held in
check before any mishaps occurred. Even in his own surname, the
irony wasn't wasted. A crozier: the implement of choice along the
tricky little path around the very real edges of reality. But the one
thing he did feel was slightly out of his control was Fitzjames and
his infernal hold over the Admiralty and accordingly, Franklin.
He'd seen nepotism constantly throughout his long naval career
but for some reason, the powers that be had seemed completely
bedazzled by this young prig from the Home Counties.

Regarding dinner, Crozier, having had little option but to lose
his precious anchors and davits, was in no mood for stomaching
Franklin's *bon vivre*. Throughout the evening, he would catch the
eye of Sir John's steward to refresh his infernally ever-empty wine
glass, but as PO Hoar went to oblige once again, he noticed that
the young steward hesitated for a moment and, on following the
lad's worried glance, thought he could see Franklin with a barely
discernible shake of the head to his steward. Crozier, without
taking his eyes off Sir John, gripped the decanter off the now
vexed steward and filled his own glass – right to the brim.

Shortly after, speech tinkles could be heard from Sir John's
glass. His warm, gravelly tones affably quelling the chatter
around the table. 'Gentlemen… gentlemen… thank you. For
those of you whose glasses aren't yet full' – the commodore made
a point of looking pointedly in Crozier's direction again – 'I
invite you to charge them now.'

As the officers complied willingly with the commodore's

excellent claret, Sir John, as per naval etiquette, remained seated and made the loyalty toast.

'Gentlemen, the Queen!' After an enthusiastic response, Sir John continued, 'Thank you for joining me this evening. I just wanted to announce that I have made a few new appointments to help get us through next winter and, as you are no doubt already aware, we have several esteemed academics in our midst and they have very kindly agreed to help any hand who cares to avail their minds to the three R's of readin', 'riting and 'rithmetic: Lieutenant Irving, whom I happen to know has an impressive capacity for figures and has even won a silver medal for it, has kindly agreed to lead the charge of teaching mathematics to those who want to get their navigational ratings up.' There was a polite round of table rapping before Sir John broke in again. 'And the good Dr Peddie has very generously allowed his able assistant Dr McDonald, who has already had some admirable publishing success, to reveal the mystery of words to any man who is willing to sit and listen.' The two men blushed a little as the 'hear hears' died away. Dr Peddie nodded munificently as if it were he himself who was about to tutor the men before Sir John continued, 'Also, I am very grateful to announce that I have a volunteer who has very generously agreed to take over all aspects of the magnetical surveying – Commander Fitzjames.'

The officers around the table went quiet for a stunned moment before remembering themselves and applauding. As they did so, every man took the earliest opportunity to eye Crozier whose cheeks had reddened as he slowly rolled the stem of his glass between his thumb and forefinger. After all, had he not been with Parry at his furthest north attempt in '27? Or James Ross's furthest south in '39? Had he not been awarded with fellowships from the Royal Society as well as the Royal Astronomical Society for his contributions to magnetical surveying? Crozier felt his stomach begin to knot as Sir John began to rap the table in applause as he called for Fitzjames to make a speech. As everyone else joined in the call, Fitzjames looked suitably bashful and surprised before unfolding what looked like a page ripped from a book. 'Thank you, Sir John, this is an honour for which I am not worthy—'

'Hear, hear!' Crozier interjected loudly with raised glass, slopping some of the contents in the process.

A very uncomfortable moment followed before Fitzjames smiled it off and raised his glass to Crozier. 'Sir John... gentlemen... Captain' – the blatant insult was not wasted on anyone – 'I beg you will forgive me if I use the words of someone far wiser than me to do honour to all the big brains gathered here this evening, and, er, I'm sure Captain Crozier, more than anyone, will appreciate much of the sentiment.' He then squinted at the torn sheet. 'A little knowledge is a dangerous thing...' He paused to allow for one or two bleats of recognition. 'Drink deep, or taste not the Pierian spring: there shallow draughts intoxicate the brain, and drinking largely sobers us again...'

Crozier stood up. He had left the dumbstruck cabin even before the back of his chair had hit the deck.

HMS 'Terror'
Whalefish Island, Greenland,
10th July 1845

My DEAR Kate, I sit down at last to take a long farewell of you, for it will be probably a couple of years, if not more, before I have another opportunity to write. I wrote you from Orkney, where we stopped three days. We left there on the 2nd of July and had a voyage of a month, with the usual variety of fair and foul weather. We made the coast of Greenland on the 25th and arrived at the Whalefish Islands on the 4th instant. We have been very busy shifting our stores and provisions from the transport, which has convoyed us so far. We have now cleared her of everything, and we all sail tomorrow – she on her voyage back to England, and we, in the first place, for Barrow's Strait, and after, as we best can. Only three of the cattle on board the transport have survived the voyage; however, we leave this with three complete years' provisions, so, even should we not cast up for so long, you need not think we have been eating our shoes. About the last week of September we shall fix our ships somewhere for the winter. We shall be frozen up for ten months, several of which in total darkness.

At present we have constant daylight, and for the last fortnight we have had sunshine all night. There is plenty of ice floating about and scraping our sides, and we have sometimes a little snow. All very well for July.

I have every cause to be pleased with my shipmates, and barring the want of all communication, I ought to enjoy myself very much, as everything is new, and, after all, there is nothing like variety – at least it is so at sea.

The Whalefish Islands, where we now are, consist of four or five barren rocky islands like Inchkeith, and the openings betwixt some of the islands are choked up with ice. We have passed many icebergs, which are huge piles of ice and snow floating about. Some are 200 feet high. These are formed by avalanches from the Greenland Mountains, which are very high and precipitous, and one sheet of snow to the water's edge. There are some families of Esquimaux living here – most wretched people, half starved, living on seals (when they can catch them); but they seem happy, and they can read their own language, and have Bibles sent from Denmark, printed in Esquimaux, and they have been taught to read by a Danish missionary who was here some years ago. They are dressed in sealskin jackets, etc., women and all alike, and their children, of which there are great numbers, are very curious-looking creatures, more like seals than anything else. They have rosy cheeks, and round, good-humoured faces though rather greasy. Their canoes are just long enough to sit in, and the sealskin frock is tied round the edge of the hole they sit in, to keep the water out; so they can go right under water without taking any in. They are made of sealskins covering a frame made of bones and are so light that a man can carry them. You will see all these things far better described in the Polar voyages of Parry, Ross, and Back, which perhaps you may now have a little interest in looking at, as they describe exactly what will be our difficulties; and you will, I daresay, like to know a little what I may be about for so long; at least, I am sure you have no friend that takes a greater interest in you than I do. I send you a little Polar chart, and I have put the track of the Expedition in red, and proposed route dotted red. We hope to reach Melville Island before the end of September, and pass the winter there, and try to reach Behring's Straits the following summer.

Should the ice not clear away enough, or should we meet land instead of water, we shall have to pass another winter and try again, and either to go on or come back in the third summer. The former Expeditions were stopped by a barrier of ice so thick and solid that the summer, which is only ten weeks long, passed away without dissolving it. However, I trust we may have a warmer summer, either this or the next, or find some channel which they overlooked. We have the advantage of all their experience and will save much valuable time in not looking uselessly for a passage where land has been laid down in their charts, which we have with us. We have a library of the best books of all kinds, consisting of 1,200 volumes, and shall be able to pass the time very well, as there shall be some exploring parties sent out on foot while the ships are frozen in; and we will eke out our provisions with all the game our guns can procure. We shall be very busy sawing the ice and working the ships on, whenever a single mile can be gained. I have written my father a letter which is very much to the same effect as this. You might send him the little chart, as our proposed route is shown in it, and he is much interested in geography generally; I daresay you may see my letter to him. And now you are in possession of all I can tell you. The sudden change from summer back to winter has caused us all to suffer from chilblains. Some are so bad that they cannot put on their shoes. I have had my hands much swollen; but they say that in two or three weeks all this will go away. There are many tons of ice within five or six yards of me now; but it is not cold, and the sun shining all night, we don't think of going to bed, but go shooting after working hours are over, and it is supposed to be night. We shall have it dark for a long time by and by. I must now finish, my dear Katie. May every good attend you and yours. My kindest love to my dear father and Lewis.

Yours ever affectionately,

John Irving

PS – I have been making sketches; but you will see all of them when I next come to Falkirk. I have eight hours' watch out of the twenty-four to keep on deck, and I have charge of our chronometers, which are little clocks. I have to wind them up and compare them and write an account of their goings on – there are ten of them in each ship – and also various astronomical observations to make, and calculations. All this is much more interesting than the dull routine in a regular man-of-war, which is like a barrack or a workhouse. Now, goodbye. God bless you.

We are going to have a school for the men. Our Captain reads prayers on Sundays. We are exempt from many of the temptations of the world, and I hope we shall have grace to find that it has been good for us to have been separated from the world, and that God has been with us in all our wanderings. May we submit ourselves to His pleasure in all things. I send you a small piece of Tripe de Roche, a sort of lichen growing on the rocks, which was the food of Sir John Franklin in his Expedition. I send you a sketch of our ships at this place. The 'Erebus' is alongside of the transport getting her provisions, and the 'Terror' is a little to the left. The Danish house is in front, and two Esquimaux sealskin tents, which they live in during summer.[1]

---

1 Last known correspondence from Lieutenant John Irving RN, 10 July 1845.

Lancaster Sound, 14 August 1845

Instruction addressed to Sir John Franklin (cont'd)…

5. Lancaster Sound, and its continuation through Barrow's Strait, having been four times navigated without any impediment by Sir Edward Parry, and since frequently by whaling ships, will probably be found without any obstacles from ice or islands; and Sir Edward Parry having also proceeded from the latter in a straight course to Melville Island, and returned without experiencing any, or very little, difficulty, it is hoped that the remaining portion of the passage, about 900 miles, to the Bhering's Strait may also be found equally free from obstruction; and in proceeding to the westward, therefore, you will not stop to examine any openings either to the northward or southward in that Strait, but continue to push to the westward without loss of time, in the latitude of about 74 1/4 degrees, till you have reached the longitude of that portion of the land on which Cape Walker is situated, or about 98 degrees west. From that point we desire that every effort be used to endeavour to penetrate to the southward and the westward in a course as direct towards Bhering's Strait as the position and extent of the ice, or the existence of land, at present unknown, may admit […]

The grimacing able seaman shuddered involuntarily at the end of what seemed to have been another interminable watch. His tired eyes had stared unblinkingly at the seething grey as sea wraiths took it in turns to vault over the bulwarks and stab at everything with their daggers of ice.

Now relieved after turning the half-hour glass and ringing the last dogwatch bell, John Hartnell stumbled below, drunk and numb with the cold. As he entered the ship's insides it was as if he had slipped into a hot, steaming second-hand bath. He stiffly shrugged himself out of his oilskins before helping the next watch to change into them while they were still warm.

Proceeding towards the crew's cramped mess deck he vigor-ously rubbed his upper arms in an attempt to get some of the blood flowing again. As he entered the mess the fug hit him like a blacksmith's anvil: within the smoke and steam of the cook's galley various cohorts gathered together in clumps of friendship. Stokers demonically playing cards for 'abel-wackets' next to the wiry upper yardman pushing press-ups, all combined to make the air seethe with restless brotherhood. At the epicentre stood the fire and the deck's principal source of light and warmth. Hartnell clasped his hand on the shoulder of his Kentish mate Tommy Tadman as he was jabbing a sailor's barn swallow tattoo into the thumb web of Bill Orren. But as Hartnell did so, the ship lurched, causing the sail needle to go in pretty much to the bone of Orren's hand. Tadman, as the needle's guide, looked aghast at Orren, but instead of wincing, the needle's new host sneered as he plucked it out of himself – almost with relish before raising his narrow eyes towards the mortified culprit.

Hartnell started spluttering, 'Oh, God, so sorry, Bill!'

Orren thumbed away the growing dot of blood from the wound. 'Yeah, don't be sorry, lad – be careful,' he said, with a measured menace that was utterly chilling to anyone who had seen the man fight.

Tadman, a small, twitchy sailor, who seemed to be a sort of

deputy to Orren, snarled at Hartnell in a sort of diplomatic effort to diffuse the situation, 'Jesus, Harty, mind where you're going, seghead!'

Tadman then mercifully dismissed Hartnell with a tap on the back of his neck. 'Now, bugger off and see your brother – there's got a job for yer.'

Hartnell, didn't need to be asked twice and scuttled aft. Tadman dipped his needle delicately into his ink again as he frowned after the young lad.

Orren's eyes narrowed suspiciously. 'Where's he off to then?'

Tadman replied breezily, 'Oh, just a bit of business with that stoker: couple of tins.' Tadman winked before recommencing jabbing his needle into Orren's hand.

Hartnell set off towards 'Officers' Country'. Passing the ward-room, he could hear the officers inside singing around a large, squawking hand organ:

Come, cheer up, my lads, 'tis to glory we steer,
To add something more to this wonderful year;
To honour we call you, as freemen not slaves,
For who are so free as the sons of the waves?
Heart of Oak are our ships,
Jolly Tars are our men.
We always are ready:
Steady, boys, steady!

He took a quick look behind him before slipping into a store that had been already unlocked. Inside, his brother Tommy was shiftily waiting with something wrapped in a spotted neckerchief.

'Here you go, Johnny, Tadders says it's four – for the stoker.' Tommy looked down into the bundle to inspect it.

'Aw, Jesus! All the way down to the engine room – I'll take the freezing cold any day of the week than being down there. Hand me your candle, Tom.' Hartnell snatched the bundle, along with his brother's candle before continuing along the dark companionways and stepladders that led below. Eventually, he opened the heavy iron hatch for the boiler room.

The Hartnell boys had always been a bit light-fingered. Nothing nicked off little old ladies or anything: just various items left lying around by those who wouldn't miss it: toffs or big firms such as the Royal Navy was all fair game – anything to buck the system. As kids, they had been part of a Kentish gang called the Hop Pickers. There were a few of them who had found their way onto the expedition. William Orren, Abraham Seeley, Thomas Tadman and the Hartnell boys were, as the saying goes, *thick as thieves.* Their little gang had been eight-strong originally but three got caught stealing booze and Sir John had offloaded them at Whalefish.

Over time, all the Hoppers followed each other into the 'Andrew' where they could escape the long arm of the law and as a boon, see a bit of more of the world (as well as sneak some of its shinier bits and pieces back home with them). They had all grown up together – mainly around the docks of Chatham where they had eked out a living by stealing rigging, gear and anything else that was left loafing around for however long it took for some warehouseman or stevedore to turn their backs for a moment or two. They gained considerable notoriety too, along with their nickname, when they brazenly made off with an anchor from a Shepherd Neame barge loaded with hops as it waited for the tide – whilst it was still holding the thing to the mud. As the story went, the ship's skipper, who had expected to fetch up his flashy new stockless anchor the next morning, was appalled to discover that it had been replaced with a scuppered harbourmaster's jollyboat. Swiping had all been part of life; it was almost part of the fun. And, if anyone could make a quid or two here or there selling things that didn't belong to them, such the odd cask of rum or any other provisions of the 'broad arrow' variety, then that was hunky-dory.

At nineteen, Leading Stoker Torrington was one of the youngest petty officers in the Royal Navy. He also happened to be well up for a bit of moody scran off these iffy little southern lads. Torrington's knack with steam engines really had propelled him past so many old shellbacks in a navy that was being dragged kicking and screaming into the nineteenth century. The old admirals who had once been so steadfast in their opposition to any new-fangled gadgetry in their warships were now involuntarily wincing a little at the fact that the Americans were already leading the way in motorising their own men-of-war ships. So now men like Torrington were seen as the new guard: a whole new mess-full of specialists who had found themselves rapidly shoved up the ratings list. As a young lad with no family, Torrington was earning more money than he could shake a stick at, so what better than to spend it on a few home comforts? At best, whatever was in the red tins, it had to be better than hardtack and salt pork from the ship's galley. Torrington was a smart lad and, if push ever came to shove, there was no way *he* was going to starve.

En route down to the engine room, Gorgeous, the ship's cat, had startled Hartnell and made him drop one of the tins that he'd been swaddling in his spotty neckerchief. In the dim light of his candle, he could just about see it rolling around in among the various bracings and extra beams before dropping his candle and cursing loudly. Shortly, another sailor's voice could be heard somewhere among the various hisses, clunks and clangs as the engine's boiler that now steamed for the sake of the ship's heating.

'Hello, who's that?'

'Me... Hartnell!'

Hartnell emerged into the light of the lantern Torrington held out in the gloom. The young AB didn't care for being below much and was acting even more twitchily than usual. 'Only gone

and lost one of me bleedin' tins, didn't I! Your bloody cat, it was
– scared the shit out of me.'

'Where is she now? Is she all right?'

As the ship lurched and groaned with the swell, Torrington
lowered his lantern and moved towards the bulkhead with
it. Down in the bilges beneath the old de-wheeled locomotive
he could already see that Gorgeous had found the tin that the
Kentish lad had dropped. It had split at the seam and she was
already lapping at the contents. Torrington's face lit up with relief
at the sight of his cat as he shouted above the din of the engine,
'Oi-oi, you – stick with the rats, you fat knacker!'

Hartnell was far more concerned about their commerce.
'You're still going to pay for that, eh? It was her what made me
drop it.'

Torrington handed over the agreed ship's tokens in payment.

'Yeah, yeah, lad – keep your hair on.'

Hartnell hurriedly counted the silver discs as the wiry north-
erner scoffed at the lack of trust, 'Bloody hell, you're a right little
worrier you, aren't you, mate? It's all there.'

Barrow Strait

THERE WASN'T MUCH THAT SHOOK Commander Fitzjames. He'd acquitted himself admirably in battle in a number of wars and even dived into a cold, filthy River Mersey in peacetime, but heights were one thing he couldn't bear. In fact, even standing on a footstool gave him the collywobbles. Now, seventy feet above the rolling black-blue depths of Barrow Strait he needed all the mettle he could muster to take his white knuckles off the ratlines and reach across for something else to cling to on the main top.

Showing blithe indifference to the commander's evident disadvantage, Ice Master Reid moved about the tiny observer's top as if pacing around on the fireside rug of his Scottish croft. Fitzjames, finally with his clammy back pressed safely against the main topmast, was in no mood to protract his current situation.

'Er, right, Reid… this had better be good.' Reid pursed his lips a little. The two men had been quietly at odds with each other ever since their 'Whalefish Wanderings', as they had jokingly become known. Reid grimly up-nodded towards the west: 'Ah, now… thar's i-i-i-ice blink, Mister Jems.'

The commander, following his ice master's squinting gaze, looked out at the clouds that loomed ahead and could see that beneath them they lent an almost celestial glow of diffuse white light. Fitzjames wrapped an arm around a stay to stabilise himself before unsteadily pulling open his telescope as he asked for clarification. '*Ice blink*, Mr Reid?'

'I-i-ice, and a lot of it afore us, s-sir.' Reid waggled his fingers almost dismissively at the phenomenon. 'The light from it we'll be seeing in the clouds.'

'Ice… that's a pity.' But then, as Fitzjames continued to stare through his telescope he almost forgot himself for a moment until Reid touched his shoulder – making him bob so much that he nearly dropped his optics as he clutched at the shroud even more tightly.

The ice master indicated to starboard with another nod. 'But she'll be fine, s-sir – that thar's a w-w-water sky.'

In stark contrast to the ice blink Fitzjames could now make out a much darker almost foreboding patch of low cloud and it put him in mind of one of John Martin's more apocalyptic biblical paintings. 'Right, water sky? And what would that mean, Mr Reid? Rain, I suppose?'

The ice master took a deep breath in an attempt to gather his stammer. 'Noo-noo, noo… it means w-water, s-sir – noo ice at arl about it, sir.'

Fitzjames still seemed at a loss.

Reid sniffed. 'F-f-f… fair-sized body of open water, sir: could be a sound or a chu-chu-chu-chu…'

Fitzjames, ever impatient, cast his optic over the horizon as he absentmindedly finished Mr Reid's sentence for him. 'Channel.' The commander was transfixed as he gazed through his lenses and said, more or less to himself, 'Well, well, well – this is all very exciting! Perhaps the furthest north record will be ours after all, Mr Reid.' Fitzjames, wondering why Reid had grown so quiet, lowered his telescope again. 'Mr Reid?'

Fitzjames found himself to be perfectly alone on *Erebus*'s top. The old ice master, having slid down a mainstay was already back on deck and straightening his cap. Looking up at Fitzjames's flailing legs shakily trying to grope for the first step down through the lubber's hole, John Reid couldn't help his sly grin. 'P-p-prick.'

Cape Riley

Instruction addressed to Sir John Franklin (cont'd)…

6. We direct you to this particular part of the Polar Sea as affording the best prospect of accomplishing the passage to the Pacific, in consequence of the unusual magnitude and apparently fixed state of the barrier of ice observed by the 'Hecla' and the 'Griper,' in the year 1820, off Cape Dundas, the south-western extremity of Melville Island; and we, therefore, consider that loss of time would be incurred in renewing the attempt in that direction; but should your progress in the direction before ordered be arrested by ice of a permanent appearance, and that when passing the mouth of the Strait, between Devon and Cornwallis Islands, you had observed that it was open and clear of ice; we desire that you will duly consider, with reference to the time already consumed, as well as to the symptoms of a late or early close of the season, whether that channel might not offer a more practicable outlet from the Archipelago, and a more ready access to the open sea, where there would be neither islands nor banks to arrest and fix the floating masses of ice; and if you should have determined to winter in that neighbourhood, it will be a matter of your mature deliberation whether in the ensuing

season you would proceed by the above-mentioned
Strait, or whether you would persevere to the south-
westward, according to the former directions [...]

'Right, gentlemen – north, or south?'

Per their somewhat prophetic instructions, their progress to the west did indeed look like it was about to be *arrested by ice of a permanent appearance.* Now unable to investigate any further due to a complete absence of wind and a reluctance to break into their limited reserves of coal for the auxiliaries, *Erebus* and *Terror* were rowed into the glassy harbour of Cape Riley by the ship's boats. Once the anchors had been dropped, a trestle table had been set out on *Erebus's* quarterdeck for charts and afternoon tea. Sir John's two captains and their ice masters considered the chart that was spread out before them as it gleamed beneath the bursts of glorious sunshine.

Fitzjames knew exactly where he wanted to go. 'We must go north, Sir John, surely? Our instructions would favour it and Mr Reid and I descried a water cloud only yesterday – did we not, Mr Reid?'

Blanky eyed Reid briefly and the two ice masters struggled to hide their smirks as Reid replied, 'Aye, sir – *water cloud.*'

Crozier frowned witheringly at the two ice masters, until any mirth on their part soon evaporated.

Sir John was deep in thought so was too distracted to look anywhere else other than the chart. 'So, Ice Masters... west is absolutely out of the question, is it?'

Using the tip of his pipe, Blanky slowly traced the Parry Channel westward and as far as the mysterious fuzz drawn around Melville Island.

'Happen as the ice blink that was spotted yesterday would tell us there's now more ice than even Parry ran into, sir.'

Crozier expanded, 'Parry headed west, sir – then was caught there... at Melville.'

Fitzjames cut in. 'Exactly, so why would we waste time following him to his own dead end?'

Crozier shrugged. 'Unless he missed something along the way – something to the south perhaps?'

Franklin was doubtful. 'If he'd seen anything to the south whilst en route, he would have charted it, surely, Francis?'

'I'm sure he would, sir – if he'd seen anything. But that's no guarantee that there's nothing there. This channel is nearly forty miles across and you know yourself how tricky it was to spot the Whalefish Islands last month.'

Sir John, Fitzjames and Reid shifted uneasily as Crozier continued, 'Stands to reason: Parry was always so sure of glory to the north too, eh, James? It's understandable, I suppose.'

The commodore took a sip of his tea. 'Ice Masters? Wellington?'

The chart indicated that to the north lay Wellington Channel in written word only. There were no actual markings for the channel itself – just typography where the cartographer had only been able to make a guess at the whereabouts of a channel named after England's greatest general.

Mr Reid smoothed a gnarled finger over the white plain paper as if attempting to divine the answer in some way before shrugging. 'As far as the i-i-i-i… ice is having it, he's been pushed out to the west last season, s-sir… Could have kept the north, fine sir – f-fine if there's a ch-ch-chu… channel, but there's no counting on what's at the end of it, s-sir.'

Fitzjames's impatience with his ice master was beginning to show again.

'But at least all the signs are pointing to a channel there, are they not, Mr Reid?'

Mr Reid shrugged. 'Aye, sir, that's as maybe, but…'

Fitzjames interrupted, 'But at the very least this could lead us to a splendid opportunity for a crack at the northern record, could it not?'

Crozier pushed his hat a little further up his forehead and

shook his head. Blanky took a long puff on his meerschaum before offering his thoughts.

'Aye, sir – looks like we're good for a channel north, make no mistake. It's very tempting to take her however far she runs – but it's to the north, sir. Unless she bends to the west again I reckon we've got no hope. Happen as we'd be better off looking south now – seeing as the summer seems to be a good'un.'

Crozier stuck his bottom lip out and frowned. 'Hmm, I agree with you, Mr Blanky. Reckon the further north we go, all we'll have at the end of it is ice – just like the Great Barrier we found in Antarctica.'

Sir John helped himself to a slice of Dundee cake and sighed. 'Well, Francis, you might well be right there, but at least to the north we know that there's some semblance of a clear channel there that could lead us to something very exciting indeed – even the discovery of a Great Northern Ice Barrier would be something of a coup, would it not? Didn't do James Ross's career any harm, did it?'

Fitzjames brightened. 'Precisely, sir! And what if the Northern Sea was, in fact, open? Imagine that!'

Sir John spooned cake into his mouth and ruminated, 'Mmm, indeed… I fail to see anything that presents us with any such opportunities south, Francis.'

Crozier folded his arms and shrugged. The commodore knew a potential loggerhead when he saw one looming, so dismissed the ice masters. 'All right, Mr Reid, Mr Blanky – thank you for your wisdom. We will keep you apprised of the next steps, gentlemen.'

The ice masters touched their peaks and took their leave as Sir John set his cake down heavily and leant his knuckles on his chart.

'I must say, I'm very tempted to go along with you on this, James. We have a definite indication of clear leads with the water sky and I'll not hide the fact that I'd be delighted at the possibility of beating Parry's furthest north record. What did he reach, James?'

'The 88th parallel, Sir John.'

'Gosh, he did have rather a lot of luck, did he not? Francis… thoughts?'

'Well, I'd say we should pay attention to the ice masters, sir.'

Fitzjames scoffed, 'Pah! I wouldn't be so certain, Francis. We've had our fingers burnt once already from listening to Reid at Whalefish, have we not?'

Crozier allowed his deadpan face to speak on his behalf. The commodore, still appearing to be a little tender about Whalefish, shuffled awkwardly.

'Please, Francis – continue.'

'Thank you, sir… I think this is a summer that's stickin' out for sure and that we should milk her for all she's worth.'

Sir John seemed confused. 'So head north then?'

'No, south, sir – we might well get a northernmost record but we're more certain to get nipped in the ice with these currents and the wind… and who knows when she'll let us go again? No, I reckon there's nothing for us to the north – just a lot of ice and an unnecessary waste of a season, aye.'

Fitzjames stirred his tea and touched the rim with his spoon before daintily placing it on his willow pattern saucer. 'But what if there are no channels south, Francis? At the moment, we have absolutely no idea what's there and the chart tells us precious little else.'

'Well, that's the whole idea of us being here, is it not, James?'

Fitzjames sipped his tea but eyed Crozier's shaky finger resting on the blurs of the imaginary coastline south of Parry's channel.

'I say we should look at this area here,' Crozier continued. 'Cape Walker… It looks interesting to me. I'd be surprised if there wasn't a sound there, trending south – parallel with Prince Regent Inlet… Why not?'

As he ran his finger along the chart it had the effect of steadying

itself until he stopped at the huge body of water that lay below
Victoria Island where it began shaking again. Sir John and
Fitzjames noticed Crozier's shakes before catching the doubts on
each other's faces. Sir John frowned before taking his hat off and
wiping his white dome with his handkerchief.

'You might well be right, Francis, but if we did head north, we
would have the opportunity of accomplishing our instructions
in a single season…' The commodore replaced his headdress as
he continued, 'As you say, we're here to add to the charts.'

Fitzjames added enthusiastically. 'And, who knows, if this
weather holds out there's even a good chance we'll snag the furthest north record to boot.'

Sir John lifted his beaming face up from the chart. 'North it
is, gentlemen – north it is.'

Crozier repeated the orders before touching his peak and
heading off back to *Terror* to brief his officers. Once alone, the
two officers of *Erebus* took another sip of their tea awkwardly
before Sir John broke the silence, 'Mmm, meant to say earlier,
this tea is awfully good, James – where on earth did Hoar get
hold of it?'

Fitzjames made an unconvincing show of rummaging around
in his memory. 'I believe it was a gift from Fortnum & Mason, sir.'

Cornwallis Island

SIR JOHN AND HIS TWO ships ascended Wellington Channel on its eastern side. With a light southeaster blowing astern they made an average of twenty-three nautical miles per day, but on the fifth, the heavens bombarded them with a hailstorm of such ferocity that the men on deck were forced to run for cover. As the tars huddled below, the hailstorm's two-inch shots of ice on the decks above their heads sounded as if they had been boarded by a flock of panicking sheep while the ships' bells rang hysterically as if the hail itself was warning them of its own assault.

Once the two ships had emerged from the freakish storm, the crews were presented with the pale vista of an insurmountable range of mountains which they estimated to be at least 1,500 feet in elevation. Crozier's initial assessment was that this would mark the cul-de-sac of their northernmost record but then, as they picked their way around several islets to the west, they were pleasantly surprised to find a clear route as they then bent to the north again. Sir John even dared to dream of attaining the North Pole as they slipped through another clear strait that ran due north after the islets there.

Clearing Cornwallis, Bathurst and Devon Islands, they found open water as far as the horizon but then, just as they cleared for a further twenty-four miles, the lookouts yelled for another heart-sinking omen of ice blink beneath the low clouds – entirely as Blanky had feared.

At least so they could attempt to add to their charts, they

pushed further until the inevitable thin strip of white appeared on the horizon. At first, the ice masters thought that it might have been land, but it soon became evident that they were now presented with an unassailable field of ice to their north, east and west: the eternally ice-bound Polar Sea. The expedition's miraculously clear run had reached its natural conclusion.

The day before turning about, both ships moored with a huge iceberg that had grounded itself in 144 feet of water. It was soon discovered that the berg offered a spectacular grotto that had formed within it and so it was decided that the officers of both ships should take advantage by dining together within the magnificent crystalline cavern. Life-sized ice sculptures of mermaids and even a grand dining table were carved out of the ice and upon the latter Hoar, Sir John's steward, had done himself proud once again with a freshly caught char which was duly poached and served with sauerkraut and scalloped potatoes. But despite the very agreeable fare and the magical surroundings, the commodore nursed an uncomfortable stone of peevishness in his gall at their thwarted attempt at the Pole. Initially, every accommodation was given to his disappointment but by the time pudding was served, everyone else's spirits had lifted with many raised and drained glasses of claret. When the time for pudding had arrived there was a great roar of approval when Hoar tiptoed across the ice with an intriguingly covered silver server. The steward placed it on the table and lifted the lid with a flourish to reveal a magnificent jam roly-poly which prompted Lieutenant Gore to rub his hands together excitedly. 'Oh, bravo, Hoar! Can't beat a bit of dead man's arm!'

The big lieutenant's coarseness proved too much for the smouldering commodore. 'Mister Gore! Please show a little decorum – you're not at Harrow now!'

Gore was abashed. 'I'm so dreadfully sorry, sir, I, er… I wasn't at Harrow.'

There were a few barely suppressed titters as Sir John stared witheringly at Gore. After what seemed like an eternity, Sir John managed to let it go before quietly asking Fitzjames to pass the custard. The chatter recommenced to subsume any further awkwardness but Crozier could see that Gore remained a little crestfallen. He leant into him quietly. 'You not eating your *dead man's arm* then, Mr Gore?'

'Um, no, sir – seems somewhat improper to do so now.'

Crozier swapped bowls with the lieutenant and as he tucked in, he gave Gore a wee wink and spoke softly beneath the chatter around the table. 'Don't worry about the commodore, Graham – he's just miffed that he didn't get to beat Parry's furthest north record.'

Gore grinned. 'So it would seem, sir.' And as he watched Crozier polishing off his pud another question occurred to him. 'Were we very far short, sir?'

Crozier wiped his mouth with his napkin and folded it neatly, leaving it beside his plate before replying, 'Oh… only by about a thousand miles.'

The two men tried not to grin too noticeably. As they managed to straighten their faces again, the lieutenant thought he'd exploit this rare loosening of Crozier's armour. 'So, sir – you were on St Helena with my father, were you not?'

Crozier held up his glass for the steward to refill since he always seemed to miss it these days – most likely, Crozier suspected, on Sir John's instruction. He gulped at his sauterne before answering, 'Aye, son – I was one of his lieutenants on HMS *Dotterel* there. How is he? Still exiled himself to Australia?'

'Indeed, sir, and he's very well, thank you for asking.' A smirk appeared on Gore's face. 'He, er… he once told me you used to slip letters into Napoleon's post bag, and he'd open them – only to find that one of them always had a completely blank sheet of paper inside.'

Crozier allowed himself the hint of a grin as he recalled the memory, 'Ah, yes – the Blank Notes… I believe something of the kind had occurred.' Crozier took another sip of his sticky wine and reflected on happier times. 'I was a daft young pup, so I was… but I do remember Boney being very easy to rattle: used to scream and stamp around like a wee brat if his coffee wasn't hot enough – gave the servants a hell of a time, so he did.'

As had become the tradition at any of Sir John's suppers, tinkles and throat clearing could be heard from the commodore's end of the table. Crozier found himself inwardly groaning as Sir John was preparing to speak.

'Gentlemen, I am to congratulate you. We have made the 77th parallel – and, accordingly, we have set a new record: we have achieved the furthest north, er, in open water.'

The rest of the officers filled the grotto with their cheers until the commodore raised his hand and nodded his head in benevolent equity.

'And it is your energy and zeal that has, indeed, brought us so far, but, alas, Our Lord God and the ice – ha-ha – has deemed our prolonged presence here unnecessary…'

Sir John allowed more cheers from the officers before continuing, 'We are still a little way off beating Parry's record and I'm certain that if we, like him, had set out on foot we would have beaten him there too…' The officers booed good-naturedly before Sir John raised his hand once again. 'But that is perhaps a challenge for another time – so for now, we can certainly eliminate this area from our enquiries and concentrate all our efforts southwards.'

More cheers – apart from Crozier, who instead opted to use the moment to have his glass refilled. Sir John joined his hands and put his index fingers to his lips before continuing, 'So, in the morning, we'll push off and head south with the knowledge that once more, we have added greatly to the Admiralty charts and extended mankind's understanding of the world in which we live.'

The officers' cheers filled their icy cavern once more as the commodore raised his glass: 'Gentlemen, the Queen!'

Later, after the cigars, the officers filed off back to their ships. As they did so, Sir John smiled pleasantly to Crozier and motioned for him to take a seat again. 'Um, Captain – won't you stay and take a coffee with me?' Both men stared at Fitzjames and he tactfully elected to excuse himself with a curt bow before following the rest of the officers off the berg. Crozier took a seat and once the two men were alone Sir John's smile shifted into a benevolent purse of concern as he poured his second-in-command some coffee.

'How are you, Francis?'

Crozier nodded his gratitude for his coffee and answered truthfully. 'Couldn't be better, sir.'

Sir John shifted uncomfortably in his high-backed chair and looked deeply into Crozier's eyes. 'Are you? Really, Francis?'

'What do you mean, sir?'

'Aside from this evening, you haven't seemed in the best of spirits to me… You seem somewhat, er, *burdened*.'

Crozier shrugged. 'Not at all, sir – I'm fine. Thank you.'

'Yes, well, forgive my bluntness, but you're drinking far more than I care to mention, and this, er, *friction* between you and James is beginning to make itself most apparent – we're all meant to be working as one, Francis.'

Crozier eyed his coffee and pushed it away a little. 'Might I speak candidly, sir?'

Sir John's benevolent little purse reappeared. 'Of course, Francis – always.'

Now it was Crozier's turn to shift uneasily. 'It doesn't much feel like we're *working as one* from where I'm sitting.'

'Oh, it pains me to hear that, Francis. How so?'

'Well, it strikes me that like you'll take his word over mine, any day of the week and it seems most decisions that concern the expedition are already made well before they are presented to me.' Crozier nodded backwards to where Fitzjames had been standing.

'I just don't understand why you hold such store by the man. His magneticals are a travesty and his cocksureness worries me.'

'Ah, so that's what this is all about, is it? Do the magnetic observations mean so much to you, Francis? If it does, I'm sorry but it's quite out of my hands—'

Crozier interrupted him. 'There, exactly – things are even out of your hands… It leaves me feeling like I'm the half-wit brother of the Prodigal Son, just having to sit back and take it all. It goes against every instinct I have.'

Franklin seemed genuinely pained. 'I'm sorry you feel that way, Francis. I know some of his notions are rash, but sometimes we must all push ourselves to places that might, well, seem uncomfortable and dangerous, don't you think? Lord knows, you yourself have been in some tight spots in your time, have you not?'

'Aye, but it takes its toll, you know, sir.' Crozier tugged at his white hair and held out his hands in order to make the point. 'Look at me!'

The two men smiled a little before Crozier continued, 'I'm just disappointed about this position we're in now: by the time we get to Lancaster Sound we'll have wasted three priceless weeks of the season when we should have been trying to head as far south as possible.'

'Yes, well, for that I make no apologies, Francis. We had to try the Wellington Channel… I know you've never seen any worth in it but it's done now and we did manage to get a record out of it, did we not?'

Sir John spooned some Stilton onto a fragment of ship's biscuit as he noticed Crozier's frown with some discomfort. 'Is there any way I can make it up to you, Francis?'

Crozier puffed his lip and nodded. 'Aye, sir – head south as smartly as we can. We're already late in the season so the weather's going to jack it in any day now. We'll be too late to make any further heading south. I reckon we find a decent harbour for winter so we can make the most of it, sir.'

'Very well, Francis, do you have somewhere in mind?'

'Aye, sir – Beechey Island.'

Crozier Strait

AS THE TWO SHIPS BENT south again towards Beechey the heavily laden vessels pitched and rolled precariously so that few matelots could avoid the awful biliousness that accompanied their bluff, beamy bomb ships as they descended the western coastline of Cornwallis. Then, as if in the eye of a storm, they suddenly found themselves becalmed. Franklin used the opportunity to celebrate the fact that they were the first to sail around Cornwallis and in doing so, had established it as an island. He needed a name for the 1,300-foot-deep underwater canyon between itself and Bathurst Island, so thought it fitting to name it after his second-in-command, which Crozier and the officers celebrated over another supper on *Erebus*. The crew too, having received extra rum for their efforts and not caring much for records, seized the opportunity to enthusiastically regale all those sailors who had entered the Arctic Circle for the first time with *up spirits* for the Order of the Blue Nose.

The chief engineer at Chatham dockyards had been most assiduous in his modifications of the '*Bilious* & *Yeller*' for the Arctic, but what the two bomb ketches lacked in grace, they more than made up for in strength. Within a very much-abridged part of his report the engineer had stated:

The ships had been fortified externally by solid chock channels, the spaces between the channels being similarly fitted. Within-board, the spaces between the bands at the floor heads, &c.,

are fitted in with six-inch oak plank within the entire surface of the hold. The upper ends rabbet into the lower deck beams [cont'd …]

It was just such a grotesquely hewn piece of woodwork that the unfortunate Welshman, with his blue-painted nose, just managed to locate with his forehead. His Brythonic mind had been set on delivering a couple of unattended cups of grog without spilling any of the contents, but now any thoughts he had at all had been wholly stunned by *Terror*'s unpredictable carpentry.

'*Iesu facking Mawr!*' The little Welshman swayed so much with the pain that he looked like he was going to go down after butting the beam. Desperately wanting to clutch his now rapidly swelling forehead, Taff offloaded one of the tin mugs onto his mucker, Eddie Lawrence – slopping him with most of the remaining grog so that he could cup his 'egg'. 'Captain's gone over the top with these extra bracings, hasn't he – I've got an 'ed like a bloody manatee, here.'

Lawrence frowned at the grog running down his shirt. 'Oi-oi! S'true what they say about you Welsh then?'

'Whassat, mate – that we are widely admired for our lovely singing voices due to our big, hairy balls, like?'

Lozzer scoffed dismissively. 'Ner, ner, ner… I'm not talking about your women, Taff. All I mean is that you're a skinny bunch of whining sheep shaggers.'

Taff thought this through for a moment or two before grinning to himself. He snatched back his tinny and proposed a toast. '*Hiraeth!*'

Black Joe, the giant AB from Nova Scotia, glanced quizzically at Lozzer. The cockney had obviously been through this before and shrugged. 'Oh, some bollocks about homesickness… ain't that right, Taff?'

Before Taff could respond, a sickening crump was heard behind him – closely followed by the mother of all expletives:

William Orren, one of the Kentish lads who had been brought across from *Erebus*, had smashed his head on the same eccentric joinery hazard. Taff winced. 'Oh bless – sounds like someone else who wishes they weren't here.'

Orren palmed his forehead before the blood ran between his fingers. He growled, 'Why don't you fackin' shut it, you little ginger ringpiece?'

'Hey, butty – no need to lose your French.'

Orren, with shocking ferocity, uppercut his fist into the Welshman's diaphragm. Taff went down like a sack. Ordinarily, that would have been enough to assuage most aggressor's rages but Orren began swinging his boot wildly into Taff's now foetal body as he struggled to clear his eyes of his own blood. He was about to swing into Taff yet again when Joe stood his full height. Orren screwed up his face and spat, 'Oh, sit down, nigger,' as he produced a wicked-looking balisong knife in a swirling, flipping, flashing blur. Black Joe calmly put his hand on the pommel of the Bowie knife that was sitting on his belt. Orren spotted the huge knife and grinned, but then Joe swung his boot into his balls and it was Orren's turn to collapse onto the deck and writhe.

Joe straightened his shirt and ran his fingers through his long Nazarite locks, before grabbing a mug from one of the other gawping blue-noses and toasted, '*Heer-eye-th*, or whatever it was that Taff said!'

But as he drank, he began to wonder why the entire mess had become so uncharacteristically demure all of a sudden. Even Orren's cronies had stood off and the big American soon realised there was someone else standing behind him. Joe sat down resignedly to reveal Crozier who had evidently also been celebrating that evening.

'All right, sit easy, lads...' He continued with a little more languor than was becoming of a British naval officer, 'No one likes a stooshie more than me... but there's a time and a place, eh?' Crozier rested an elbow on Joe's broad shoulder as he eyed every man present. 'On this run we're going to need every man jack one of yous. It's going to be a hard old slog, so start looking after yourselves, as well as the man next to you – whether you're out on the ice, or down here in the mess decks, eh? Oh, and, er, watch out for the bracings there, lads – they're all we've got to stop us being crushed like a box of frogs, eh?'

The captain, distracted by more moans from Orren, shook his head and curled his lip. 'This new lad off *Erebus* isn't very nice, is he? Toss him over the side.'

The matelots froze in uncertain horror.

'Jesus – I'm just baiting you, lads! Where's your sense of fun?' Crozier grabbed Lozzer's tinny. He squinted with one eye at the contents before proposing a toast. 'Welcome to the Frozen Bosom of the North, lads.'

The Engine Room

Bloody cat.

Torrington had searched all the usual places: down in the orlop where the rats sometimes nested in the big tuns of carrots packed in sand, or down in the bilges where she might have fallen… or any number of her prime nooks and crannies where she would usually sequester herself during a swell to nurse her biliousness.

If the taste of ox cheeks in gravy didn't bring her home, then nothing would. He had tried it for himself too – on a bit of hardtack, declaring it to be a 'decent bit of scran'.

'Gorgeous! Where the hell are you, you bloody article!'

For three days he'd left out meat from the can that had split in order to try and coax her back, but all he caught were rats. Eventually, Torrington found Gorgeous in the most obvious place: high up on one of the hot water pipes.

All curled up.

Nose tucked under her tail.

Dead.

Beechey Island, 3 October 1845

Instruction addressed to Sir John Franklin (cont'd)…

*9. If at any period of your voyage the season shall be so
far advanced as to make it unsafe to navigate the ships,
and the health of your crews, the state of the ships,
and all concurrent circumstances should combine
to induce you to form the resolution of wintering in
those regions, you are to use your best endeavours to
discover a sheltered and safe harbour, where the ships
may be placed in security for the winter, taking such
measures, for the health and comfort of the people
committed to your charge as the materials with which
you are provided for housing in the ships, may enable
you to do – and if you should find it expedient to
resort to this measure, and you should meet with any
inhabitants, either Esquimaux or Indians, near the
place where you winter, you are to endeavour by every
means in your power to cultivate a friendship with
them, by making them presents of such articles as you
may be supplied with, and which may be useful or
agreeable to them; you will, however, take care not to
suffer yourself to be surprised by them but use every
precaution, and be constantly on your guard against
any hostility: you will, by offering rewards, to be
paid in such a manner as you may think best, prevail*

*on them to carry to any of the settlements of the
Hudson's Bay Company, an account of your situation
and proceedings, with an urgent request that it may
be forwarded to England with the utmost possible
dispatch.*

*10. In an undertaking of this description much must
be always left to the discretion of the commanding
officer, and, as the objects of this Expedition have
been fully explained to you, and you may have already
had much experience on service of this nature, we
are convinced we cannot do better than leave it to
your judgement, in the event of your not making
the passage this season, either to winter on the coast,
with the view of following up next season any hopes
or expectations which your observations this year
may lead you to entertain, or to return to England
to report to us the result of such observations, always
recollecting our anxiety for the health, comfort and
safety of yourself, your officers and men; and you
will duly weigh how far the advantage of starting
next season from an advanced position may be
counterbalanced by what may be suffered during
the winter, and by the want of such refreshment
and refitting as would be afforded by your return to
England [...]*

'Let go anchor!' the boatswain cried.

As the rodes noisily clattered out, there was much to do in preparing the ships for overwintering on Beechey. Ever craving contingency, Crozier had made extensive notes in his survey of the island whilst they had stood off at Cape Riley.

In its starkest description, Beechey was a ring of scree surrounding a menacing 643-foot-high plateau with cliffs covered in the guano and squawks of a million guillemots: the last safe harbour at the very entrance to the Great Unknown.

It took the boatswain three attempts to anchor before Crozier was anywhere near happy. In his appreciation, the captain wanted both ships to be within easy walking distance of the shore once they were beset, but deep enough at fifty feet to avoid being ground onto the rock and putty by any significant push from the ice.

As the anchor chains finally stopped paying out, all that could be heard was tinnitus and the wheeling of outraged guillemots. Something of a frisson hung in the air too as the crews of each ship knew this would be their home till the next thaw and, with it, the start proper of their Arctic odyssey.

Aloft, David Young from Sheppey had never seen anything like the strange, brutal-looking island that loomed up before him as he and the foretopmen helped to prepare their sails and spars for overwintering. Since he was the youngest hand in the squadron PO Armitage, the officers' mess steward, had seconded Davy to the foretop so that the boy could get his ratings up. As captain of the foretop, Petty Officer Peglar could see that the lad was beginning to get a little too distracted by his exciting new world aloft. Peglar was also amused to note that the lad was wearing two left gloves with little hearts embroidered on the palms. Davy ripped them off and tucked them away bashfully.

'Sorry, Chief, er… my little sister knitted them for me.'

Peglar couldn't help but notice that the boy's delicate white hands had a newly tattooed swallow between the thumb and forefinger. 'Yeah, they're very sweet, but gloves have no place up here, lad. Cold hands are better than lying cold on the deck because you couldn't find your grip.'

The captain of the foretop recognised something of himself in this fawn just trying to find his feet, trying everything to make the leap from boy to man. He didn't have to look down at his own blur-blue versions of the swallows that were leaching into the skin and merging with the blood of his own hands to know how much the two sailors had in common. Peglar glanced doubtfully at the knots that secured the sails. 'And have another look at that gasket will yer, boy?'

'Aye aye, Chief.'

Young Davy Young, as he had come to be known, checked his clove hitch: there was nothing wrong with it. The chief just wanted him to look slippery – check again, leave nothing to chance – everything seamanlike. Regardless, the PO's resolve melted a little. 'I know the older hands make it look like a cake-walk up here, lad, but if you fail once, you won't get to fail a second time. You catching my drift, Young Davy Young?'

'Aye, Chief.'

'And them swallow wings won't help you fly anywhere in this life, boy – just the next.'

Over on the mainmast, a gull laughed as it took a perch on its eight-inch-wide truck: the highest point of *Terror*. Davy caught the PO's eye and smiled. 'Chief?'

'What, lad?'

'Is it true that you've stood where that seagull is now?'

Peglar frowned before begrudgingly replying, 'Aye, lad. Daftest thing I ever did – got a lot of baccy for my troubles though.' Davy held on a little tighter as he went a little weak at the knees at even the thought of balancing on the mast's truck: a lump of wood the size of a small cob loaf on the top of a mast that was nearly a hundred feet above a rolling sea. Peglar narrowed his eyes at the wincing young lad with mock suspicion. 'But don't you be getting any ideas, young man.'

'Oh, no fear there, Chief – I don't smoke.'

Peglar laughed before shaking his head. 'Good lad! Funny thing is, as I bent down to climb back off, do you know what I could see, scratched on the top of that truck?'

Davy, dumbstruck, shook his head before Peglar continued.

'Someone's initials was already carved there.'

'Go on, Chief – you're having me on! Whose?'

By this time, Peglar had shuffled daintily across the yard to make his way down. He tapped his nose enigmatically to the boy before swinging himself over the futtock shrouds and shouting back as if it was the most obvious thing in the world. 'You'll have to find out for yourself lad!'

Over the coming days no topman would get a minute's rest during the unbending of the upper works for winter in the pack. They really would earn the right to wear their flashy neckerchiefs – along with the swagger of an invulnerability born from blithely swinging around on lengths of Chatham hemp from a great height in all sea states, day or night. The sails were the ships' wild horses and the topmen, as their riders, were now leading them to the stables.

The race against winter setting in was on as they unbent the sails and stowed the top spars and yards. All the yards nearest to the deck would be lowered and braced fore and aft to form a ridgepole for the sails themselves to be stretched across to provide a weatherproof awning over the deck. Just as they had done four years prior, back in Hobarton – for the dancing.

Van Diemen's Land, 1 June 1841

THE PERFECTLY STILL EVENING AIR had been coloured with the fragrance of blue gum and golden wattle when Sophia had first danced with Francis Crozier. Only two people in the world had ever felt comfortable enough to call him Frank and both were with him at a big dance on a small colony off the southernmost tip of Australia.

Sophia hadn't known what to make of Crozier at first. He'd seemed aloof and not in the least bit interested in her, and, to a beautiful young woman who was accustomed to getting her way, this came as something of a shock.

The Ross expedition had touched at Hobarton in order to refit *Erebus* and *Terror* before continuing onwards with their daunting mission South. Back then, Sophia was young and flirtatious – constantly craving attention but soon finding herself regretting her suitors. With the glamour of Ross's visit, her Uncle John, as the bored and homesick Lieutenant Governor of the Colony, had found the perfect opportunity to fill Hobarton's season with as many parties and functions as his stipend would stretch to. Over the summer, Sophia had become greatly intrigued by Captain Crozier but she had found the man to be consistently diverted by everything else but her. Whether it was summoning a drinks tray after her dark, twinkling eyes had met his; or the Irishman starting a most genial chat about the weather with a domestic after she had made a point of casting him what she knew to be her most comely smile. There was even a lengthy discourse on sail adjustment between the Governor and Crozier after he had absentmindedly picked up the handkerchief that she had dropped *en passant*. Even while promenading on Collins Street one evening, she could have sworn that he had crossed the road to avoid her by offering his arm to a fairly elderly lady who seemed entirely able to cross the road under her own steam. Had it not been for the rather charming way his cheeks reddened every time his and Sophia's eyes met she would have given up on him long ago.

During most social occasions Sophia Cracroft would habitually find herself swarmed by young bucks trying very hard to outdo each other with their suspiciously familiar tall tales or studiously casual mentions of family connections. But as she sat behind her fan either yawning or wincing, through her haze of braggadocio and courtliness she would catch glimpses of Crozier lugubriously peering at his watch or patting a dog. The thought of one of the most outstanding explorers of the age appearing to be so obviously out of place, so lost, made her smile. And she noted too that although his face rarely went out of its way to express itself, his silver eyes constantly sparkled with wit and interest. And she was also amused to note that the way Crozier moved completely failed to portray him as a leader or an intrepid explorer. His movements, counterpoint to Ross's swagger, were slow and unimposing – as if his back couldn't possibly bend. But then when Sophia had made enquiries regarding the captain's somewhat stolid bearing, one of his particularly keen young officers, enthused that when the occasion demanded it, Crozier could assail rigging like a maintopman, and his imperviousness to any form of discomfort was preternatural. In fact, tales of Crozier abounded about how, as a young lieutenant sitting on spray-lashed rocks, day-in-day-out dutifully scribbling his observations for a tide's rise and fall for the betterment of science, or whilst toiling at sea during the wildest storms, he could be wholeheartedly relied upon to make instruments that had been delicately set and tested in the warmth and tranquillity of the Greenwich Observatory yield their measurements perfectly. It was also well known that as a fearless midshipman on Parry's expedition, he had once carved his initials on the very top button of HMS *Fury*'s mainmast after standing upon it to salute 'the wind, the rain and the rolling sea'. And though he was a man of frustratingly few words, Crozier could reduce a man to a gibbering confessor by the mere pursing of a lip, a grunt, or – far more troubling – the fixing of a stare. But on the rare occasions when he happened to raise his low, mumbling brogue, any man who doubted Crozier would soon be convinced that he could sink a whale, or part clouds, or move icebergs if that was what his captain required of him. However, as for matters of the heart, Crozier was utterly hopeless.

James Ross's expedition found it necessary to touch at Hobarton three times during their assault of Antarctica, and over the course of their refits, Francis Crozier and Sophia Cracroft did manage to fall in love. It brought both joy and relief to Ross to see his bashful friend finally at ease with a woman – her, jabbering on about nothing in particular as he listened mutely with a smile of amusement playing on his broad face. But, by the end of the expedition's various refits, she had privately become resentful of the prospect of letting him go again, sick of not knowing if he would ever return. Sick of yearning. She hadn't wanted to fall in love with him but Crozier was not the safest of harbours in which to secure her feelings.

After their success of finding its northern counterpart, Ross and Crozier's ultimate mission was to find the South Magnetic Pole but with the sheer vastness of the continent they were only able to infer the existence of a constantly shifting phenomenon. But by the end of their toils what they did achieve eclipsed their wildest dreams: not only did they map more of the Great White

Continent itself, but they discovered the Great Ice Barrier – along with the long, slow rise of the Transantarctic Mountains behind it. Where the two converged, they discovered a bay with an island formed by two volcanoes. One of the volcanos seemed to be in a state of constant eruption, and when the entire crew was on deck to witness a particularly dramatic crescendo in the igneous firework display, Ross clapped Crozier's shoulders as the Irishman observed through his telescope. 'Well, what do you think, Frankie – who shall we name those two devilish pinnacles after?'

Crozier grinned slyly as he responded, 'Well, James, there's the calm sturdy feller there but it seems to be under the shadow of the big blustering one… How about we call the big one *Terror* and the wee one *Erebus*?'

Ross guffawed, 'Capital suggestion, Frankie – Erebus and Terror, surely.'

Despite not accurately locating the South Magnetic Pole, their accomplishments would turn out to be an embarrassment of riches, with the expedition's scientists able to record a boggling array of new species: from birds, to seals, to the first definitive charts on magnetic declination, dip and intensity. Even their twenty-two-year-old botanist, Joseph Hooker, was able to make his name by producing six illustrated volumes bursting with the descriptions of over 3,000 new species, whilst the expedition's discoveries and observations regarding the ice were even respon- sible for founding a new branch of science called glaciology. In short, the Ross expedition was an out-and-out success and the last major expedition carried out entirely under sail returned without the loss of a single soul. But if any of this came at any expense at all then perhaps it was its two captains who had borne the cost as they toiled throughout with the terrifying Southern Ocean. Each time the expedition touched at Hobarton, their leaders arrived pale and spent – their hair whiter than the last time and with hands less able to be steadied after the weight of the ordeals they had suffered.

Now, as the two ships lay at anchor in the glassy bay below Government House, Ross and Crozier felt like they were a world away from the turmoil they had endured. The nearby shore lights danced in the black, quopping satin of the water and the absence of any wind allowed the sound of tiny little shore breaks to be magnified in the stillness. Even the chirrups of the cicadas in the eucalyptus trees helped to add to the gentle, rhythmic sibilance.

A cable offshore, *Erebus* and *Terror* had been rafted together to form the venue of 'the Glorious First of June': a grand ball thrown in gratitude to the Governor and people of Hobarton. The ships' stout black hulks, topped with the intricate tangle of masts and spars, normally rose out of the water forebodingly like palisades of bramble – but tonight, nothing at all was unwelcoming about the two warships and their cheery festoons strung with their signalling flags.

The glowing prism of an awning seemed to be floating amidships, and from the decks within, the sound of waltzes and merriment could be heard. Leading up to the prism, a pontoon for the guests had been rigged from the ships' boats connected via planks. Bunting and fragrant little yellow flowers of wattle lined the rope handrails to help the giddy revellers negotiate the planks towards the sound of Strauss via the Hobarton Town Quadrille and the band of the 51st Regiment. Once aboard, the main decks of both ships, cleared of gear, boats and lines revealed the 'most solid-sprung ballroom in the southern hemisphere'. Whilst above, a magnificent chandelier, fashioned from the marines' polished bayonets had been hoisted so that its serried, shards of light would catch 248 looking glasses that had been positioned around the rails of the decks. This was the Royal Navy: a shimmering reflection of the Motherland, rising to any occasion with the 'pride, pomp and circumstance of glorious war'.

Up until this point, Sir John Franklin had been the Lieutenant Governor of Van Diemen's Land, but it had not been going well. The island was both a free colony and a prison and there had been an inevitable conflict of imperial and colonial interests. The free colonials profited by the convict establishment, which provided them with a market for their products along with cheap labour. So much so that Franklin, or more specifically his wife, had been appalled by the way the convicts lived and the way in which they were treated. And it wasn't as if they'd done anything particularly harmful to get transported to the colonies either: anything from poaching a rabbit on the wrong estate to letting a room to a homosexual would land offenders of almost any age a one-way ticket to the colonies. Lady Franklin's interference had made the governor one or two malicious little enemies who were beginning to make life difficult for her husband whilst they snarlingly referred to her as 'the Man in Petticoats'.

Perhaps it was the two heroic officers with their smart ships and perfectly disciplined crews that made Sir John yearn for an infinitely more straightforward life than the petty, self-serving politics involved in heading a colonial backwater as he gazed out across the dance floor of *Erebus*'s magnificent floating ballroom.

Sophia Cracroft was feeling pangs of a different sort. Dancing with Captain Crozier, her heart skipped beats as his two left feet stepped on and off her delicate little toes. As she avoided Crozier's boots, she couldn't help but peek round his epaulettes to see the Franklins begin to waltz to 'Non Più Andrai' as if they were all alone in the cockpit of their private yacht. 'Look at them, Frankie. How could anyone possibly find two people more in love?'

But Crozier's mind was elsewhere. 'You're very quiet, this evening, Captain. Is it something I said?'

'Huh? Oh, Lord, no! Sorry, Sophy, it's just that I've...'

Crozier squirmed awkwardly before leading Sophia to the rail at a pace that was a little too much for her already bruised toes.

Crozier strode towards the rail to check the lines and fairleads on the quarterdeck.

Once there, Sophia started to giggle. 'Oh, Frankie, what is it – you seem dreadfully worried?'

Crozier, in one sleek and probably well-drilled movement produced something from his waistcoat pocket: a ring box. Sophia put her hands up to her cheeks as Crozier peered into her eyes earnestly, 'I'm hoping that after we leave for England you'll follow me back?' He opened the little box to reveal a huge opal secured to a ring of gold. 'Sophia, my darling, the last three months have been the most delightful I've ever spent with another human being – will you marry me so that we can be together, always?'

Sophia, on seeing the ring, seemed entirely delighted at first, but then another notion came to her and her attitude quickly hardened. '"Together, always" – do you really mean that, Frankie?'

'Well, yes my love… of course!'

'So does this mean you'll leave your other mistress for me?'

Crozier was more than a little perplexed. 'Mistress? My darling, I promise you, I…'

Sophia put a hand on his chest and patted it. 'I'm talking about the Navy, dear heart.'

Crozier's shoulders seemed to slump as awkwardness began to set in. The notion of leaving the navy had never even crossed his mind. After all, it had been his home, his school and his livelihood. It had been all he had known since he was fourteen years of age. How would he possibly afford living on land? Keep a wife who was used to getting whatever she wanted? The prospect of leaving the Navy filled him with more dread than anything the sea could ever toss at him.

'Well, er…'

Sophia's eyes narrowed a little as she tried to find Crozier's. 'Now you suddenly seem unsure, Captain?'

Crozier eyed the ring before looking up again into Sophia's eyes. 'Well, I suppose what I really want is to have a reason to come home – to someone I love. Someone like you, Sophy.'

Sophia peered over the side and into the pulsating water as her vista began to blear.

'I'm sorry, Francis. I'm not sure that's enough for me – if I'm to be truthful to you. I don't think I would be able to just sit around sewing patiently as I wait with hope for you to come back to me from places that aren't even on any maps. You're a marvellous man, Francis Crozier, but as long as you're in the Navy, I'm not sure I can marry you.'

She reached over to the ring, still in its box, still in his shaking hand – and tenderly closed it again for him.

Erebus Bay, 7 October 1845

CROZIER WARMED HIS HANDS AROUND his teacup as he gazed for-
lornly at the glassy calmness of the bay. Through the poky little
stern lights of his Great Cabin he mused at the silkiness of new ice
forming in the water: *shuga, grease, slush, nilas, pancakes; they will
all conspire against me any day now... sea scabs for my wounds. The
darkness will follow again... the one thing of any certainty in my life.*

He'd been out on deck all morning overseeing the preparation
of *Terror* for overwintering, but now, as he smelled the malt of the
whiskey mingle with the steam of his hot pusser's tea, he could feel
some of the warmth creep back into his body, temporarily easing the
knot that was beginning to twist and turn in his stomach. Overhead,
he could hear the scuffling of busy sea boots on the quarterdeck
above – along with the muffled voices of struggling men as they
prepared to take the strain of *Terror*'s rudder. Crozier listened miser-
ably as it was unhitched from its pintles before the men above began
to haul away so that the rudder's full weight graunched unwillingly
up its Woolwich-designed transom channel. The innovation of a
detachable rudder had been truly revolutionary but what captain
could ever feel entirely comfortable in a rudderless ship? No one
understood better than Crozier how sacrifices had to be made from
every quarter when it came to preparing the ships for overwintering,
but as the five-ton timber rumbled its way up towards the deck, he
felt nothing but despair in the planned disablement of his ship. To
his ears, it was the grating of a tomb being sealed as he tried to ready
himself for yet another long, dark winter trapped in the ice.

Beechey Isthmus

Instruction addressed to Sir John Franklin (cont'd)…

11. We deem it right to caution you against suffering the two vessels placed under your orders to separate, except in the event of accident or unavoidable necessity, and we desire you to keep up the most unreserved communications with the commander of the 'Terror,' placing in him every proper confidence, and acquainting him with the general tenor of your orders, and with your views and intention from time to time in the execution of them, that the service may have the full benefit of your united efforts in the prosecution of such a service; and that, in the event of unavoidable separation, or of any accident to yourself, Captain Crozier may have the advantage of knowing, up to the latest practicable period, all your ideas and intentions relative to satisfactory completion of this interesting undertaking.

13. We have caused a great variety of valuable instruments to be put on board the ships under your orders, of which you will be furnished with a list, and for the return of which you will be held responsible; among these, are instruments of the latest improvements for making a series of observations

*on terrestrial magnetism, which are at this time
peculiarly desirable, and strongly recommended by the
President and the Council of the Royal Society, that
the important advantage be derived from observations
taken in the North Polar Sea, in co-operation with
the observers who are at present carrying on a uniform
system at the magnetic observatories established by
England in her distant territories, and, through
her influence, in other parts of the world; and the
more desirable is this co-operation in the present
year, when these splendid establishments, which do
so much honour to the nations who have cheerfully
erected them at a great expense, are to cease. The only
magnetical observations that have been obtained very
partially in the Arctic Regions are now a quarter of a
century old, and it is known that the phenomena are
subject to considerable secular changes. It is also stated
by Colonel Sabine, that the instruments and methods
of observation have been so greatly improved, that the
earlier observations are not to be named in point of
precision with those which would now be made; and
he concludes by observing, that the passage through
the Polar Sea would afford the most important
service that now remains to be performed towards the
completion of the magnetic survey of the globe.*

*14. Impressed with the importance of this subject,
we have deemed it proper to request Lieut.-Colonel
Sabine to allow Commander Fitzjames to profit by
his valuable instructions, and we direct you, therefore,
to place this important branch of science under the
immediate charge of Commander Fitzjames; and
as several other officers have also received similar
instruction at Woolwich, you will therefore cause*

*observations to be made daily on board each of
the ships whilst at sea (and when not prevented by
weather, and other circumstances) on the magnetic
variation, dip and intensity, noting at the time the
temperature of the air, and of the sea at the surface,
and at different depths; and you will be careful that
in harbour and on other favourable occasions those
observations shall be attended to, by means of which
the influence of the ship's iron on the result obtained to
sea may be computed and allowed for.*

*15. In the possible event of the ships being detained
during a winter in the high latitudes, the expedition
has been supplied with a portable observatory,
and with instruments similar to those which are
employed in the fixed magnetical and meteorological
observatories instituted by Her Majesty's Government
in several of the British colonies.*

*16. It is our desire that, in case of such detention,
observations should be made with these instruments,
according to the system adopted in the aforesaid
observatories, and detailed directions will be supplied
for this purpose, which with the instruction received
at Woolwich, will be found, as we confidently
anticipate, to afford full and sufficient guidance
for such observations, which will derive from their
locality peculiar interest, and high theoretical value.*

*17. We have also directed instruments to be specially
provided for observations on atmospherical refraction
at very low altitudes, in case of the expedition being
detained during a winter in the high latitudes; on this
subject also particular directions will be supplied, and*

you will add any other meteorological observations
that may occur to you of general utility; you will also
take occasions to try the depth of the sea and nature of
the bottom, the rise, diction and strength of the tides,
and the set and velocity of currents […]

Winter arrived with a ruthless efficiency that saw everything turn cold, white and hard before their eyes. As Crozier had anticipated, the pancake ice appeared in just a matter of days and *Erebus* and *Terror* were made ready. From the shore, the two ships with their ochre-coloured hatch lines and what remained of their standing rigging took on the appearance of two colossal bumblebees that had been pinned onto their backs by a demented collector.

Overwintering could now begin in earnest. With the establishment of various buildings ashore such as a storehouse, two washhouses, the blacksmiths' forge and even a magazine for the ships' gunpowder on the far side of the spit. No detail was too small to be overlooked and every comfort and contingency had been considered. Through careful planning, and the lessons learnt from the many expeditions before them, Sir John and his men would settle into the winter routine easily. A frisson of excitement ran through those who had not gone through a winter on the ice but for those who had been there before, it was a chill that quietly leached into their bones.

As if winter herself had magically constructed a new garrison around them, various sporting events were organised whenever the weather permitted. Cricket, football and rugby teams trotted out onto the ice three times a week and, despite Sir John's hint that it was possibly *overly familiar*, Crozier often involved himself in the rugby where he played loosehead in the scrum and could be relied upon to keep his elbows high and his fists loose. Concurrently, and almost as a form of constant applause, the rippling crackles of fire from the other officers' fouling pieces could be heard in the distance as they hunted.

The only exception to the din and the hubbub of sport was the quietude that Sundays brought. On Sir John's orders, these were strictly set aside for the Lord, with bible studies in between matins and vespers given by the commodore himself.

Throughout the season, despite any weather, exploratory parties were sent out to reconnoitre the lie of the land. These sledging crews were deployed so that by the time the ships were released from the ice, Sir John would have a proper appreciation with charts updated accordingly for the next season's endeavours and, at the very least, they could rule out routes that were impassable or were of no use to their cause.

Any officers and men who remained aboard dedicated their full attention to the meteorological, hydrographical and magnetical surveys in order to keep the Magnetic Crusader, Edward Sabine, happy back home in his Woolwich citadel. To this end, a portable observatory, insulated with snow blocks, was set up on the ice away from any interference from the ships' iron in order to house the notoriously sensitive declinometers for hourly observations of magnetic variation. The Admiralty had a seemingly insatiable desire to reveal the great remaining mystery since Newton's work on gravitation, and as such, these responsibilities now lay before the shining boots of Commander Fitzjames.

Despite this inexplicable snub, Crozier hated to see any job done sloppily and, still feeling a weight of responsibility for any observations taken during the expedition, he had asked his own Lieutenants Irving and Hodgson to step forward and assist the commander. Both lieutenants had shown outstanding aptitude whilst on their various courses at Woolwich whereas Fitzjames's own efforts, whilst under the beady glare of Colonel Sabine, had been found to be eye-twitchingly inept when it came to anything regarding accuracy and diligence. Irving and Hodgson's assistance with the bewildering, scientific observations came as a great relief to Fitzjames.

As far as the rest of the men's schedule was concerned, it was beginning to verge on hectic, but if there was still any other free time, most of those who cared to hunt were fully encouraged. In fact, hunting was seen as a vital addition to their provisions and had become so bounteous that it was assumed that the tinned provision would be unlikely to be used in anger. Parties would often bring back sacks of game, such as ptarmigan, willow grouse, and sometimes even more exotic species such as owl. Peregrine falcon was a particular favourite, with Commander Fitzjames even going as far as to declare it 'the best beef in the country'. As well as bird, there was plenty of larger game to be had too. Musk oxen were found to be excellent eating whilst young and in the right season, but utterly revolting under any other circumstance, whereas seal, reindeer, polar bear, and even wolf, provided a far more agreeable staple on the tables of every mess. The fresh meat was eaten whenever available and as for everything else, not a bone, lump or lip was wasted, and if anything remained after that, it was rendered into fuel oil for lighting and cooking.

However, nature being nature, adaptability was inevitable. If lucky enough to stay out of the reach of shot or a 0.796-inch ball, most of the animals learned very quickly to take a far wider berth of the dark silhouettes of men on the ice.

'The Royal Arctic Review Hall'

Were I laid on Greenland's Coast,
And in my Arms embrac'd my Lass;
Warm amidst eternal Frost,
Too soon the Half Year's Night would pass.
Were I sold on Indian Soil,
Soon as the burning Day was clos'd,
I could mock the sultry Toil
When on my Charmer's Breast repos'd.
And I would love you all the Day,
Every Night would kiss and play,
If with me you'd fondly stray
Over the Hills and far away

'Over the Hills and Far Away', John Gay, *The Beggar's Opera*

Within the High Arctic, the thirteenth day of November always sees the setting of a sun that will remain set for the next 126 days. In preparation for this, both ships had all but four of their ten guns unshipped and the provisions that had replaced them had now been relocated to their new storehouses on the beach. With the gun deck cleared, various activities such as meetings, education, communal messing and even entertainment could take place per Sir John's desire for every soul to spend as much time in as many different people's company as possible during the dark months. This was the one thing that Sir John and Crozier did actually see eye to eye on. Being from the Parry School, and beset eight times already, Crozier knew all too well that one of the best ways to avoid any 'dark or mischievous thoughts' creeping into the men's heads was to bring officers and sailors together to lark about. So, under Sir John's patronage, they rehashed the *Royal Arctic Revue*, which had first been established by the crews of *Hecla* and *Fury* some ten years prior.

A guest officer would manage each of the productions that would be rigged for the first Monday of every month aboard alternating ships, and over time, the expectations for each production rose appreciably with each airing. At the start, there were many shows of amateur dramatics – usually involving the surprisingly deft application of make-up, abundant Union flags and an extensive wardrobe – the bustling gowns of which had been generously donated by Lady Franklin's wide social circle. But from there, things began to escalate. Productions ranged from theatricals, musicals and revues that featured many skits such as a faithfully reproduced mock-up of an infamous matelots' pub in Blackwall called The Gun. This production, complete with permanently apoplectic landlord, Bob Hall, was made incarnate by the hilarious, and no doubt frequent observations of Marine Sergeant Tozer. Even the expedition's big, black dog, Neptune, put in a turn whilst wearing a little velvet cape and matching bonnet and the beast would sit and pant patiently as Sergeant Bryant, the usually gruff West Country man, waggled his fingers elaborately under his moustaches to produce a bewildering array of birdcalls. At the end of each one, the great dog would give a single deep bark before various members of the audience would heckle their own guesses on the birdcall. The sergeant would pause teasingly for a moment before appraising both the dog's and the hecklers' responses accordingly by saying things like, 'Yes, boy – it were a marsh warbler.' Or, 'No, babba – get it together! That were a little Jenny Wren.'

Sprinkled throughout the running order of these

entertainments would be musical delights from 'some of the country's most talented performing artistes' such as caulker's mate Cornelius Hickey on his squeezebox joined by AB William Wentzall on the fiddle to belt out much-loved shanties. (Cornelius, being completely toothless, had the added appeal of being able to gurn as he played.)

And then there were truly unexpected delights such as Graham Gore on the flute – which he played like a virtuoso; or any of Mr Irving's strange, yet beguiling poetry, such as an 'Ode to Chilblains', or 'Cocoa, How I love Thee More Than Tea'. But, inexplicably, the all-time favourite was the pairing of the gunroom steward Thomas Armitage and captain of the foretop Henry Peglar. As Macheath and Molly from *The Beggar's Opera* the pair would elicit damp eyes from even the saltiest of matelots with their enchanting duet of 'Over the Hills and Far Away'.

Another particular highlight of the Entertainments Calendar was the increasingly lavish masquerades. These were 'Ordered to Attend' but really needn't have been as the men wouldn't have missed them for all the tea in China. As far as the order of dress was concerned, a domino was the bare minimum dress-up requirement for admission, but for the majority of the tars, nothing less than a huge over-the-top ensemble of imagination and mirth was what would materialise at the entrance. Highly competitive levels of elaboration included monks, monkeys, sultans, sheiks, mandarins and other wryly observed characters (usually from foreign climes) with each characterful confection met with raucous cheers of mockery or admiration. Obviously the British Royal Family was sacrosanct so any get-up that portrayed them was wisely avoided. That said, one particularly chilly evening did see Quartermaster 'Old' Davy McDonald chance his arm as Britannia herself. Pulling up at the bottom of *Terror*'s torch-lit snow ramp, she looked truly majestic on her hessian horse-drawn chariot drawn by two somewhat retarded-looking pantomime horses (two stokers in each, front and rear). She even had a six-strong retinue of face-blackened footmen – all rather smart in their ostrich-laced tricorn hats and scarlet coats. They also came equipped with multi-coloured breaches that the pusser suspected had been cut from some of the adrift signal flags that the captain of *Blazer* had made a something of a fuss about whilst back at Stromness. Overall, Old Mac's depiction of Her Britannic Majesty would have been supra-magnificent were it not for her constant insistence on prodding her trident heavenward and shouting, 'Winter – you can kiss ma fat one!' at the top of her far more than ample lungs.

In preparation for each of these monthly shindigs, officers and men would toil together for hours over costumes, sets and rehearsals to make each of their ship's events a point of pride and a thing to be recollected for years to come. The fact that officers and men were working together as equals was unparalleled in a normally hierarchical navy that lived and breathed on everyone rigorously knowing their place.

Christmas was fast approaching and the caulkers, together with the carpenters, had done *Erebus* proud with a gilded trompe l'oeil proscenium arch for the 'Christmas Review':

THE ROYAL ARCTIC THEATRE PRESENTS... THE TEMPEST

Playing before the squadron for Christmas had grown to become a somewhat daunting challenge. Director Little, feeling rather buoyed, introduced the crews to what he felt was one of The Bard's more relevant works within the two pages of *The Fort Nature Weekly Chronicle*. *The Chronic*, as it came to be affectionately known, was a gazette, published weekly from *Erebus's* printing press and it mainly comprised humorous contributions consisting of anything from lengthy jibes at shipmates, droll reports regarding various calamities on the ice (of which there was a never-ending supply) and, with predictable regularity, poems dedicated to either various stages of the weather, or lovingly crafted odes: to ailments – or, of course, food. These were all posted anonymously in a box at the forward skylight and were ruthlessly edited by Commander Fitzjames under the pseudonym 'General Frost'. One for his substantial rejection pile seeped from what he suspected was the dark quill of Lieutenant Irvine:

> We are all at sea.
> Floating on the darkest soup of uncertainty.
> Supped by none but the slave of the moon
> Oh, God please grant us safe harbour soon
>
> In cahoots with the wind which art thine brother,
> We slosh and swill from one shore to another
> As we hopelessly cling to your wide, blue back
> Till our sails rip and our masts doth crack.
>
> Often deeper than our most infinite ropes,
> But in a trice shallow to dash all hopes;
> One moment flat and useless –
> The next, a range of tyrannical mountains,
> To be dashed against rocks in their terminal fountains.
>
> The sea lets good men sink whilst deadwood floats
> Let's toss our oars and man the boats.
> Confounded by the deep and ruled by the waves,
> Are we not all this limpid slave's slaves?
>
> Unfathomable fathoms,
> Unnavigable passages,
> Bearings lost, and in the direst of straits!
> The briny, the oggin, the deep, the main,
> You are the devil's piss in all but name.
> There's land ahead but her shore is a lee
> Alas, my lads
> We are all at sea.

Regarding the big Christmas production, Crozier had his doubts about 'Billy Bloody Waggledagger' too, but the actors and the audience seemed to really take Shakespeare to their hearts. By the end of the month every man jack knew almost all the characters whilst the cast knew almost every line.

So it was that on Christmas Eve 1845 nerves were getting to everyone. Give or take the odd costume malfunction or wobbly canvas rock, the show started off promisingly enough and, despite her gaunt looks, Lozzer made a thoroughly convincing Miranda. Every time *she* appeared on stage with her huge bosom and enthusiastically applied rouge the men would go wild with roars and applause so that poor Lozzer found himself struggling to get his next lines out. Only after some time waiting for the catcalls and wolf whistles to subside, he would actually start basking in the furore and even play to the room a little with what he imagined to be a comely smile. However, it was an icy glare from Sir John that pricked the cockney blowhard onwards. Regardless, the production romped on – Torrington's Caliban, carrying his burden of wood and delivering his 'All the infections that the sun sucks up' speech, was particularly well received until, completely unprompted, he began to wave and dance before appearing to stumble – taking some of the flimsier props down with him. The audience rose to their feet in rapturous appreciation of his incredibly convincing *exeunt*. Sir John, knowing the play well, was somewhat confused regarding this unexpected twist in the plot.

Through his Dollond compound microscope, the assistant surgeon of *Terror* was observing the stool sample on the glass slide. He could clearly see the sausage-shaped bacteria reproducing at a startling rate. Goodsir was an excellent surgeon and he had superb instincts but at that point, all the young doctor knew with any degree of certainly was that poor Torrington, lying there in his sickbay, in his vomit-ridden mooncalf garb, was about to breathe his last.

The Main Deck

Drag, drag and drag some more,
Like the Asses of a cart that go before
Cough, cough and cough it all out
Spit or swallow, but never have doubt.
Never give in lads; we've got pulling mastered,
And never let the boss hear you call him a –
Drag, drag and drag some more,
Like the Asses of a cart that go before.

'The Pully-Hauly Song', Anon.

Petty Officers Armitage and Peglar were overseeing the Watch. Or, more accurately, they were staring into the sky with mouths agape. They had seen many things during their service together on HMS *Wanderer*: during campaigns in the Opium Wars they had carved their names on the alleged 'Tomb of Genghis Kahn'; whilst in Liberia they'd liberated slaves from the traders' barracoons on the Gallinas; and in Borneo they'd even skirmished against pirates and lived to tell the tale.

They had already been through so much together, but they'd never seen anything like the Aurora Borealis. The Northern Lights they were now witnessing had utterly entranced them with its green glow that writhed and pulsated across the crisp night sky. Armitage slid his cap off his head as he emptied what was in his mind. 'Fuck me, Pegs – you seeing what I'm seeing?'

Peglar eventually managed to lift his dropped jaw. 'Certainly am, Tommo.'

Peglar was in a reflective mood as he broke off from gawping to pack his pipe. 'Jesus, we've seen some things together, haven't we, mate?'

'Yeah, them lights put me in mind of the glow we made when we set fire to them slave prisons in West Africa.'

'Yeah, lit 'em up good and pretty, didn't we?'

Peglar took out a notebook from a breast pocket. Armitage spotted it and nodded. 'What you got there then, Pegsie?'

'Oh, it's just me personal bits and pieces, you know, there's a letter in there for me old mum and that...' Peglar rubbed his beard. He was going to say something but thought better of it, before Armitage pressed him. 'What is it, Pegsie?'

Peglar was still unsure. 'Ah, it's nothing – you'll just think I'm being soppy.'

Armitage frowned. 'Come on, me ol' mate – course I won't!'

Peglar gripped his little book even tighter before offering it to Armitage. 'Well, I want you to keep hold of it for me, Tom... Just for safekeeping, like... Just in case I don't make it back.'

Armitage looked puzzled. 'Back from where?'

'Back from here... Home.'

Armitage scoffed, 'What are you going on about? Of course you'll make it back – soppy bastard.'

Peglar squinted for a moment or two, but insisted, 'Yeah, thought you'd think that... All the same... it'll just gimme a bit of peace of mind if I know it's in your hands, Tommo.'

In the end, Armitage agreed but only on the proviso that Peglar did the same with his own pocketbook, just for safekeeping.

With seemingly no end to the entertainment laid on for the watch that evening, a hauling crew filed off the other ship to divert them further. *Vixen*, one of the smaller whaleboats, was lowered from the after davits and shipped onto heavy sledge runners. The great black hulk of Neptune was shoved down a canvas chute to get him onto the ice. Sergeant Bryant was waiting for him in an attempt to arrest the great hound's descent, only to be completely bowled over for his troubles and almost licked to death afterwards.

The huge dog had been brought to the Arctic because he had an almost supernatural nose for smells and so could act as an early warning system for polar bears. The other reason for bringing a twelve-stone hound into the Arctic was that he could swim like a fish in any water – whether it was sea, lake or river, no matter how cold. Should any man find himself submerged in water in the Arctic, the drill (practised ad nauseam) was for the casualty to hang onto the dog's tail and allow the beast to drag him to the side of the lead. Usually, a man in freezing water had around twelve minutes before losing consciousness and, unless the casualty could be warmed within twenty minutes of immersion, death would be in attendance very soon after.

What the watch was observing now was the latest of Franklin's sledging parties setting out for a bit of 'pully-hauly'. They were off to recce the lie of the land and get every hand used to pulling the one-ton sledges – or adapt them accordingly. The party consisted of a few of the more able ABs but mainly marines, as this was what they were made for: endurance, stamina and good old-fashioned bullheadedness. Johnny Hartnell, pulling his woollen hat down over his curly mop couldn't have felt more excited. Finally, he was out doing some proper work – anything to avoid polishing silver in the mess or picking up napkins for toffee-nosed little *jimmies*.

Lieutenant Le Vesconte pulled out his silk sledging pennant from his breast pocket and secured it to the flagstaff off the boat's transom. As the men readied the boat, Lieutenant Little, who had been given responsibility for the daguerreotype camera came down the ramp and began to clatter around with his device's ungainly tripod as the men prepared for the off. After much fiddling, he attempted to rally Le Vesconte and his men in a pose beside their boat but it was like herding cats. No sooner would he have the men settled when someone would fiddle with a cap or the device itself would sag as if it was wilting in the cold. Finally, Edward Little was happy. 'Right, you lot, er, in this light, I've calculated that you're going to have to stand as still as you possibly can for about twenty-three minutes.'

The men looked to Lieutenant Le Vesconte. He frowned and said, 'Yes, right, well, we'd love to oblige you, Edward, but we've got the Slough of Despond to find – perhaps we could reschedule on our return?'

The well-drilled men took up their positions on their harnesses and the lieutenant nodded to his sergeant.

'All right, Sergeant Bryant, cast off, please.' As the heraldic-looking standard fluttered in the breeze the lieutenant saluted *Erebus* and the sergeant gave the order to pull, as if they were off to fight at some wintery medieval tournament. 'One, two, three…'

The men took up the slack, then, leaning in together with their full bodyweight, they all shouted and pulled together. 'Heave!'

The one-and-a-half-ton boat finally creaked forwards, and if he had ever been stoic enough to brave the Arctic, Sisyphus would have been up there, trying to keep up with the best of Le Vesconte's men as they hauled away at HM Sledge *Vixen*.

The Great Cabin, HMS Erebus

BY ANY MEASURE, SIR JOHN Franklin's table was sumptuous. A huge silver salver of perfectly hung venison was placed upon the crisp, white table linen. The commodore, seated at the head of the table, reached into his waistcoat for his pocket watch as the rest of the officers chatted politely. After noting the hour, he pressed the little catch and it flicked open to play a pretty chime arrangement of 'Non Più Andrai'. He smiled a little as he thumbed the inscription within the watch's case:

In time, we will be together.
J.

He gently closed his watch before tucking it away again. Evidently at a loss, he started toying with an imagined hang-nail on his perfectly manicured fingers whilst dubiously eyeing the steam rising from the perfectly cooked meat as if it was the spectral soul of the reindeer rising heavenwards. As if talking to the haunch, he quietly mumbled two words: 'Captain Crozier?' Fitzjames, sitting to his right, responded by shaking his head curtly as if this made his information more rapid for his superior to absorb in some way.

Whether it was the recent bad news, the constant darkness, the loneliness, or the huge weight of responsibility, Crozier was the owner of what the poet Horace would refer to as a 'black dog'. He had once attempted to describe to James Ross that it was, 'as if a powder keg exploded within my very core – always a few hours before dawn.' Ross knew exactly how he felt: like his heart had been carefully lifted out of his ribcage whilst still attached to all the various plumbing and lines and whatever else that made the thing secure and pump the claret around his being. Then, the fingers cradled around it would open and his heart would fall to the floor. The ensuing jolt would usually leave him immediately upon waking, but, increasingly, the feeling would stay for days to make him a prisoner of his own bed so that the smallest task would be a major struggle: reading a book would be rendered unthinkable; standing – herculean; and button-ing one's waistcoat – an ecstasy. Ross had slapped his back and laughed as he admitted that when the same happened to him, he found great comfort in drinking himself senseless. Crozier embraced Ross's remedy wholeheartedly and hid it from no one, but when he did drink, he considered it best for everyone that he sequestered himself to his bunk so that he could curl up with his pet of self-loathing alone.

At his long table, Sir John, now chewing his lip, gazed absent-mindedly at the officers chatting quietly around him – almost as if they were not present at all.

'All right, um, right, gentlemen...' The chatter petered out immediately and all eyes were on him as he continued with the formalisation of the rumours that had been given wings. 'I'm sure most of you will have heard already but, er, it is my very sad duty to inform you that one of our men, er...'

He looked beseechingly at Commander Fitzjames for a prompt but was met with an unhelpful grimace of awkwardness.

Dr Stanley tactfully stepped in as he mumbled at the lip of his wineglass: 'John Torrington, sir.'

'Thank you, Doctor – er... Able Seaman?'

The ship's surgeon shook his head and Sir John corrected him-self: 'So sorry... Petty Officer Torrington died this morning.'

The commodore let the news sink in a little before he spoke

again. 'God willing, let us hope he is the last casualty of our mission here in the north.' Franklin held an open hand out to the surgeon, who nodded his head sagely. 'Dr Stanley here, assures me that young Torrington more than likely died from a miasm which he may well have been harbouring for years before venturing onto the ice with us.'

Dr Stanley shook his head regretfully and sighed, 'Yes, most unfortunate indeed – poor fellow. Naturally, I shall be confirming my diagnosis with a full autopsy to establish the cause and shall keep you all apprised accordingly.'

Sir John smiled his appreciation. 'Thank you, Doctor – seems that here the climate can be something of a Pandora's box when it comes to revealing a man's true physiology: all very sad indeed, but once Dr Stanley has completed his examination let us bury Petty Officer Torrington in the right and fitting naval manner… in the meantime, let us pray.'

'Sacred to the memory of John Torrington, who departed this life January 1st, A.D. 1846, on board of HM ship Terror, aged 20 years.'

From behind the stern lights of *Terror's* Great Cabin, Crozier could see the lanterns of both ships' crews in a procession twinkling across the ice before constellating high up on the beach.

There, the crews shivered as they mustered around the grave. Anything less than a proper burial had been wholly unthinkable to Franklin, and it had taken four men six hours and three broken pick helves to chip their way through the permafrost to form an oblong slot in which to post Torrington's body to the afterlife. His grave had even been set on a bearing of 105° so that it faced every new dawn, faced England, faced *home*. His fellow stokers had wrapped the PO's head in a scarf, and for his coffin, they covered it in navy serge and inside, the carpenters lined his bed with their wood shavings. All of these things they did in the heartfelt hope that they could somehow make Torrington more comfortable as he rested in the loneliest place in the world.

Sir John shuddered as he removed his cocked hat before producing his Bible. As he started to speak, huge snowflakes fluttered down gently to join the men's glittering breath on the coffin. The commodore involuntarily shrugged again as he read with a trembling fervour:

"'They that go down to the sea in ships, that do business in great waters;

These see the works of the LORD, and his wonders in the deep. For he commandeth, and raiseth the stormy wind, which lifteth up the waves thereof.

They mount up to the heaven, they go down again to the depths: their soul is melted because of trouble.

They reel to and fro, and stagger like a drunken man, and are at their wits' end.

Then they cry unto the LORD in their trouble, and he bringeth them out of their distresses.

He maketh the storm a calm, so that the waves thereof are still.

Then are they glad because they be quiet; so he bringeth them unto their desired haven…'"

Franklin detested the cold. For him, it was both a terrible emotional and physical reminder of the awful privations he and his overland expedition had endured on the Coppermine River in what now seemed a lifetime ago. Any cold now just seemed to prey upon his old frostbite wounds with an excruciating throb in his feet and, despite a pair of silk stockings and two pairs of thick woollen socks, he still couldn't feel his big toes within his sea boots. This he knew was a sure-fire sign that there would be hell to pay once he was back in the warmth – when the blood would

flow back around his ruined nerves once more like darning needles being tortuously worked into the skin beneath his toenails.

The marines fired off their volleys, and afterwards the first
spaded shingle rapped upon the coffin's lid that had been pep-
pered with snowflakes – preserved forever like frozen tears. Sir
John snapped his Bible closed, replaced his 'fore and after' and
stepped off back to *Erebus* at a brisk pace to get his circulation
going again. The rest of the officers hurriedly joined the commodore to form a marginally solemn cabal around him as thoughts
now turned towards the big lunch that *Erebus* was laying on for
the officers' wake.

Goodsir and McDonald, the assistant surgeons, chose to hang
back with the rest of the men as they lingered round the graveside. As they stared down at Torrington's grave being filled, Sandy
McDonald attempted to brighten the mood. 'I say, Goodsir, the
commodore is quite the bishop, isn't he?' Goodsir's mind was
elsewhere as it pondered why Dr Stanley had breezily dismissed
his offer to carry out an autopsy as a waste of time – despite the
fact that the younger doctor had won prizes for anatomy whilst
at Edinburgh: *We will do well to bear in mind that a disappointing morbidity of stokers prevails – probably attributable to their
exposure to constant heat, smoke and coal dust and other similar
afflictions suffered by their sickly coal mining brethren.*

Regardless, the two assistants had taken it upon themselves
to take various samples. This they did in the hope of trying to
ascertain a more conclusive diagnosis, and when they had shown
Dr Stanley the rampant microbes writhing on the glass slide
of their microscope he had dismissed it all as *some sort of bug –
heaven knows it was cold enough for anything to manifest itself in
this godforsaken place.* The ship's surgeon had quietly warned the
assistants not to press their case as it would serve no one to cause
panic among the men and wished them all luck with any attempt
to persuade Sir John to return home over such a trifle.

As Torrington's coffin disappeared beneath the shovel-loads

of schist and shingle Goodsir, almost speaking to himself, said, 'Miasm, my arse!'

McDonald frowned. 'So, you're not entirely convinced by Dr Stanley's diagnosis then?'

'I just don't understand why he and Dr Peddie seem to be making light of this – their indifference staggers me… I'm assuming that it's because they're too busy diagnosing Burgundies and Bordeauxes.'

'Yes, well, they certainly seem to know their onions there, don't they?' McDonald grinned as he unsuccessfully tried to catch Goodsir's eye. 'So is there something else troubling you, Dr Goodsir?'

'Um, yes, it's just that I've never seen anything take a grip so quickly.'

McDonald offered his thoughts. 'Well, assuming our seniors are incorrect, and that there is something else with us, what could it be that would present itself so quickly?'

Goodsir squinted at McDonald as he wiped ice from his spectacles. 'Working on Stanley's hypothesis, how about consumption?'

McDonald pondered this. 'Possibly… If it was tubercular consumption, the ships' heating for one would make perfect conditions for the incubation of any diseases, would it not?'

'Yes, it's possible, but what if it was something else – something in the water perhaps?'

'Well, Goodsir, that's possible too, but as you know, if no one else has gone down with anything yet, then we have no model to compare it to. Every soul on the expedition is drinking the same water and eating same food, so it might rule out typhoid as the symptoms aren't consistent – and I would say it was safe to rule out cholera too as there's no evidence of rice water stools, so far.'

Goodsir dropped a glove, and, instead of picking it up, could only stare at it in the daze of his tumbling thoughts – as if observing a flattened woolly mammoth dropped from a great height. 'Well, let us pray that it's neither of the two – otherwise we'll be back here very shortly with "the bishop" and more of his stirring verse.'

'A depressing prospect indeed,' McDonald said as he picked up his friend's glove for him.

Goodsir, stirred from his reverie, looked askance at McDonald as he blew into his glove. 'I would say we should be worried, Dr McDonald.'

As they headed back towards the ships, McDonald noticed a small grave marked 'Gorgeous' and even as he spoke, his words seemed hollow. 'Yes, *worry* – the symptom of those who feel helpless. We might be far away from help but that doesn't mean we are helpless just yet, Dr Goodsir.'

The Hare & Billet, Blackheath, 14 May 1845

THE NIGHT BEFORE SETTING SAIL from Greenhithe, Francis Crozier and James Ross had supper at the old coaching inn that stood beside the little village pond. As they settled into their high-backed chairs near the fire, Ross slowly rolled the end of his huge Uppman over a splint and contemplated his dearest friend as he sucked his cigar into life. Ross waggled his forefinger at the young girl who had been serving their supper and gave her his most engaging smile. 'Where's the rest of that bottle of port, my dear?'

'I'll fetch it right away, Sir James.'

Ross inspected the end of his cigar and, satisfied that he was correctly lit, reclined. Without taking his eyes off Crozier, he began to grin from ear to ear.

Crozier, already sitting back in his chair, shook his head and smiled back uncertainly. 'What?'

'Why are you looking so worried, Frankie?'

'Am I?'

'Of course you are, brother – you're even more miserable than usual, you Irish bastard. Show me your hands.'

Crozier leant forward to oblige and held out his hands. They were shaking like an old man's and his fingernails were a bitten disgrace. Ross clenched his cigar between his teeth as he held out his own hands for inspection: they were also ablur with the tremors. The two men laughed before Ross said, 'Hell of a storm, wasn't it? Old Man's Disease after just one night of hell… and I still can't believe you got in the way of *Erebus*, Frankie. Very rude of you.'

Crozier frowned. 'And I'm still not biting, James – I seem to remember you gybing into me, you big, flapping sissy.'

The two men laughed again before the soothing crackles of the settling embers took them off to other places in their heads. After a moment or two, Crozier let slip of what was in his. 'God, I just wish it were you I'm sailing with tomorrow, Jimmy – Franklin's sound enough but he's never had what you have.'

'Oh, and what's that, Frank?'

'Luck. Sir John has never had any luck, has he?'

'Ha! Luck is merely experience and skill applied with an air of indifference.' Ross let out another rolling blue cloud. 'So why the hell did you put yourself forward, man?'

Crozier seemed pained as he replied, 'I don't know, Jimmy – Barrow can be very persuasive when he's after something. He pretty much told me that Franklin would fail unless I joined him.'

Ross's eyes narrowed as he whistled out another plume from his cigar. 'So what of it? You don't owe Franklin anything... But that's not the reason you volunteered, is it, Captain Crozier?'

The Irishman's cheeks began to redden. 'Well...'

Ross raised his eyebrows as an insistence for his friend to elaborate. Crozier was having difficulty – then Ross twigged. 'You old devil! It's that sweet little thing from Hobarton, isn't it – their daughter?'

Crozier's cheeks reddened more deeply into big blotches. 'Niece, actually – er, Sophia.'

'I knew it!'

Evidently squirming with embarrassment, Crozier reluctantly expanded, 'Lady Franklin took me aside. She was worried about Franklin too but was sure that if I did go north with the expedition she would feel certain that by the time we returned, Sophia would be perfectly ready to marry me.'

'Wouldn't surprise me if Lady Jane hadn't put the lass up to turning you down in the first place,' Ross scoffed.

'That's not very fair on Sophia, James. I'm sure she has her own mind... and heart.'

'Hmm, possibly, but what I'm sure she doesn't have is her own income. You're just a poor bloody sailor and they are her only family – she's not going anywhere without their nod, old son – is she?'

Ross's eyes narrowed as he saw his friend peer gloomily into his port. 'When was this, Francis?'

'What?'

'This cosy little gathering around the cauldron with Lady bloody Macbeth?'

'Lady who...? Oh, it was at their Christmas reception in Bloomsbury.'

'Ah, yes, I remember... Gave me the utter cold shoulder all night once she'd found out I'd been approached before Franklin – couldn't do enough for me before that.'

Ross's face beamed again, but not for Crozier: it was the girl returning with the port. Crozier was shocked to note how she was now bending over in front of Ross in a most wanton manner as she set the bottle down on the table. Ross gave her a shilling and patted her derrière as she turned to leave. He caught Crozier frowning at him and dismissed it all with a shrug. The man whom Lady Franklin had once referred to as 'the handsomest man in the navy' raised his glass without saying a word and the Ulsterman couldn't help but grin as he raised his own snifter. 'You're a shocker, Jimmy, so you are.'

After savouring the smooth tawny before it slipped away, Ross laughed. He wasn't naturally predisposed to laughing, but when he did it was always a sort of sudden blurting of astonishment – as if he was surprised to ever chance upon something that could actually amuse him. 'You silly coot, you! I've just realised what you're putting yourself through all of this nonsense for... a bloody woman!' Ross refilled their glasses before holding his own aloft. 'Frankie, dear boy – here's to you and your mission to find Sophy's Passage. I wish you nothing but good luck, dear boy, but if I don't hear word from you within three years… no, two years… I promise I'll drag you back here myself.'

Radstock Bay

Instruction addressed to Sir John Franklin (cont'd)…

*18. And you are to understand that although the
effecting a passage from the Atlantic to the Pacific
is the main object of this expedition, yet, that the
ascertaining the true geological position of the
different points of land near which you may pass, so
far as can be effected without detention of the ships
in their progress westward, as well as such other
observations as you may have opportunities of making
in natural history, must prove most valuable and
interesting, and to call that of all the officers under
your command to these points, as being objects of high
interest and importance […]*

On a rare day that was clear of mist, fog, snow, blizzard or rain, Lieutenant Le Vesconte called a halt for lunch. He thought it would be helpful if the men could occasionally see what they were doing within the rare light of the timid sun that was beginning to gingerly slink along the horizon once more. January daylight in the High Arctic was only seen for one hour and fifty minutes at their latitude. They had made little headway and their every step had been hard won. Fresh snow on the new, flat ice had been blown into sand-like ripples – only to be reshaped and hardened again into razor-sharp ridges and jags called zastrugi.

These came up to the men's knees and gave the sledge the same characteristics of a carriage being pulled over a buckled, tangled railway line running across a field of daggers.

On reaching the far side of Erebus and Terror Bay, Le Vesconte had intended to do what the men had affectionately referred to as 'guttersniping'. This involved coming off the sea ice and taking advantage of the small, deceptive frozen waterways, valleys and inlets that occasionally offered a relatively flat, sheltered route. But here they just found cloying mud and shingle that slowed their progress dramatically like the colossal prehistoric glaciers that had slithered across their Silurian limestone foundations over millennia had left the terrain looking more like a battle-scarred bailey of a massive fortress. And for its moats, narrow furrows and valley-sized undulations had inevitably filled with water and ice at their points closest to sea level. Typically, these gutters extended into anything from a few hundred yards long to major navigable routes of hundreds of miles, but every time a gutter was taken on, the parties were gambling with what had become the Hauling Party's Equation: Distance = Weather x Load over Food.

Sometimes these gutters could provide relatively sheltered shortcuts that could shave days or even weeks off the men's struggle and if they were really lucky, they could sail their ships through historical feats of discovery of their own making. But usually they were just a disappointing waste of time, effort and provisions which no sledging parties could afford to lose.

Caswall Tower loomed up over 600 feet into the air like a great rotting molar pushing through a black gum of scree to form an ominous sentinel for Radstock Bay. Whilst on the isthmus heading towards the Tower, marines shot at some red-throated loons and four of them had the munificence to tumble back down onto the ice for them. Despite taking five hours to put the last mile behind them, the men's morale was still reasonably high as they slumped in their pulling traces and caught their breath after a halt was called. Any time spent standing still on the ice risked people getting too cold so it was vital that they tried to salvage some energy by resting as they shipped as many calories into themselves as they could. Sergeant Tozer and his corporal had gone for 'a rummage' with the dog and a telescope up Caswall Tower to look for eggs, birds and the lie of the land. In the meantime, Lieutenant Le Vesconte took the opportunity to make magnetic observations via a dip-circle: an awkward-looking device that put one in mind of what would happen if a banjo should be swung violently into the various brassy innards of a grandfather clock. On its production from its protective mahogany case, it often prompted various wags among the men to make enquiries regarding the time of day as they impishly nodded their heads towards the 'thingmibob'. Or, in the case of the officer being particularly naive, the more brazen sailors would sometimes beg for a tune to be played on it.

As a mess steward, part of 'John the Light' Hartnell's responsibilities was to get a brew on for everyone. This entailed him lighting the seven wicks of the spirit stove which would take an hour and a quarter to melt enough snow to provide twenty-eight pints of tea. It was a bit of a faff – especially as the rest of the men were able to hobble around clutching their thighs as they swore at their lactic burn. Hartnell's nickname was acquired due to him being a dab hand with brimstone and tinder, and he was even rumoured to have produced fire from a knapsack on one occasion during a particularly brusque Atlantic hurricane in the Orkneys. Despite the onerous responsibility, Hartnell did manage to find that making the 'gossip broth' also came with certain perks.

With the cooking utensils simmering away on the burner with the lids on, Braine, one of the older marines, hobbled over to Hartnell to sort his feet out next to the heat. Struggling to get his boot off in a hurry to avoid the cramp that was beginning to bite, the marine began to wince. 'Quick, quick mate – get me boot! Hartnell obliged with a tug and the boot came away easily enough. As Braine kneaded his throbbing foot, Hartnell inspected the wet boot now in his hands and marvelled at the huge split straight across the shank. 'By the Blessed Beck, Brainy, what happened to your boot, man?'

Marine Braine grabbed the boot back and waggled a finger through the gash. 'Zastrugi, mate.'

'You what, mate?'

'Zastrugi.'

Hartnell looked out onto the ice, the foreboding jags of Caswall glowing orange in the sun's low light, whilst beneath it, the rays also caught the tips of zastrugi, putting him in mind of the Kentish farmers burning stubble in their wheat fields. The young mess steward shook his head. 'Jesus, we might as well be pulling a dead walrus over a fuckin' big cheese grater, eh? The marine fished out a fresh sock that he'd been keeping warm in his vest.

'Oi, John the Light?'

'What?'

The marine flung his old wet sock at Hartnell's face. 'Do you want some cheese with that wine?'

Hartnell, repulsed by the stink of rotting feet, began to gag. 'Oh, bleedin' hell! You been walking through dog shit, mate?'

As the two lads laughed together, a shifty look soon appeared on Hartnell's face. 'Actually, Brainy, I might be able to do a bit better than cheese...'

Hartnell beckoned Braine to come closer to his cooking dixie. He looked around again before sliding back the lid a little to reveal a red tin rattling around in the bubbling tumult within. Braine's eyes lit up at the prospect of some extra food.

'Will a quarter of "Pusser's Rough", do yer, Johnny, lad?'

✳

Sergeant Tozer and Corporal Firemark made it to the summit of the tower in an hour and a quarter. They'd sent the dog back to *Vixen* with the birds tied around his neck as they didn't want to risk his paws on the sharp the rocks they had to scramble up and around. Breathless from their climb, they leant heavily on their rifles as they looked out over the frigid bay.

Firemark was the first to be able to speak again. 'Looks like a decent gutter running to the northeast, Sarn't.'

Tozer, still panting, handed the corporal his weapon and took out his telescope. 'Aye, she'll do – can't see no end of her.'

Firemark, now looking behind his sergeant, spotted some filthy weather coming on. 'Not sure you'll like the look of that though, Sarn't…'

Tozer followed Firemark's gaze and just as he was about to swear, the two marines saw a maroon flare pop from *Vixen*'s direction.

Erebus and Terror Bay

TERROR'S ALARM BELLS RANG. SERGEANT Tozer and Corporal Firemark's vanguard stumbled out of the swirling curtains of the squall. As the crews of both ships rushed onto the ice to assist, they met with the rest of Le Vesconte's party. They'd had to abandon *Vixen* five miles away in order to bring back the two rapidly deteriorating souls who had collapsed just before the storm.

With just five sailors able to pull they were lucky to have made it back at all. The extra effort required to haul the vomiting duo of Braine and Hartnell back to the ships had taken Le Vesconte and his men an extra three days. Even the considerably freshened westerly joined the conspiracy against his party and they were on their last legs by the time they had returned to the ships. As for what was wrong with the casualties, it was anybody's guess, and, as Dr Stanley had observed, it was common to find that men just collapsed when they were out on the ice. Whether it was man or gear, the Arctic would soon find holes and pick at them until everything was left tattered, gaping and empty. In the case of men who had illnesses that hid among their carcasses in regular climes, they were soon betrayed when they went to the Polar Regions. Sometimes it would be consumption, rickets or even venereal disease, but a man falling ill on the ice was all part of the landscape – all part of the inexplicable things that happened to people when they visited places where they didn't belong – like the picking of a scab, or staring at the sun. As Franklin had put it, it was like 'opening Pandora's box in a snowstorm'. The other thing that was found to be inexplicable was why Hartnell's effects had contained extra provisions that had not yet been on general issue. They had found pemmican and spirit of wine and they would have also discovered the full extent of their crimes if Hartnell and Braine hadn't eaten the contents of the cans before burying them in the ice.

When Sir John found out about the thievery, he privately wept. Not out of pity for the men who were now gibbering and hallucinating with pain and fear, but with genuine anger at their lack of Christianity. To him, it was treachery of the lowest water – treachery towards their brothers, their ships and, most importantly, to God. Through Divine Service, Sunday schools and a substantial supply of Bibles bought with his own money, the commodore had always done his best to steer his men's morality off the shoals, but then something like this still happened and it made him wonder what more he had to do to make his men better people.

In the surgeon's bunk Hartnell went first. This time Goodsir was granted permission to perform an autopsy. He made a one-and-a-half-foot-long Y-shaped incision along Torrington's thorax: from the iliac crests at his hipbones to his umbilicus before proceeding northwards to his sternum but despite Goodsir's best efforts, Dr Stanley's stance had been proved right when the post-mortem had thrown up more questions than answers, but the two ship's assistant surgeons the only question they felt needed answering was the decision not to abort their mission and return to England as soon as the next thaw would allow – given that that they still had no idea what it was that had killed two men, and looked set to take a third.

When Hartnell's brother, Tommy, found out that they had cut his brother up, he was distraught – and then there were the words that Sir John had ordered to be carved into his headstone that hurt him even more when they were read to him. In his valediction, Franklin wanted to send a very clear message to the rest of his men that issues of loyalty and greed were always dealt with in the most severe ways possible. Not, in this particular instance, executed by the hand of naval law, but by the ultimate judge Himself. In recognition of this, he had Hartnell's grave marked with the most merciless text he could muster from within the thin, jaundiced pages of his Old Testament:

Sacred to the memory of John Hartnell, AB,
of HMS Erebus, died January 4th 1846, aged twenty-five years.
"Thus saith the Lord of Hosts, consider your ways." Haggai, I, 7

The ship's companies found themselves at another graveside next to Torrington's. After the service, the Kentish lads stayed behind and gathered around their Johnny's grave. Little Tadman produced a blue flask of spirit of wine and those who smoked lit their clay pipes. Tommy swore and began to weep bitterly again. 'Consider your ways? What the fuckin' hell is that supposed to mean!'

Orren heeled at the ice like a restless cob. 'Ah, pay it no mind, Tommy, boy.'

Tadman handed the flask to the lad who took a swig and coughed.

Orren smiled conspiratorially. 'He did ship some of them tins when he went out onto the ice though, didn't he?'

Tommy dried his eyes on the back of his mitten. 'Course… took a few with him… see if he could make a few Abrahams off of the marines, like.'

Orren's face twitched involuntarily as he sniffed. 'Fair enough, thought as much – s'why Tadders and me got a notion, lads…' Orren looked around the men suspiciously. 'So, any of you been tucking into them tins y'selves, like?'

Seeley looked genuinely abashed. 'Fore God, you know we ain't, Bill – them's for the rainy-day fund, ain't they?'

Orren sniffed as he nodded towards the graves. 'Yeah, well, if you're selling me a dog, you'll be grinnin' at the daisy roots next to these two poor sods – make no mistake.'

Tadman shivered and folded his arms as he nodded in Tommy's direction. 'Tommy, you and your bruv rolled a couple of tins by way of that stoker feller there as well, didn't yer?'

Tommy handed the flask to Seeley. 'Aye, Bill – what of it?'

Orren scratched his scalp with his Welsh wig and a mixture of frustration and impatience. 'See, I reckon it's the tins what did 'em in.'

Seeley also coughed after taking his swig. 'Nah, them tins is on the square.'

Orren seemed to seethe. 'Oh, yeah – an' 'ow would you know?'

Seeley shrank back into his shell a little. 'Er, well, I just heard Sir John banging on about how we'll be letting us belts out after a season or two on 'em.'

Orren snatched Seeley's pipe and relit his own off it. 'Yeah, well… Old Baldie was only 'ornin', weren't he? Telling everyone what he knew, eh?'

Tadman chimed in, 'But what we do know, lads, is that them tins is a Jonah. First the stoker, then our Johnnie and that bootie, Braine – looks like he's next, poor sod.'

The Hoppers fell silent again as they listened to Tommy's quiet sobs and sniffles.

Orren put his arm around the lad's shoulders and said quietly, almost in a whisper, 'I tell you, it's the tins what's fed them two holes in the ground there – they's been baned like rats.'

Seeley shook his worried head. 'So, if they's poisoned by them tins, we's all gonners, ain't we? What happens when the rest of us needs them tins?'

Orren nodded darkly as he sucked and blew on his pipe, the wind carrying the smoke off through his awful teeth like a cold mist through a graveyard. 'Very good question, mate.'

'We should tell… the bloody… captain!' Tommy hiccuped through his sobs.

Orren shook the lad almost soothingly by the shoulder and whispered, 'We should tell no one nothing.'

Tadman slid his sleeve beneath his running nose. 'Yeah, we need to keep this tight, lads; make sure we look after us first – then give 'em the gypsy's?'

Orren snatched the flask back off Seeley who was going in again on the ethanol.

'Jesus, no, lads! What did I just say? No warning to no buggers. If anyone found out that we knew, they'd then ask how we knew it, wouldn't they?'

Tadman, like any good henchman, instantly changed his tune in order to support his leader. 'Then they'd have us swinging from the yardarm as soon as you could say Jack bleedin' Robinson.'

Seeley shook his head doubtfully. 'So, what if the marine sorts hisself and starts blabbing about them tins, like?'

Orren palmed the cork back into the flask. 'Oh, I wouldn't worry about him, lads.' The Hoppers' stunned silence spurred Orren into expansion. 'I ain't no doctor, but I reckon he'll be next to go.'

Barrow Strait

Instruction addressed to Sir John Franklin (cont'd)…

19. For the purpose, not only of ascertaining the set of the currents in the Arctic Seas, but also of affording more frequent chances of hearing your progress, we desire that you frequently, after you have passed the latitude of 65 degrees north, and once every day when you shall be in an ascertained current, throw overboard a bottle or copper cylinder closely sealed, and containing a paper stating the date and position at which it is launched, and you will give similar orders to the commander of the 'Terror,' to be executed in case of separation; and for this purpose, we have caused each ship to be supplied with papers, on which is printed, in several languages, a request that whoever may find it should take measures for transmitting it to this office.

20. You are to make use of every means in your power to collect and preserve specimens of animal, mineral and vegetable kingdoms, should circumstances place such within your reach without causing your detention, and of the larger animals you are to cause accurate drawings to be made, to accompany and elucidate the descriptions of them. In this, as well as

in every other part of your scientific duty, we trust that
you will receive material assistance from the officers
under your command, several of whom are represented
to us as well qualified in these respects [...]

'Lay aloft and loose all sail!' It had seemed like an eternity since
any instruction to move the ships had been issued and it brought
joy to the men's ears. Crozier squinted skywards as he watched
what the wind was doing to his sails. The benevolent northeaster luffed the canvas and *Terror* was first away. The captain's
orders became more clipped as he prepared to increase the wind's
involvement in the ship's movements. 'Set the courses – smartly,
lad! Boatswain! Put your toe up that twerp's hole, will yer!'

The Arctic's thaw of 1846 had arrived early. To the twitchy ears
of the men, the sound of the cracking and growling of the ice
moving again once more was like a nerve-wracking Devil's
Symphony, as they called it. But to Franklin the sound came
as nothing but a balm: the heralding of a thaw. He ordered the
ships to be made ready to sail.

The upper masts were stepped and re-rigged; the canvas
awning that formed 'the crust on a pie' over the decks was struck;
and the last of the packed snow, which had done so well to insu-
late the decks during the winter, was cleared off. Soon, the bay
was sufficiently clear of ice that the ships gaily swung about their
anchors with the ebb and flow of each new tide, and with no
further threat of the ice crushing them like crabs, the ships' rudders were lowered back down to resume their position on their
pintles once again.

However, their last remaining time on the island hadn't passed
without incident. One of the storehouses on the shore had
gone up in smoke after one of the younger hands had evidently
dropped a lantern in there whilst fetching pickles for Sir John.

The fire was eventually quelled but not before well over a hundredweight of pemmican was reported lost. The other thing that they had lost, almost two months to the day after John Hartnell, was Marine Braine. He had really shown how tough and stubborn a marine could be and even seemed to be rallying for a short time but then unexpectedly took a turn for the worse one night. It was Orren, who, after volunteering for orderly duties in the sick berth, had raised the alarm – but, sadly, all was too late for Marine Braine.

As the order was given for the anchors to be weighed, the men couldn't help themselves and gave three cheers with breath that was thick with rum. An extra ration had been issued the night before and they had raised their tinnies with joy whilst quietly remembering the three men they were leaving behind in the small grave garden they had so seamlessly grown. *Sandy bottoms to Torrington, Hartnell and Braine.*

But now, on that splendid July morning, the ships' crews were able to put all of that behind them as *Erebus* and *Terror* ran well out of the bay and back into Barrow Strait. Everything from here on out was about discovery, with everything to the south a cartographic white marble of which it was Franklin's mission to chip away and find its form. For the best part of that first afternoon of freedom every top on both ships was filled with men and officers brandishing their 'looksticks', keen to sight land that had never been seen before – at least not by Englishmen. Down in the water, the ships' crews witnessed all manner of fantastical aquatic life: hundreds of small albino-like whales bobbed in and out of the azure sea as if they were the smiles of breaking waves; Narwhal parried and countered against each other within the inky sword-fencing pistes of their leads; panicking walrus almost walked on water en masse as they flapped and skittered from the acute, sinister dorsals of a grampus hunt; and polar bears brayed victoriously as they furnished the smaller bergs with rugs of red after smearing a kill across them.

As the quartermasters negotiated giant bergy bits that were often like blue explosions frozen in time, it was palpable that the full colour of life had returned to Franklin and his people. Whaleboats were lowered away before shortly returning with their gunnels nearly dipping into the sea from the sheer weight of fish and blubber. Sir John laughed joyously at the sight of Lieutenants Gore and Des Vœux with cigars clenched between their teeth as they hung over *Erebus*'s rail and poked around with nets and poles. Aboard *Terror*, Crozier gladly drank in the fresh winds of change as he held his face to the warming, rejuvenating sunlight.

The expedition wasted no time in crossing Parry Channel where they found the colossal bluffs of North Somerset that looked like they'd been built using set squares and plumb lines. From here, they intended to push west like so many of the forebears who went before them only to have their ardency quenched by ice fields that extended to the ends of their world.

On paper, west had seemed the most obvious route possible between the Atlantic and Pacific seaboards – but in the past it had been like chasing rainbows. What might have been the path of least resistance for millions of tons of ice and water was very rarely shared with anything else – especially not with men in their puny ships. So often, explorers had to defy the mighty dynamics of weather and water and cheat their way through their own paths of desire. And in Cape Walker, the Franklin expedition had found theirs. Their new rainbow pointed south.

Bending with the southern coastline, the current of the turning tide seem to suck them down a seemingly endless sound. At one point, Crozier was so worried about the strength of the currents pushing them onto shoals or rocks that he made them lay up so that the tides could turn again and they could avoid the full flow. The waterway that had eluded everyone for centuries now seemed to embrace them with open arms.

Physically, this new sound hadn't looked particularly promising from the Parry Channel but as it was the only fuzzy area left on their chart's coastline, Crozier found it very enticing. At first they could plainly see how Sir Edward Parry and all the others before him had so easily missed it, but when clear water kept yielding itself before them, it was impossible for them to resist pressing on to the south.

Even two days after passing Cape Walker, their southerly horizon kept stretching out before them. Sir John was so excited about this unexpected progress that regardless of what this mysterious body of water turned out to be, it was now substantial enough to be named in honour of their great Prime Minister – or at least the one who had been in office when they had shoved off from the shores of England.

Erebus and *Terror* hugged the huge bluffs that trended along the west coast of North Somerset and at around eighty miles, whilst they just still had the cliffs' lee, Crozier insisted on having the ships hove-to again for the sake of the incredibly powerful tidal currents. As they waited for slack water, the lookout thought he could see someone waving from a promontory above what looked to be a small bay. Moments later the port sides of both ships bristled with telescopes as the officers craned to get a better look. Mr Hodgson, as *Terror*'s officer of the watch, was particularly eager to establish what they were looking at as he stood next to his ice master – who also happened to be keenly glassing the coastline. 'So, Mr Blanky, what are we looking at?'

Blanky grinned as he handed over his telescope. 'Well, sir… it's either a local what's frozen to death wavin'… or it's a cairn.'

The lieutenant squinted through the optics. 'A cairn?'

'Aye, sir. Eskies, I reckon… Don't make 'em out of little stones like us… they stack boulders till they look like folks.'

Lieutenant Irving arrived on deck and was so excited by this new discovery that he began patting himself for his notebook so that he could make a sketch of it for his next letter home.

As they were stood off, Sir John felt that this was a perfect
moment to share a few words with the men of both ships over
fortifying hot toddies on his quarterdeck.

'Welcome, gentlemen, welcome all' – Sir John beamed with
genuinely heartfelt pride at his people – 'I just wanted this
opportunity to take you through how things stand: we are at the
very gates of history, gentlemen…' With this there were polite
sounds of approval and Sir John continued to beam. 'We have a
healthy, rejuvenated crew and last season we added six hundred
and twenty miles of coastline to our charts' – there were more
sounds of approval – 'and though we came away without our furthest north record, we have been able to confirm that Cornwallis
is indeed an island! Ha! Can't wait to see Admiral Parry's face!'

With this, every soul became a little more raucous at the news
that they had just got one up on one of England's greatest explorers. Crozier made an effort to clap and smile with everyone else
but there was no hiding his doubts – after all, he had actually
been a midshipman on Parry's expedition where he'd helped him
achieve the furthest north record, as well as being with Parry
during his third crack at the North Pole as commander of *Hecla*.
Remembering at that point all of his other polar *jaunts* he played
out all the scenarios and their outcomes in his mind: ice melts,
sail through the Passage… collect medals, fellowships, extra
pay, hopefully marry Sophia, retire. Or ice melts; sail further,
then ice sets in again… another overwinter until next thaw and
then push on until clear – repeat until the Barents Sea. After all,
having learned so much from the bitter lessons of so many others
who went before them, they'd planned for a three-to-four-year
campaign and, at the very worst, they could always hunt in the
summers and crack into the sixteen tons of preserved stores –
should the fresh provisions became scarce. They had a long way
to go yet but for all of them to get home again safely was another
matter. To Crozier, it was all very well patting each other on the
back now, but the main thing that niggled him was the need for

some kind of insurance: a contingency of some sort – a way back out for when the ice inevitably returned.

Per their instructions, both ships had tossed their pro forma messages rolled up and sealed into copper tubes. Each day they had faithfully dropped them over their transoms, but for Crozier, he felt they might as well have been chucking sausages over the side for all the good it would do them. Crozier's instinct had been to land caches of supplies at regular intervals, marked by cairns for all to plainly see – just like the one they were looking at now. But as nothing of the kind found itself in the orders from the Admiralty the commodore was only thinking forwards, not backwards – trying to make up for the time they had lost last year in their attempt to eliminate the north from their enquiries.

The worry had evidently shown itself on Crozier's face as every eyeball on deck was now levelled on him now that they'd clapped and cheered themselves out. Crozier had been too deep in thought to hear Sir John who had asked him the usual rhetorical question in the spirit of unanimity – in the hope that his increasingly *difficult* second-in-command would now be onside.

'So, Captain Crozier, perhaps a few words, if you will?'

Crozier raised his tumbler of hot, sweet rum in an effort to recognise their achievements. 'Well, lads, you've done well – there's no taking it away from yous. But we've a wee way to go yet. The ice masters are saying that they've never seen so much old pack ice loose at this time of year, but we must assume that it is indeed an uncommonly mild season—'

This wasn't the direction that Sir John wanted to go so he stepped in to help steer Crozier's course. 'So, we'd be fools not to follow the open leads into the last unmapped five hundred miles of the Passage, would we not, Captain?' said the commodore encouragingly.

Crozier shrugged. 'Perhaps, sir, but who knows what we'd be sailing into? I'd be worried if all that ice we saw up north breaks up and chases us south… We'd get caught good and proper. If we

couldn't get out of the ice again next spring it would be like finding ourselves in a field full of bulls with the gate closed behind us.'

Fitzjames saw an opportunity and seized his moment. 'But,
thank the Good Lord, we are not farmers – we're explorers, are
we not, sir? The good captain here has said it himself that we're
having a wonderful summer and these currents are an absolute
gift – plain for all to see, surely?'

Fitzjames eyed the men: the ardent fresh faces of the juniors,
along with the sceptical ones of those more salty – he desperately
wanted to make an impression on them all. 'Sir John… men…
even in the unlikely event that we do get caught in the ice we will
be but the seeds of raspberry jam caught in a tooth at breakfast…'
As Fitzjames paused for effect, some of the men could barely con-
tain their cynicism whilst others were genuinely fascinated to see
how their foppish officer could explain himself. The commander
continued, 'Any besetting will be infuriating initially but with
a bit of a prod with a toothpick there's always a happy ending.'

Blanky scoffed, 'That's wonderful, sir – so are you saying we
can always unstep the main and use her as a toothpick, sir?'

As the men laughed, Crozier couldn't hide his grin before
Fitzjames continued to drag out his point. 'Don't be ridiculous,
Ice Master! Why would we fiddle with sticks when we could take
advantage of something that no other expedition before us ever
had…' As the entire group of assembled men began to lose their
patience, Fitzjames stamped the deck with his boot three times
and splayed his palms towards the engine beneath the decks:
'Steam power – let the engines be our toothpicks – let them smash
us through the ice… smash through any gate of yours, Captain, so
that we can crack on with enjoying the rest of our breakfast!'

As everyone cheered, laughed or shook their heads in bemuse-
ment Crozier put a hand to his mouth in an effort to hide his
incredulity. It almost made him laugh at witnessing how Fitzjames's
weighing scales of ambition was a perfect balance of confidence
and inexperience. He was often amazed and sometimes even a little

envious of how some Englishmen were so driven by their burning need of advancement that was nearly always at the expense of everyone else's. Decision without knowledge; risk without experience; power without wisdom. He thought Fitzjames might well be an outstanding officer to have around on a man-of-war – he was brave and even had the medals to prove it, but perhaps his pluck showed a man who felt he had much to prove to others – rather than to himself. Here was a man who had spent but a single winter on the ice but now felt brave and prepared enough to compare polar exploration to eating jam.

Crozier had overseen *Terror*'s first sea trials with the auxiliary engine on the Thames and had found its performance to be risible. He saw that even the five-knot flow of the outgoing tide of the river provided a very worthy adversary for the thirty horsepower engine. If that was the case on Old Father Thames, then what chance could they possibly have against millions of tons of shifting ice along with who knows what sort of weather buffeting and bouncing them around the Arctic's waters. Even if they could spot leads within the ice and warp the ships, their 180 tons of coal would only give them two weeks' steaming. In his experience, that coal would be far better put to use as fuel for heating. And what would happen if the engines didn't hold out? Crozier knew that it would be folly to depend on machinery of any kind in the Arctic – never mind unproven machinery. Sir John saw the doubt in Crozier's eyes. If he wasn't careful this would turn into an open forum – and in his precarious empire of oak, any form of democracy would never succeed. He quickly moved to wrap matters up whilst everyone was still stoked. 'All right then, gentlemen, that is it. Let's push on. In a week, perhaps two, we will, God willing, have sailed into the very heart of the Northwest Passage and into the history books forever.'

The Great Cabin

'SO WHAT IS IT THAT you would have us do, Francis?' The three officers stood around the chart. Crozier hesitated to answer the commodore's question but felt it important to get everything off his chest: get everything out in the open – albeit *in camera* and with Commander Fitzjames very much as Sir John's lapdog.

'I propose that I take *Terror* back along Lancaster Sound, sir… cache depots of emergency supplies along the way, build a few message cairns – couldn't hurt. At best we would have something to fall back on… at worst, if any parties ended up looking for us they would have our last positions along with our next intentions.'

Sir John grunted before walking over to his stern lights. 'Hmm, how long would you need, Francis?' the commodore said as he looked out at the open sound and its infinite potential.

'A week, sir… perhaps two if the weather isn't humming our tune?'

Sir John shook his head. 'No, no, no – that won't do at all, Captain – I'll not butter the bacon.'

He stomped back to the chart on his table and rested his knuckles on it as he grumbled, 'We don't have time for such unnecessary precaution… We're racing against nature and as you well know, the ice isn't a particularly good timekeeper. Also, if anything were to happen, how would I explain splitting up our ships to the Sea Lords when they have instructed us quite specifically to the contrary?'

Crozier's mouth went dry. He could feel ire pumping through his blood. 'Well, sir – their Lordships aren't here, are they – they're in London, busily sailing their desks through their tranquil lakes of bureaucracy.'

Sir John's face reddened. 'Captain! That sort of language will not do, sir. You will do well to remember that those men you are so easily dismissing are our superiors – men who had insisted on you being here, actually.'

Fitzjames picked at some invisible fluff on his sleeve at the thought of such an unnecessary inclusion. Crozier wanted to kick himself for his hot-headedness and attempted to mine some of his diplomatic reserves.

'I apologise, sir – I'm out of order. What I should have said was that if any of their lordships were here with us now, I'm sure they would encourage us to form some sort of contingency at this moment and that anything less would be an unacceptable risk. In fact, sir, may I respectfully request that my suggestions of contingency are added to the log, please?'

Sir John stared disbelievingly at Fitzjames for a moment or two before blinking back his frustration at Crozier. 'Yes, well, Captain, as you are at great pains to point out, our masters are not here with us at this moment in time… so, as ever, it's down to me, isn't it?'

Crozier bowed his head in recognition of the commodore's unenviable position as Franklin continued, 'And all I've got to work with is a vaguely marked chart and the Admiralty's exceptionally clear orders – all down in black and white.'

The commodore rapped at his table and shook his head as he sighed. After a moment or two's consideration, he looked up at Crozier. 'I'm sorry, Francis, you were perfectly correct about last season, and I accept that. We should have been at this point last year but then hindsight is a wonderful thing, isn't it? And I'll tell you something for nothing: I find the thought of missing out again to be wholly intolerable. I've made that mistake once, and

I shan't make it twice… But I do take your point, Francis, and your comments will be duly added to the log.'

Sir John stared down at his chart again. 'I do appreciate we shall be caught again at some point. But then, the further in we get, the closer we will be to finishing what we came here to do: find a passage between the Atlantic and the Pacific.'

Crozier tried to add something else, but Sir John cut him off by holding up an index finger. 'So, Captain, if we commit to another year in the ice, it will make our provisions even more precious. And to that end, I certainly can't afford any of our stores to be wasted in caches… no, the whaling fleet will just have to make do with getting fat off what they drag out of the sea – rather than pilfering our stores.'

Franklin Strait

THE TWO SHIPS ANSWERED WELL to the strong currents and a following wind so that they made unprecedented progress further south. En route, they often found themselves overtaking more and more loose icebergs of every hue and imaginative form possible that seemed to mark their progress like a sequence of huge, marble buoys – pilotage as if put out by Poseidon himself.

On their charts, every day that passed saw them adding various twists, turns and bends in ink as they reshaped the western extent of Boothia Felix so that it started to transmute from the barriers of continent – to the borderless potential of a peninsula. But each time a mirage of ice or a trick-sky persuaded them that they were about to be bitterly repulsed by a dead end or a field of ice, their horizon to the south remained enticingly clear. Their initial suspicions that they were just beating into an inlet soon dissipated and hope replaced doubt with every mile that was run as they pressed for 250 miles.

Then, one morning, just as the humility of their hope was beginning to be taken over by expectation, nature chastened them with a blanket of fog that came on so thickly that even the topgallant sails of both ships were hidden from those on the deck below. As *Erebus* led the way and the bells of both ships tolled dolefully for each other every two minutes, Ice Master Reid would hail and flap his hands as if swimming as he guided them through and around various bergy bits. Some were the size of cottages and when they complained bitterly against *Erebus*'s ironclad hull he would swear at the sweating, pale-faced quarter-master as he grabbed and grappled frantically at the wheel. After four hours of the unbearable tension of being blind fools in a graveyard, the ice master could finally report back to the commodore, 'Sir, a-a-arl the fog'll be g-g-garn ahead.'

Fitzjames couldn't help himself as he quipped, 'Oh, that's wonderful news, Mr Reid – perhaps we'll be able to go back and hit some of the bric-a-brac we missed?'

Just as Mr Reid was about to gather his retort, the lookout began shouting and as everyone looked forward, the mists were lifting like the curtains of a fantastical stage: nothing but sea – limitless horizons all about them. A gulf of potential and their gates to the Kingdom of Everything. They had found that the inlet was indeed a channel – widening into a large open sea that converged with four significant waterways. To the south, there was the sizeable sound already marked on their charts that they could finally link with the new marks they had added. For this sound, Franklin had his trusted Canadian friend Warren Dease to thank as he had mapped the area twenty-six years prior.

Frobisher, Cabot, Ross, Back, Parry, Cook, even a teenage Nelson, had all sued for the Passage, but all had failed. All the flesh and oak that had been lost over the years; so many men pulling tiny boats, so many men sailing great ships – so many, lost forever. But here, now, in the very cold heart of the Arctic, Franklin had finally outdone them all: he had found the Northwest Passage.

At that point, he could have turned about. Back up the channel, and back home as fast as the wind and currents could carry them. Franklin would have been immortalised forever as the man who had found the last link of the Northwest Passage and lived to tell the tale. He and his men would be fêted, and their families would want for nothing else for the rest of their lives. But Franklin wanted more. He had always detested being known as the man who ate his boots. To him it came to signify all the failures in his life, along with all the opportunities he had striven for but never been able to seize – particularly when so many of his peers had received so much recognition, promotion and respect. Now he wanted to make sure there was absolutely no lack of clarity regarding his legacy. He needed to safeguard against anything making his clear blue waters of history murky and he wasn't going to be overshadowed by some privileged young buck with a lucky wind behind him, who, in the next year or two, would finally sail straight through *his* achievement. No, he had come so far, and he had no intention to leave it at that. He was going to *conquer* the Northwest Passage by sailing clean through it and prove, for once and for all, that there was a clear way across the top of the world; a sovereign channel and yet another first for the British Empire, its science, its leadership and its boundless reach.

The officer of the watch was Lieutenant Gore, so Sir John, in his delight, had him run up a flag signal to mark the moment for the cheering officers and men on *Terror*:

THE PASSAGE IS OURS. WE WILL ADVANCE.

Later that night, the two ships heaved to and gammed once more so that together, the crews of *Erebus* and *Terror* celebrated with much grog and singing. They had sailed 650 miles into the Northwest Passage. It existed, and it was theirs. On Commander Fitzjames's suggestion, they named this new, world-changing strait in honour of their leader.

Larsen Sound

Instruction addressed to Sir John Franklin (cont'd)…

4. As, however, we have thought fit to cause each ship to be fitted with a small steam-engine and a propeller, to be used only in pushing the ships through channels between masses of ice, when the wind is adverse, or in a calm, we trust the difficulty usually found in such cases will be much obviated, but as the supply of fuel to be taken in the ships is necessarily small you will use it only in cases of difficulty…

After a week of plain sailing, their achievements were punished with the coldest wind holding from the north and with it, glowing clouds revealed iceblink from the wider channel to their N.W. A knot twisted itself tightly within Crozier's stomach as he sensed his bull's gate creaking closed behind them. More growlers and bergy bits loomed at their horizon too, whilst at their bluff bows the bomb ships clattered through the ice uneasily. Then one night, the wind dropped like a stone and with it, the mercury began to plummet brutally as slushy pancake ice began to form across the water like bacteria forming on a sea of agar. Soon after, they had no option but to fire up the engines.

As they steamed fecklessly through the leads, the ships meandered through the ice as fast as thirty horses could pull 385 tons apiece. Eventually, as the sea curdled stiffly around any hope of further progress, Crozier had the men set about the ice with their twelve-foot-long ice saws, picks, axes, ice chisels and even gunpowder to keep their icy maze open. But, as fast as the ice-cutting crews could hack, saw, bang and smash, the ice was always one step ahead of them.

The men toiled night and day on the ice and the ice masters oversaw the shifting of ballast and the backing of sails. And after the engines failed them, they set kedge anchors into the fast ice before warping the vessels forward or astern a ship's length at a time like burlaks on the Volga River. Even Wentzall, the fiddler, was sent out on the ice to help the tars heave to music – until the bitter cold peevishly took away two of his fingers.

By Fitzjames's reckoning, the men made 'a very respectable' seven and a half miles in four days and nights battling against the ice. They were nearly twenty miles to the N.W. of Cape Felix when the ice finally held them under siege. At nearly a fathom thick the only further course for Sir John was to order the ships to be prepared for another winter out on the ice. Cape Felix marked the northernmost tip of King William Land, whilst ahead of them and to the south and west, lay the archipelago that formed the rest of the Northwest Passage – ready to be circumnavigated for the first time by men in ships. But for now, that would have to be left until the next thaw.

King William Land

FUNDED PRIVATELY BY HIS GENEROUS friend and gin magnate Felix Booth, Sir John Ross first named the great peninsula Boothia in 1829. To its west, lay what Ross perceived as another narrower landmass that he named after 'The Sailor King'. Ross estimated that King William Land was 'a great peninsula of not less than five hundred miles.' Ross was an outstanding leader and a superb sailor and part of his success had derived from a reluctance to stray from the lanes of doubt. So much so, that it was his undoing as far as the Admiralty was concerned. His 1829 expedition had to be privately funded as the Admiralty had washed their hands of him after he had entered Lancaster Sound and said that the way was blocked by an impassable range of mountains (graciously naming them the Croker Mountains after the then First Secretary of the Admiralty). Rather than delve any deeper, and after much protestation from his officers, he turned back for London – only for subsequent expeditions to determine that the mountains were an optical illusion, or perhaps a delusion based on what he wanted to see: an excuse to turn back. The implication being that Sir John was at best a liar and at worst, a coward. He had completely missed the very gateway to the Northwest Passage and the Croker Mountains would become the pinnacle of British hubris forever. However, Ross, in a desperate attempt to redeem his reputation, used the financial backing of his wealthy friend Sir Felix to more than make up for any such aspersions that had been cast upon him. His expedition went on to discover the Magnetic North Pole as well as make a great many ethnographical and geographical observations before catastrophe loomed – his ship, the *Victory*, was lost to the ice. But, due to his incredible leadership and miraculous good fortune, he and his men lasted an unprecedented four years on the ice before a passing whaler picked them up. Once back in England, Ross was knighted for his troubles and his crew were back-paid in full, even though they weren't actually part of the Royal Navy.

Ross was not the only one guilty of making assumptions when it came to King William's Land. George Back, tasked with a search and rescue party for Ross from the south, had the opportunity to determine that King William Land was, in fact, an island. If either man had taken the risk of further incursion, they would have discovered a clear navigable run along the entire eastern side that was clear of ice during most seasons. Had Back determined this, he would have found the only possible escape route from the ever shifting, choking ice that was all part and parcel of the Northwest Passage – perhaps he might even have gone on to discover the Passage itself.

From *Terror*'s maintop, it was Ice Master Blanky who was the first to spot the thin strip of dull grey that acted as the dividing line between the grey sky and the grey sea that indicated the northernmost tip of King William Land.

The black leads which Franklin's people had broken their backs to carve out all week were now completely gone and the ships were gripped by solid ice that was now anything between ten and twenty feet thick. The pressure it bore on the ships was immense as they creaked and groaned and listed as if wounded, the wind over the sea ice howled unceasingly in its cruel victory over them.

Unlike Beechey Island, this time they were twenty miles off-shore and were granted no lee to shelter in and no relief from any landscape – just the feeling of utter desolation and on the rare days when the wind didn't blow, a bleak limbo of mist determined everything. The combination of utter silence along with the dull, dreary uniformity of their seascape helped to trick their brains into believing that all their senses had been placed in suspended animation.

Haggard by the unrelenting management of the warping, Crozier had denied himself food and sleep in order to not miss a moment of trying to meet Sir John's wish to commit the ships as far into the pack as was humanly possible. Finally, beset once more, Crozier sat on the stool beside his bunk and studied his ever-shaking hands. He reached into his locker with them and produced a bottle of Bushmill's. Uncorking it, he looked around for a glass. He couldn't find one so just drank from the bottle.

Galatz, Moldavia

Stephen Goldner, a newcomer to the naval supply business, had undercut all the other suppliers by a sherry-spilling thirty per cent. At the time, no one quite knew how he did it, but as long as he came in on budget and on schedule, the Admiralty didn't care. Donkin & Gamble who had been supplying the navy for over thirty years had been genuinely shocked that their Lordships could deign to do business with unproven, untrust-worthy upstarts, and James Cooper of Clerkenwell had nearly been put out of business by the whole affair.

Green turtle soup was a delicacy originally discovered by matelots in the warmer oceans of the Orient. It went on to become something of a sailor's staple as the huge thirty-stone beasts could be kept alive for months on board the ship. Soon, all the finest tables in England became obsessed with the hearty stew, seasoned with Madeira and cayenne and served with force-meat balls. At the height of the soup's success, more than 15,000 green turtles were imported into England each year and it wasn't long before the poor creatures flapped away awkwardly towards the brink of extinction. However, a sustainable alternative was soon found that was exceptionally agreeable to the Victorian palate and purse: mock turtle soup. Specially formulated from any parts of calf, veal or even sheep, it was an epicurean delight of brains, eyes, tongue, heels, knuckles and everything else that had the same taste and texture as the real thing.

So, as an entrepreneur, it had been music to Stephen Goldner's ears when he had heard that one of Franklin's favourite dishes was turtle soup – a dish consisting of cheap bits and bobs that he could get away with pricing as a delicacy. Goldner was doubly delighted to discover that Lady Franklin was so taken with a recipe from the revered *Martha Lloyd's Household Book* that she knew it off by heart and would often make it for her husband herself. With this priceless intelligence, Goldner made sure that the soup samples that Samuel Richie had presented to Sir John followed Mrs Lloyd's recipe to the letter. He was certain that once his supplies were seen to be feeding the most famous expedition in the world, then the supply orders from the Royal Navy thereafter would simply come flooding in.

Much of Goldner's success was attributable to his crafty agent, Samuel Richie. He had presented their Lordships with the fact that 'his little Hungarian genius' had discovered an incredible new means of preserving meats that would guarantee that there was perfect, succulent meat in every tin – a rarity in naval victualing which also meant that there was no wastage and therefore, more importantly, a very attractive cost-efficiency. 'Simply too good to be true!' pursers on every naval vessel would be saying as they bit Goldner and Richie's arms off for their delectable preserved samples.

The reality was that Goldner had indeed acquired a new French patent but had absolutely no right to use it. This didn't really matter to him though. Once he'd secured the long, lucrative contract with the Admiralty he relocated the Houndsditch meat rendering and canning concerns to his Moldova factory. That way, the grubbing fingers of the law and the sticky-beaked inspectors weren't long enough to reach him whilst he was 1,547 miles away.

The other reality was that the cost had been the real clincher for the Royal Navy – as long as he could honour the clause in the contract that stated the provisions would be there on time.

But when the order finally came from the Admiralty, even he thought he might have bitten off more than he could chew. He was to supply 22,000 pints of soup, 5,500 lb of vegetables, and 31,000 lb of meat and he would need all the cheap Moldavian manpower he could muster in order to meet the almost unreasonable demands from the Admiralty. A few corners would need to be cut here and there.

Predictably, on 5 May 1845, the superintendent at the Victualing Yard, Deptford, found it necessary to report to the Board that Goldner had failed to come up with the goods – supplying only a tenth of his order. But Goldner still promised faithfully that all the meat would be there by 12 May and the soups by the fifteenth. In his letters, he begged that he might be allowed to supply the soups in canisters larger than specified. *But, sirs, I have made a promise to you and the heroes on them boats, and I swear to you now, I shall make good my undertaking.*

Wearily, and with a ringing endorsement from Sir John, the Board of Victuallers eventually granted Goldner permission to supply the Franklin expedition later, with the larger tins.

The Ship's Stores

ALL THINGS CONSIDERED, THE STORES were holding out remarkably well. Lieutenant Osmer, as the ever-prudent chief purser, had been privately anxious about Sir John's optimism regarding 'spinning out the provisions to six, possibly seven years' and had advised Sir John to hold back on breaking out any of the tinned stores until absolutely required, but the sledging parties were a special case and needed portable food. With the lion's share of the pemmican destroyed on Beechey, it had been a necessity to issue them with tins early. Generally, if fresh supplies weren't to be forthcoming, at least they had 64,224 pounds of preserved pork and beef and all the salted fish and game that were caught whilst reaching across Lancaster Sound. After that, and only as a last resort, they had the sixteen tons of tinned provisions – not to mention 1,008 pounds of raisins and what was left of the 580 gallons of the pickles after the fire. The thought gave him much comfort. The three poor souls left on Beechey *had* been a concern, however: particularly when McDonald had taken him aside and asked him to quietly carry out a full check of all the stores as well as call for the implementation of a new hygiene regime. Apart from maggots found in one of the older ewe carcasses, and nine of the food tins on *Terror* unaccounted for, everything was in order. But now, Sir John's orders for Mr Osmer were to *fetch something that would perk his somewhat down-in-the-mouth officers. And please make sure the men have plum pudding and double grog.* It was against Osmer's better judgement, but he thought the morale of his brother officers far outweighed any deficit in provisions that might never be issued. And if Sir John wasn't a special case, then who else was?

Victory Point

28 of May 1847 H.M.S. Ships Erebus and Terror Wintered in the Ice in Lat. 70°5'N Long. 98°.23'W Having wintered in 1846–7 at Beechey Island in Lat 74°43'28"N Long 91°39'15"W After having ascended Wellington Channel to Lat 77° and returned by the West side of Cornwallis Island. Sir John Franklin commanding the Expedition. All well Party consisting of 2 Officers and 6 Men left the ships on Monday 24th May 1847.
—Gm. Gore, Lieut., Chas. F. Des Vœux, Mate

The two officers grimaced stiffly behind their blue-tinted snow goggles as they slumped behind their pile of stone shards for cover against the strafing wind and snow. Graham Gore hollered at his nearby friend as if he were half a mile away, 'Surprisingly keen edge to the wind today, eh, Mr Des Vœux!'

'It's quite extraordinary, Mr Gore. If we had any milk, it would be blown from our tea! Don't think we could hope to find a more wind-loved place if we tried!'

Sir John had dictated the cairn note from the warmth of *Erebus*'s chart table before Graham Gore's party left the ships. Their orders were to cache the note in a pillar famously built at Cape Felix by James Ross some fifteen years prior. Ross's cairn was nowhere to be seen, so they had to build their own at where they could only assume Victory Point was meant to be. Finding the material for it was a straightforward matter, using the limestone shards that lay all around, everywhere… so abundantly, so monotonously.

As the snow began to blow almost horizontally, they huddled on the leeward side of their limestone stack and felt very grateful that they didn't have to try thawing ink and writing with it in the freezing squall. Their heavy woollen uniforms had been stiffened by ice for days and any man who had left his mitten off for anything more than a moment or two found their fingers padded with plasma-filled blisters – only for the fluid to then freeze rapidly. The attendant pain would become intolerable until thawed again and pricked. But there was also something else that was beginning to creep into the two officers' dispositions: listlessness. It was beginning to grow among the men too, and it was starting to make their progress treacle-like. Corporal Hedges had collapsed several times, and his face had become so swollen that the other hands started to refer to him as 'Corporal Hedgehog'. But in reality, their mirth masked the fear of the same affliction happening to them.

A camp had been pitched on the beach below the cairn and the two officers had proceeded up the long, gradual slope alone to post the note, so that by the time they returned, it was very much hoped that the men would have managed to regroup themselves and put a feed on whilst they were away. Before returning down the slope, Gore started to read the note one last time before furling it into a canister and placing it within the cairn: '"All well… Party consisting of two officers and six men left the ships on Monday 24th May 1847."'

Gore, rendered serene with his fatigue, puffed his lip at seeing the day's date. 'My God, is it really two years since we left England? Feels like twenty-two.'

Des Vœux shrugged as he said through chattering teeth, 'Why on earth would the old man write that all is well when we've lost three men?' He stared bleakly at the miles upon miles of ice that stretched out before them.

Gore stiffly rose to his feet like a beggar. 'Well, I suppose it would read marginally more agreeably than reporting that we are stuck in fifteen feet of ice in the middle of the bloody Arctic with a senile egomaniac, an Irish dipso, and a thick lickspittle?' The two friends cracked a smile between them, and Gore held out his hand to help Des Vœux up. Like wizened old crones, they started off back down the hill towards the men until Des Vœux lost his footing.

'So sorry, old man… not feeling quite myself today. Curse this absolute arse of a place! I'm sick of it all, actually – sick to death of it.'

'Come on, Charles, old thing. Everything will come right – you'll see.'

At the bottom of the hill, the two officers joined their men again and they were just in time to be handed steaming mugs. Gore, whilst spooning his soup, winked at Des Vœux. 'There you are, Mr Des Vœux. A drop of hot soup is the answer to most things, isn't it?'

The Great Cabin

SIR JOHN HAD INVITED CROZIER and the officers of *Terror* for supper where it was understood that he was laying on a special treat to celebrate their second anniversary in the Arctic. However, with the storm whipping up so wildly, it had to be that Lieutenant Hodgson was the sole representative from *Terror* as he had gone over to *Erebus* a day earlier to assist Commander Fitzjames with some observations on atmospherical refraction. Conversely, assistant surgeon McDonald had been unavoidably detained aboard *Terror* whilst working with Dr Goodsir. They had been urgently preserving and categorising some hitherto unknown species of shellfish that had begun to disconcertingly discolour after they had dredged them from the seabed as part of their rapidly expanding collection of specimens. The truth was that Dr Goodsir found the learned company of his fellow countryman on *Terror* far more conducive than the somewhat clubbable personalities of their senior doctors Stanley and Peddie – along with their outstanding talents for delegation. As for Dr Stanley, he did find molluscs and bivalves to be of immense personal interest as long as they were presented with plenty of horseradish and washed down with a decent Muscadet, whereas Dr Peddie was quite content with just the wine.

Their two Scottish assistant surgeons had crossed over by about two years whilst at Edinburgh, passing by each other like ships in the night. But now, finding themselves on the expedition, they had become kindred spirits – particularly in light of the fact that their seniors had thrust them together so that they could work diligently on what they regarded as the more mundane elements of the expedition, such as the zoological and geological specimens – as well as seeing to the physical wellbeing of the men.

To look at the two assistants, they couldn't have been more different if they had tried: Goodsir was stubborn and sullen and had won both the praise and spleen of his praelectors at Edinburgh in equal measure with his constantly irritating correctitude which they broadly mistook for arrogance. Goodsir had never been to sea before and was constantly at a loss – especially when it came to seasickness. His misery seemed to bring much barely disguised amusement to the older hands until one day, Lieutenant Gore, known for bolting his food, was found choking on the quarterdeck and as the matelots and officers helplessly watched him silently turn blue, the scrawny doctor astonished everyone by applying a rather decent uppercut to Gore's solar plexus. He was just about to be restrained as he went in again, when the big lieutenant coughed up a particularly gristly lump of pemmican and all was made clear. Alexander McDonald, however, was entirely the Heads side of Goodsir's coin: the flame-headed doctor was elegant and charming and what he didn't know about matters medical, he more than made up for with his incredibly winning bedside manner. Sandy, as his many friends called him, had been to sea many times and had visited the Arctic aboard a whaler – even bringing an Inuk back to Scotland with him for the sake of science and the coincidental publication of his narrative regarding his journey.

Thick weather had whipped-up from the N.W. an hour before the officers were due to set out across the already treacherous half-league slog between the two ships. The squall didn't let up for even a moment of its seventy-hour tantrum but for supper that evening Crozier and the rest of his officers were quite content to stay put and make do with Diggle's famed unicorn pie, which, as most were starting to suspect, consisted almost entirely of narwhal. Too much weather came on for any sensible acceptance of a supper invitation from *Erebus*, so Crozier had the signaller run up the signal flags by way of communicating *Terror*'s regrets and apologies. For Crozier, no squall could have been more welcome.

In *Erebus*'s great cabin, the glittering terrine was slid into position on the crisp linen. To the officers who were able to dine in the Great Cabin that night, it was a sight to behold, and the smell of the rich Madeira gravy, onions and thyme was so tantalising it actually made the officers' mouths sting in anticipation. That is, to all but Fitzjames, who had been feeling rather off-colour over the last day or two.

Sir John had become anxious about Gore's party in the deteriorating weather and had asked for volunteers to go and look for them. Fitzjames made an immediate show of selfless leadership and put himself forward – along with Harry Le Vesconte as his second-in-command. But then, Sir John has insisted that he remain aboard in order to convalesce. James Fairholme sportingly raised his hand to join Mr Le Vesconte in the commander's stead.

With so many of the officers absent, supper had been somewhat quiet affair but after the cheese, cigars were lit, the port was passed and the evening turned out most pleasantly indeed. Franklin, on seeing the warm, satisfied glow on his officers' faces, toasted Stephen Goldner as the one who had blessed them with enough food in their bellies to get them up any 'Horeb' and he was grateful to the Hungarian for giving them the means to live as civilised Christians in a wild, inhospitable place inhabited by beasts and savages. In fact, in a further flourish of benevolence, Sir John asked that PO Hoar let the galley hands take full advantage of the Lord's providence by not wasting any leftovers.

Lat. 70º 05' N, Long. 98º 23' W

THE WEATHER IN THE ARCTIC that summer had been particularly harsh. So much so, that even the Swedes were feeling it. Sir John Ross, whilst serving as British Consul in Stockholm, had been exposed to robust evidence of a change in the weather systems within the Arctic Circle.

Like some sort of glacial procession, the billions of tons of ice from the northwest corner of the Arctic Archipelago were making their way back down south with a vengeance. Through every channel and sound that led to Victoria Strait it was now carrying *Erebus* and *Terror* forwards at a rate of around a mile and a half per month. The ice, as it had done for millennia, was being pushed south again, down the western coast of King William where the colossal weight of more ice crept in from the west to join a creeping, inexorable floe of biblical proportions.

From the sophisticated data-gathering of the Swedish meteorological office Sir John Ross had been deeply impressed with the accuracy of their science regarding the climate – particularly as a man who had witnessed the full fury of nature's belligerence first-hand. As a consequence, Ross's somewhat patronising manner towards Franklin had been pushed aside by anxiety and even a little guilt for not being able to do more to stymie Franklin's selection for the job. If Swedish predictions were correct, then he, more than anyone, knew that any poor souls who happened to find themselves north of the 66th Parallel were in for the devil of a time. The old polar veteran didn't waste a moment in besieging the Admiralty with both his privileged intelligence and the full bluster of his concerns for Franklin and his men – each time, prompting Barrow to quietly grimace at yet another acute communiqué from the 'Weather Cock', as they now privately referred to him. What the Swedes had been observing was a notable drop in climate temperature; particularly in their lands to the north and they were starting to refer to the phenomenon as the *Liten Istid*. Theories abounded regarding the cause of this new Little Ice Age: some ventured that there were volcanoes erupting in the Azores that were blocking out the sun's rays, whilst others attributed it to oceanic circulation – some even blamed it on variations of the Earth's axis.

Crozier was on deck taking a midday fix on their position as the sun showed itself anaemically for brief moments through the scudding clouds. He was always staggered at how the weather could switch so quickly, but now, with the first let-up for over a week, he had meant to send a bottle of Burgundy over to Sir John by way of an apology for *Terror's* poor show regarding his anniversary party. Looking through his sextant's eyepiece, he could that see Sir John had already beaten him to it as a runner from *Erebus* was making his way across the ice at quite a lick. Shortly, a breathless Young Davy Young appeared on deck, only just remembering to salute before blurting his dispatch. 'Commander Fitzjames… requests your presence… at your earliest convenience… sir?' Crozier grunted his acknowledgement to the lad, but as he tenderly placed the sextant back its case, various thoughts crept around his head: *Commander Fitzjames requests your presence?* He made a note of their position: it had evidently changed.

Victory Beach

MR GORE'S PARTY HAD BEEN expected back three days ago. Granted, they must have had a rough time with the weather of late, but it was only twenty miles from the ships to the Ross Pillar, so with eight fit hands on pully-hauly they should have easily been able to pull for around five miles a day – even taking into account the pressure ridges and the winds. But with the keenest eyes of the marines posted on the tops there had been no sign of Gore. Even before they left the ships to pursue them, the weather for Mr Le Vesconte's party was forecast for grimness. Sir John had even relaxed his normally stoic stance on their apparel in order to give them as much advantage as possible, and for the men's long leather sea boots, under Carpenter Honey's suggestion, they had put brass tacks through their soles to give them better purchase on the ice. The men had also made use of another resource that was readily to hand: animal skins. It may not have looked seaman-like for a modern navy, but to feel entirely comfortable even at -60°F was an entirely welcome novelty. Usually, the standard slops of pilot cloth greatcoats and shorter, double-breasted monkey jackets quickly became wet with sweat before turning into unhelpful sheets of rigid armour. But Sir John, ever keen to maintain standards, normally thought it crucial for his men to keep up appearances whilst on the ice: furs were fine for ladies, or as part of a humorous theatrical production, but it was wholly inappropriate for any member of Her Majesty's Navy to traipse around looking like a savage. But now, after Crozier had pointed out that even the normally martinet-ish John Ross had found the wearing of 'northern slops' to be of great benefit to sledging parties Sir John had finally relented. He made a big show of it during one particular Sunday sermon where he quoted from the Book of Judges where Gideon was asking God to give him a sign by putting out a fleece. Some of the men could see the parable about never questioning faith, but all of them could see the joy of feeling less cold.

Northern slops aside, the taking of the sea bears was readily embraced as it gave the sailors unfettered access to fresh meat that was gamey and generally found to be excellent, but it was their fur that was the real prize. The previous ban on wearing furs for non-sledging hands did ensure the steady growth of a stock-pile which the tars, being ever resourceful, soon managed to find another use: for polar bear sleeping bags. These instantly become a distinct improvement on the standard sleeping equipment that comprised of wool blankets folded into modified hammock canvas and perhaps inaccurately referred to as *sleeping* bags where any such event rarely took place. Instead, the poor soul interred within usually ended up chattering his way through the night.

Whilst they were alive, the donors of these skins had become troublesome to say the least. The bears had made travelling between the two ships even more treacherous, prompting the men to call it the Bag Bait Run. Whenever any people were sent to either of the ships, it was necessary to post marine sentries on both watches with their Brunswick rifles made ready. The Bag Run almost became something of a sport and a book was alleg-edly started among the marines to see how close they could let a bear get to its typically hysterical victim before felling the beast – usually with just yards to spare. On one such occasion whilst on Beechey, Marine Firemark, who was the finest marksman in his regiment, was covering the progress of a stores party as they transferred sacks of dried peas over from *Erebus* on little sledges. However, the party led by PO Diggle, were soon perturbed to hear the huffing of a white bear as it cantered across the ice to meet them. Understandably, the men immediately abandoned their load and ran. Seeing this, the bear's gait developed into a more determined gallop, covering the remaining five hundred yards in a flash. As the bear was closing in on the now frantic men, the somewhat portly PO found his acceleration to be no match for the bear who was now in full-tilt. From his vantage point in the ship's tops, Firemark left it so late to squeeze off the action that the bear actually slumped dead on top of an exceedingly disturbed Diggle.

Afterwards, some of the hands argued that the quality of the food did improve considerably for at least two weeks afterwards, and if the sharp-shooting prankster had been anyone else other than Firemark, he would have doubtless had Diggle's rolling pin wrapped round his neck for giving him such a scare. But somehow the marine had a way about him that always seemed to allow him to transcend blame or offence.

Firemark's actual name was Henry Wilkes, but he had acquired his moniker for two obvious reasons: his impeccable prowess with a rifle – and the port wine stain that covered his left eye and cheek. His birthmark was a fascinating thing to look at and it even came with an attendant shock of white hair that heralded how his malformed capillaries extended past his hairline. After the Diggle incident, Commander Fitzjames was so amused that he saw fit to have the young private made up to corporal (acting).

Cape Felix

LIEUTENANTS LE VESCONTE, FAIRHOLME AND THEIR men had set out with their boat sledge to look for Mr Gore. Ahead, the wind whipped up the loose snow from the zastrugi and carried it across the ice as if it were the spray of a raging sea. They had made steady progress but were in need of rest.

In an effort to slake his thirst, one of the hands had developed the habit of scooping up snow and eating it. This would only lead to further dehydration as the culprit's body wasted more energy thawing the snow, which would eventually cool the body temperature and lead to hypothermia.

Sergeant Tozer spotted him. 'Oi, you! All my eye and Betty Martin, what do you think you're doing, lad! I've told you before: melting ice in yer chops will do yer summin' chronical. Catch you one more time, and I'll shove my bandook up yer arse and flick you to Greenland, right, boy?' The sergeant leered at the ragged-looking marine before cracking a wee wink. 'Good 'ere, innit?'

The two officers nearby caught each other's eye and could barely conceal their grins. Fairholme coughed a little and reached into his armpit to retrieve his watch where he kept it on a lanyard in order to keep it from freezing.

Perhaps carried by the wind, Sergeant Tozer thought he could hear something up ahead in the swirling white mayhem of the weather. He quickened his pace as he unwrapped the cloth insulation from his rifle's working parts and pulled the hammer back. As he passed the men, then the officers, he held his fist over his head as a signal for them to halt and get ready for something or, *hurry up and wait* as some would mutter. Now away from the din of the men and nothing but the wind for company Tozer could definitely hear something... the deep, almost beseeching bark of Neptune. As he made for the waterline on the beach, he could see Lieutenant Gore's ragged silk pennant flapping horizontally in the wind. Pitched round it was a Holland tent that had been half absorbed by drifts of snow – the sergeant called for the rest of the men. They shrugged off their harnesses and broke into a stiff run towards the camp. Once there they fell to their knees and worked quickly at the tent's fastenings with numb hands and no sooner were they undone, the wind took the canvas flaps from their blistered fingers to reveal hell itself within: among the gear, clothes and various detritus lay the bodies of Gore's people still in their sleeping bags. Their expressions did not belong to men who were peacefully at rest, but rather as if they had died mid-nightmare; their faces, blackened and taut from the frost, staring out with pearled, frozen eyes. As if their bones were trying to burst from their skins. The cold had desiccated the corpses and the flesh around their mouths, eyes and even noses had withdrawn back to make the men look like a choir scream-ing with the wind for all eternity.

Neptune had finally stopped barking but had resorted to a low growl as he lay across the cold, lifeless legs of Sergeant Bryant and had to be dragged out of the tent by Sergeant Tozer and his corporal. Lieutenant Gore's body was eventually identified, and they found his journal, still clutched tightly to his chest. The two officers were just about able to make out Graham Gore's last words written in a delicate, spidery scrawl:

27th May 1847
To whomsoever may find this,
    Our souls are now in the hands of a far greater Being. Please assure our loved ones that the journey to Him was

painless and swift and that we are now in a far better place. Having entered a peaceful torpor, the men's eyes, along with their speech, dulled before slipping into a fathomless sleep. We have no idea what the cause of this affliction was but if it assists our doctors, please let it be known to them that its early signs started to appear four days after setting off from our ships. Having done all we could to make the men as comfortable as humanly possible here, our intention was to strike out for our ships and raise the alarm. However, the recent blizzards, coupled with our own lessening ability to move, conspired ably against us. My great friend, Lieutenant Charles Des Vœux, at last, closed his eyes this morning and I feel both certain and grateful that the same sleep will visit me next.

With the greatest affection, admiration and brightest hope for your own endeavours,

Lieutenant G. Gore RN

You will find the men's valuables and letters at the bottom of their sleeping bags.

The Commodore's Bunk

Instruction addressed to Sir John Franklin (cont'd)…

21. In the event of any irreparable accident happening to either of the two ships, you are to cause the officers and crew of the disabled ship to be removed into the other, and with her singly to proceed in prosecution of the voyage, or return to England, according as circumstances shall appear to require, understanding that the officers and crews of both ships are hereby authorized and required to continue to perform the duties according to their respective ranks and stations on board either ship to which they may be removed, in the event of an occurrence of this nature. Should, unfortunately, your own ship be the one disabled, you are in that case to take command of the 'Terror,' and in the event of any fatal accident happening to yourself, Captain Crozier is hereby authorized to take command of the 'Erebus,' placing the officer of the expedition who may then be next in seniority to him in command of the 'Terror.' Also, in the event of your own inability, by sickness or otherwise, of any period of service, to continue to carry these instructions into execution, you are to transfer them to the officer next in command to you employed on the expedition, who is hereby required to execute them in the best manner he can for the attainment of the several objects herein set forth […]

Sir John began to come to as the concerned faces of his two captains peered down at him. In his delirium he was muttering to
himself as if drunk and every part of his body had puffed up like
a balloon. He, seven officers (including the two senior surgeons)
and four of the men were all in the same beleaguered boat. The
ships' assistant surgeons had done all they could over the last ten
days since Crozier was summoned to *Erebus*, but whatever they
tried was futile. Dr Goodsir had been incredibly diligent in collecting and observing stool samples and had discovered the same
sausage-shaped bacteria writhing before him on his microscope's
slide. It dawned on Goodsir and McDonald that whatever it
was that Torrington, Hartnell and Braine had suffered from, the
twelve officers and men now had the same mysterious bacteria
multiplying inside them.

At odds against everything, Sir John seemed to be at peace
with himself as he lay on his bunk clutching his pocket watch.
Attempting to open his eyes through their impossibly engorged
lids, he was rewarded with the vision of Lady Franklin standing
over him. She tucked the sheets tenderly around her husband
and as he instinctively reached for her, he found that she had
swaddled him in the Union Jack she had sewn. He was horrified
and began to thrash and kick hysterically.

'There's a flag thrown over me! Don't you know that they lay
a Union flag over a corpse!' Then, another pair of hands gently
restrained him. McDonald, almost in a whisper attempted to
console him. 'Sir… Sir John – please, calm yourself. You have a
fever, sir.'

The commodore sobbed as he begged for his wife. 'Where
is Jane? Why am I covered in this flag?' Sir John looked down
again at his bedclothes: the flag had vanished, of course – along
with his wife. Sir John blinked with confusion as Crozier joined
McDonald at his bedside. 'Oh god, Francis! Things have fallen
out… so unluckily.' In one more convulsion, their leader tightened his grip on Crozier's arm before finally letting go. Dr

McDonald gently placed Sir John's hands together on his belly and took the watch that he had been clutching. Carefully pouring the fob chain into his cupped palm he then handed it to the expedition's new leader. Crozier flicked open the watch and peered at its inscription as Mozart's tinkles played out:

In time, we will be together.
J.

Crozier gently closed the watch up again as he shook his head. 'We really have become fortune's fools, haven't we?'

As soon as the door was slid open Crozier's face contorted with the stench.

Inside, the two surgeons worked with towels tied around their faces, whilst Fitzjames and Pusser Osmer held wads of unravelled bandages to their mouths and noses. Osmer offered a similar bundle for Crozier, but he dismissed it with a distracted wave of his hand as he saw inside the small forward bunk filled with seemingly lifeless men and their bedpans and vomit-lined blankets. Crozier shortly held out his beckoning fingers towards Osmer – he did need something to cover his mouth and nose after all.

'What the hell is going on?'

McDonald answered as he hovered the back of his hand over the normally stoic Lieutenant Hodgson's mouth and nose, 'We have no idea, sir – we've no experience of such symptoms.' Satisfied that the lieutenant was still breathing, he clutched the patient's hand and spoke as if addressing an inattentive child. 'Mr Hodgson... George... can you hear me? Squeeze my hand if you can hear me.'

Hodgson did as he was told and the doctor patted his patient's hand. 'Well done, George, very good.'

The doctor gently laid Hodgson's hand at his side as he said to Crozier, 'We've seen this sort of fever before with cholera, but Dr Goodsir has found a reference of it in one of his gazettes that shows the cholera bacteria to look nothing like this under the microscope.'

Goodsir was just making some more notes about the rapidly deteriorating Dr Stanley and didn't waste any time by looking up as he said, 'The only thing we've been able to establish is the men started to go down after the Anniversary supper.'

Dr McDonald took a scrap of paper from his coat pocket and began to read. 'The commodore... er, seven of the officers – including both of the ship's surgeons and two of the galley hands – at this rate we'll need to expand the sick berth into one side of the main deck, sir.'

Crozier looked around the sickbay and shook his head in bewilderment. 'Yes, of course... and none of the men from the other messes are showing any signs?'

'No, sir – not as yet.'

Fitzjames noticed that the blood had drained from the purser's face. 'What is it, Pusser? You look like you've seen a ghost.'

Mr Osmer, now too distracted for stenches, lowered his handkerchief. 'The soup!'

Crozier was nonplussed. 'Soup?'

'Yes, mock turtle, sir.'

Crozier was tempted to lift Osmer by both ears. 'Make yourself clear, Pusser.'

'I, I cracked into the tinned provisions as the commodore wanted to lay on a treat for the officers. I did have to try a lot of the tins, but they were off – made a dreadful hum. But those that weren't bad tasted like they were made yesterday... absolutely fine, sir.'

'Well, they're obviously not fucking fine, are they? Has anyone else been at this shite?'

Osmer's face went even paler. 'Yes, sir, the sledging parties, sir: Gore's... and Le Vesconte's... Oh, dear Lord...'

Terror's Great Cabin

WHEN CROZIER'S STEWARD FOUND HIM the next morning he had been worried enough to fetch the commander urgently. Fitzjames, thinking the worst, was almost relieved when he saw the wreckage of Crozier sprawled on his bunk: smashed bottles and the thick, fruity stink of stale whiskey and cold piss.

'Couldn't wake him, sir – 'e's gunna bust my eye when he finds out I hollered for you, sir, but I ain't never seen him this bad.'

'Does anyone else know about this, Jopson?'

'No, sir – not a soul, sir.'

'Please make sure it stays that way and wait outside.'

As Jopson closed the door gently behind himself Fitzjames wasted no time in flinging open a few of the stern lights to let the wind bring both a flurry of snow and a means of escape for some of the stench. He turned the captain onto his back and shook his shoulders before attempting to drag Crozier away from his bunk and back near the little open windows. Crozier, more out of reflex, tried to get to his feet before languidly swinging his fist at Fitzjames – just catching the commander on the lip. Fitzjames responded with a smart slap across Crozier's face. The captain attempted to put up his fists again but fell heavily against a shelf of specimens, sending them crashing to the deck with him.

Fitzjames shook his head. 'Call yourself a leader?'

'That's one thing I've never called myself, boy!'

'Well, whether you like it or not, Francis, that's what you must be now.'

'Who the fuck are you to tell me anything… you jumped-up gobshite!'

Tasting rust, Fitzjames touched his lip and inspected the blood on his fingers.

'Well, Captain, I'm not entirely sure who I am myself, but I'm certainly not someone who has given up on themselves – quite the opposite, actually.'

'Oh, really?'

'Yes, *really*, sir! I can only imagine what the sea and the ice has done to you over the years, but…'

Crozier closed his eyes as the sting of the cold on his neck and the warming of his cheek began to bring a return of his senses.

Fitzjames pulled up a chair and sat down in front of him. 'But all I know now is that you can lead us out of our troubles or just add to our woes – Sir John is dead and the men will be looking to you for answers, Francis. You're one of them and they have faith in you…' Fitzjames eyed the pathetic state of Crozier: 'Far more than you do in yourself, evidently.'

Crozier scoffed, 'Well, more fool them.' He covered his eyes with his palms and began to sob. 'I'm broken, James. I'm scared and broken.'

Fitzjames hesitated before putting a hand on his shoulder. 'Of course you're scared – we're all scared – out of our wits. Any man who says he isn't is either a liar or insane. But whatever you might be feeling, Francis, the men need to be shown leadership; the officers need a leader… and heaven knows, *I* need a leader. We need someone who can hold us all together, and that *someone* is not me. I wish to God it was, but you know as well as I do that the men wouldn't follow me as far as the ship's rail.' Fitzjames shook out his folded handkerchief and held it to his lip. 'Look at all the men you've sailed under, Francis: Parry… both Rosses… Sir John Franklin… yes, Sir John Franklin – I know you and he didn't see eye to eye, but even you have to admit that he was a brave man, Francis.'

Crozier wiped his eyes and shivered. 'Aye, well – it was either face coming here or stay at home with that missus of his, eh?'

Both men smiled.

'So, what do you think James Ross would do if he was here now, Francis?' Fitzjames put his handkerchief away again as he continued, 'I've read James Ross's narratives and by all accounts he would have made his presence felt on every yard and every deck. He would have made himself more unreasonable than any storm and he wouldn't have given anything or anyone an inch… would he not, Francis?'

Crozier nodded a little at the accurate assessment of his friend. 'Yeah, perhaps, but what you wouldn't have read in any narratives was the fact that he was always just as terrified as the best of us.'

'So, what's the difference between him and you, Francis? What would he have that you don't in a situation such as this?'

Crozier shook his head at the thought about how, just like him, Ross often sought to look at fear through the dulled lens of a bottle. It was almost miraculous how it made everything seem far further away than it actually was – especially pain and fear. Crozier smiled wanly as he answered, 'Dunno – perhaps he just learned to hide his fear better than anyone else?'

'Well, then, that's what you must do now, Francis. Surely to God?'

The Main Top

A NEW WATCH HAD JUST come on and Peglar, perched aloft, could see the pall of black smoke some five miles off. Mr Little, as officer of the watch, set out with a party of marines to investigate the source of the smoke. But, as a quick reaction force, their progress was slowed somewhat by hummocky ice ridges that had acted as hedgerow-height hurdles every ten yards or so.

As they got closer to the smoke, they could identify its source: Le Vesconte's boat had been set on fire, he presumed, by the four or five Inuit who were surrounding the boat. However, on spotting the approach of Little and his men, they began to flee with their dog sledges, running eastwards along the ridges. Mr Little gave Firemark the order of 'prime and ready', but Firemark was already rammed. He set his leaf sight to 300 and fired. The closest Inuit was dropped, but in the eight seconds it took Firemark to reload, the remainder were well out of range as they howled off into the distance with their quick dogs.

Mr Little and his men, on finally reaching the burning boat, saw the helpless condition of Le Vesconte and his men and began their evacuation back to the ships.

Firemark, on catching up with his quarry turned the body over to reveal not an Inuit hunter but a young girl: she was unconscious and bleeding heavily from the knee. As she began to groan, he removed the percussion cap from his rifle's lock and gently eased the hammer.

The Fire Hole, Erebus

Sunset and evening star,
And one clear call for me!
And may there be no moaning of the bar,
When I put out to sea,

But such a tide as moving seems asleep,
Too full for sound and foam,
When that which drew from out the boundless deep
Turns again home.

Twilight and evening bell,
And after that the dark!
And may there be no sadness of farewell,
When I embark;

For tho' from out our bourne of Time and Place
The flood may bear me far,
I hope to see my Pilot face to face
When I have crost the bar.

'Crossing the Bar', Alfred, Lord Tennyson

On 11 June 1847, both ships' companies were assembled around
the fire hole that had been cut into the ice beside *Erebus*. Crozier

led the service and Commander Fitzjames and Lieutenant Irving both gave readings. Afterwards, Sergeant Tozer brought the men up to attention and his marines fired off their salute. As the last remaining sergeant, and with his best friend now gone, he felt that leading his firing party was the least he could do.

Finally, the Still was piped as the tenderly swaddled bodies of Sir John, five officers and ten men slipped away from beneath their Union flag palls and into the cold, dark enigma of the sea.

Crozier stood next to the now limp flags and asked for the men to be stood easy. From his breast pocket he produced a small book of verse wrapped in a medal ribbon which he used as a bookmark. He took out the attached medal and peered at it for a moment or two before looking up again. His pale grey eyes seemed to pierce the souls of every man who stood there shivering from the cold and the fear.

'Some of you may well be starting to question yourselves about your decisions to be part of this expedition... You might be asking yourselves why the hell we are here in this cold-hearted bastard of a place... and you'd be forgiven for thinking that we probably don't have much going for us, right now. But, lads, you would be wrong there.'

He held up Sir John's medal. 'This here is Sir John's Grand Cross of the Royal Guelphic Order. King George awarded it to him. On the back it says something in Latin, which Dr McDonald assures me means "hardships do not deter us."' Crozier looked around again at every man. 'These were words that Sir John lived by, gentlemen. But there is one word in there that is easily overlooked: the only little word that can deliver any Latin promises, gestures or oaths scratched into silver, or carved into stone.'

He paused, so that he could catch every man's eye again. 'What we have is *us*, lads. With *us*, we can hold out a hand from a dark, lost place and know that someone will be there to take it. With *us*, we can stand back to back and fend off savage beasts – and then afterwards, get drunk and probably laugh about it.

With *us*, we can cross the unknown with the strong hands of friends pushing us forward – but with the surety that those same hands will readily turn into fists to defend us. And we each know that we would, in turn, do the same for the man standing next to us. *Us*: together, as *us*, we are everything and no hardships in this place, or any other will ever deter *us*.'

With his ever-shaking fingers, he replaced the medal within the pages of his book and bound the covers once more with its ribbon.

Gore's Bunk

IT WAS DIFFICULT TO PUT an age on the Inuk girl who lay there in the serenity of unconsciousness beneath her black, sooty grime. She had perfect teeth and shining hair and she could have been anything between seventeen and thirty. McDonald, in an attempt to limit her exposure to infection, set about dabbing the smut from her face with the care of an archaeologist dusting away the sands of time from a long-lost idol to Venus. With soap and hot water, he soon revealed a girl with flawless olive skin and the rosiest cheeks the men gathering around his shoulders had ever gawped upon.

The ball from Firemark's rifle had passed through her left leg at the knee, taking with it both the lateral and anterior ligaments. The top of the tibia and its attendant meniscus had gone too. Never again would her leg be of any use to her – just a hindrance. McDonald did all he could to reassure the young woman before the pain set in again to bring her the mercy of unconsciousness so that Goodsir could set to work removing everything below the knee with tourniquet, catkin and tenon saw. It was all over in thirty-five seconds. At the very least all the articular cartilage was clean and there had been plenty of material to bring together for sewing up the wound. Throughout, the corporal with the port-wine stain never left her side.

※

It took three days for the girl to come to. When she opened her eyes in the little bunk room with all its other-worldly straight lines and timber work, she assumed that she had died and been transported to the afterlife and that the man with the blood face, dozing on a little stool next to her accordingly became her *anirniq*.

In Christian terms, the *anirniq* was roughly the equivalent of an angel or celestial being. Her people, the Netsilik, believed that the *anirniq* of any animal or person was liberated through the death of its host, and that once freed, it had the power to either take its revenge or dispense benevolence such as their fate would dictate. The *anirniq* could either be appeased or inflamed by the deceased, depending on their obedience in life. The girl, convinced that her beliefs had been made real in the afterlife, did not feel any fear at that moment. Instinctively, she reached over and touched her *anirniq*'s face. He woke with a start that made her recoil into the corner of her bunk. It was only then that she felt the pain in her leg. She yelped and covered her mouth so that she didn't displease her *anirniq* further. Firemark corresponded by retreating a little towards the tiny bunk's doorway, saying softly as he did so, 'Please... it's all right – please calm yourself, miss... you're safe here.' He glanced down and could see that a spot of blood was widening on her sailor's shirt where it hung by her knee. She had evidently opened the wound on something during her panic. 'I'll go and get the medic, miss...' She followed his gaze, saw the blood and where her leg had been, and began to scream uncontrollably.

The Glory Hole, Terror

PUSSER OSMER, ON CROZIER'S INSTRUCTIONS, had gathered the tinned provisions that had bloated or split – along with all that had contained 'mock feckin' turtle soup'. Then, every one of them was dumped into the sea through the fire hole. They soon found some of the tins to be so full of air that they wouldn't sink, so men wearing thick scarves and mufflers over their faces split them with axes before kicking them into the sea.

With twenty-one officers and men from the two parties dead, along with the other officers who had supped the treacherous soup with Sir John, Crozier was furious with himself, more than anything. The expedition was an unmitigated disaster. In his thirty-five-year career he'd never witnessed such a loss of men before. He shook his head with the bitter irony of history repeating itself for an expedition under Franklin – having lost half of his people to starvation in his Coppermine expedition back in '22. It felt like the man's over-compensation to avoid such disaster happening to him again was now the cause of even greater calamity.

But what Franklin couldn't possibly have foreseen was the foulness that Crozier and his men were now inheriting with the tins. Crozier, feeling a bile of a different kind rise within him, was disgusted that his sailors, in a modern navy, had been provisioned with such filth – poisoned by those whom they had depended upon to sustain and support them. He and his people were now the victims of accountants seeking to claw back money for greater efficiencies. Efficiencies that had brought about chaos with factory workers who had sabotaged their greedy, money-grubbing bosses' businesses as revenge for their shocking working conditions. Crozier didn't take it personally, but he thought that if he ever got hold of the scrawny runts who did this to his people, he would strangle them with their own oily little cravats.

Out of 60,000-odd pounds of essential provisions, they were left with just half a hundredweight that were deemed anywhere near usable. That, along with the hunting, would have to do it until nature would trot past their keenly traversing gun muzzles in the spring.

A blaze aboard a ship was one of the greatest fears for sailors. The irony of ships being surrounded by water but threatened by fire was never lost on matelots, but anyone who was ever fortunate enough to survive a floating mass of tinder and powder consuming itself in the middle of a bottomless sea will know indeed what the fires of hell truly look like. To any sailor, the threat was constant – especially in light of how effortlessly the storehouse on Beechey was lost. Each ship's fire holes were cut as a precaution against any such incident and the blocks that were cut from the ice were then used to build a storage hut for the ship's pumps so that in the event of a fire the pumps could be deployed rapidly. The Glory Holes, as the men soon referred to them had many other uses too: they were used as a dump for gash from the ships or the buckets from the heads. One of the better by-products of this was that a lot of wildlife was attracted to the hole – whether it was fish, seals or even the odd narwhal coming up for air. Sailors would often exploit it as a fishing hole where many a record fish was caught and yanked onto the ice gasping and flickering.

On one occasion, during a particularly gloomy day, AB Seeley, who was one of the more stoic pole worshippers, had just caught a magnificent char and was on his knees struggling to disgorge the thing from his hook when he felt a slap on the back. With hands full of livid, flapping fish, Seeley shouted back at whom he thought was Tommy Hartnell (who had gone off to relieve himself) only to receive another, rougher shove on the back. Spinning round, with gritted teeth, ire instantly turned to abject horror at the spectacle not of Tommy still wiping his hands on his thighs, but of a huge, veteran polar bear slavering at the sight of fish. Seeley, without missing a beat, flung the fish at the bear like a bride's bouquet at a wedding as he ran away screaming.

As 1847 blew its way into 1848, winter looked like it was set to outstay its welcome yet again. At the start, the solid ice was a boon to good hunting. Shooting parties went out regularly to shoot willow grouse, ptarmigan and little auks. Often the sky would darken almost biblically as bands upon bands of migrating passenger pigeons flew in convenient waves over the ships. With each new suicidal squadron, volleys of officers' and marines' 'lead poisoning' brought a renewed shower of dead birds bouncing onto the ice as if they were on a grouse drive on one of the more generously stocked private estates. Mr Osmer, as he double-gunned with Mr Little as his loader, was even prompted to declare the dependability of passenger pigeons as the Wheat Fields of the Sky, as he harvested them for all they were worth. Game such as fox, lemming, ermine and, of course, bear would even sniff round the ships – only to be despatched almost breezily by anyone who happened to have a fowling piece within arm's reach. However, the flesh that most of the men came to treasure was that of seal. Between the two ships, 357 seals were taken during their first six months on the ice. The pusser, a keen deer hunter in civilian life, had developed a means of stalking any seal that dared loaf about the ice for too long. His system involved sliding up to the creatures on a small, lightweight sledge that he lay prone upon – inching himself forward with his toes. To facilitate the latter, he had the blacksmith refashion a broken ice saw and screw it to the soles of his sea boots for greater purchase on the ice. He also had a screen of No 8 canvas fixed to his sledge and in its middle he cut a slit through which his barrel covertly prodded. On one occasion, he got so close to a harp seal as it lay there itching itself like some bloated, watery-eyed dog in a sleeping bag, that he was able to rest his muzzle on the poor creature's temple before gently squeezing off the action.

A decent-sized seal would yield about 30 pounds of the lean, fresh meat that the crews had come to cherish, but, over the months, the seals became reasonably shy of any hole in the ice near any ships. Above the water too, any wildlife, with its essential genetic need to adapt, soon disappeared completely: resorting to a far less perilous route to wherever it was they were headed.

Eventually, the pusser let it be known that he was worried about the provisions and so Crozier had no option but to start a more swingeing regime by putting the men on half allowance.

On the Ice

THE GIRL HOBBLED ONTO THE ice with Corporal Firemark. Throughout her convalescence, the two had become inseparable. Initially, Firemark had been the only one whom she would let near her. She had depended on Firemark for everything: from emptying her chamber pot to fetching her raw fish or seal meat since the cooked foods she was constantly offered were repulsive to her. But over the ensuing months she had almost settled into her strange 'afterlife'. Each day, regardless of the weather, she and Firemark would take to the decks arm-in-arm as she learnt how to walk again under the shelter of the awning. So much so, that she went from hobbling around slowly and unsteadily, to almost skipping with a crutch as fast as Firemark could walk. For this, she would use her free arm in a peculiar swinging motion that helped give her the momentum she needed in order to compensate for the weight of her lost limb.

One day, as they were resting, Firemark presented her with a fragment or two of chocolate and by the expression on her face, he thought she was going to spit it out or weep as the cocoa and sugar melted on her tongue. She was in ecstasy. *Toklat* was her first word of English and, within a fairly short space of time, both she and Firemark's vocabulary in their respective new languages rapidly grew as they pointed at things and shouted nouns repeatedly in English and Inuktitut. He understood that her name was Aguta and she understood that his name was Henry, but somehow it always came out as Anirniq.

Perhaps it was down to the corporal's diligence with her dressing changes that her leg had healed better than even the eternally optimistic Dr McDonald could have hoped for.

Though she became quite deft with the crutch, getting up and down any steps had presented her with great difficulty as even the most able-bodied still needed both hands on handrails in order to safely haul themselves up or down at the best of times. So, Firemark had asked the carpenters to make her a wooden leg in return for his month's tobacco allowance. They had initially set to work on a decent piece of spruce but were soon caught by their master, Mr Honey, who was disgusted when he discovered what his carpenters were doing for the girl. The chief admonished the men and swiped the spruce away from them – only to return sometime later with a flawless piece of mahogany he had earmarked as a spare for *Terror*'s jackstaff. Finally, when little Aguta's wound was healed enough, the carpenters presented a deeply polished wooden leg to her with a bashfulness that tried its best to conceal a brimming pride. It had a reindeer-lined harness that was secured with shiny admiralty buckles and inlaid around the top of the block in polished brass letters was the inscription: TOGETHER WE STAND. In return, the corporal gratefully handed over his tobacco as agreed – only for the carpenters to then slide the pouches back to him with the assurance that they had all suddenly given up smoking.

By the time she had been with them for a month, every man jack had taken a shine to Aguta and although there was nothing particularly ladylike about her, to the men's eyes, she exuded a femininity that made them yearn for their own women back home. Her very presence to them was a breath of fresh air in their cold, dark pit of despair. Even Crozier's heart would melt a little when he saw her and the corporal promenading around the decks during her rehabilitation and it somehow brought him closer to Sophia.

The entire ship's company came to regard Aguta with a

sibling-like tenderness that was touching to observe and though Aguta still had very few words of English, any matelots who absentmindedly swore in her presence covered their mouths in shame or were elbowed harshly until they apologised. The other consequence of Aguta's presence was that no man felt able to fully enjoy another piece of chocolate without offering it to Little Aggie, who, to give her her due, never said no. With every gift of chocolate she would giggle nervously before quickly wrapping it up in a swatch of parchment-like seal gut which she had taken to always keeping tucked away in her pocket. She, in turn, responded after seeing so many of the sailors shivering in the cold whilst wearing their woollen uniforms. Their standard Royal Naval slops would become sodden with water, only to then freeze solid and split like card. So she showed them how to make their own slops from the hillocks of pelts the crews had accrued from all their bag runs. She showed them how to make *atigi*, which were a sort of undershirt of sealskin worn with the fur against their own skin, and then for outer layers; *parka* smocks with the longer fur of bear, caribou and wolf turned outwards to the weather for the best protection. She showed them how to sew bird skins together, making sure not to pluck the feathers but instead keep them on for smocks that would still be comfortable in the foulest conditions. And she even had them carve out their own protection against snow blindness from bone, driftwood and ivory to form narrow goggles with little slits that allowed the wearer to see just as much as they needed without exposing their retinas to the searing effects of the Arctic light. Also, a vast improvement on their hopelessly soggy woolly mittens, were her hare and rabbit versions. But, perhaps for men out on the ice, the greatest gift of all was the ability to keep their feet warm with waterproof boots crafted from the skins of the ever-bountiful seal.

And as for her corporal, she was able to keep him warm in other ways – after all, he had become her *life force*.

21 Bedford Place, 1 December 1847

'WAIT!'

The driver of the fly pulled up outside the imposing townhouse in the cold, foggy Bloomsbury morning. The wheels had barely come to a standstill when Sir James Ross leapt out and strode towards the front door as he issued his short but comprehensive instruction to the driver. Inside the house, Ross heaped his hat, sword and his heavy wolf-lined greatcoat onto the aged butler and proceeded into the drawing room where Lady Franklin and Sophia Cracroft were standing anxiously by the fire.

'Good morning, James, how are we?' Lady Jane enquired.

'I'm worried, Jane – worried and vexed.'

'Oh, dear – why so?' Despite trying to maintain some semblance of dignity, a fusil bomb had detonated in Jane Franklin's stomach at the inkling that Sir James was about to deliver some terrible news. She had to sit down as she covered her whitening lips with her hand as she felt her treacherous physiognomy begin to betray her.

'Er, please, Sir James… won't you sit?'

'I've sat around for long enough, Lady Jane.'

She had been expecting him. She hadn't responded to any of his letters and if there was one thing Ross couldn't bear, it was being ignored.

'Well then, perhaps some tea?' She nodded at Sophia, who obliged by tugging the bell pull at the fireplace.

Painted into a corner of etiquette, Ross begrudgingly took a seat on the somewhat dainty sofa. 'Lady Jane… Jane, I've come to you directly from a meeting with the First Sea Lords and, to cut a very long story short, I am to mount a search for your husband.'

'And the Board has agreed to this?'

'It has, Jane, yes.'

'But why? Isn't this all a little premature? I know you've always assumed Sir John would fail, but he will not this time, James. No, he can't – I've made sure of it.'

'You've made sure of it? How so?'

'Well, I've…'

'Even you can't intervene here, Jane, it's something well beyond your control – unless you're the Goddess Nike incarnate?'

'I don't follow you, James – what has happened?'

'It's not what *has* happened, but what *is* happening: the weather. Every whaler in Baffin Bay has reported a massive build-up of pack ice that is unusual at such low latitudes – even for this time of year. Do you happen to remember my uncle?'

Jane smiled a little at the thought of Admiral Ross. 'Sir John? Of course, how could anyone forget such a welcome thorn in the Admiralty's side?'

'Yes, quite – well, he has now been appointed the British Consul to Sweden and as such has been privy to most of their weather studies there. It transpires that Scandinavia's northernmost weather stations are reporting something of an event within the Arctic Circle that corroborates the whalers' observations entirely.'

Lady Jane's elderly servant arrived with the tea. He peered worriedly at Sir James for a moment before setting the tray down next to Jane.

'Er, shall I pour, my Lady?'

'No, no – leave it with me. Thank you, Potter.' Potter left the silent room as if on casters. As the two long doors creaked shut again behind him Sophia seemed particularly eager to continue their conversation.

'An *event*, Sir James?'

'Yes, Miss Cracroft: an epoch of particularly severe winters. As one might imagine, Admiral Ross has already been lobbying the Board heavily but I'm afraid the 'Barrow Boy' won't give him the time of day, and well...'

Jane poured the tea as she interrupted, 'Don't tell me – it falls upon *you* to do what you should have done in the first instance...? You always had your doubts, about my husband, didn't you, James?' She handed Ross his tea and in his quivering hand, it began to rattle noisily on its saucer. There was no occasional table within reach and he seemed marooned on his chintz. Caught between the need to set his tea down and the urge not to make a fuss over something so distracting as a rattling bloody teacup, he imagined that Lady Jane had done this to him intentionally.

'Yes, I did have my doubts, actually, Jane.'

'What sort of doubts?'

'Courage, Jane... courage. Sailing into the ice, some days it's there, then other days, nothing – pack ice one day, then all broken up and threatening to grind our ships to splinters the next.'

'And you doubt Sir John's capacity to cope with such matters, do you?'

'No, no, you quite misunderstand me – I have no doubt of your husband's courage whatsoever: it is my own that I have doubted.'

Sophia, feeling that Ross need relief from the burden of his cup and saucer, fetched a small three-legged table and placed it next to him.

Ross set his teacup down clumsily as he said, 'But I have to go back to the ice one last time. I have to return because I'm now more afraid of living out the rest of my days knowing that I could have done something but didn't. And if that comes at the expense of anyone's ego, then so be it. I also feel a duty to my greatest friend Francis Crozier. He is there and I am not, and you are entirely correct – if I had agreed to lead the expedition in the first instance, I would certainly have felt more sanguine than I do now.'

He gazed at Sophia briefly before speaking again. 'But for what it's worth, Captain Crozier also shared his reservations with me and, if I am to be completely candid with you both, he is there under some duress… is that not so, Miss Cracroft?'

Sophia anxiously thumbed at the opal ring that she'd taken to wearing on her right ring finger immediately after Crozier had departed. Looking down at the ring now through her tears she had been disturbed to notice how the sparkling flecks of rainbow-like colour had somehow started to pale since he had given it to her in what now seemed like an eternity ago. She hoped to God that it wasn't some sort of talisman that faded with time – washing away any colour, or vitality, or signs of life as hope faded.

'What else could I do, Sir James? I do love the man, I really do. But I resent his job and I have a duty to my uncle and aunt, do I not?'

'Of course, Miss Cracroft – just as I have a responsibility to my own wife and children. But now your duty has been made a problem for my friend and I'm going to help all I can…'

He stared intently at Sophia for a moment or two before gazing over towards the fire as if back in the Hare & Billet with his old friend. 'He took your refusal to marry him quite badly, you know, Sophia?'

Lady Jane stood up like an arrow plucked from a quiver. 'What is this guilt you lay at our feet! You have no right to betray such a confidence, Sir James!'

She seemed to glide away to the window where she attended to her tears privately with the same lilac handkerchief both she and her husband had cried into on the dock at Greenhithe.

Ross tried his best to hide his own squirming discomfort as the room fell into silence. The only response came from the ormolu clock's pendulum as the machine strove as best it could to keep pace with the unstoppable process of time. 'Forgive me,

ladies, but there is a far more pressing matter than your hurt
feelings…'

Sir James checked his own watch against the filigreed fingers on the mantelpiece and stood up. 'Apparently, there was no
summer in the Arctic this year and they can't rule out the same
happening next summer. We need to pull them out, Jane.'

'We can't, James.'

'Oh, how so?'

'I promised my husband that we'd all have a little faith and
give him at least three years before anyone came looking for him.'

'Well then, in that case, I'm not looking for your husband,
Jane – I'm going to look for my friend, Captain Crozier, and his
men. There is no need for Sir John to be offended.'

Lady Jane fought back her tears admirably, but it was hopeless. 'But we can't go sending men out to look for them after only
two years! That will just confirm what they already think of Sir
John, won't it?'

'Well, Jane, that would be a small price to pay. Look, I'll speak
plainly: you knew he wasn't up to it, didn't you? You even put
your own niece up to stringing Francis along just so that your
husband had the best chance.'

Jane blinked back the tears and covered her eyes with both
hands and when she slowly removed them again, something in
her manner had changed: the sort of rage mixed with frustration
that Ross had seen something of in his own wife when he had
announced that he was going back to the ice once again. Jane
rallied with a sort of resignation that was disconcerting.

'Yes, James – you're utterly correct! I would do anything for
my husband. But you know, he would rather die up there on the
ice… in the miserable stinking ice than live a long life here as a
mockery – as a silly man who failed at everything he touched. I
only ever tried to help him, help him to be the lion that he truly
is, rather than the donkey that everyone else thought he was.'

'Oh, tosh! You just tried to help yourself, Jane. You used him

like a puppet to pursue your own crackpot ideals, and your…
pet projects.'

'Pet projects! How dare you! Is that what you call anything
that a woman finds to be of any worth?'

Sophia rose. 'You men who are so sure of yourselves – so cocksure, so… entitled! Do we women not count for anything but
petit point and flower arranging?'

Jane went to her niece and clutched her hands to calm her as
she retorted, 'Whatever we women do, James, we *always* do it all
for others first. And we do so gladly – even though we have no
choice. But whatever you men do, you do for yourselves… for
glory, for money, for power. The world is merely a man's arena,
and at its sidelines, we women are expected to just sit as specta-
tors and clap and cheer for you accordingly. So just… just go and
do what you feel you must do, James, but don't say you're doing
it for us; we refuse to give up hope just yet.'

The Ship's Rail

During Spirits Up, the men had collected their grog and just lit their pipes when the ship's bell sounded the alarm. As the men mustered on *Terror's* deck clutching any weapon they could find to hand, they squinted into the January gloom to starboard. The marine on watch was transfixed – seemingly by the darkness. The sailors joining him did the same till silence pinged the night air and they could detect what had prompted the alarm: the sound of a slow, unrelenting beat.

Boom… boom… boom…

The men watched for what seemed like an eternity but then, as their eyes became accustomed to the darkness, they saw it. A figure with the big, shallow drum slowly emerged into the arc of the ship's lamplight on the ice – one footstep with each beat. The marine made his rifle ready and trained it on the huge moon-like face with its two big round circles for eyes that seemed to stare with unsettling impassivity from the fur-lined fringes of wolverine.

The overall effect made the mask seem to radiate and float above the stocky conical form of a white bearskin parka like a cold, blue moon rising over a distant mountain. Once completely out in the open, the figure halted then, gradually increased the beats as forty-five to fifty of his people stepped into the light: first the men, then the women, and then the children. Their dogs, left to their own devices in the remaining darkness, started barking and whining as their owners gathered on the ice around *Terror*.

Crozier gently pushed aside the muzzle of the marine's weapon and said softly, 'Mr Irving?'

Mr Irving appeared at his shoulder. 'Sir?'

Crozier continued without taking his eyes off the *moon*. 'Please fetch Aggie – I believe she's on *Erebus*.'

'*Kabloonan teyma Inueet*.' We are white men – friendly to Esquimaux.

Generations of Viking, whaling and privateer fleets had done much to make the Inuit wary of Kabloonas. In 1576 Martin Frobisher, on a mission to find gold, had his men pin a group of Inuit against a shoreline with the intention of kidnapping one of them to act as an interpreter. The Inuit were so certain that the sailors were going to eat them that they threw themselves head-long off cliffs and into the waves crashing onto the rocks below.

Regardless, Frobisher went on to fill his three ships up to the gunwales with 1,350 tons of gold ore, which, after years of smelting at great expense, turned out to be nothing but worth-less iron pyrite that was eventually used to bolster walls and fill in potholes on London's streets. Perhaps this was what Dick Whittington was referring to when he thought that London's streets were paved with gold?

Fortunately, for anyone after Frobisher, the Inuit people had an almost unfathomable capacity to forgive. For the subsequent European expeditions that had deigned to interact with the Inuit in a more collegiate spirit, only good things would come. The Inuit had thrived on the ice thousands of years before Christ and yet, whether it was down to prejudice or an innate sense of superiority, it was astonishingly unusual for many Europeans to adopt any wisdom outside of their own civilisation. The rare exceptions to this had been Edward Parry in 1821, who had used

Inuit knowledge to draw his maps and charts, and Sir John Ross
some fourteen years later, who, as well as adopting some Inuit
hunting techniques and their technology, was so enamoured by
their 'glorious giggles and consistently sunny disposition' that
he shared an *iglu* with one for an entire season. Perhaps because
of their wise interactions, both Edward Parry's and John Ross's
expeditions had been history-making successes. The other thing
that Parry's and Ross's expeditions had in common was that
Crozier had been a witness during both.

Much to the surprise of his crews Crozier invited the 'neigh-
bours' aboard *Terror* by beating his chest as he shouted '*Kabloonan
teyma Inueet*.' He had initially observed this peculiar greeting
with Parry and, like him, had come to rather admire and respect
the Inuit, so it seemed both wise and polite to take on some of
their customs.

At first, the Inuit were unsure whether to board *Terror*. But
then when the shaman removed his mask, his black eyes were
agog at Sergeant Tozer's red coat. The *angakkuq's* face was
streaked with tattoos which radiated down from the peak of his
forehead in thin straight lines and maintained their continuity
through his lips via ivory labrets that had been carved into the
shape of whale flukes.

Tozer seemed incredibly uneasy and completely at a loss of
what to do next, with either fight or flight appearing to be his
most base options. Crozier, seeing his sergeant's fists begin to
clench, asked him to remove his red coat. The sergeant complied before Crozier then duly offered it to the shaman with his
outstretched right hand, whilst he started to beat his chest again
with his left. The *angakkuq* appeared to be awestruck and, as
if hypnotised, dragged his huge, magnificent parka off over his
head and let it slump at his feet to reveal a tiny little man dressed
only in a thin caribou *atigi* tucked into his fluffy satyr-like polar
bear breeches. Still without saying a word, the little man slipped
his narrow shoulders into the scarlet jacket. There was a stunned

silence as they waited for the *angakkuq*'s next move as he stroked
the red felt… his entire face then exploded into a grinning mosaic
of cracks and lines before wailing and whirling and gyrating in
triumph. He then picked up his parka and handed it to Sergeant
Tozer before reaching towards his head in an attempt to take the
sergeant's shako too – a marine would give you the shirt off his
back, but his headdress was asking too much. Regardless, the
shaman was delighted with the prize of the tunic and continued
to reel in his joy.

Once they were a little more settled aboard the ship, the
Inuit were agape as they found themselves in a ligneous world
in which they didn't even know they could dream. Everything
on the ship seemed to astonish: the magic of glass, the luxury of
wood and the mystery of metal. The matelots did all they could
to good-humouredly prise all their pans, spoons and equipment
back from the locals' eager, oil-burnished fingers before replac-
ing everything with needles, buttons, coloured ribbon, brass
rings, beads and other essential trinkets that the expedition had
brought along especially for just such an occasion. Regardless, an
ancient woman with no teeth still managed to be caught carting
off Fitzjames's cursed magnetometer that had always given him
so much grief.

The Inuit, having a totally different appreciation of possession
than the white men, couldn't help but grab at all the treasure that
lay about them so bountifully. Items such as the almost breathtaking efficiency and precision of sewing needles – rather than
bones or claws, were far more precious to them than gold or
precious gems were to Europeans.

If anyone had been able to hear above the joyous chirrups
of the natives they would have heard the approach of clunking
footsteps negotiating the ladder down to the deck. But the little
angakkuq did – above the hustle and bustle of his jubilant people,
he was stopped dead in his tracks. There, almost celestially, was
Aguta, one of their own who had been thought dead, suddenly

being helped down the steep steps by the tall warrior with the blood face. Before long everyone else around stopped what they were doing and followed his gaze. At first her people were overwhelmed with joy to see her, taking their turns to rub noses – until the *angakkuq* noticed her leg. Getting down on his knees and smoothing a hand up it he was feeling for some kind of pulse, warmth or other signs of life within it. Then, springing up, he began barking orders to his people. Some began to weep and wail as if their hearts had been ripped from their chests. Their demeanour had completely changed and as they shuffled off the ship none of them could look any of the sailors in the eye. They took their now-deformed daughter with them – almost having to prise her desperate hands as she sobbed with her corporal. Firemark looked to his captain beseechingly for a moment and in response, Crozier shook his head regretfully. Firemark carried Aguta down the gangway in his arms and, once at the bottom, he set her back on the ice and embraced her as hard as he could as he whispered his sorrow, '*Aullamna*, Aggie – *aullamna*!'

As she broke away from him, she said, 'I leave you here, but you are my *Anirniq* – we are everywhere. *Nagligivagit!*'

She shivered as he wiped a frozen tear off her cheek. '*Nagligivagit…* I love you too, Aggie. We will be together again, I promise.' She tried to smile before turning back towards her people, and as they slipped away into the darkness, the sound of their eager dogs faded with them into the night. The silence seemed to roar back at the mortified sailors. As they stared dazedly into the wan pool of light from the ship, Aggie's wooden leg was hurled back at them – clattering to a standstill onto the ice.

The Retreat

Sick Berth

AS THE SWEDES HAD PREDICTED, the winter of 1847 had been harsh. Nature had forsaken Sir John's people in every way possible. The sun showed itself so sparingly that a false night prevailed as the ever-mithering winds took turns to howl from every point of the compass. Even if the visibility allowed the sailors to hunt, any sort of edible quarry had absented themselves from the sailors' hooks, harpoons, nets or guns with great alacrity so that a great strain was put upon the ships' provisions. So much so that food had to be issued in tiny instalments with an almost laughable parsimony. The men's clothes had begun to swing limply about their frames too as they shuffled and lolled about their day-to-day duties. Overall, each day was very much like the other as the men fought with monotony, hunger and coldness with every waking moment with the wind mocking them. During rare breaks in the weather, hunting parties shuffled out into the poor light but brought back little enough to justify the danger and the extra energy they had expended. Perhaps if they were lucky they would bag the odd fox or ptarmigan. It was far from enough but at the very least it gave the men the opportunity to kill some boredom – along with their intensifying sense of utter helplessness.

Irritability and lethargy escaped no one, as the early signs of various ailments associated with poor diet started to take a grip. The main culprit was the same that had, throughout history, killed more sailors than any enemy action ever could: scurvy.

Every captain feared it more than any storm or enemy action. Crozier had seen the sad havoc it could wreak on the poor souls of the *Viewforth*, and it was entirely why they had shipped 9,300 pounds of lemon juice in big brown bottles. However, any efficacy that the lemons yielded seemed to rapidly dissipate soon after their first year and with the men now relying exclusively on their salted and pickled stores they were barely getting the essentials that would help them to stave off scurvy. In desperation, they had even resorted to raiding the specimen jars of McDonald and Goodsir's precious collections where a trove of undiscovered species had been carefully collected to take back to a ravenous scientific world to feast their knowledge upon. Even a fraction of them would have been enough to make the names of the two surgeons – just in the same way that Joseph Hooker had done in botany whilst on *Erebus* under James Clark Ross. But for now, the priceless discoveries, fastidiously categorised in their rows upon rows of specially made pigeonholes, would have to serve as a meagre supplement to the provisions as the ship's cooks dangled their fingers into jars of legion-legged arthropods, walrus foetuses and yet-to-be-named monsters that resembled mouths with fins.

Of course their meagre 'pickled nightmares' were far from enough. The men needed fresh meat. To Crozier, it was as if his ships were sinking as he watched helplessly as his people lost weight, teeth, hair and spirit.

For him, the decision was straightforward to conceive but dreadfully difficult to execute. If he and his people stayed on the ships they would die. That was their only certainty. With rapidly depleting provisions they had enough to survive for a few months but with the hunters' sacks returning resolutely empty there was nothing to stay for – other than starvation. Any thaw in the ice would not be for at least another six or seven months, but, as they had learned from experience, drawing up any sort of timetable based around nature's movements had become notoriously unreliable. However, even though the weather was so cold, it actually gave them an advantage as far as good, dependable ice to pull across was concerned. Otherwise, during the more clement months, the ice usually became a tenacious, sticky porridge that was torture to haul through and the perfectly round pools of azure melt water would hopscotch their every avenue.

April would be the time to go – before the sun would eventually rise in the sky and stay there for 150 days to reduce the ice into a giant pit of slush, or, hopefully, melt it completely.

As for a heading, if they went east or west they would be faced with the prospect of treacherous pack ice, open water or both to get their little boats across. If they left the ships and went back up north and to the east, perhaps they could pull to the edge of the pack and hope to be found by a whaler on Lancaster Sound. But Crozier likened those odds to 'stepping in rocking-horse shit'. To the north he even knew that there were food depots there that John Ross had left in '32, but even if the Inuit or whalers hadn't raided them already, they would be woefully inadequate when it came to sustaining 106 men. No, his only option was south. If they hugged the coastline, Crozier knew that the nearest certain point of civilisation would be the whalers at Wager Inlet and Repulse Bay – the 'North-Western Passages' above Hudson Bay. He knew the area well from his days under Parry and he also knew that most of the way there, via the Back's Fish River and the Hayes Tributaries, had been well mapped and documented after the considerable efforts of George Back and Thomas Simpson.

But the mouth of Back's River was over 250 miles away and Repulse a further 200 eastwards. Crozier also considered the option of following Back's River to Fort Resolution on the Great Slave Lake, but that was 500 miles away and had eighty-three rapids to portage over – a monstrous prospect considering his people's current state. But, in all events, the further south they headed the more likely they were to encounter fairer weather, animals to hunt, or possibly even a rescue party. South would be their only hope but for some, or perhaps many of his men, they would be embarking upon a death march.

What Crozier needed more than anything was to buy himself and his men some time in the hope that the Admiralty was actually launching a search on their behalf, and at the very least, he knew that James Ross and his uncle would be making themselves incredibly tiresome flies in the Admiralty's ointment.

Crozier assembled all hands in the gun deck during Spirits Up and privately thanked Christ, on his men's behalf, that the grog hadn't run out just yet. 'Listen in, lads: we're going to leave the ships.'

Had a pin been dropped, it would have clanged like the ship's bell.

'Man was never meant to sail this deep into the Passage. I neither know nor care about records, but I reckon that no living soul has ever pulled off what yous people have up here. It was a freak that we got this far but it was testimony to your seamanship that we did: two winters here on this bloody ice with no thaw and who knows when the next one will come? But what I do know now is that we're not going to wait around for it. No doubt you'll have heard all sorts of rumours about our provisions, but the truth is that the suppliers of our tins had, er, cut a few corners, shall we say – so, it would appear that we had been giving precious stowage space to sixty tons of shite that we need to leave at the bottom of the sea. But we do have some tins that are usable. We will bring them with us and they will be held back as a last resort. In the meantime, we'll have to make do with what's left in the dried stores… These will have to last us until we find game. I know it's not much, so steel yourselves, lads. It's going to be hard, but let's pull together and go home. We'll bend south, follow the Great Fish River and from there we'll crack on until we get to Repulse Bay. Then, we'll wake the buggers up, eat like pigs and drink our bollocks off, eh?'

This went down well with the crew, but in among their noisy

enthusiasm, a lone dissenter at the back shook his head disbe-lievingly. The Hop Pickers had been doing well with their stolen pemmican, but they'd never get away with taking it with them off the ships. Orren needed immediate clarity from the nearest authority next to him at the back, his lips turning taut and white as he spoke. 'Mr Irving, sir… this *Repulse Bay*, how far is she, like?'

'Um, I believe it's just under five hundred miles, Orren.'

'You what, sir?'

Mr Irving replied in a whisper in the hope that it would make Orren lower his voice. 'Yes, five hundred…'

'How in Jesus' name are we going to do that! Pull for five hundred miles? We ain't pullers – we're bloody sailors. We sail!'

Tadman and Seeley were quick to rally round in case Orren got into something he couldn't get out of, coaxing him into silence before anyone of any significance heard.

Crozier continued, unaware of the minor fracas, 'What I'm asking of you, lads, is everything. Regardless of the pain, hunger and the cold, we need to pull together as brothers and if we don't, then we'll all die here as fools.'

Orren punched at one of the bracings and as his knuckles started to swell like apples he quietly swore to his Hoppers. 'Ner, we ain't going to be no one's bleedin' fools, you mark my words, lads – mark 'em well.'

Lat. 69º 45' 36"N, Long. 098º 52' 12"W.

22 April 1848

On the last day of July we encamped near the mouth of a river, much larger than the Coppermine, with a strong current, that freshened the water amongst the reefs for some distance from the shore. Its banks appeared much frequented at this season by reindeer and musk cattle, and no fewer than five fat bucks were killed by some of the party whilst the rest were pitching tents and preparing supper. A couple of Esquimaux sledges lay by the riverside; and as we had found many old stone caches, both upon the islands and points of the mainland, it seemed more than probable that, like many of the natives near the Coppermine, the people to whom they had belonged had come from their winter stations over the ice in June to ascend this fine stream.

Thomas Simpson, *Narrative of the Discoveries on the North Coast of America; Effected by the Officers of the Hudson's Bay Company During the Years 1836–39*

The 'fine stream' Thomas Simpson had so happily reported was the *Thlewechodyeth*, or the *Haningayok*. *Thlewechodyeth* roughly translates as the Great Fish River. What people called it depended on where they lived along the river but if they lived in England they called it Back's River.

One of the few books in Crozier's collection above his bunk was Thomas Simpson's account of his overland expedition some six years earlier. Crozier had studied it with a keenness that was bordering on obsessive. On reading Simpson's meticulously detailed chapters, Crozier marked his observations and experiences well and got to know most of it off by heart. To him they were the perfectly detailed instructions of an escape plan. It had motivated, encouraged and reassured him, and if he and his men could find even half the animals that Sir George Back and Thomas Simpson claimed to have gorged themselves upon, then they would be saved. All they needed to do was take their boats upriver and eat their way towards the nearest Hudson's Bay outpost. Once they were in this perceived Garden of Eden that was Back's Great Fish River they could take as much time as they liked – but for now, the urge to get there was extremely pressing.

Good Friday fell on 21 April, so Crozier waited till the next day to evacuate their ships. The weather brought a temperature of -24ºF – along with an exceptional stillness to their position in the Arctic. The work on adapting the ship's boats had taken Mr Honey and his Daedalus-like carpenters two weeks to complete – including work on strengthening the removable skids for the boats as they would need to bear much weight.

The entire 104-strong ships' companies of *Erebus* and *Terror* were mustered on the ice and standing by in grim readiness to pull their four heavily laden whaleboats away to a place that Jesus, bleeding alone on His cross, only knew.

PO Peglar had shimmied up the main mast with a Union flag tucked into the breast of his monkey jacket. It was the same flag they had covered their commodore with before commending his body to the deep. On the ice below Peglar, all hands had formed three ranks and the shrill of the boatswain's whistles filled the still air as Peglar formally nailed the ships' colours to the mast.

Crozier had refused to give up his ships to the ice or anyone else for that matter: they would leave them deserted, rather than abandoned. To Crozier, desertion left open the contingency of their return or, at the very least, the possibility of the Royal Navy being able to legally reclaim Her Majesty's property. Under salvage law, a ship that was abandoned relinquished the owners of any right to the ships – should they ever lay claim to them in the future. *Abandon ships*: that was what happened when a vessel had floundered on a lee shore or was stove by reef, rock or solid shot. Nothing of the sort had happened here.

To reinforce this, Crozier had both ships' decks cleared, and all hatches secured with the same pride as if they were paying off the ships whilst below, every mess, bunk and deck had been thoroughly scrubbed, polished and inspected. In his Great Cabin, Crozier made a précis of the expedition's log to date and, along with a few personal letters to family and friends; he secured them all in the top drawer of his desk. Out of habit, he even closed the door of his bunk behind him to keep some of the warmth in and the cold out – despite leaving the Great Cabin for what he hoped was the last time.

Over the last months, having carefully pored over his charts with his ice masters, Crozier had finally formed a plan for their retreat. He had already sailed with Ice Master Blanky three times and trusted this tough, wiry little man from Whitby with his life. His presence had been one of the few provisos that Crozier had insisted upon before joining the expedition – just as James Ross had done in 1831 when he selected Blanky and just three other trusted men to accompany him on his death-defying final push to discover the North Magnetic Pole. But if Blanky was to be relied upon for dogged determination on the ice, his forthrightness often put him at odds with leaders. When Sir John Ross's expedition subsequently had to abandon the *Victory*, it was Blanky who had taken it upon himself to represent the crew's feelings – only for the overbearing John Ross to make himself very difficult to misconstrue by pointing a loaded pistol between his eyes before waving it as a signal for him to go back to the men with the news of an utterly unaltered itinerary.

But Blanky's experience, combined with Ice Master Reid's lifetime on whale ships made them both indispensable assets. If they couldn't work out what was happening with the ice, then no one else, certainly from the Western world, could.

Like Thomas Simpson before him, Crozier had assiduously studied the narratives of all his glittering forerunners who had diligently written accounts of their heroic deeds that had helped forge European understanding of the Arctic: Edward Parry, John Ross, James Ross and even George Back. To the cynics, these men had published their either florid or laconic prose along with weightily scientific addenda – mainly to ensure their own fame, legacy, awards or further patronage. But for Crozier to call these narratives essential reading would have been an understatement. Whatever was about to follow for himself and his men, the knowledge of their forebears would be the outline of their escape plan. This was particularly vital for the preparation of the little boats they had brought along with them on the ships' decks and davits. For this, the ship's boats would need careful refinement, so Crozier turned to the detailed account of George Back for the modification of his own boats that served him so well on a treacherous river filled with rapids and currents. Crozier entrusted no one else other than his own diligent number two, Edward Little, to personally oversee the refit of the ships' cutters: *Dasher, Prancer, Comet, Vixen, Dunder* and *Blixem*.

Thomas Honey and his chippies set to work immediately on readying the boats so that they could carry every man across water in all its condensed guises – whether ice, snow, sea or river. At the possible expense of strength, the carpenters were to make their boats as light as possible for the men to pull, so they had the carvel-built vessels stripped of the planks in their upper strakes and replaced by lighter fir clinkers. They were fitted for sails too and had rudders and oars that could be unshipped if the need for paddling kayak-fashion arose. Finally, they were fitted with a weather cloth that was battened down at the gunwales to protect the extensive goods and chattels that would feed, protect and carry the men.

Since the death of Sir John, the men had been encouraged to wear Aggie's northern slops and, accordingly, had been able to perform far more favourably in the cold. Only two more of the men went down with the sausage disease (as the sailors had started to refer to it) and it had been suspected that those sufferers must have, at some point, been too weak to resist chancing their arms with the noxious tinned provisions.

After the colours were ceremoniously nailed to the mast, the men waited on the ice as Crozier ran a loving hand down *Terror's* ironclad cutwater whilst muttering to his ship. 'Sorry to leave you here, lass… You've taken me to the top of the world… as well as the bottom. You've been the wife I never married and the home and family I longed for since I was twelve. Bless you, girl. Thank you.' He dusted off the rime from his mitten before crunching off with slow deliberation towards his awaiting men.

Crozier had anticipated that it would take a fit crew sixty days to haul their one-and-a-half-ton boats 400 miles. With his already eroded, hungry people he had adjusted his appreciation to eighty days but he only had enough allowance for forty. Unless they were able to kill animals en route, they would die on the ice. He knew his jittery, superstitious, gossipy sailors would work this out eventually, so, shrouded with loosely guarded secrecy, Crozier ordered Pusser Osmer to fill four stout chests with what remained of Goldner's un-bloated tins. These were then stowed in the boats under lock and key. Crozier wore the only keys as a necklace and the men assumed that he was guarding the last of the serviceable tins and that they would only be used as a last resort. He had hoped that this would reassure his men of some semblance of a contingency.

He initially wanted to take six boats but under their trials this seemed too much for the men so he whittled the gear down to a slightly more tolerable load and if the corrected weight still proved too much, at least they could make a depot of the super-numerary items once they touched land.

Two of the boats remained aboard *Terror* and for the four they were about to pull, extra traces had been made so that fifteen men could pull together with five resting (in the slightly less arduous role of pushing at their boats' sides). The only exception to this was Neptune – the great hound would remain at his trace regardless. Six men from the crews were already too sick to pull on anything more than their boots so they were to walk beside the boats and their duties were to keep a weather eye out for any game so that the marines could be stood to with their rifles. The officers and non-commissioned officers would of course push and pull where necessary but were also expected to read the ice ahead and lead the men to as smooth a run as possible.

Everything was crisp, and frigid, and still. Crozier searched for Osmer as he walked towards the lead boat where he found the purser as he was slipping his best shotgun under the boat's weather cloth.

'Pusser, are you happy with the load?'

'Aye, all present and correct, sir.'

Crozier then lowered his voice and rubbed his chin. 'Grand… and the, er…' Before Crozier could finish, Osmer handed Crozier a clutch of four keys on a lanyard. 'Aye, sir – the sundries are secured.'

'Good man – thank you, Charles… And the other wee matter?'

Osmer touched his nose before switching back *Vixen*'s weather cloth to reveal a case of whiskey. Crozier reached into the boat and pulled it out before walking back into the middle of the men and setting it on the ice before them. They all formed a circle round the Bushmill's and they passed the bottles around solemnly. As they partook, some men crossed themselves whilst others took swigs that were as long as decorum would allow after toasting the ships they were about to leave behind – or the families and friends they dearly hoped to see again. It didn't take long before Crozier was handed the last swig of the last bottle. He swirled the contents around then caught Fitzjames's eye… He offered it to him with an outstretched arm and flickered a smile. The commander refused politely but Crozier prompted him with a waggle of the bottle as he quoted Sir John Franklin, 'Temperance is the ship that fairs better in a storm.' Fitzjames nodded and smiled. As had been his habit, he was about to wipe the top of the bottle but then thought better of it before taking the remaining dregs back in three gulps.

The crews' collective breath hung in the air to almost create their own climate of a warm, malty brotherhood and every sound seemed to be magnified as the men crunched about on the ice like nervous cattle before settling into their positions on the pulling traces. They were ready. There was a moment of total silence as Crozier slung his shotgun and shifted the position of his telescope across his chest before almost muttering the order to leave their ships. 'Let's go home, lads.'

Instantly, the chaos of shouting began with the officers, non-commissioned officers and men all urging themselves and each other to pull and push but instead of the scene exploding into action, it was delayed by the stubbornness of their burdens before the boats relented and slowly creaked forward.

Camp Clear

Instruction addressed to Sir John Franklin (cont'd)…

22. You are, while executing the service pointed out in these instructions, to take every opportunity that may offer of acquainting our secretary, for our information, with your progress, and on your arrival in England, you are immediately to repair to this office, in order to lay before us a full account of your proceedings in the whole course of your voyage, taking care before you leave the ship to demand from the officers, petty officers, and all other persons on board, the logs and journals they may have kept, together with any drawings or charts they may have made, which are all sealed up, and you will issue similar directions to Captain Crozier and his officers. The said logs, journals or other documents to be thereafter disposed of as we may think proper to determine […]

Crozier and his men had made landfall in three days. Though the ice had been hard and even, its surface had been coated with a thin layer of almost moss-like crystals that would coat the sledges' runners so that their sledges would stick to the ice 'like shit to a blanket,' as the men observed. Fifteen miles in three days: one hundred and six men pulling both themselves and just over five tons of kit across the ice. This was murderous progress but at

the shoreline they were promised the luxury of jettisoning extra
clothes, tents and kegs – and even some of their scientific instruments. This, combined with no longer having to bide their time
for fate to catch up with them on the ships felt like progress
proper. Their burdens lightened in every sense.

Crozier was loath for any of his men to take a single unnecessary, energy-sapping footstep so had chosen a heading a little
further south of Victory Point called Back Bay. Previously recon-
noitred by the winter teams, Back Bay had been found to lead into
an inlet that promised Crozier and his men a little more lee from
the savage winds of the sea ice as well as make the route as direct
as possible for the crews to pull along. This way Crozier's people
would also be spared the sight of the mounds where Le Vesconte's
party had laid stones over the bodies of Gore and Des Vœux's men
as they lay in their tents. Le Vesconte's men had done this to make
it more difficult for animals to scent the carcasses. It was also the
easiest method for men who were too exhausted to dig through
permafrost in order to bury their dead brothers.

Whilst dragging themselves across the ice, Crozier and his crews
had spent three days and two nights alternating between grunting
and shivering. The extra energy that the men were expending made
them feel constantly on the brink of collapse, frostbite or both –
especially those who hadn't been able to swap their standard-issue
navy slops for Aguta's more useful garments. Crozier, eager to get
the men off the ice as swiftly as possible, made brutally limited
provision for resting with just one halt per day. For this they would
hove to at midday for the sweet, alcohol-laced hot chocolate which
the energy-sapped men cupped their hands around like gibbering
opium fiends. The expedition had brought along 9,500 pounds
of the stuff from Mr J. S. Fry & Sons, so chocolate was one rare
luxury they could actually afford. Mixed with spirit of wine, they
melted the brick-hard slabs on their oil stoves: their allowance
being a quarter of a pint to melt enough chocolate for seven sailors.

The salted and pickled goods having long-since gone, the only semblance of food they could look forward to for supper would be an insipid burgoo consisting of a negligible amount of seal meat with pea powder and some oats. So now, to Crozier's men, the chocolate they sipped at lunchtime had become more precious than gold. Perhaps even more precious than a letter from a loved one who wrote of everyday things such as chicken pox, April showers and new frocks.

In the mornings, whilst out on the ice, it took the men four hours to get up and away as they hacked and hobbled about like drunkards after another sleepless, miserable, frostbitten night. Breakfast consisted of tea with sugar, if for no other reason, to incentivise the men before tackling the almost monumental struggle of rolling and stowing their frozen bedding and tents with fingers and backs that wouldn't bend.

On their second morning on the ice, Divine Service was given as it was Easter Sunday, and, as it coincided with St George's Day, extra cocoa and a very slight upping of the biscuit allowance was given. During the service, Commander Fitzjames, who wasn't particularly religious, did however prove himself to be a devout Englishman. Reading all six lengthy verses of Robert Southey's 'Ode for St George' he even managed to make some of the Colonials among the men brim with pride.

And England and St George again prevail'd.
Bear witness, Agincourt, where once again
The bannered lilies on the ensanguin'd plain
Were trampled by the fierce pursuers' feet;
And France, doom'd ever to defeat
Against that foe, beheld her myriads fly
Before the withering cry,
St George, St George for England! St George and Victory!

Throughout the many verses, PO John 'Lucky' Cowie, a normally fidgety stoker from Bermondsey, was observed to be listening with uncharacteristic tranquillity as he sat cross-legged with his elbows on his knees to prop his chin. Afterwards, as the men stiffly rose to leave, he could not be stirred from his evidently blissful reverie.

Not wanting to leave his body on the ice, Lieutenant Irving's party was given his corpse to take with them to the high-water line since they were going there anyway on another matter. Once there, they laid him to rest beneath canvas and limestone. Some of the men privately felt happy for Lucky and thought he'd probably had a better Easter than all of them put together.

On 25 April they arrived in a small bay and set up a base on the high water mark that Crozier named Camp Clear. Meanwhile, they would wait for Lieutenant Irving, who had been tasked to take a small party to find and retrieve the note in Ross's Pillar that Gore and Des Vœux had left in it so that it could be amended with their latest progress and intentions. Irving and his three men had set out on foot across the island and, despite a leaky boot, he found walking again without having to haul was almost a pleasure, but he and his party couldn't find the cairn in the snow. Initially, the lieutenant had thought he'd got the coordinates wrong but after triple-checking he had determined that Ross's Pillar simply wasn't there. Perhaps the locals had ransacked it and the ruins lay under the deep snow and ice? They searched everywhere and found nothing. Then, on the route to meet up again with the main body, they found a five-foot-high drift. Clearing it, they discovered a cairn – four miles out of place from where it should have been. Irving observed that it had no signs of lichen growth which would otherwise have betrayed the fact that it was far more recent than Ross's visit in '31. But, despite its recent construction, the cairn had been there long enough to be welded together by the ice and Irving's men had to break their way into it – even splitting a pick in the process. After four hours of backbreaking work they found Graham Gore's message deposited within the stones and retrieved it.

The Officers' Tent

THE WEATHER HAD TAKEN ANOTHER turn for the worse and by the time Irving and his men had trudged back to camp they were drunk with fatigue. The lieutenant's foot had become very cold where his boot had split at the welt. Despite this, Irving managed to report that Gore must have been unable to find Ross's original cairn and taken it upon himself to build his own, albeit in a *slightly amended* position. This frustrated Crozier immensely as he was relying on the famous cairn and the precision of its location. Without correct coordinates he would be unable to relay his own progress and whereabouts to any subsequent search parties so this meant that the existing note would need to be carefully updated before Ross's pillar was reinstated at its correct coordinates.

That evening, Crozier dictated another note that was written out word for painfully written word from various entries from his log. He would have written the note himself, but his hands now shook so violently that he could barely lift a mug to his lips without having to steady it with both hands. His 'Dog' was starting to strain at his leash too, and this wasn't helped by the fact that he had refused to soothe the beast with drink. Within Crozier's ribcage the feeling of utter desolation and emptiness tore at his heart as he summarised their grim status from his log via Fitzjames's pen nib: 'April the twenty-fifth, eighteen forty-eight... Her Majesty's ships *Terror* and *Erebus* were deserted on the twenty-second of April... five league north-north-west of this, having been beset since... Where are we?'

Fitzjames looked quizzically at Irving. 'Beg pardon, sir?'

'How long have we been here?'

'Oh, I see – in three weeks it will be, er… three years, I believe.'

'Three years? God, how the time flies.'

Crozier checked the dates in his log again. Nearby, Irving attempted to rub some blood back into his right foot: the lieutenant had taken the opportunity to look at it briefly whilst the men were hacking away at the cairn and had noticed that all his toes had turned a clean, milky white. At the time, they had ached so much that it made him want to whimper like a child. But now, he could see that the same toes were now starting to turn black and bruised but at least the waves of pain were now beginning to abate.

Crozier had finished working out their coordinates and continued his dictation to the commander who had to keep pausing to thaw the ink for his pen. Fitzjames was now running out of space to write on the document so had resorted to rotating the paper and scratching their notes around the margins of the standard navy pro forma they had brought with them. Most of the valuable space was taken up with printed advice for any finder of what to do with the document in five different languages – with not one word of them in Inuktitut. It had ample space for details about the vessel, position, dates and signatures but only three lines for any form of elaboration. The clerk who had composed the document from his well-buffed seat at the Admiralty could not possibly have foreseen what the Sir John Franklin expedition would have needed to elaborate upon. Their endeavours so far had been anything but *pro forma*.

Fitzjames blew on his fingers as he spoke. 'Sir, I read back: "The officers and crews, consisting of one hundred and five souls, under my command landed here in latitude, er… sixty-nine degrees… thirty-seven minutes and, er… forty-two seconds, longitude… ninety-eight degrees and forty-one minutes, sir?"'

'Correct – thank you, James. To continue…' Crozier then began to read directly from his log: 'Sir John Franklin died on the eleventh of June eighteen hundred and forty-seven; and the total loss by deaths in the expedition has been…'

Crozier's concentration wasn't coming easily to him as he thumbed the pages of his log carefully back and forth. '*To this date, nine officers and… fifteen men.*' The captain closed his logbook gently. Fitzjames finished scratching up the note before handing the pen to Crozier, who seemed to be searching for something in his mind, 'Er, what are they calling the Great Fish River nowadays? Is it Back River or Fish River?'

'I believe it is now named after Sir George Back, sir.'

'*Back?* Such a bluffer. Daft name for a river too.'

Fitzjames handed the pen to Crozier. He blew at his fingers in an attempt to warm them again as he said to the captain, 'Well, I for one am very glad I didn't have to try and squeeze *Thlewechodyeth* on that scrap of paper, sir.'

Fitzjames's attempt at levity was wasted on Crozier as he was investing all of his senses on steadying his trembling hands so that he could sign and add his postscript: *And start on tomorrow 26th for the Back's Fish River.* Crozier then wafted the note near the stove to dry the ink before handing the note back to Fitzjames.

As Fitzjames began to furl the note he couldn't help but notice that Irving was cradling his foot and shaking his head despondently, tears running into his beard. Fitzjames slipped the note into the slim copper canister as he casually enquired after the lieutenant. 'Irving, dear fellow – everything all right?'

'So sorry, sir. It's just, um – feet are letting me down, rather…' Irving closed his eyes and was prompted to continue. 'Oh, it just all seems like such a waste. Why on earth are we here? We've done so much to map the Passage, but it seems about as productive as to draw the anatomy of a… a flea's toe.'

Crozier, recognising the despair in Irving, caught Fitzjames's eye and raised his chin. His second-in-command dutifully made his excuses. 'I'll, er… I'm just going to carry out my rounds, sir… make sure all the necessaries are done for the cairn party in the morning.'

Crozier nodded his quiet appreciation of Fitzjames's tact before turning his attention to Irving. 'Aye, well, even a flea needs to find his feet, does he not? But this is what we do, Mr Irving. This is the nature of our work, and nature is a hard-faced bastard of a superior, eh? The world keeps turning, and we're just visitors here just trying to feel our way around. Someone has to find new paths or, at the very least, places that should be avoided, eh?'

Irving closed his eyes with the pain that was now soaking through his nerves. 'Yes, I suppose so, sir – but it all just feels so, um... pointless.'

'How could it possibly be pointless, John? No one knew for certain that we couldn't sail straight through here to the Pacific; but *we* do now. What we've achieved here is to show people that there is no passage here: no path to anywhere – just damned ice and hardship... a place where we are not welcome.'

'Yes, well, I'm so pleased I could help in some small way.'

Crozier grinned at the quip. 'Aye, well, just let the surgeons see what can be done about your feet, eh?'

'Yes, of course, sir. Thank you.'

Over the next few days, the slow, unrelenting sleet had made the ice impossible to pull across, so Crozier had no option but for them to stay put for a few more days and allow the men to recoup their strength. This suited Irving as his feet had deteriorated to the extent that he was now finding it impossible to walk, let alone pull. He realised that he would ultimately have the indignity of having to ride in his boat as his men pulled, and the thought of adding to their woes felt far more excruciating than his now horrifically bloated foot.

The deep bruising had been rising up his leg at an astonishing rate and the two surgeons had come as soon as they could to see poor Irving.

Back Bay Inlet

THE THREE GAUNT, SHIVERING FIGURES shuffled across the ice as the sleet fell in straight lines through motionless air. Taff, Lozzer and Joe had been given the inlet's northern shoreline to see what they could forage. The scene would have been almost serene had it not been for Neptune's incessant barking. The dog had been tetchy all morning. Someone thought they had seen a brace of loons further along the inlet, so anyone who could shoot was sent out to see if they could bring them in. Those without fowling pieces were sent out too as Goodsir had read in George Back's narrative that there was a particular species of fish that was the size and appearance of a cod known as a burbot. Apparently, the burbot made a habit of getting caught in the ice – only to come back to life again in the next thaw.

If not armed with guns and rifles, the men equipped themselves with whatever they could find that could club, cut or jab at anything that resembled something to eat. Failing that, they were to comb the rocks of the coastline to scrape away at a sort of lichen exotically called tripe de roche. At best the lichen stopped the men sitting around in the cold as they waited for Fitzjames's cairn party to return from Point Victory, and at worst the rock tripe offered negligible nutrition whilst allowing them to fully appreciate what a gritty, bitter scab tasted like.

Chilled through to the bone, Taff walked with his arms folded as he struggled to speak through his chattering teeth. '*Iesu Grist!* It's w-wetter than an otter's pocket out here!' After a few more paces Taff continued his whining. 'And that bloody dog is pissing me off too… We should eat him.'

Lozzer wasn't in the mood. 'Taff, yer big, bleedin' cough drop – you just gonna do a moan all day?'

Lozzer suggested that they spread out a little to give themselves a better chance of finding something. They would also be out of earshot of Taff, who had now begun to expectorate hideously. Joe, having already pushed out further onto the ice had started to prod about with a long brass rod that, if now redundant as a magnetical marker, he hoped would serve him well as a harpoon.

Taff, ambling towards the waterline where big round rocks seemed to bubble up from out of the snow, thought he saw something move. Then it looked up at him: two watery eyes with a little shiny nose beneath them – a polar bear cub. Taff's first instinct was to call out to the others but he managed to resist. Instead, he resorted to tiptoeing towards it but as he got closer, he couldn't help but break into a halting run-walk. The little bear just stared back, perhaps in fascination but more likely frozen by its own instincts to trust the camouflage of its own pelt. The two other men, already alerted by Taff's sudden lack of carping, spotted his peculiar run-walk and started closing in to join him. The hunt was on. The bear, losing faith in its camouflage, panicked and started to dig itself into the snow. But before it disappeared completely Taff rugby tackled the little bear before grabbing it by the scruff. As Taff held the cub aloft, he wailed, 'You bloody beauty!' The bear immediately protested by making a noise akin to a fat little lamb having its throat cut. The scene resembled something from the Book of Isaiah declaring that *the wolf shall live with the lamb*. But then, Neptune's distant barking intensified and Taff could see his shipmates had now stopped dead in their tracks – as if in awe. But the awe was aimed at what was behind him: the cub's livid mother half-running, half-tumbling but now fully roaring down the long snowy incline towards her cub. Taff began to run with the little bear and headed back out onto the ice to follow his friends, who were by this point running like the wind. Lozzer looked back and saw that Taff was still being part of the problem, so he shouted back, 'Taff... put the bloody bear down!' Taff, finally twigging, dropped the cub and ran as fast as his clicking, aching bones would allow. Behind him, instead of giving up her pursuit, the mother bear continued her lolloping gallop after the sailors with the speed of a horse. Joe, seeing her closing in fast, turned about and started running back towards Taff and his ursine nemesis. Roaring, with his brass rod as if in some medieval joust with the huge snow beast, Joe stopped and held fast with one end of his brass lance braced into in the ice and tilted towards the bear. A hundred and fifty yards off... a hundred... fifty... twenty... 'To me, Taffy – to me!' Joe heard a crack that made his ears ring at almost the same time as he saw the bear stumble for a moment before swiftly continuing her charge. Then, just as Taff was beginning to think that his number was up, another crack... This time the bear tumbled end over end, coming to rest with her chin on the ice. She growled lowly as the blood from the gunshot wound started to run from where her eye had been and onto the wet ice. Spellbound, Joe cautiously approached the bear before finishing her with lunges from his rod again and again into the back of her head until the blood pulsed away with her slowing heartbeat and her growls ceased.

It was Neptune of course that had alerted Sergeant Tozer so that he could get the initial shot off, closely followed by Corporal Firemark's very welcome follow-up.

Taff, with a mixture of adrenaline and relief, started screaming hysterically. Lozzer, still bent over with his hands on his knees, spoke with difficulty as he attempted to catch his breath. 'Taffy, mate' – he waggled a finger – 'you should have seen your face.' Behind them, the cub bayed. Taff doubled back to fetch it.

The fresh bear meat that had been brought in couldn't have come at a better time. They used every part of the mother and cub: from the meat and blood to the offal, skin and the marrow from the bones. Not a morsel would escape Diggle's pot – apart from the poisonous livers that were begrudgingly tossed – and the big heart. The latter, Sergeant Tozer had claimed on behalf of Neptune as a reward for saving the day.

The dog had already ably proved himself to be an incredible asset and had become a beloved friend of the men. Ever since reports came back of the beast lying across the body of Sergeant Bryant, they had grown to appreciate him more than ever as they realised that any other starving beast would have resorted to the reasonable recourse of using any dead body as a means of survival – but not Old Nep.

Neptune, a particularly large specimen from the Newfoundland breed, had initially been brought along on the expedition on the insistence of Fitzjames since he had read about the loyalty and bravery typical of the breed and their ability to swim strongly in freezing cold water. Indeed, it was a Newfoundland that had stood guard over his dead master after he had been drowned at sea. Captain John Boyd and his men on HMS *Ajax* had been attempting to save the ship's company of the *Neptune* that had broken up on the rocks off Dublin Bay but a freak wave had taken them all over the side and they were never seen again – apart from Captain Boyd. His body was washed ashore days later and next to it was the big black dog that had been trying to keep his master warm. Captain Boyd was buried in the churchyard at Glasnevin, but even then, the dog never left his grave – instead choosing to die of starvation rather than leave his master's side.

In short, Neptune had become an integral part of the expedition. He was part of the family and they had felt that he was far more valuable to them both spiritually and practically than to be slaughtered for mere sustenance. These latest events had proved Neptune's worth beyond measure and even for starving men like

AB Jerry, whose minds had been deafened by their screaming bellies, slaying the dog for food was inhumane.

For the latest of their doctors' rounds to Mr Irving, McDonald and Goodsir thought it beneficial to bring Neptune into the tent with them in an attempt to bring him some cheer. On seeing the dog, the lieutenant's face lit up before wincing in pain as he shifted to let the dog lie beside him. His foot had become putrescent. No doubt aided by scurvy, the so-called wet gangrene had taken a grip with a ferocity that was appalling. As McDonald gently peeled back Irving's dressing, the two doctors instantly recognised the stench as the pus percolated out of the lieutenant's engorged foot. His toes had gone within two days of the swelling and had been reduced to black, twisted stumps lined up beside his impossibly swollen, purple big toe. This gave his foot the overall appearance of a smashed lobster claw that had been pulled out of a fire. Irving saw the doctors' reactions, but this alerted him to nothing he didn't know already.

'I'm, um, assuming the prognosis is poor, gentlemen?'

Goodsir and McDonald eyed each other in order to try and decide who would speak first. Goodsir, the blunter of the two doctors began.

'Well, you've left it very late, Irving and—'

McDonald interjected with a little more delicacy.

'However, there are options, John… but it will require some rather radical action I'm afraid.' McDonald swallowed hard before he was able to continue. 'Obviously, your toes are gone and, well, they are clearly past any debridement.' He eyed Goodsir and, managing to secure a brief nod of agreement said, 'We could try and save your foot and… well, the infection is still very likely to fester and spread further.' As McDonald continued his inspection of Irving's foot he could see almost the entire red colour spectrum from pink to black; then, from the ankle to the middle of his thigh the flesh was grey and almost crisp to the touch – nothing but rotting conduits of sepsis leeching into the rest of his body.

Irving reclined onto his bedding and put his arm across his eyes until his body started to convulse with grief.

McDonald touched the lieutenant's elbow lightly and, after some time, Irving was able to bring himself to speak again.

'Um… and what if I ask you to do nothing?'

The two doctors eyed each other again and nodded almost imperceptibly.

'Well…' began Goodsir, 'you'll probably not see the morning.'

Irving looked to McDonald for perhaps another less frank response. McDonald didn't have one so just nodded sadly in agreement.

Irving closed his eyes and sighed deeply. 'Well, then, gentlemen… I wonder if you would do me the incredibly kind service by leaving Neptune and me to turn in? It all seems to have caught up with us, quite suddenly, hasn't it, old boy.'

Goodsir was about to say something in protest but McDonald interjected. 'Yes, of course… sleep well, dear friend.'

Irving, once left alone, sank his fingers into Neptune's thick pelt and felt the warmth of the dog's skin and the life it represented as he spoke softly to the dog. 'Goodnight, old boy, I hope you have more to look forward to than just the past.'

Comfort Cove

CLOSE TO THE CAIRN, THEY used a pall of No 8 canvas for Irvine's body as if for sea burial. Drunk with fatigue, the crews had stumbled giddily around as they prised the larger slabs of schist from the frozen ground with picks and bars. They had scraped out the grave and lined it with the slabs so that the lieutenant was interred within his own shallow tumulus. Beside him, they placed his silver medal as the only plaque they had to mark his honour, whilst in his arms they placed his telescope almost sceptre-like. PO Armitage, as the last gesture of appreciation, folded his silk neckerchief and placed it tenderly under the young officer's head for a pillow.

All hands were formed up around the graveside quietly sniffling and shuffling around on the eggshells of shingle as Crozier gave the service. Afterwards, when he asked if anyone else wanted to say something, PO Peglar stepped forward like a nervous bird. He produced a small leather pocketbook that he clutched with both trembling hands. He caught his breath and began to read from it.

'I just wanted to say a few words on behalf of the lads because… well, that's what you gave a lot of us, Mr Irving, sir: words. I for one can now read this here note what I have in my hands… and it was your kind patience what taught me how to write it. So that now, I can tell my loved ones how I really feel… with a pencil… without ruining it all with the sound of my rotten voice. It's because of you, sir, that I can read a book and get to escape this terrible place whenever I feel like it… but not for nearly as long as I'd like, though' – at this, some of the men grunted their solidarity – 'and it's coz of you, sir, that my family wouldn't believe their eyes if they could see me here, today… readin'.'

Peglar was imagining exactly how his family might react if they could actually see him at that moment – all skin, bone, hair and dirt; rocking from side to side in order to keep some life in his toes. He pretended to look down at his notes for a moment or two in a hopeless attempt to stop his chin from quivering as he continued. 'But anyway, Mr Irving, sir – we wish you well on your last journey, and we thank you from the bottom of our hearts. God bless you, sir.'

Crozier nodded across to the boatswain's mates and the all too familiar shrill of the Still was piped. Once they had finished, all that could be heard was the gentle rattling of rocks and stones as the men tottered around on them before picking some up and placing them carefully on top of Mr Irving's body. As each stone was laid, it became a token of each man's warmest affection and in hardly any time at all the grave began to take on the appearance of an upturned boat hewn from stone.

Greenhithe

WHEN JAMES CLARK ROSS HAD toasted Crozier at the Hare & Billet with his promise of launching a rescue mission after two years, he had meant it. With continual weather updates from his uncle that verged on harassment, Ross had started the ball rolling whilst, outwardly at least, everyone else at the Admiralty still seemed to be entirely sanguine regarding Franklin's prospects.

HMS *Enterprise*, a barque-rigged merchant ship of 471 tons was purchased from Money, Wigram & Son of Blackwall's shipyard. Next to her, HMS *Investigator*, her sister, was moved in next to her for their Arctic fit-outs. The first to be ready was *Enterprise* and at her launch it was remarked upon how moving Lady Franklin would have found it all. However, Jane had chosen to mark the occasion from the Shetland Islands where she was rowed out to a cold and lonely outcrop. The rock there, which had been smoothed by a million storms, was called *Ootsta* by the locals but marked on the charts as Out Stack. Here then, was the northernmost part of the British Isles, but for Jane, this bleak, windswept place brought her as close as was humanly possible to her husband.

Sir James' wife Lady Anne, though heavily pregnant with their second child, broke a bottle of gin across *Enterprise*'s bow. Booth's Gin was the preferred christening tipple over champagne in this instance as Sir Felix Booth had been persuaded once more to generously part with money for the sake of continuing the *Arctic War*.

As soon as their compasses were set further downriver at
Greenhithe Ross managed to clear off a week shy of three years
after Franklin's expedition had left from the very same dock. Ross
cursed the extra week he'd lost due to the necessity of having to
patronise dignitaries eager to attach themselves to his endeavour,
but now he was under way to the Arctic.

Comfort Cove

ALL LOADED AND READY FOR the off, the men were chatting quietly as they filled their pipes with Old Osmer's Rough Shag. This was a concoction of what was generally assumed to be a subtle blend of tobacco, tea, some dried rosemary – and an ample quantity of finely rubbed sawdust which, when combined and sold by the pusser, was referred to as Pusser's Rough for short. The blend tended to produce a cough that was both rich and rewarding but it did also have the advantage of staying alight in anything up to a seven on the Beaufort scale. Young Davy Young was staring at Joe with the daze of fatigue as the big man scraped away at his scrimshaw languidly with a huge Bowie knife.

'Big knife, Joe.'

'Yeah, she's got me out of some big scrapes. Belonged to my father before me... got him out of some bigger scrapes.'

'Was he from Africa, Joe?'

'No, little man – born and raised in the Carolinas.'

'The Carolinas? Sounds pretty. Where is it?'

'America, son – Pop was a second-generation slave. Fought for the British in the War.'

'War?'

'The American War.'

The boy was evidently none the wiser.

'The War of Independence, Davy,' Joe continued. 'The Brits promised to make him a free man if he fought.' Joe smiled to himself. 'Huh... by *free* they gave him and Momma the choice of shipping out to fly-blown West Africa… or ice-blown Nova Scotia.'

'So why didn't they go to Africa?'

Joe stopped carving and weighed up the boy. Was he stupid, or just naive?

'What do you know about Africa, son?'

'Nothing much, just that the animals are big and fierce… and that you'll probably need a big knife if you're going to live there.'

Joe shook his head and frowned. The boy was just naive.

'Well then, you know about as much as my ma and pa, son.' Joe, in between scrapes, kept eying the youngster. Davey's mind seemed elsewhere. 'You all right, kid?'

'Yeah.'

'You don't look it. What's wrong with you?'

'I don't feel hungry anymore, Joe. I just feel empty.'

'Yeah, well, you'll be home soon enough with your ma cooking you roast beef and taters. That'll put things right – you'll see.'

The thought brought a smile to the lad's face. 'Yeah, nothing tastes better than how my mum cooks.'

'Sure, Davy, every mum is the best cook in the world.'

Something else came to Davy's mind as he wearily straightened his pulling traces. 'So, is your mum and dad still alive, Joe?'

Joe shook his head. 'Pop died when I was eight. Momma, five years ago.'

'So that makes you an orphan, Joe?'

'Guess it does.'

Davy pondered this carefully. 'When my dad died, they called my mum a widow… and if she had died, they'd have called him a widower, wouldn't they, Joe?'

Joe nodded as he continued to carve. Davy continued driving his train of thought. 'So, if I died, what would they call my mum then?'

Any answer that Joe might have had just hung in the air before Sergeant Tozer began to raucously circulate among the men in order to rouse them; catching the eyes of those who were awake but kicking at the boots of those who weren't. 'Ready to move, lads... get ready to move.'

Joe returned his knife into the sheath on his belt and blew the swarf off his little doll before tenderly tucking her into the breast pocket of his jacket. The men creaked and groaned as they wearily rose to their feet before taking up their positions on their harnesses once again. Davy, still dazed with fatigue, couldn't work out his harness so the big man helped untwist Davy's shoulder straps before attending to his own.

'Guess folks would be too sad to think up a name for something like that, huh?'

Joe mussed the boy's hair. 'But there's no call for you to go worrying about notions like that, kid. Just keep pullin' with me and you'll be fine – you'll see.'

Royal Clarence Victualling Yard

HMS *VICTORY* LAY ROTTING ON a mooring at the mouth of Portsmouth Harbour. After years of neglect and underfunding, the Admiralty had officially designated her as a tender for the third-rate HMS *Wellington*. Paying civilians had even been allowed to clamber aboard her for tours.

Over on the Gosport side of the harbour, four men smoked as they shook their heads ruefully at the peeling paintwork and dangling spars of what was once Nelson's flagship and the pride of the British Navy. The smokers had arrived early at Royal Clarence Victualling Yard, where, for over 140 years, the 'Larder of the Navy' had been responsible for provisioning the greatest naval fighting force in the world. It had brewed its sailors beer to slake their thirst, it had baked their biscuits to fill their bellies and, accordingly, to feed their gripes, it had even supplied them with the weevil too. Of late, crooked dealings with an Admiralty that had been obsessed with value for money and any other cost-cutting schemes seemed to be getting out of hand. It was felt as though there was now a new enemy to defend Her Majesty's Navy against: suppliers.

The four inspectors had gathered at the yard gates an hour before any workers were due to arrive. They had been dispatched to investigate a batch of tinned provisions that had caused some concern after they had bloated and split having been warehoused inside. The 300 food canisters had been due to be reconsigned to the troops in the Mediterranean and the inspectors were keen to get on with the matter in hand, but as they began to open the cans they were repulsed beyond belief. It wasn't until they opened the nineteenth canister that they found anything even near fit for human consumption. The ordure they found inside most of the tins was so rotten that afterwards, the stone floors of the warehouse would need to be coated with chloride of lime to neutralise the stench. Throughout the day, the inspectors had been so overcome by the fetor that they had to regularly take their leave for fresh air before resuming their grim task – gagging and honking like geese. During their ordeal, they had fished out lung, horn, gums and palate from dogs or sheep 'quite rotten, and garbage,' roots of tongue and large quantities of coagulated blood, lumps of tallow, a whole kidney 'green, perfectly putrid,' intestines (still filled with the value-adding weight of the animal's undigested last meal), ligament, tendons and a mass of pulp. Some organs had evidently been cut from diseased animals and, afterwards, one of the more philosophical inspectors, almost in admiration, had observed that the suppliers had managed to stuff 'everything but the pig's squeal' into the tins. In their report concerning the Clarence Consignment, the inspectors concluded that the tinned provisions had been reallocated after they had been delivered too late for an expedition after its departure. Initially, the tinned provisions had then been sensibly kept in cold storage, but after a long, hot journey to Clarence Yard, the cans had warmed enough to split, making their contents unavoidably apparent. The inspectors condemned 273 cans that day, dumping them unceremoniously into the sea at Spithead – perhaps in the hope that if the crud didn't kill the crabs and other bottom feeders, maybe there was a chance it would keep them off Old *Victory* for a tide or two. The expedition that had departed without them had been Sir John Franklin's and the ensuing public scandal was so great that the Admiralty dispatched inspectors to naval dockyards all around the country as part of a nationwide moratorium. But the tins, like a crated-up venereal disease, would turn up in the most unexpected of places; even years later when there was a report from the *Plover*, stating that they also had to throw 1,570lb of canned meat into the Bering Straits. The captain's subsequent report had stated that, '… we found it in a pulpy, decayed and putrid state, and totally unfit for men's food.' Those tins had been traced from the same supplier as Franklin's too: Mr Stephen Goldner.

21 Bedford Place, Bloomsbury

LADY FRANKLIN, WHO HAD MADE good her promise to her husband by deferring any action on her part for three years, was now free to do what had to be done. Making up for lost time with a vengeance, she had waged a masterfully orchestrated war of attrition upon the Admiralty – beginning with an unrelenting lobbying of Parliament using lengthy, heartfelt letters urging anyone with a conscience to rise from their inertia and help return her husband and his men. So much so, that within parliamentary circles, their continual bombardment from the Franklins' London townhouse had become affectionately referred to as *the Battery*.

For a while at least, Lady Jane's battles also came up against another front: the terrible famine that seemed to be worsening in Ireland – but it was surprising how quickly a fatigued readership needed a story that offered more hope than the poor, starving souls across the Irish Sea. With Lady Jane's intervention, the *Illustrated London News* had never sold so many papers as they regularly splashed Franklin articles on their front pages and even dedicated entire sections regarding the concerns for Sir John and his 'heroic men'. Even the Franklins' very good friend Charles Dickens had waded in by writing impassioned articles about the matter in *The Examiner*. So taken was he and his readership by the Franklins' plight he was even prompted to write a new play called *The Frozen Deep* with his long-time collaborator Wilkie Collins. The first showing was a command performance with Dickens himself on stage in front of the Queen – along with

most of her family, all of her Cabinet, and the key European
heads of state. At the curtain's fall even Hans Christian Andersen
and William Thackeray rose to their feet with tears streaming
down their cheeks.

But it was only after the scandal was discovered at Gosport
that further expeditions for the west, east and south were coa-
lesced by the now stuttering Sea Lords. Clutching their orders,
expeditions of all shapes and sizes poured out of the Thames
Estuary in their droves before turning left to head up into the
North Sea.

Sir James Ross's two ships, having stolen an early march, were
already answering well to the Baffin Bay currents and the decent
winds. At this rate he would be in Lancaster Sound by late July if
all went to plan. Ross was leading the game by almost a year, and
once he and his squadron had reached Baffin Bay, they were met
with various whaling ships whose captains all confirmed most
of Ross's doubts. Captain Hill of the *Lady Gambier* mentioned
that he had passed Sir John's ships two winters ago as they were
moored to an iceberg. He offered that all had seemed well with
Sir John and his men and they all appeared to be in excellent
health. But it was now evident that they would have sailed into
a winter that had been so brutal that most of the channels Ross
now faced would already have been choked with ice.

This news only served to heighten Ross's anxiety for Franklin
and his men. Firing guns on the hour and dropping message
capsules along the way like droppings from an albatross, Ross
pressed on into Lancaster Sound using every means at his dis-
posal to make his ships' presence as evident as possible to any
souls who had ears to hear and eyes to see. He even had his
motorised steam pinnace lowered into the leads so that he could
send crews on regular patrols to cover as much as 330 miles of
coastline and, it being early in the season, when it would still

turn dark at night, Ross had blue lights struck – just as Crozier had done for him many years ago in a stormy southern ocean en route to the Falklands.

Erebus Bay

THE WHITEOUT CAME ON FROM the N.N.W. and the brutal wind that brought it lashed at their starboard beam mercilessly as Crozier's men dragged themselves and their sledges across the ice. Appearing as if they had all caught some sort of contagious affliction, the men had developed an involuntary rictus with their right shoulders hunched into their ears to somehow shield themselves from the stinging whips of the weather. As visibility was so low, Crozier had faithfully led them to bend to the shoreline. As the men hauled, the officers assisted all they could by pushing the boats from the stern as they toiled over the innumerable ruts, ridges and stacked slabs. Even Fitzjames, who prided himself on a *correct* leadership style, lent a shoulder whenever he thought no one could see.

Suddenly, Neptune seemed very pre-occupied with something out in the fog. He began to growl lowly like the onset of distant thunder, his eyes fixed and his jowls quivering. Then the barking came on so unrelentingly that there was barely time enough for each bark to escape before the next one would succeed it. The dog transformed into a wild beast and began to gnaw at his trace. Sergeant Tozer, on fearing for the gear, released him from his bonds and the big dog immediately bounded off into the enveloping whiteness. At first, they couldn't hear anything, but then the escalating sounds of other snarling beasts came – four, perhaps five – quite dog-like. Then the snarling became an almost savage chant... closely followed by frenzied snarling... before agonising yelps. Then, the most disturbing sound of belligerence took over: silence. Fitzjames began to run into the fog but was quickly overtaken by his marines pulling back the hammers of their rifles as they ran into the maelstrom. Shortly after, a couple of shots were heard before the bootnecks came back dragging the bodies of two white wolves as they bled on the ice like freshly dyed ensigns. Fitzjames was the last to reappear with Neptune limping to heel with a mauled shoulder and most of an ear missing. All the same, the big dog still managed to look somewhat pleased with himself.

After lunch, the sea haar rolled away to reveal the route that lay ahead of them: a ruined crystal graveyard filled with giant, crooked monuments dedicated to hardship and misery. The condition of the ice and the brutal headwind had taken its toll on men, who, by this point, had been hauling for three days but had only managed to make fifteen miles. The sailors had begun to murmur darkly among themselves and Crozier knew that if he didn't watch it, poor morale would grow faster than a foolish thought and fester among them like a pox.

For exhausted men, humour was always the first pillar of morale to collapse and it was the bellwether looked for keenly by any adept leader. Once morale was lost, their path would become increasingly treacherous as enthusiasm, confidence and discipline crumbled. From here, physical erosion would take over via hunger, cold and fatigue. Almost anything was bearable until morale was lost. Morale was the caulk that kept the sea out of their vessels – however troubled their ocean. As Crozier looked about his people, he could readily identify those individuals whom he could depend upon – as well as those who depended on everyone else. Adversity and suffering always brought out the worst in most, but sometimes, it brought out the best in a few. So much so, that Crozier often thought that tired, desperate men could often take on the qualities of other creatures struggling to survive within God's Kingdom. In his mind, the greater part of any suffering group consisted of Oxen: stoically pulling together – the quiet masses – capable of almost anything with firm guidance and enough fodder, but then, utterly hopeless if left to their own devices. From a leader's point of view, the Oxen were relatively straightforward to herd, but equally, their faith in others made them easy to lead astray. After the Oxen came the Bears. They were the few who rose to any occasion – the mainstay and the backbone of any group whom the leaders could depend upon. And finally, there was a third, and mercifully, rare minority – those who were usually the cleverest and would do whatever it took to survive. Typically, they were the ones who were constantly needy, but never there when needed. They thrived during the fog of fatigue and when they found weakness they exploited it ruthlessly: they were the Wolves.

With several of the men now in no fit state to pull, they set up camp on a sandbar that was about 500 yards in length and seemed to have been formed by the outflow from an inlet. Crozier was never really able to fully rest when he called halts – instead preferring to go for what he called 'a wee dander'. During these halts he would often explore the immediate area so that he knew they weren't missing some sort of trick or opportunity. In this particular case, he walked a little way up the inlet that appeared to run southwards as straight as a die. From the condition of the ice he could see that it was brackish so he imagined that this could be a narrow inlet and perhaps a shortcut if it did indeed continue south. Perhaps it would give them a guttersniping opportunity so that they could avoid the grossly unappealing option of the route that now lay ahead of them…

During the night, the wind died and the men had slept well after a relatively decent meal of a wolf burgoo, and in the morning they woke to a clear, crisp day. Crozier, still intrigued by the inlet, left the main body to sort themselves out in preparation for another day of pulling and, together with Sergeant Tozer and Corporal Firemark, headed up the higher ground with his telescope. As he broached the crest, the true extent of the ground they were to cover revealed itself to him. They were about to round a peninsula that extended westwards for about six miles before trending south.

More disturbingly to Crozier, he could see a huge field of ice that had been pushed from the rear so that it crumpled and slumped upon the shore, whilst at the western extent of the peninsula he could see that this intense pressure of ice from the north had choked itself at the islet-strewn funnel of Alexandra Strait. Crozier almost gasped at the thought of his men pulling through the mayhem of the ice there. Twitching his telescope to the south he could see the new inlet's extent and Crozier found it tempting. It ran like a furrow grubbed straight through the middle of the peninsula and they could perhaps avoid the awful prospect of clambering around, over, and through the fearsome palisade of rime that defended the peninsula. If they were supremely lucky, it would shave off a week of troubles. Crozier couldn't help himself and pivoted back behind him to the N.N.E. where he could just about see the dim tops of *Erebus* and *Terror*. He imagined them being sucked slowly and inexorably into the icy vortex of the Northwest Passage, nature's supernatural crew sailing on without them.

One of Crozier's legs was causing him some discomfort so he asked the two marines to continue their recce without him as they would be far more agile. Once they'd disappeared out of sight he collapsed his telescope and sat on a rock for a moment to rub some life back into his leg. As he gazed down between his boots, Crozier noticed a small dirk-like shard of sandstone. He picked it up and saw that it had a thumb-sized arthropod fossilised into its widest part. The hopelessly trapped animal put him in mind of an oversized flea, and he smiled at the thought of handing it to Irving and asking him to draw the anatomy of the creature's toe. Crozier slipped the immortalised flea into his pocket before setting off stiffly down the slope again towards his men.

Little Point

IT MAY NOT TAKE MUCH to douse the morale of tired, cold, starving people, but then it doesn't take much to stoke it either. So when the sergeant and his corporal returned from their recce with the confirmation of a route cutting through to the other side of the peninsula, Crozier privately let out a huge sigh of relief as his people's spirits visibly lifted again. Sergeant Tozer had added that the inlet did have a kink in it that they would probably have to portage over, but this was a small price to pay for the luxury of moving through a flat, relatively protected area. When the men were briefed about their new course, Sam Honey, the blacksmith, had helpfully suggested they name the inlet Shit Creek after it had reminded him of a similar-looking feature back home in Plymouth. Crozier surprised everyone by adding the name *Shit Creek* to his chart.

On Commander Fitzjames's suggestion they marked the rest of the peninsula on their charts with Graham Gore's name because, 'Like the man, it stuck out and would forever be missed.'

The fifteen miles or so along Shit Creek offered benevolently sheltered sides that rose steeply to around fifty feet as they ran through the pockmarked gashes of sandstone. At some point in distant history, the creek must have been carved by unbearable weights of ice and rocks that had slithered across its surface. However, nine miles up the creek, just as Sergeant Tozer had logged, they reached a point where prehistory had dumped its boulders. Here, the boats were portaged, with each of them having to be unshipped and their heavy sledges removed before the reverse could take place once the men had pulled and pushed and graunched them clear of the obstruction of the boulders. The three smaller boats went over – just. But *Blixem*, being the bigger boat and weighing 900 pounds unladen, proved to be just too much for the men to lift. Crozier's only option was to send her back round the peninsula – the long way. Mr Little had drawn the short straw but Crozier gave him the lion's share of the fitter men whereas Crozier's own party would consist almost entirely of 'the Sickies' so that they would have the best chance to regain their strength as they waited for Little's return. But for this, he still needed the support of the odd 'Bear' in order to succeed.

As Mr Little was overseeing the stores being transferred Crozier picked up one of the books that were also about to be unshipped. '*Great Expectations…* at least we finally found a use for Franklin's books, eh, Mr Little?'

'Sir?'

'There's nothing better than curling up next to a good book when it's chilly.'

Mr Little appeared to be still none the wiser so Crozier expanded, 'Kindling, Mr Little.'

'Ah, that's what we brought them along for – I thought you were losing your marbles for a moment, sir.'

'Marbles? Yeah, well, I reckon they rolled off the deck a long time ago, Edward.'

Crozier picked up another book and smiled to himself. 'We're probably already damned for burning books but don't set fire to this one, will you?'

Little studied the cover: *A Manual of Private Devotion.* He opened the book and studied the inscription: *G. Back to Graham Gore.*

'I'm sure he would have wanted you to have it, Edward.'

'Thank you, sir… if it gives me an ounce of Gore's resolution, it will be my most treasured possession indeed.'

'There's nothing wrong with your resolution, Mr Little. Nothing at all.'

Crozier unslung his shotgun and handed it to the lieutenant. 'You may need this too.'

As Little clutched the weapon Crozier maintained his grip for a moment as he looked his number two in the eye. 'Cunning buggers… always come from the place you least expect.'

'I'm sorry… who do, sir?'

'Wolves.'

Once the last of *Blixem*'s load was unshipped and the weather cloth was battened down, the men wearily slung the yokes of their traces about their shoulders once more. As the order was given, they pulled and strained but nothing happened: the runners had frozen to the ice. Seeing their brothers struggling, the men from the portage crews trotted in to help start them off.

Lozzer, appearing at Taff's shoulder, slapped his back. 'Up the arses of the English, eh, Taff?'

Taff smiled as he nodded: 'Aye, *twll dîn pob Sais.*'

Tadman, on a trace nearby, sneered to Orren, 'Aw, bless me soul, why don't he blow him a little kiss while he's at it – bleedin' little Mary.'

Lozzer retorted instantly by raising the back of his hand towards Tadman. 'Shut it, Tadpole, you little twerp.'

Tadman flinched outrageously – much to the glee of everyone who witnessed it. Lozzer and Taff cackled mercilessly at Tadman's lily liver. Even Orren smirked as the little man fought down the bile of his humiliation.

Once the heavy boat's runners were cracked out of their icy bonds they were away. Lozzer, Joe, the marines and everyone else who had helped shove them off stood with their chilly hands in their armpits as the *Blixem* lads grunted and strained, pulling their boat back towards the coast.

The Boat Place

LIEUTENANT LITTLE WAS FEELING AS buoyed as he was apprehensive. Getting his men and their load over the ice and round the peninsula was a daunting prospect but at last he'd been given his own command and, as he'd so selflessly put himself forward for going back, Crozier had named the point to which Little and his men were returning after the young lieutenant. Little Point. The irony wasn't lost on the already hungry, tired sailors. Such a herculean effort that required them to go back on themselves. But despite the predictable purging among a certain Kentish knot of his thirty men, they made good progress. The favourable surface condition of the six miles of ice in the inlet helped them to drag themselves to the point in just under eight hours.

Despite the skeletal spectre of the ships over the horizon, Little and his people made camp on the beach in reasonably good spirits. They did all they could to gird themselves for the brutal day that was to follow – trying not to think about wading into the exposed chaos of the sea ice that had been pushed up upon the long, muddy plains of the peninsula's coastline.

As the wind died, the rain came on in big, slow, depressing drops – each like a galling, prodding finger goading them into either pulling their coats around themselves tighter and just giving up or to rally and sort themselves out. Mr Little managed to chivvy them all in the nick of time to put up the tents, and finally a sheet of canvas was stretched over *Blixem* to form a good-sized 'summerhouse' for the watch. The boat was now unloaded enough for a watch routine to be established within her thwarts so that they could be in relative warmth and safety as they guarded against any opportunistic animals that wandered within blasting range of the camp. And if any poor creature did find themselves within the watch's arcs, they would be reached out to with two double-barrelled shotguns that had been packed with enough coarse wire shot to split a mammoth.

While the rest of the men were waiting for their wolf burgoo to thaw, Orren and his gloomy-looking Kentish mates had taken the uncharacteristic step of volunteering to look for firewood. Whilst they were out on the beach's hinterland, Abe Seeley was thinking about their supper and was already anticipating bitter disappointment.

'I'm fair banded and all we've got to look forward to is more pully-hauly and that bleedin' bow-bow broth for our troubles.'

Tadman started to grin, which didn't help Seeley's mood.

'What you got to smile about, Tadders?'

Tadman caught Orren's eye conspiratorially. 'Shall I tell 'em, or will you, Bill?' Tadman's smile broadened to such an extent that he began to take on the appearance of a demented little toby jug.

Orren remained expressionless as he looked up resignedly at the weather as it began to jab at them once more. 'Yeah, go on then.'

Hartnell peered at Tadman excitedly. 'Is this what I think it is?'

Tadman jerked his chin over towards the ships. 'We're going back, ain't we?'

Seeley's head swivelled between the men and the direction of the ships. 'Who is? Back where? Oh, beggar me, Tadders! I'm not in the mood for yer yarns.'

Orren sneered. 'We're going back to the ships… Collect our rainy-day fund, eh?' Orren held his hand out for a few drops of the rain to bounce off. Tommy Hartnell was already dancing round with excitement.

'Coz it's starting to rain, innit?'

Seeley's grey, gloomy face finally cracked into a smile and he clenched both fists with joy. 'Oh, fackin' yeah… it's about bleeding time.'

Whilst back on Beechey, nearly three years and a few hours before Tommy had dropped his lantern in the food stores, the Hoppers had spirited enough pemmican to *Terror's* orlop for about thirty men to last for a couple of months… or for four men to last, well, ages. At the very least, it was enough to buy them some time – perhaps enough for the ice to melt again, or for help to arrive? Seeley was just about to join Tommy's dancing when Mr Little approached, having returned from a recce further along the beach. He didn't care for the way the men suddenly went quiet. Nor did he care for the way their twitchy, shifty eyes began to look down at their feet.

As he passed them, they knuckled their heads and he returned the salute. 'Don't stop dancing on my account, gentlemen – unless it interferes with your firewood collecting, of course?'

Tommy called after him, 'Aye, sir… just keepin' our tootsies warm, sir.'

After supper, the lieutenant mustered the men and read through the orders for the night's watch. Once done, he asked them if they had any questions.

Orren scratched at his beard with an almost manic impatience as he gazed at his boots. 'It's funny, innit, sir?'

'What is, Orren?'

Orren looked up from his boots and his twisted face had an air of mischief about it. 'Well, that we've called this place Little Point?'

The lieutenant was just about to respond when Orren cut him

off. 'Especially as how me and some of the lads was reckoning our ships looked a bit closer from when we last left them?'

Little looked back doubtfully towards the ships: they could hardly see the ships at such a distance even with a glass, so he suspected he was being had for some sort of goose.

'Well, you must have jolly good eyes to see that from here, Orren – the ships are drifting by about two hundred yards or so each day, I'd say.'

Orren shook his head doubtfully. 'They look closer than that to us, sir.'

Little blinked with misgivings but made an attempt to diffuse the situation. 'Well, perhaps if we waited here for a few months, I'll wager we'd probably see them drifting past… just don't expect to see a bright bone at her cutwater, Orren. Now, if I may continue…'

Mr Little turned back to the rest of the men who were now shifting uncomfortably at Orren's nerve. But Orren still wouldn't let it lie.

'Yeah, so we could wave to them as they bobbed past, couldn't we, sir?'

Mr Little was about to continue, but he was interrupted yet again by Orren waving his arms in the air. 'Bye-bye, ships!'

Little was a very patient and kindly officer, but his nerves were beginning to jangle in response to a situation that he guessed was rapidly deteriorating into sedition. 'Do you have something you need to get off your chest, Able Seaman, or do I need to put you in the Report?'

Orren's lips went white in an instant and he felt a sort of spontaneous emptiness in his stomach as his adrenaline was sent squirting through his blood vessels and into every fibre of his being. He stood up and turned to the rest of the men with arms outstretched, as if in victory. 'Aye, sir – I do have something I want to get off my chest, actually. I'm putting it to yous all that we get back on the ships and sail 'em.'

Mr Little's confusion was plain for all to see as he almost squawked, 'What on earth are you talking about, Orren?'

'You heard, sir – sail!'

The young lieutenant involuntarily looked in the direction of the ships again. 'They're caught in seventeen feet of bloody ice, man. I'd like to see you try.'

'Well, it's a better scheme than pulling these bleedin' boats all over the bazaar... Sir.'

Orren's *sir* was added as an obviously contemptuous after-thought that prompted Taff to pipe up. 'Orren – mate!'

Orren closed his eyes and ground his teeth before cutting Taff off. 'Button it, Taffy boy, or, so help me, you'll get a bastard.'

Tadman touched Orren's shoulder to calm him before turn-ing round to Little, who was about to protest. 'Sorry, sir – we's all a bit tired and overwrought, but 'appen as we'd have a better chance without the others... Stands to reason, doesn't it, sir?'

The rest of the men had become very quiet – agog with eyes that swivelled between conflicting views; torn between their loy-alty to Crozier and the rest of their friends, and fear of falling foul of Orren. For some of the weaker sailors, certain thoughts began to course through their fragile minds: justifying their actions by imagining that their return to the ships would somehow assist the rest of their comrades by not being such a burden on their already punishing allowance.

It was also often the case that sailors, once they were adrift from their ships, felt less inclined to adhere to the stricter discipline that they would far more readily submit to whilst on board. But what-ever had prompted the shift in their mood, Mr Little was starting to worry about the integrity of his men and the general dark demeanour they all had about their faces. Almost involuntarily, Mr Little's hand clutched at the leather of the sling that held his gun around his shoulders as if it were Crozier's own reassuring arm.

'Orren, what the hell has got into you, man? And, Tadman, what do you mean "without the others"?'

Orren felt his pulse quickening again – just like it always did before that red mist came on from behind his eyes – only to clear away again to reveal someone lying at his feet, bleeding and quiet. Tadman, the only man on earth who ever seemed to be able to reason with Orren, noticed his lips were whitening again as his knuckles tightened, so he caught his eye and shook his head. Orren's snarl dissolved again. 'Yeah, you're right, sir – what *was* I thinking? Pardon me, sir.'

The young officer, doing his best to hide his fear, reinstated his authority by telling the men that they were *in the Book* regardless and would have a case to answer with their captain later on. After this threat, the men seemed to settle down again but Mr Little felt that he had come within a gun barrel's length of an outrage.

After their meagre supper, the lieutenant made sure all the men had half a cup of hot tea to go to bed with and most of them crawled into their blankets and furs reasonably happy – but among the better men there were some who were still shocked at the brass-necked temerity of Orren. He had always been a bit of a loose cannon, but tonight, he'd taken it too far with the young officer. It had been a distinctly uneasy evening, but most put it down to the fact that they hadn't eaten a proper meal in over four months and, coupled with the weeks of extra exertion out on the ice, they were living life at the bitter end. There wasn't even the boost of rum left to help with their misery. Whatever the case, Orren knew that he would now have the devil to pay when Crozier found out about his behaviour.

In the morning, as a chilling, dense haar drifted onshore from the N.W., few hands had been awake enough to be troubled by the sound of the two gunshots. Most were too exhausted to even stir but those who were motivated enough to wriggle free from the bonds of their frozen bedding stumbled out of their tents to see the foggy silhouettes of Orren, Tadman, Seeley and Hartnell leaning against *Blixem*. As they got closer to see what was going on, Orren and his men appeared to have the queerest edge about them – something that ranged between a quiet smugness and a barely contained gibbering excitement – whereas, inside the boat, the last watch lay silently, still: Taff and Lieutenant Little. All that was left of the two men's skulls were their steaming jaws still attached to what remained of their spines.

Orren, having leant the shotgun he'd used against the side of the boat, blithely started packing his pipe with baccy as he sang:

'There is all sorts of Fowl and Fish,
With Wine and store of Brandy;
Ye have there what your hearts can wish:
The Hills are Sugar-Candy...'

He looked up from his pipe at the puzzled faces of the men as he continued to sing to them, before breaking off: 'Morning, lads – there's been a change of plan.'

Dunder Bay

ONCE AT THE SOUTHERN OPENING of Shit Creek, Crozier and Fitzjames's crews met with the sight of a rather bleak, frozen bay that was six miles across. Running past the bay's mouth, the jagged jumble of sea ice was shunted from behind by the millions of tons of pressure coming from the north – just as it had done on the other side of the peninsula.

Crozier and the seventy-four souls dragging *Prancer*, *Dunder* and *Comet* skirted around the bay and set up camp on a beach on the far side. They found the best protection afforded to them was near a frozen creek and Crozier wasted no time in establishing a routine to keep the blood circulating through the minds of his spent and famished people. In an attempt to keep up with his many orders from his Lordships regarding the recordings of cartography and readings for magnetic variation, he sent Fitzjames out with parties to note the lie of the new land ahead of them, and for his own part, Crozier took over dipole readings for the sake of determining magnetical observations. In the middle of the bay a hole was cut into the ice so that its bottom was sounded at around thirteen fathoms. As was his habit, the captain observed in his log that the bay would make a superb anchorage for any future expeditions looking for a decent overwintering harbour – should anyone ever make it so far.

Fitzjames's discovery parties returned with a fairer idea of what lay ahead of them, and it was determined that they were a quarter of the way to the mouth of Back's River.

Having taken just under two weeks to get this far from *Erebus* and *Terror*, some of the men were already rapidly deteriorating. Some had lost toes and fingers to frostbite and collapses due to malnourishment were an almost hourly occurrence. Even more worrying to Crozier and his surgeons, the snare of scurvy was beginning to tighten. The only thing known to hold it at bay was a better diet consisting of fresh meat, fish, fruit or vegetables. With this very much in mind, those not otherwise engaged or too sick were sent off to look for something to eat or burn. With a distinct dearth of animals to hand, hunting had mainly con-sisted of scraping rock tripe off schist, sandstone and whatever else it could find to cling to, whilst, out in the middle of the bay, the hole in the ice fed the men on the hope that fish and seals coming up for air would be caught. Their new glory hole was manned permanently during the daylight hours, which in late May was twenty hours and twenty-five minutes.

Overall, the men did have some luck in the first few days with Firemark and Tozer bringing in three ravens; whilst others brought back around twelve pounds of bitter disappointment in lichen. Fish and seals, however, remained a complete and utter enigma to them.

They had been in Dunder Bay for a week and Edward Little's people had been expected back three days earlier. The weather had been fairly steady but Crozier, remembering what became of Gore's sledging party, was beginning to have déjà vu. Having consulted with Fitzjames, Crozier took the necklace of keys from around his neck and ordered Osmer to bring all four chests to his tent and summon all those responsible for provisions and diet.

'All right, gentlemen. We're going to have to go back and look for Mr Little. This'll help to buy us some time.'

As the first chest's lid was opened Dr McDonald couldn't help himself. 'Oh, dear Lord – it's bloody Christmas!'

Diggle shook his head in disbelief: Crozier may as well have opened the Lost Ark and found the Holy Grail inside: it was a hundredweight of pemmican.

'Oh, stone me! I thought we'd lost all at Beechey, sir?'

Crozier nodded towards Mr Osmer. 'Well, we have the diligence of the pusser to thank, actually.'

The pusser started beaming. 'Well, I was just making my ships' inventory before we paid them off, when, upon my inspection of the orlop, someone had sealed up the large tuns for the carrots and potatoes – so my suspicions were instantly aroused when—'

Crozier closed the chest's lid quite brusquely in order to cut what was evidently going to be a long story short. The men hushed as Crozier began to speak. 'The fire at Beechey was no accident – whoever the culprits were, they must have been squirrelling away some of the pemmican for their own dirty little needs.'

McDonald was dumbfounded. 'Who? Who on earth would do such a thing?'

Crozier shrugged. 'No idea – that's why I couldn't afford to have anyone know we have their wee stash… Not even you gentlemen – my apologies.'

Something else occurred to Fitzjames. 'Well, one thing is certain – they must have been jolly miffed at having to leave their little *shop* behind.'

'Aye, I reckon they'll try and get back to retrieve it at some point, so we need to be on the lookout for this, gentlemen – any mumbling among the men… Use your eyes and ears.'

Crozier opened the lid again and lifted out a slab of pemmican. He gingerly held it to his nose and grimaced. 'God-awful stuff, forgotten how much I hate it, but…'

Goodsir interjected, 'Needs must when the devil drives, sir?'

Crozier grinned at Goodsir's uncharacteristic joviality as he returned the precious ingot of fat and gristle to the treasure chest.

'Indeed, Dr Goodsir – Mr Osmer has worked out that there's probably going to be enough to keep us going for…'

Crozier looked to his purser to assist.

'About three weeks, sir: an allowance of six ounces per day, per man. It's not much, but it'll help keep the wolf from the door for twenty-three days of work.'

Not for the first time, the notion of wolves crept into Crozier's thoughts.

The next morning, Crozier had all-hands mustered and, together with Fitzjames and their surgeons, he inspected the men to assess who could or could not pull their way back to Erebus Bay. Thirty-two men were put in the sick report and made to stay behind where it was hoped that they could rest and recuperate under the diligent eye of Goodsir, who would, without doubt, have his hands full as he coped with the rise in casualties.

Once again, anyone who was deemed fit to pull found themselves standing in their reins with a mixture of fear and dread at the prospect of more excruciating labours on the ice. Finally, when it was time for Crozier's party to depart, the men said their goodbyes to each other with a mixture of guilt, sadness and apprehension on both sides.

McDonald felt a dash of leadenness flow around his knees at the thought of parting from his brother medical officer.

'I, er, left you an extra bottle of a smart cathartic, Goodsir. I really don't think I'll have much use for it whilst we're pulling.'

Goodsir appeared to shift his feet uneasily too. 'Oh, yes – excellent, Sandy. Thank you. And, er, do you have plenty of laudanum? I imagine you'll be needing plenty of laudanum…'

Sandy was taken aback. He had never heard Goodsir call him anything other than by his surname or title before and found it inexplicably touching. The young doctor did have plenty of laudanum, but all he could do was smile fondly as he slipped his mitten off and held out his hand for his dearest friend. 'Goodbye, Harry.'

Erebus

ORREN AND NOW HIS TWENTY-NINE people had left *Blixem* exactly where she stood. A few of the men had covered the bodies with a bearskin or two as if to help keep them warm or perhaps cover their disgrace in some way. The mutineers rolled their sleeping-skins and slung them around their shoulders. Lighter and faster without the boats or their tents they made it in two days but had to leave five of their number where they lay as there was precious little they could do for anyone who *fell overboard* whilst out on the ice.

Once reinstated aboard the ships, the men were reinvigorated with a new sense of purpose – perhaps even with a modicum of their old discipline renewed due to some sense of survival that most possess or, again to perhaps compensate for their treachery in some way. Shame could be a great motivator, but as a stone cast into water creates ever-increasing circles, that same stone, once beneath the surface, enters a downward spiral until it finally rests at the very the bottom of their pond.

Immediately on re-boarding, Orren had ordered Tadman and the rest of his Hoppers to go and retrieve their 'rainy day fund' from their sand barrels. There were six of them in total and when the men reached the orlop with their lanterns they were exactly how they had left them. They jemmied the lids off and plunged their arms up to their elbows into the sand with the grappling hands of children at a country fair's bran tub – but instead of pulling out oilskin-wrapped packets of their pemmican prize, they pulled out tins of Ox Cheek in Gravy, Pork in Gravy, Beef in

Gravy, and plenty of Mock Turtle Soup. Tadman, peering into the last tub of tins, clutched his chest with horror as he leant heavily against a bracing. 'Tommy… better get Orren down here, lad.'

Like the grimmest of ministers about to give sermon, Orren gripped *Erebus*'s rail with blood-blotted knuckles as he stared out over the ice that was now beginning to creak and groan restlessly.

As the bearer of the bad news regarding the orlop, Tommy Hartnell had been beaten so badly by Orren that his own brother would barely have recognised him. It had been more out of frustration than any ill-will on Orren's part. Fully aware of the tins' corrupted innards, Orren still held hope that some of the contents could be eaten, so ordered them all to be fetched up to the Great Cabin so they could be held under lock and key as thieves always instinctively know who can be trusted in a time of crisis: absolutely no one. Some of the tins were fine – about a fifth of them, but eventually, they knew not to touch any of the bloated ones after being nearly floored by the escaping funk. Instead, they tossed the stinking things straight through the stern lights and onto the ice below.

Even with some of the tins that hadn't bloated, it was noted that some of them had been filled with an almost humorous list of ingredients: one of them had what appeared to be a single turd bobbing in a *jus* of very dark piss, whilst another had been filled with eyeballs – the square pupils betraying that they had once provided sight for a small flock of sheep. Regardless, the mutineers salvaged what they could. The eyes were added to a broth and as the brew bubbled around in the ship's iron dixie, the gristly ingredients could easily have belonged to the cauldron of one of the more deranged witches from *Macbeth*. For a sweet couple of days, Orren and his men had more food in their bellies than they had eaten in months, and all seemed well with the world. But they knew that these salad days were numbered.

As the weather improved, the sun sometimes raised itself to a daytime temperature up to 50°F and upwards and, combined with the stench of the carelessly disposed of tins, brought with it a cloudy plague of mosquitoes that efficiently displaced any feelings of wellbeing they might have had. At night, the temperature dropped like a stone, and only then were they granted sweet relief from the wrath of the *bastard mozzies.*

Another consequence of the warmer weather was the ice continually hissing and shrieking as it shifted. The disconcerting din of the ice and the whining mosquitos played together in concert to jangle the men's nerves. The Devil's Orchestra was warming up again for the final movement of the famine-ridden hellhole they had dug for themselves.

Orren had mustered everyone on the quarterdeck as they lethargically slapped or swatted themselves at the sites of their wretchedly irritating lumps and sores.

'Right, lads… before you start giving me any poor mouth, do you want the shit news, or the not-so-shit news?' The men were in no mood for banter, so Orren continued, 'Well, the shit news is that there ain't much fodder left, yeah.'

Normally there would have been groans or protests at any such news, but the men, somewhat more chillingly, didn't even stir. Orren shifted nervously from foot to foot and sniffed. 'All right then, the good news is that the ice is gonna be off soon. There's enough of us what can sail us out of here, and – who knows – maybe some schnurglies'll jump into our fishin' nets, eh?'

Young Davy Young, who was as thin as a rasher of wind, looked utterly forlorn as he pleaded, 'What we gunna eat, Bill?'

Orren's affable demeanour began to curdle. 'What do you mean?'

'Well, you said that there was going to plenty of grub, Bill.'

Orren rubbed the top of his head impatiently before his face turned puce. 'See, what did I just tell you about givin' me mouth?'

Orren grabbed Davy and raised his fist in readiness to pound his jaw into dust. All the men stared silently, as if urging Orren to carry on – as if daring him to try and beat them all collectively through a child, with eyes bulging in fear, who was so weak that all he could do was spray flecks of spittle as he tried not to cry through gritted teeth in anticipation of pain. For the first time, Orren seemed to lose his resolve and begrudgingly let the lad go.

Tadman stepped in to diffuse the situation. 'Come on, lads – wasn't our fault Crozier found our scoff, was it?'

One of the older hands, a tough, sinewy Scotsman called Tom Work, shook his head grimly as he folded his arms defiantly.

'Aye, but it was nae yoors in the fest place, eh?'

Orren couldn't help himself this time. He exploded – pinning the Scot to the bulwark so that he didn't even have time to unfold his arms. He then picked up one of the tins nearby and smashed it into Tom Work's cheek again and again until both split and the blood and the gravy ran like a sewer. Tom slithered down bulwark and onto the deck. The ferocity of the attack was so unexpected and so rapid that every man present froze in horror, any leanings towards dissension quelled in an instant. Orren, sweeping back a stray lock of hair, seethed at them all as he caught his breath again. 'Anyone else wanna do another whinge, just step forward and I'll gladly remind you of the way it is!'

No one moved or made a sound, other than the old Scotsman who was now finding it difficult to breathe. Orren leered at him and sniffed, 'Ner – didn't think so. Fuckin' jellyfish, the lot of yer.'

The Boat Place

WITH CROZIER WALKING ON AHEAD with his telescope, the crews behind him took on the appearance of a herd of steaming Highland cattle as they hauled their giant wooden plough-shares through a desert of salt. By the time Crozier, Fitzjames and their forty-five souls had dragged *Dunder* and *Comet* round Gore Peninsula they were just about ready to spit blood. They had gone the long way around assuming that they would have bumped into Mr Little en route but with every footstep towards Little Point, their hope of finding all to be well with Mr Little and his men diminished until, eventually, they found themselves right back where they had started in Erebus Bay.

Crozier, walking ahead, called a halt. He continued alone towards Mr Little's partially drift-covered boat. Dread and fear rose with every step. As he peered over the boat's gunnel, several Arctic foxes suddenly leapt out. Instinctively Crozier swung his telescope, catching one of them painfully on the rump. Then, returning his attention to within the boat, he groaned. He gripped the gunwale. It was all he could do to stay on his feet as he surveyed the absolute wreckage of two human beings within the boat's thwarts – his heart sank even further as he spotted his own shotgun leaning beside what was left of Edward Little. He took the weapon and pulled back the hammers to remove the spent percussion caps. He sniffed at them delicately as if to scent the stench of the culprits.

Shortly, Fitzjames approached to see what was going on and

instantly blanched. 'Oh, dear Lord... dear Lord.' Holding a hand to his mouth, he spoke through fingers that were trying to hold back bile, 'What would do this... Animals?'

Crozier turned to the direction of the two ships skulking just over the horizon – *Erebus*'s pall of smoke betraying them before replying. 'Aye, animals indeed, James – only this breed walk on two legs and can evidently light fires. As for the foxes, they have my blessing.'

'Poor Edward. Who is the other soul?'

Crozier saw Fitzjames's tears and placed a steady hand on his shoulder. 'James, tell the men to slip their harnesses and file past to pay their respects. I want them to let this be the motivation to get them back on the ice.'

'Back on the ice, sir?'

'Aye, back to the ships – whoever did this can't get away with it.'

The ice was on the move again. The pressure from the north had been piling in, driving the ice together like a rugby scrum to form concertina-like pressure ridges that meant the sailors had to portage the boats almost as much as they were able to haul them. These pressure ridges had risen up with monotonous regularity so that Crozier's people would have to pull, and push, and heave over one ridge, only to be then faced with another just yards afterwards. Occasionally, they could smash a course through them with axes and picks, but more often than not, they would have to make more portages; painstakingly emptying the boats in order to lift them over before re-stowing and carrying on once more. And if they were very lucky, they could pull along the ridges when they ran in a direction that corresponded with their heading, but mainly they were not lucky and so their lot was just a relentlessly soul-destroying rigmarole of pulling, unshipping, lifting and shipping their increasingly resented boats.

One of the caulkers had fallen on the ice and died where he

lay. All Crozier could do was begrudgingly call a halt and detail a party to drag the body to just above the high-water line. They had pulled themselves a world away from the heady days of carved headstones and coffins lined with wood shavings for the dead minority – now they were the dead-on-their-feet majority.

As the rest of the matelots rested, some filled their pipes using numb, trembling fingers as they listened to the sound of their own pulses banging against the backs of their eyeballs. Eventually catching their breath, they plugged their pipes into their mouths and puffed languidly with blank absentminded stares which they had come to term dead-eyes. McDonald had diagnosed this as the unfortunate consequence of shot nerves, exhaustion or both; that their vision was taken over by awful re-visitations that played out in the reclusion of their own heads.

What were they turning into? Crozier's own dead-eyes replayed their own image of the two men he had left crumpled in the bottom of a boat with their heads disintegrated by shot, powder and depravity. Life didn't seem to count for much anymore – instinctively outrunning death was all that mattered now. That, and perhaps retribution: the only other instinct that seemed to be buoying some of the men after what had been meted out on Taff and Little. Both primal instincts that were impossible to shrug off. Of course, it could be countermanded by an innate sense of decency and morality that most human beings are blessed with through experience and learning. But those lessons can become completely obsolete once one's own body, deprived of even basic nutrients, starts to feed itself on its own fatty tissues until, when that's depleted, the muscles, kidneys, eyes, liver, even brains, start to waste away too. Under such conditions, only the very strongest of men would be able to cling to any vestiges of humanity.

Crozier looked northwards towards *Terror* and *Erebus*. He knew that those who had blown Taff and Little's heads off had settled back into the ships like the worms that gnaw and burrow into the timbers beneath the waterlines of great ships before undermining them completely and sending them to the bottom of the seas that they were built to rule.

He couldn't let the ringleaders get away with what they had done. At the same time, he recognised that there must have been Oxen and Bears among them who wouldn't have had a say in the matter. But the ringleaders; the Wolves… yes, they would need to be taken in hand.

Creek Camp

IN DUNDER BAY, SANDY MCDONALD was doing all he could for the sickies left in his charge, but with the bulk of the men already dying of scurvy, malnutrition and the gangrene from frostbite, there was only so much he could do with filthy bandages, surgical knives, saws and ethanol. The only other thing he could do to perhaps help was to make sure the men were as warm as possible and not wasting any of their precious body reserves unnecessarily. The pemmican had long since gone and so they were relying on rock tripe, flour and powdered peas. Even some of their animal skins had been roasted – just as Sir John had done during his disastrous Coppermine expedition.

The fitter men were sent shuffling out onto the ice to take it in turns to fish from the Glory Hole, but their hooks remained resolutely unattached to anything that could be eaten. Other hands were sent looking for food and some of the scant bog rosemary kindling for their fires. But mainly the men just staggered back empty-handed and with even emptier stomachs and souls.

Then, during one particularly calm, crisp night, as they listened to the rumblings of their tummies, Ice Master Reid was heard to be talking in his sleep. Without even the hint of his stammer he declared, 'I'm volunteering fae galley duties, lads.' In the morning, they were found to be his last words.

Erebus Bay

A NORTHERLY WHIPPED UP AND blew tenaciously into the teeth of Crozier's men as they struggled to drag their two boats across the ice. They were at least another day away from reaching *Erebus* and *Terror* when they heard the first explosive crack in the ice. The men, almost too physically weakened to act with any valid response, fretted uselessly instead. Knowing that they were in constant danger but being too hungry, tired and cold to care just heightened most of their anxiety so that their feelings of utter helplessness gripped them by their throats relentlessly.

Another crack was felt beneath their feet and Crozier signalled a halt as he struggled to listen above the din of the squall.

'Sergeant Tozer! Tell the men to get down!'

Sergeant Tozer, who was having equal difficulty hearing above the raging wind, cupped a mitten to his ear and shouted, 'Say again, sir?'

A sound akin to giant timbers splintering could be heard as a huge crack raced towards the sailors like a felled tree. Crozier, the closest, was the first to react as he turned and ran back towards men. The captain didn't need to repeat himself as Tozer realised what was happening and shouted to the men, 'Rotten ice, lads! Get down!'

As the sergeant dragged some of the men closest to him down, a calving plate of ice rose out of the water and crashed down onto the floe. Pressure from the storm to the north was forcing the ice to break up and as it lost its integrity it began to rock with the sea's swell beneath it.

The furthest boat was *Comet* and the men pulling her could only watch in horror as another calving plate of ice rose up like a giant hand of God looming over them. The weight of the plate on the ice then formed a slipway which *Comet*, on her runners, intractably began to launch herself down… down towards the dark, newly opened lead. The men, still attached to her harnesses, clawed pointlessly at the ice as she dragged them into the frigid, roiling sea with her.

Prancer's crew, coming to their senses, wriggled clear of their own harnesses before running towards their friends to help. As they reached the edge of the lead, they were greeted with the sight of *Comet* bobbing about in the waves as if set free whilst all about her, sailors, blinded by panic and the shock of the cold, turned the water white as they scrabbled and thrashed themselves to her starboard side. Crozier called for them to leave the boat alone but as he did so, *Comet* began to dip with their weight on her gunnels. The big Nova Scotian dived in clutching his knife and hacked away at as many of the hands' harnesses as he could before the numbing cold forced him to retreat. Neptune jumped in after him, barking incessantly as he dragged two of Joe's liberated men back towards the waiting hands of their brothers.

But one of *Comet*'s people who couldn't swim refused to let go of the boat and those near him attempted to drag him off. As they did so, *Comet*'s load shifted. She lurched over to starboard and her gunnel dipped beneath the surface, greedily sucking in water.

As she did so, Stickland, a tall skinny AB from Portsmouth, was able to grab a line tossed by Tozer. He managed to get it through *Comet*'s painter ring, but by this time his fingers were so frozen that he couldn't possibly do anything about her knot. Fitzjames, seeing the futility of the lad's fumbling, took off as many clothes as he could before diving in to assist, but by the time he was able to secure the line at *Comet*'s bow, she began to sigh almost resignedly as the last of the air within her weather cloth was displaced by seawater. Her bow rose hopefully for a

moment before she began to sound. This prompted some to state
the obvious as they shouted desperately, 'A'mighty God, she's a
gonner!'… 'Be quick lads!'

The sailors on the ice began to pull at *Comet's* line for all they
were worth but she was too heavy with water as she hissed and
creaked with increasing vehemence. Then she took on the appearance of an enormous whale's fluke for a moment before slowly
slipping beneath the surface. All the poor souls who were still
attached to her could do was shiver uncontrollably until the slack
in their ropes was taken up as *Comet* began her seventy-fathom
descent to the bottom. Treading water next to each other among
the utter chaos, two Scottish friends said goodbye to one another
in their own way through violently chattering teeth. 'It's baws –
eh, Jimmy?'

'Aye, Willy – pure baws.'

Some began to scream with wide, terrified eyes as they came
to terms with their terrible, inevitable fate. Some called for their
mothers, some for Jesus Christ and some for nothing that made
any sense. One or two were still desperately trying to free themselves to the very last; gnawing at their bonds till their mouths bled.

On the ice, every man had joined in at the painter with all
the strength they could muster. But they couldn't get enough
purchase with their feet as the frozen line slipped through their
useless hands – dragging them to the edge of the lead as close as
they dared before letting go and running towards the end to bind
on again. But *Comet* was already set on her determined course
for the bottom of the sea. On the ice, the line paid out, whilst
in the water, the slack was finally taken up on the swimmers'
harnesses. The screaming men's heads were snatched beneath the
waves in the bat of an eye.

Four minutes, nine souls and the last of the pemmican: gone.

Creek Camp

And thou shalt eat the fruit of thine own body, the flesh of thy sons and of thy daughters, which the Lord thy God hath given thee, in the siege, and in the straitness, wherewith thine enemies shall distress thee.

Deuteronomy 28:53

Dr McDonald was in the business of saving of lives through his understanding of science. It was what he had been trained for at Edinburgh's Royal College of Physicians and it was what he had done extensively during his own promising career before volunteering for this expedition. Crozier's party were meant to have returned within days, but instead it had been weeks since they had started out for Lieutenant Little and his men and so he had assumed the worst. With no food, and fruitless hunting, the twenty-seven remaining souls in his charge were days from death.

The men were wasted away to around sixty per cent of their bodyweight, reducing them to listless, hacking skeletons. Hair and teeth were falling out by the handful and some men were so poorly, they could barely swallow tea, let alone food. Despite this, the bellies of some of the sailors grew so large that the skin covering them became as tight as a drum, prompting one or two of the more irascible sorts to become initially suspicious – accusing them of stealing food somehow. This led to several punch-drunk scuffles and some half-hearted shouting, but nothing much ever came of it. They were all too far gone to really care.

From inside the jury-rigged marquee, the men could hear a storm developing on the other side of the canvas. They had joined two tents together by lacing an awning between the two so that all of them could cram in for Divine Service. With the wind picking up outside, the doctor had to raise his voice to be heard.

McDonald knew that he had only one option if he was to keep any of his men alive. They needed to eat, and the only thing they had to eat was the dead. McDonald had thought that he could start planting the seed while they communed with God. He selected a verse from Deuteronomy that mentioned Moses' threat to the Jews to follow Jesus otherwise, without his love and protection, all they could expect was the awful prospect of eating their own children. The doctor wasn't a religious man – he was a scientist through and through – but, by God, the Good Book did have its uses sometimes.

McDonald went on to reason in his sermon that the Bible never said that eating human flesh was a sin but rather acknowledged that it was the last resort of the desperate: a necessary evil. Standing before those men who were still capable of listening, he held his Bible aloft so that there was no doubt that their salvation was there – clenched in his hands.

'The Holy Bible is harsh, gentlemen… because life is often harsh. We may feel like we're being punished for some reason, but we have done nothing wrong. In fact, our deeds, as well as our intentions have only ever been pure. But nature has seen fit to be hostile towards us – like the people of Jerusalem, nature has lain us under a siege of her own. But this is not a fault of God. It is merely the fault of circumstance, and the truth is—' At this point the squall blew so hard that the men thought their tent was going to be carried away by the Lord God above. The doctor, returning to his notes, continued, 'Er, the truth is that God lives in all of us, therefore, we must do everything within our power to stay alive… and, in turn, keep God alive. We have nothing to fear, but God, brothers… amen!' The sailors' amens were given with a gusto that was redolent of mewling lambs.

The next day, it was with a barely concealed breath of relief when three sailors *let go* during the particularly brutal night. But instead of commending their bodies to the deep or returning ashes to ashes, they had their non-celestial hosts moved to the doctor's tent.

Alexander McDonald, using his skills as an anatomist, made short shrift of the bodies. He removed anything that looked remotely human-like. The head, hands, genitals, feet and any tattooed skin were immediately rendered into fuel oil for cooking.

He took the meat and the giblets and added them to everything else in a big kettle for boiling.

The doctor didn't bat an eye throughout the entire procedure of turning a human being into food. In fact, he recorded in his notes how tough in texture the meat had become. Its colour had become lighter, almost greyer, the amino acids having very little fat to absorb. The bodies had started to consume their own muscle-tissue and as a consequence, the meat's value had been much reduced in both calories and nutrients. The meat could have come from any number of the more suspect butchers of Smithfield Market, and McDonald didn't know whether to laugh or cry as he recalled the words of a famous French gastronome who once wrote, 'Tell me what you eat and I will tell you what you are.'

During supper, as the men ate, they made whimpering noises as they laughed and cried at the same time with the prospect of not feeling hungry anymore. Those who were too poorly to eat were coaxed into sipping a burgoo made from meat stock that had been fortified with a little flour. The surgeon noted an improvement in his sickies almost immediately and over the subsequent days started to see the men talk again. Then, just as they were running out of meat and having to resort to cracking bones to pick out the marrow, another poor soul for whom the nourishment had come too late had volunteered for 'galley duties'.

Over the weeks, even some of the scurvy started to skulk off back to whatever black place it came. Of course, the men had known from the onset that the meat they were eating was that of their shipmates but despite this, they seemed relatively serene – perhaps with the notion that they had been brought back from the abyss by their dead brothers.

One night, as Billy Wentzall and Reuben Male lay awake with stomachs aching with fullness and the almost pleasant gurgles of food snaking around in their digestive systems, Wentzall noted, 'You know, 's funny, I don't feel nuffin'.'

Male seemed confused. 'Well, just keep wiggling your toes there, Billy lad… keep the blood moving, eh?'

Billy Wentzall shook his head. 'Ner-ner – nothing to do with the cold – 's the meat, innit… I don't feel nuffin' about eating a, a…'

Male's kedge finally caught. 'Oh, right. Yeah.'

Both men fell quiet for a moment or two before Reuben piped up. 'I mean, it's sad to lose mates and that, but I don't feel sorry for them. I feel happy for them not having to go through what the rest of us is going through: makes me really feel like I owe them.'

Wentzall was about to say something but coughed and spluttered.

Male baulked at the Londoner's appalling rattles and wheezes. 'You right, Billy?'

'Aye… I was just going to say, like, I wonder how many folks would have any sympathy with us, if we ever get home again?'

Male crossed his heart and hoped to die. 'If we ever get home again, I swear to Jesus I'd never tell a living soul about what we did up here.'

Wentzall, managing to bring his cough under control, shook his head. 'By Jabers, I wouldn't dare – they'd probably put us in some sort of freak show.'

Male, almost to himself, said, 'Then turn us into gallows fruit.'

HMS *Terror*

ORREN CLUTCHED VARIOUS LENGTHS OF chord in his fist so that they could draw straws. As the men on *Terror* ran out of meat again, Orren asked for volunteers. Initially, there were a few who came forward, happy to be put out of their misery, and there were one or two who were too enfeebled to offer any protest, but over time, as the weakest were winnowed out, the volunteers evaporated as their bellies and their hope filled. Up on deck, the men, as thin as sticks in winter, stood around wittering about anything that would take their minds off the awful process that was taking place below decks. There, three of the 'most ready' men had been selected and carried into the sick berth.

As Orren went around each bed so that the poor souls could draw straws, he seemed almost upbeat. 'This is all above board – it's the custom of the sea, yeah? When it comes to necessity there are, well… how do I put this… certain sacrifices that have to be made, don't they? It's all about giving us, your brothers, the best chance of survival, innit?'

Orren, like a surgeon on his rounds, shuffled between his *patients'* hammocks as he chatted breezily, 'If you think about it, you're all winners here today: it's you what gets all the glory… All we're left with is some gristly meat and a swing from the highest yardarm for our troubles if we ever get back. Don't seem fair on the rest of us, really.' Tom Work, who had been so enfeebled since his beating had been barely able to speak or move. His cheek and nose had swollen to such an extent whereby he could barely breathe. Speaking was an impossibility. Seeing the help-lessness in Tom's Work's eyes horrified the men nearly as much as it shamed them all – all but Orren, that is.

Orren now greeted Work with the patronising tenderness of a parent helping a child. 'Ah, Tommy, Tommy, Tommy – you are definitely looking like a winner here today, wee man!' He picked up the skin and bone of Work's hand and kneaded his fin-gers around a single straw. The next 'volunteer', Josephus Geater, was just able to clutch his own straw: it seemed very short. He swallowed hard but before he could start protesting, Orren del-icately plucked Tom Work's straw from his fist and inspected it. Obviously shorter, he swapped it and put Geater's smaller one in Work's helpless fist. He winked at Josephus jovially. 'Don't say I didn't do nuffin' for yer, Joey.'

Orren was just about to move to the next volunteer when scuf-fling was heard on the deck above before men started shouting.

The weather had become perfectly calm and the open leads now enabled Crozier, Fitzjames and their thirty-two men three days to return to the ships. They had taken turns in warping *Prancer* and *Dasher* through the water – a far less arduous procedure than dragging her across ice. Where the leads had to be crossed, they would pull the boat back and forth across the water like a ferry with the sounding line or, if the lead was narrow enough, slide the boats across on her oars bound together to form fascines.

Now they were within hailing distance of the ships. As they approached *Terror*, they could see smoke coming from the cook's chimney stack near the forecastle – almost like a romantic croft-er's cottage, whilst perhaps inside, the good wife's stew bubbled on the hearth as fresh bread rose in the oven. Perhaps even a jug of ale waited on the table?

On a rare calm day in the Arctic it is possible to see and hear everything as if magnified; preternatural powers bestowed upon the senses. Smell was another sense that was particularly height-ened for starving men and the unmistakable aroma of cooked meat almost lifted them by their cold, frost-nipped noses.

They were about four hundred yards away and they could hear a man shouting something to them from *Terror*'s beak. Crozier put his eye to his telescope to see a sailor waving his arms at them and shouting before another man appeared behind him swing-ing something into the back of his head.

The next moment, they were fired upon. The ball had gone wide of Sergeant Tozer's head by about three feet – enough to make his ears ring and for him to get his belt buckle down onto the ice. Before the next shot was fired, sufficient time had lapsed for Firemark to get into a defilade position and spit his lead into the direction of the ship. The second man tumbled back as a small, pink cloud puffed at his shoulder.

After that, all had become quiet. As Crozier scanned the ship again, he could see more men hesitantly appearing on deck with their hands in the air. One of them waved a white flag.

HMS *Terror*

AS CROZIER'S MEN BOARDED *Terror*, they found Orren bleeding all over the compacted snow of the decks where he had been felled. He was clutching his shoulder, but instead of reeling in pain he seemed more enraged at the inconvenience than to be put out by agony. As the marines rushed him, he managed to stagger to his feet and grab a nearby belay pin before wielding it like a one-armed boxer. His eyes burnt with an unreasonable hatred as he flecked spittle whilst he ranted, 'These are my ships now, if you want them back, you'll have to see me first!' Sergeant Tozer, having had enough of Orren's noise, parried him in the mouth with the butt of his rifle. The sergeant sneered at the man who lay sprawled at his feet, 'Yeah, well – consider yourself seen.'

As Crozier, Fitzjames and their men went below on *Terror* they were greeted with the appalling sight of a ship that had been turned into a floating charnel house: dixies filled with bubbling, rendering body parts and marrow-scraped bones lay all around.

Despite this, the twelve remaining mutineers were beside themselves with joy at being reunited with their brothers. At the very least they were still alive, but it had evidently come at a great price as they shuffled around like aimless beggars with less spirits than the dead they had just consumed. Their delight was soon subsumed by shame, offering their best seats and putting up the hammocks of Crozier's men as if they were returning heroes. But despite their evident gladness, there was now a pale planted between them as they busied themselves with idle chat and menial tasks. Tadman, on seeing Crozier and Fitzjames, began to giggle with a manic, mirthless wheeze. He was a pitiful sight, saluting nervously as he stooped and flinched as if he was constantly expecting to be beaten.

'Ha, Captain! Welcome aboard, sir. You're just in time for breakfast, sir... ha, ha! No eggs I'm afraid, but I'm sure your lads will find the, er, fried kidneys very nice indeed... ha, ha, ha!'

Sure enough, from the direction of Sir John's Great Cabin the unmistakable smell of fried meat could not be avoided. Every man jack of Crozier's men had cheeks that were stinging involuntarily as their mouths slavered. Crozier looked at his men who had only eaten pissy burgoos of pemmican since leaving Dunder Bay and thought they looked far worse off than the deserters by comparison. The latter seemed the picture of health, relatively speaking. At least they could still move around without the constant pain they felt in their every limb. But Crozier wondered how they could ever bring themselves to eat a human being when they couldn't even eat their dog!

But then they needed to eat. If they didn't, then that would be suicide. Truth be known, Crozier himself no longer wanted to live, but if he gave up now, his people were as good as dead. Morale, not morality, was all they had to help keep them alive, but it wasn't enough. As a God-fearing man himself, what could possibly be the lesser of the two evils in the eyes of the Lord? In performing the unspeakable last taboo, there, possibly, lay salvation and deliverance. If they didn't eat, then they would be committing a mortal sin.

Eating their dead was the only way for Crozier and his men to live and in defeating death then their transgressions could perhaps be forgiven. Crozier had to decide that if they wanted to live, they were going to have to do it through the sacrifices of their dead brothers. And if Crozier and his men were to be spared, could it ever be possible to live normal lives again? He very much doubted it, but all he knew for certain was that a large part of their souls would forever remain with the ice of the White North.

Port Leopold

HAVING BEEN CAUGHT BY THE ice in Baffin Bay, John Clark Ross's position had been 200 miles to the N.E. in Lancaster Sound. As they limped behind the ice towards Cornwallis Island, Ross could see that there was nothing for them to either the west or the north – just biblical amounts of ice. Worried about being caught too far in, Ross had searched high and low for a decent harbour for *Enterprise* and *Investigator* and he found it at North Somerset. Here, he had the ships prepared for overwintering as a well-versed Royal Navy had been doing for nearly thirty years, and James Ross, as the most successful Polar man in the world, had known exactly what he and his men were getting into. Once the routine had been established for that winter, Ross and his ships' companies went about the business of finding the Franklin expedition with a vengeance and a rigorous sledging schedule.

As Ross sent his parties out to all points of the compass, he had them build cairns but, unlike Franklin's men, instead of making monuments to desolation, their stony markers were beacons of contingency and hope with stacks of provisions and anything else that might be of assistance to Franklin's people. His sledging parties even took out roving parties of 'Twopenny Postmen'. These were trapped Arctic foxes. For these wily little animals, Ross had the blacksmith put copper bands round their necks with messages attached that stated the positions of the ships and the food caches they had deposited for them.

Over the ensuing months, Ross's parties had drawn a blank

north, west and east, but south, the last place where he thought of looking, now seemed to be the only option left for them. 'Maybe the old duffer did manage to punch through the ice after all?' thought Ross. So, with the only option remaining, he and his steadfast number two, Leopold McClintock, set off as far south as their dwindling sledging provisions would allow.

The Gun Deck

SOMETHING HAD TO BE DONE about Orren, who, whilst secured down in the orlop with his empty barrels of sand, had taken to singing hymns raucously. Even from down there, he managed to have a very unsettling effect on the men. Crozier had determined the need for summary justice. It was the only way to guard against any more mutinies and it was the only way he would be able to maintain the morale of his people.

On questioning all the mutineers, it had become apparent that most had been unwilling to return to the ships with Orren, but with the example he had made of Mr Little and Taff – along with the promise of food – they felt they had no option but to go along with Orren and to some extent, his deputy, Tadman.

Under the Articles of War, Crozier had the authority to try the pair whilst at sea and, if found guilty, had it within his power to carry out capital punishment. According to the Articles, *any member of the Fleet found guilty of mutiny, mutinous or seditious threats, or striking a superior officer was to be automatically punished with death.*

Crozier set up a drumhead court martial on the gun deck with every man present.

The captain appeared uneasy as he sat behind his mahogany table that had been fetched from the Great Cabin. Orren's men were left to stand in a roped off dock like a flock of lost sheep whilst AB Orren, with his arm in a sling, had a chair in the middle of the deck so that he could hear the evidence. For his

Oath, Orren was offered the Bible and, after studying it inso-
lently, dismissed it with a sniff before languidly spitting on the
deck. 'Yeah, I'm not going to lie to you, lads.'

From the drumhead, Crozier looked across at the defaulter
who sat slumped, leg bobbing vigorously as he gnawed away at
his filthy thumbnail with what remained of his teeth after Tozer's
rifle butt. Throughout, as Orren heard the evidence, stalactites of
drool depended off his palm and onto his sling as he occasionally scoffed at his former co-conspirators' versions of events and
when he found the testimony to be too tedious, he made a point
of shifting his eyes about the men in a manner that unsettled
them greatly (having been frightened witless by him prior, none
of them could bear to catch his eye). It amused him to note how
some had adopted various techniques for avoiding his gaze: one
man just closed his eyes and seemed to be praying quietly to
himself throughout, whilst another retained a fixed stare as if
hypnotised by a knot in a timber plank.

Hearing other men's testimony, Crozier learnt how they had
been lured back to the ships with the promise of pemmican –
only for Orren to claim that someone had replaced it all with the
rotted tins. At first, the men had suspected foul play on the part
of Orren and his gang, so three of the disgruntled sailors were
going to double back to Little Point first thing in the morning.
Orren had said that they were free to leave and even promised
them some extra allowance to take with them. In the morning,
the turncoats were found with their throats cut. After that, the
rest of the poor starving souls were putty in his hands.

Orren had ordered the three men's bodies to be wrapped in
canvas and stored up top on the forward deck, and they took what
they needed from them as and when required. After nine days,
when there was nothing of left of them to eat, volunteers were
asked for. Crozier heard that when no volunteers were forthcoming, Orren resorted to drawing straws and the man who drew the
shortest would be killed by the hand that drew the second shortest.

As the horrific story unfolded, Crozier also had a dilemma with Tadman in that he had initially appeared in cahoots with Orren regarding each of the counts of mutiny, but Tadman, with his head still bandaged from being clubbed by Orren, reasoned that he was actually able to temper Orren a little and, therefore, could impose a greater degree of fairness (this was indeed borne out by most of the other witnesses). Tadman also begged for clemency because it was he who had alerted Crozier and his men as they approached the ships after all – though, there were those who had suspected that Tadman, realising the game was up, had hedged his bets in order to be looked upon more favourably in any subsequent investigation.

Crozier, after conferring with Fitzjames, decided that whilst the men had obviously suffered a severe breakdown of moral fibre, they did have good reason to take their awful recourse. Crozier was also mindful that they needed every man possible, and that they should perhaps consider deferring any decisions until the men were back home where the more dubious suspects such as AB Tadman could be tried under courts martial. Two further men were also singled out as mutineers: ABs Abraham Seeley and Thomas Hartnell. Hartnell, in mitigation, claimed that after his brother had died, he felt like he had nothing left to lose, and as for Seeley, he was evidently just a village idiot.

When asked if he had anything to say for himself before sentencing, Orren regarded his fellow mutineers with disdain as he cleared his throat.

'Sir, in my defence, I would like to say me and the lads was just exercising the custom of the sea – ain't that right, lads?' All the men behind the rope, stared at their feet intently, in silence. Orren seemed hurt by their reticence for a moment before puffing his cheeks and making a sort of bobbing motion as he sneered, 'Fackin' jellyfish – the lot of yer.'

Young Davy burst into tears. 'You never gave us no choice, Orren… Sir, he never gave us no choice!'

Orren mocked the kid by imitating him with an insipid falsetto version of his plea.

'Surr, he never gave us no choice!'

Crozier looked up from his knitted fingers. 'And you'll give me no choice but to flog you if you don't stop this contempt for my court, Able Seaman.' Orren knuckled his head in mock deference. Crozier proceeded through gritted teeth. 'So, what "custom of the sea" are you referring to, Orren?'

Orren stopped chewing his thumbnail for a moment and smiled at the thought of being able to illuminate something for his captain. 'Well… the one that says that you can eat them what's dead if it's a, er – *necessity*, sir.'

Crozier sighed. 'I see. And what you did to Lieutenant Little and Able Seaman Jerry was all part of that *necessity* too, was it?' Orren's reply was almost absentminded as he returned to what remained of his thumbnail. 'Ah, yeah, well… there you have me, sir.'

Crozier was finding it difficult not to fly across at Orren and beat him unconscious. What he really needed to do was to have Orren court-martialled in England, but he couldn't afford to let such a destructive force continue to walk among his people again. Of course, under the Admiralty's agreements with most civilised countries, the expedition was to be regarded as neutral, but, at that moment, they were under siege with the greatest adversary of all: the forces of nature. He, his men and his ships were being attacked constantly – by the day, by the hour. He couldn't afford to lose even one more man, but with Orren, he was more than willing to make the sacrifice. They were at war and he needed to invoke the Articles. Orren accepted his death sentence by laughing in such a demonic manner that one of the men behind the rope pissed his pants with fear.

Regarding the rest of men who had gone with Orren, Crozier exonerated the majority but warned Able Seamen Tadman, Seeley and Hartnell that as the ringleaders, they would have to face the music when they returned and his report on them would depend entirely on their conduct from here on in. Naturally, any possibility of annuities for their polar service was gone – along with their pensions. He asked the remainder of the men to see it from the mutineers' points of view: they had evidently been guided by their exposure to extreme duress from a monster of a man. Crozier appealed to the remaining innocent men, as Christians, and as brothers together, to let bygones be bygones. But not for Orren – he was beyond forgiveness.

> *All the sons of Israel grumbled against Moses and Aaron; and the whole congregation said to them, 'Would that we had died in the land of Egypt! Or would that we had died in this wilderness! 'Why is the LORD bringing us into this land, to fall by the sword? Our wives and our little ones will become plunder; would it not be better for us to return to Egypt?' So they said to one another, 'Let us appoint a leader and return to Egypt.'*
>
> Numbers 14: 1

In the morning, the wind howled steadily from W.N.W., its lament whistling and rattling through *Terror*'s standing rigging. A line had been run up through a block on the main mast and back down to the deck where all the assembled sailors now stood. On one end, a simple noose had been placed over Orren's head and on the other, every man who had mutinied with him was waiting for the order to pull. This was part retribution as well as a show of their commitment to the men they had let down.

Crozier read a passage from the Book of Numbers about having faith in leadership in order to dispel fears. After closing the Book he asked Orren if he had anything to say. As seemed to have become his custom, Orren grimaced as he pulled at some phlegm at the back of his throat before spitting it out through twisted lips – only for the wind to catch it and swing it all round the side of his face. He shook his head sardonically as he grumbled, 'Just not my day, is it?' On Crozier's nod the blankets were removed from the defaulter's shoulders. Orren began to shiver so violently that he almost seemed vulnerable for a moment – before quickly rallying and raising his face from the deck to look every man in the eye again. He nodded his head slowly as he sneered, 'Anyways… I hope you all choke on my flesh and break what's left of your teeth on my bones, you fackin' jellyfish.' Crozier looked to the sky as he shouted, 'Able Seaman Lawrence!' Lozzer appeared and knuckled his head, 'Sir?'

'You'll take the lead on Orren's line please.' Lozzer took up his position on the line. Without taking his eyes off Orren, he spat on his hands and shouted, 'Right lads, take up the slack!' As the sailors pulled softly, the knot behind Orren's left ear started to rise, causing his head to press down and to the right in a way that made the already contorted man even more gargoyle-like. Lozzer shouted out the cautionary part of the order to pull: 'One, two, three…'

Orren began to gasp and seethe like a snared wildcat as the rope tightened around his windpipe. Lozzer, without taking his eyes off Orren's, mouthed, '*Hiraeth.*' Before letting his hand drop to his side. Then every man shouted together, 'Pull!'

Whether the block had frozen, or the deck too slippery, or the men's strength too pathetic, they could only manage to lift a bucking and choking Orren as far off the deck as the tips of his toes so that he appeared to dance a last Jig of the Ship, mocking the men even in his death throes. Lozzer yelled again and they all pulled again but Orren's rope remained fast. Their weakness became his strength as the veins on his forehead and neck bulged as he tried to utter something past the very tongue that was now choking him. Perhaps it was the last of his rage, or even a plea as he bore down at his executioners through devilish eyes that were beginning to turn red with their bursting blood vessels.

The rest of the men, seeing their shipmates struggling on the line flew to it for as many as the rope's length would allow. Those who couldn't touch rope, pulled at the shoulders of their brothers. With every hand bound on together they pulled a wildly kicking and twisting Orren right up to the yard in lusty jerks until the rope on Orren's noose jammed at the block and the men could pull him no more. The knot tightened further so that the snap of his neck could be felt on the line. All the rage that had propelled and governed him in life had now left him limp, quiet and lifeless. With his bitter end belayed, William Orren's body swayed along with a wind that seemed to sing his lonely requiem.

The Mess Deck

CROZIER AND HIS PEOPLE WERE about to eat together. Since they were on the last of the meat, he felt that equity and transparency in everything regarding food was the only way to ensure that every man was certain that they were getting the same as the next man. Each day both ships would come together for their only meal at three o'clock with the exception of hot chocolate for breakfast in an attempt to muffle the screaming pain of their hunger. The officers and men all messed together, but as leaders, Crozier had insisted that his officers were always served last. But now, as the officers waited their turn, they tried not to appear too mortified at the sight of their almost skeletal men queuing for the mere whits that represented their sustenance. Crozier felt utterly wretched and ashamed at his inability to do more for his starving people, who, with their uniform of shocking scorbutic sores, tottered about with a dismal, lachrymal air about them like exhausted children whose every effort seemed insurmountable.

As the sailors held out their plates, tins and cups with feeble hands, Diggle would carefully place tiny, scrupulously apportioned morsels in or onto their motley vessels. There were the occasional squabbles regarding imagined inconsistency but it rarely came to anything as the men were either too withered to care or too tired to persist. Once they were served their food, the men usually ate within their knots of friendship but those who had followed Orren back onto *Erebus* had chosen to disassociate themselves from their past treachery by avoiding each other. Instead, they ingratiated themselves on any group that would tolerate them. But even though the other men had outwardly allowed them to return to the fold, it wasn't the same. After all, it was only human to harbour suspicious thoughts that questioned how they could have deserted their friends – only to then eat the flesh of their very own. Not because they were disgusted or morally troubled, but because they knew that sooner or later it would be their turn to adopt the *custom of the sea* in one way or the other.

One of the older hands, AB Leys, dropped his tin plate and it clattered and spun on the deck like a dinner gong. Instead of picking it up, he could only stare with his chin trembling – utterly incapable of any sort of decision. All eyes went to the spare food that now settled on the deck's planks. Young Davy Young, seeing the slavering look appear on people's faces had the self-possession to throw himself down on his knees before anyone else could and frantically scooped what he could back onto Leys's plate with his spoon. The spoon wasn't helpful enough so the boy used his filthy black fingers to return every last scrap to Leys's plate. Straightening up again with the plate in his hands, Davy could see that the entire mess deck had become silent; every deep-set beady eye now boring into him. He was unsure whether they were going to riot for their share of the spoils or beat a young whippersnapper whom they could assume was about to brazenly steal the provisions of another man. Davy quickly felt the urge to clarify his intentions so grabbed the stick-thin arm of the Scottish stoker and led him to a nearby table. From there, he tenderly fed the shrunken sailor using a monogrammed silver dessert spoon. The scene took on the appearance of a lamb being ladled gruel by an orphan, one morsel at a time. Tears ran over Leys's bony cheekbones before disappearing again into his thin, grimy beard. As the young lad spooned him his food, he confided, 'I wasn't gonna eat it, Leysie, honest!'

The rest of the men returned to diligently scraping away at their own bits of gristle.

Lozzer, perhaps unintentionally, superseded the sound of rattling plates with a belch that had a timbre and resonance that was rich and impressive before he complained good-naturedly, 'Diggers, that was shite, that was, mate – gonnows, you ought to be ashamed of yerself!'

Yet again, Diggle found himself shrugging. 'Well, lads, I'm only as good as the ingredients I'm given to work with… I keep telling you this.'

Some of the men laughed and jeered and Cornelius Hickey couldn't help but add to the accusations. 'Yeah, but even if you was just handing out fresh, juicy apples you'd turn 'em to shite, Diggle.'

'Oi, oi, young Cornelius – we all turn food into shite eventually.'

One or two sailors *hur-hurred* to themselves as if reminiscing over some other, more carefree times. Sergeant Tozer joined the banter.

'Yeah, but that's usually not before it's been consumed, Diggle. Stripe me if you wouldn't turn a nice, crusty Cornish pasty into shite.'

Then one or two others, who began to salivate over the thought of crunching into a pasty, trotted into the baiting of Diggle like hyenas.

'Yeah, Diggle – Cornish pasties!'

Joe felt the need to have a go too. 'You'd turn a nice juicy steak with all the fixin's into shite.'

Then everyone joined in. 'Nice juicy steak!'

At the officers' table, Fitzjames was enjoying the repartee immensely and couldn't help himself: 'Or a spicy kedgeree from Simpson's?'

Understandably, this stumped everyone and they all simmered down – some even groaned. Crozier sighed and shook his head before attempting to salvage the moment. 'All right – how about a full Irish breakfast then?'

The heading returned but with adjustments: 'Full ENGLISH breakfast!'

Diggle joined in looking incredibly optimistic. 'With sausages made with my lovely unicorn recipe?'

Everyone laughed and swore at Diggle and some even threw their empty tinnies at him. Then there was another pause before Young Davy Young got things started again as he could barely talk for giggling. 'Diggle, you'd… you'd turn ginger beer into shite.'

Most felt the need to also correct the young lad – 'BEER!'

Old McDonald stood on a bench and gnashed at the air like a very convincing toothless rodent of some sort. 'The crotch out of a low-flying seagull.'

By this time, everyone roared back, 'The crotch out of a low-flying seagull!'

But then Lozzer piped up, 'What about Orren? At least you can't spoil 'im, can you, Diggers?'

Instantly, any joy was lost. No one repeated this last suggestion and the deck turned silent. Young Davy thought to say something, but luckily Joe held him down by the elbow. Lozzer held up his hands. 'Well, sooner or laters we're gunneraffto – ain't we, lads… sirs?'

During Orren's own defence, he had cited the custom of the sea and he had made a very good point about using this unwritten understanding – albeit to suit his own wicked agenda. Most sailors had heard of the custom and, over the years, it had fuelled endless nights of lively debate over that particular conundrum: what they would do if they were adrift and starving in a rudderless lifeboat caught in the Sargasso's gyre or shipwrecked on a coral atoll in the South Pacific? Most men, with rum-fuelled exultation, would swear they would bare their breast upon their honour, that they would gladly die as flesh for their brothers, but never, ever stoop to living disgracefully off their brothers' flesh. That was what they would all say. It would be a noble gesture, but most knew that it was probably a promise that was as empty as their stomachs were at that moment. And in any case, starvation came with its own flawless logic: if it was honourable to offer one's flesh to one's brothers, then why wouldn't it be honourable to accept that noble sacrifice from them? Regardless, starvation would always be the very embodiment of tantalisation and that no man really knew what he was capable of resisting in such a terrible predicament – until it became a necessity. *Living honourably*: the reality was that only one of those two words was compatible with the act of cannibalism.

Erebus Bay

THE SUMMER OF 1849 ARRIVED exceptionally late, but finally, with the temperature's rise and the aid of a vintage squall from the N.E, the ice had begrudgingly relented and began to loosen its grip on *Terror* and *Erebus*. At one point, the storm even brought with it two passenger pigeons that must have been blown off course from Greenland. In an attempt to rest, one of the birds managed to grapnel itself onto one of the ship's spars whilst the other just couldn't quite find any purchase as it pitched and yawed in its battle against the wind. Osmer, bracing himself on the deck below, used the spokes of the ship's wheel to rest his shotgun as he aimed off: waiting in ambush for the other bird to settle on the spar. But just as Osmer was taking up the pressure on his trigger, the poor creature was snatched away again by the wind. The purser swore to himself. He could have still taken the one bird that remained on the spar but didn't quite have the heart. In the end, the wind decided the pigeon's fate as the bird relinquished its grip on its perch – hopefully to catch up with its mate. Osmer smiled as he muttered to himself, 'Flock together, feather brains.'

The storm blew itself out after three days, and in the aftermath of its tumult the sea ice had cleared sufficiently so that the ships' rudders could be lowered onto their pintles once again. In their feeble state, the men who had been too weak to even haul a man up to the gallows had to now swing for all they were worth at the heavy flywheels of the Massey bilge pumps just to keep

Terror and *Erebus* afloat. The decks were cleared above, whilst below the ship's stokers blew life back into the steam boxes of their engines' cold, black hearts so that they throbbed once more beneath the feet of their captains.

With an eerie calm that seemed to goad Crozier into taking his next move, *Terror* and *Erebus* steamed lethargically through the various groaning, cracking ice leads as the engines wheezed and clanked correspondingly with their spark-flecked puffs of black smoke. The ships ground their way towards Erebus Bay but after forty-six miles, the ice conspired to hold them once again, forcing the ships to be stood off the bay as they waited for the next favourable movement of their captor. At the very least it was a relief to be out of the savage gales of Victoria Strait.

Crozier had needed to rebalance the ship's lists, so Petty Officer Diggle had been seconded to *Erebus* with POs Armitage and Gibson taking over his duties aboard *Terror*. At mealtimes, the two stewards had, on Sir John's insistence, always worn their smart stewards' uniforms complete with mess waistcoats and silk neckerchiefs and this had evidently been a hard habit to break – whether out on the ice or up a mast, they always brought a touch of eccentric finesse with them. Crozier in particular appreciated their smartness; he thought it brought a necessary dignity to a galley that couldn't possibly have needed it more. At mealtimes the rest of the shaking, haggard hands would queue in the galley for their food like old beggars but Armitage and Gibson, though never particularly chatty or familiar, just quietly and efficiently served the men their food.

On the day before the ice let them go, Gibson placed a copper dixie gently on the servery with a reverence and care that was touching – not particularly for Orren, but more for the men who, in feeding from his body, were about to consume something of themselves forever.

The chatter died down. The new men who hadn't tasted proper food for over a month attempted to be blithe at first, but ultimately, they couldn't help but gawp involuntarily at the cooking vessel with a mixture of morbid fascination and dread. PO Armitage removed the lid without his usual proud flourish to reveal a pretty routine-looking stew bubbling from within. One or two of the men crossed themselves, whilst others merely stared at their feet. Another sailor smartly left the deck, and over the heads of the quietly waiting men, they could follow the sound of his hasty progression towards the ship's side.

As every hand came forward to collect small ladle-loads with their plates they then took their seats around a collection of tables that had been laid out together, communally. Once seated, they waited quietly for everyone to be served. As was the custom, the officers were expected to lead from the front in every situation but when dining, they hung back to ensure that the men were fed first. To a morsel, Armitage and Gibson had exercised excellent portion control by finely mincing the meat. Eventually, Crozier was served his food and rested his forehead upon his knitted knuckles. The men, seeing he was about to say grace, piped down to let their silence speak for them as their captain prayed.

'For what we are about to receive... may God please forgive us.'

The men's amen was solemn and quiet. As they took their first mouthfuls, the taste of proper food had come as a shock to them and any reservations they had about eating another matelots' flesh rapidly dissipated. Within a moment or two, the slow, uncertain scrapings escalated into a noisy rattling and slurping as the men filled their shrunken stomachs with Able Seaman Orren.

Those who had mutinied privately relished their shipmates joining them in their dreadful coven of men who had eaten the flesh of their brothers. Some had thought it like the tougher cuts of pork, whilst others were reminded of goat. One even thought it was comparable to older venison, but they had their doubts as to the aficionado's claims to have ever tasted the original.

※

The ice was on the move again, shunting to the S.W. to leave them with no option but to go along with it. This meant that one of the ships had the potential to bend to the west if they used the currents well. They would also have to make the most of what little sail they could put out and burn what little fuel they had and, if fortune was smiling, they could inch their way towards the Beaufort Sea and perhaps even onward towards the Bering Strait where they had a far better chance of meeting up with another ship.

Fitzjames and Crozier poured over their charts together as they attempted to work out the logistics of this latest plan.

'It should be you who heads west, James… see what you can do there. Blanky reckons it'll be clear for a while and, who knows, perhaps you'll even make the Beaufort Sea?'

Fitzjames tried to catch Crozier's eye but his captain remained far too engrossed in the chart.

'But, er, what will you do, sir?'

'The Dunder Bay lads… I'll be going back for the Dunder Bay lads.'

Crozier picked up a set of dividers and rested his thumb on the points, as if he was testing their truth via their sharpness. 'We'll transfer the bulk of the coal over to you, James. I just need to keep enough to get me to Dunder Bay. If the ice is clear there, I'll continue south – sail her as close to the Back's River as I can…' He opened his dividers between Dunder Bay and along the western edge of King William's as far as Chantrey Inlet before placing his points on the chart's scale. He puffed his lip before thinking aloud: 'A hundred and eighteen miles… if we can avoid covering that overland, it'll make all the difference.'

Crozier felt his leg stiffening up again so he dragged up the nearest chair so that he could sit down heavily in it. He rubbed his eyes and stared somewhat blankly at Fitzjames for a moment or two before muttering, 'Sorry, James.'

'Sorry, sir? What on earth for?'

'For thinking you were a bit of a wee gobshite…'

Fitzjames grimaced awkwardly as he tried to make light of Crozier's comments. 'Ah, yes, well – there, you will not be the first, sir; and I'm fairly certain you won't be the last.'

Crozier allowed himself to catch the eye of the younger officer briefly. 'Reckon we all come with our prejudices and, well, I thought I had you all marked out, but your actions when *Comet* went down… I tell you, it was one of the most selfless things I've ever seen. I've mentioned it in the log, by the way.'

Fitzjames made an attempt to shrug it off. 'Thank you, Francis… though, in reality, I think I probably slipped… thought, whilst I was wet, I'd see if I could make myself useful for a change.'

Crozier looked over at the chart again and frowned. 'Hmm…' It was unclear whether he was dismissing Fitzjames's quip or was just contemplating the topography. Crozier rose stiffly and faced Fitzjames. For a moment, Fitzjames wasn't sure what to do until Crozier held out his trembling hand. 'It's been an honour to have sailed with you, James.'

Fitzjames took Crozier's hand and felt it steady itself like a rock as soon as the two men gripped. For some reason, Fitzjames found that the warmth and strength in Crozier's hand felt surprisingly assuring, as if this gruff, powerful, modest man had finally taken him into his confidence for the first time.

Fitzjames bowed his head a little. 'The honour has been entirely mine, sir.'

For the next day and a half, the two captains worked out various contingencies and the finer details of their new instructions as the men readied both ships for putting to sail again as best they could. They transhipped the lion's share of the coal onto *Erebus* as the two ships built up their steam before finally sailing off together. Per the plan, they rounded Gore's Peninsula and *Terror*

peeled off to port as *Erebus* carried on westwards. As the two sister ships parted company, every man hung off the shrouds to bid farewell – taking it in turns to give each other three cheers for all they were worth.

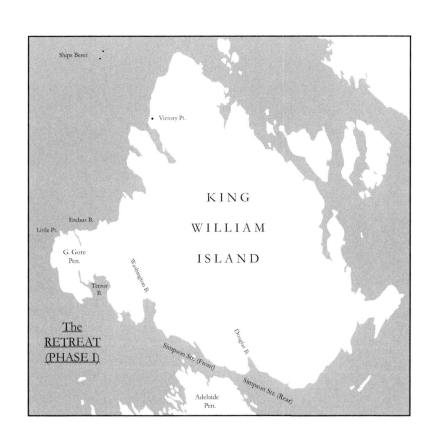

Ships Beset

Victory Pt.

Erebus B.

Little Pt.

G. Gore
Pen.

Terror
B.

KING

WILLIAM

ISLAND

Washington B.

Douglas B.

The
RETREAT
(PHASE I)

Simpson Str. (Front)

Simpson Str. (Rear)

Adelaide
Pen.

Dunder Bay

And the bay was white with silent light
Till rising from the same,
Full many shapes, that shadows were,
In crimson colours came.
A little distance from the prow
Those crimson shadows were:
I turn'd my eyes upon the deck–
O Christ! What I saw there!

Rime of the Ancient Mariner, Samuel Taylor Coleridge

It had been nine weeks since the men of Creek Camp had said their farewells to Crozier's party. So much had changed since then. So many men lost. Some had gone almost immediately but then, just as the surgeon was about to give up, so many of the men rallied directly after their ability to cook had expired. Dr McDonald had been utterly stumped at first but then he made the connection after the fuel for their cooking stoves had run out and they had resorted to serving the men's meat allowance raw. From that moment, the men's symptoms of scurvy seemed to improve – almost overnight.

Since 1834 the Royal Navy had always prescribed cooking food thoroughly in order to kill any bacteria. This had been prompted by the discovery of the trichinella roundworm first found in muscle tissue by a young student at St Bart's called

James Paget. He then found that cooking the hell out of the meat killed all the bacteria – which was all well and good when it came to halting the vector of parasites, but when it came to cooking meat, the vector of any ascorbate value was also unwittingly halted.

When some of the others questioned McDonald's wisdom about eating raw food, he had reminded everyone that Aggie had never eaten a piece of cooked meat in her life before she met them and it seemed remarkable that she and her people were in such rude health – and all without a pickled vegetable or chunk of salted pork in sight.

Now, at the end of August, the sea ice, though far from absent, had broken up so that much of it in their harbour had melted and turned into candle ice that shoved itself onto the beach in great shards that tinkled like chimes with each incoming wave. With the newly exposed sea, they had even been able to fish properly and supplement their diets with the odd char. But now, they couldn't believe their eyes: pushing through the loose sea ice that had been trapped in their bay was HMS *Terror*.

With clicking bones and aching joints, the men rose from their tents and cheered deliriously at the glorious sight of *Terror*. Some wept as they listened to the candle ice clacking off her ironclad bow, whilst others smiled and laughed with mouths that bled from cracking lips.

Dr McDonald had *Dunder* made ready and shoved off from the beach to meet the ship. They didn't even wait for *Terror*'s anchor to be dropped before tying up alongside and clambering up her ladders. Once on deck though, the doctor and his men were aghast at how much Crozier and his men had changed since the last time they saw them: captain and crew were ravaged by scurvy. Their every contour laid testimony to their suffering with missing teeth and festering open sores or black lesions everywhere else. Their grey, sooty skins were so tightly stretched that the fissures of their bones that lay beneath could be clearly seen and even heard with their every movement. The men who had lost fingers to the cold shuffled around with black hands painfully held up as if in constant prayer, and along with their missing teeth, it gave them the pitiful gurn of cadavers-in-waiting. But it was their eyes that really would have broken the heart of any witness: the glassy eyes that pleadingly flashed and flickered from the backs of their sockets – guilt-ridden eyes that begged to be forgiven for all the terrible things they had seen and that yearned to see no more.

As the ship's surgeon and the captain saluted each other on deck, it was all McDonald could do to stop himself from weeping with joy at the sight of his captain. During their separate ordeals, every man had been burdened with the dark, terrible secrets that were impossible to justify to outsiders. But, on seeing the monstrously filled kettles in *Terror*'s galley, McDonald breathed a sigh of relief as he saw that they had all become brothers bonded by necessity; bonded by a savage will to stay alive.

With nineteen remaining souls from Dunder Bay and thirty-seven on *Terror* the total remaining hands numbered fifty-six – plus the forty-two souls who were heading west on *Erebus*.

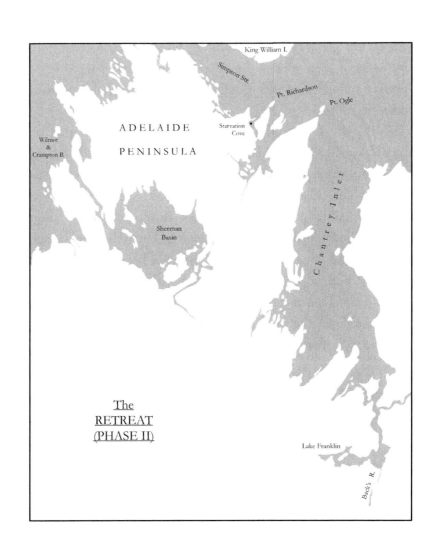

King William I.

Simpson Str.

Pt. Richardson

Pt. Ogle

ADELAIDE

Starvation
Cove

PENINSULA

Wilmot
&
Crampton B.

Chantrey Inlet

Sherman
Basin

The
RETREAT
(PHASE II)

Lake Franklin

Back's R.

Storis Passage

FITZJAMES AND HIS CREW HAD made glacial progress as they zig-zagged with the leads shifting past the Royal Geographicals, as the islands were known. When they weren't lurching from rocks or massive bergy bits, unavoidable growlers would slam up against *Erebus*'s sides – often rocking her to her very keelson. At one point, a jag the size of a carriage screeched against the hull with such force that the sailors thought they might be stove. With bilge pumps constantly manned, the caulkers worked tirelessly as they stemmed plank fountains whilst the sweating stokers spaded coal into the inferno. Six hundred miles… eighty per day… they could make the Beaufort Sea in seven or eight days if the ice went along with their plans.

Then Fitzjames started to entertain a wild notion that started to flicker in his mind: perhaps they would make the Beaufort Sea after all? What if they could actually make it through? The honour of being the first through the Northwest Passage would be his. He bit his lip at the prospect of this seemingly unassailable quest that had defeated the greatest names of navigation for centuries. Could the glory finally belong to the forsaken child of a drunkard English diplomat and a South American whore? James Fitzjames, Bastard Mongrel: Conqueror of the Northwest Passage. He grinned to himself at his indulgence before turning to his helmsman: 'Quartermaster, new course… bearing, south-east by south.' After having to repeat himself to the confused helm, *Erebus* was swung to port and towards the ultimatum of their contingency plan: to meet Crozier and his men at Lake Franklin.

Terror Bay (Formerly Dunder Bay)

TO A MAN, NO ONE had escaped without being affected by the creeping, insidious grip of scurvy. Reduced in numbers and increasingly ravaged, most were far from well enough to move anywhere – particularly since the mercury had dropped. Crozier was appalled at how lacklustre he and his men had become. Even the most sanguine of characters would fly into the most terrible rages over the smallest matter, and it wasn't unusual to find the most stoic of men weeping quietly to themselves. In fact, the weeping had become so commonplace that it had almost become part of breathing. Crozier wasn't exempt either. He felt pain every time he moved. Every vein had become a stream of needles; every bone in his body felt like it was grinding with the next, penalising him for his every move.

He had tried to establish a busy but constructive routine for all his people, but they were all far too fatigued to do anything of any use. Those sent out fishing caught nothing and those who were sent out with guns and rifles returned with dependably empty bags (though, Pusser Osmer did once swear he had winged a vixen that seemed to have been wearing something that resembled a thin hoop around her neck).

Between the hunger and the scurvy, discipline had become something of an issue too as the men didn't seem to care about anything anymore. Without purpose, they had no respect and without respect they had no humour. They peevishly bickered with each other constantly. When in each other's company, they had nothing to talk about and the once effortless banter now seemed to be a lost art – whining became their only comfort. Long-since forsaken basic hygiene had added to their woes, with the inevitable outbreak of dysentery and the deaths of three more sailors who were swiftly put to use in the galley.

The men had reached a point where they no longer cared where the meat came from and they amused themselves by cynically speculating over its provenance: a steak from an Aberdeen Angus, the shoulder of Welsh lamb, or the cheap cuts for an Irish stew. Their reality though, in the cold light of day, was the pale meat of their starved brothers that contributed little towards the men's own nourishment.

Crozier's men needed to move on in every sense. Head south and pray for some hunting and, who knows, perhaps even dare to entertain the possibility of rescue. Crozier would have been surprised if no one had been sent out to look for them after three years without word from Sir John Franklin. He knew with certainty that James Ross would already be en route, and he also knew that the man would be like a dog with a bone. He wished to God that Franklin had allowed him to go back and build cairns back at Cape Walker. Crozier assumed that any search parties, as they had done, would make their way as far west as the ice would allow on Barrow Strait and in the inevitability of them getting caught there, the likelihood would be that they would find a safe harbour in which to overwinter. From here it would seem natural to send out sledging parties – searching north or south. If north, perhaps they would find the graves they had dug at Beechey Island? If south, perhaps they too would find Peel Sound as they had done? But in the likelihood of them missing the latter, Prince Regent would seem logical recourse? The other totally different prong of any searches would be for an overland party sent up from Hudson's Bay. Crozier didn't dare imagine the luxury of coordinated searches from both directions.

From what he had seen of the ice, he knew that any parties from the north would have been lucky to make Port Leopold before the ice would have persuaded them into overwintering there. Any attempts from Crozier and Fitzjames to sail north would have been against the floes and therefore hopeless.

The truth was that even if they had been able to shake hands with such rescuers, they wouldn't have been able to do much for he and his starving, scorbutic men – perhaps drop them some food to buy them some more time, but very little else. Or per-haps send for more parties in the hope that they would still be alive by the time they returned? No, if they had any hope at all it would have to be pinned on a rescue from the south – most likely from Hudson's Bay. He felt that his plan to head to Back's River still had more *probables* than *perhapses*.

It had become evident to Crozier that they had been very unluckily caught in a plague of nothingness: a famine that had been formed by two abnormally short summers, and because of this, the animals had obviously forsaken them too. So all his hopes were again pinned on the likelihood of the wildlife retreat-ing south. Surely something lived there, somewhere, somehow – whether it was a deer, or a bird, or even a bloody fish. Anything that his men could eat that wasn't one of their own species. For this to happen they had to haul themselves out of this awful 'Land Without' and head south.

It was Dr McDonald who thoughtfully suggested that they rename Dunder Bay after their heroic ship, rather than a small boat named after a reindeer. Crozier thought it far more fitting.

Storis Passage

THOUGH IT WAS STILL LATE summer according to the calendar, that didn't stop *Erebus*'s thermometers from declaring -19°. The northeaster picked up with a vengeance as the ice pushed onwards to the west as they toiled through icy spindrift for three frightening, blood-draining days. Blue-tinged boulders started to stack up around the little islands, spits and shoals. The soundings became cause for concern, with the ship's keel complaining bitterly against rock on three occasions. The readings would jump from thirty fathoms to eight and then back again and the smooth shingle bottom would give way to jagged rock. Many breakers could be seen crashing over various sandbars and dark jags, causing the men up in the lookouts to wave their arms from port to starboard like panicking cormorants. Fitzjames eventually stood *Erebus* in Wilmot and Crampton Bay where she sounded at around fourteen fathoms. Here, he guessed, most of the more menacing icebergs would run themselves aground before they could do any harm to his ship. Who knows, maybe they would even help protect her until their return someday?

As they stood off in the rocky bay, the same wind that brought them there was now fetching ice – enough of it so that within the space of four hours of dropping *Erebus*'s best bower they were completely surrounded by loose ice. Overnight, the temperature dropped so severely that the telltale pancake ice began to form once more. Fitzjames started the preparations for remounting their boats on their sledges so that they could continue on their

same bearing on foot: straight down the inlet until they struck
Lake Franklin.

At thirty-two miles long and two miles wide, Franklin was
roughly the same size and shape as Lake Zurich and from its
middle flowed the estuary of the Back's River. The whisper was
that George Back teasingly named it after his fellow Midshipman
as it was 'rather wet, got in the way and was going nowhere fast'.

It was agreed with Crozier and Fitzjames that, regardless,
whoever arrived at the lake first would wait one week for the
other party. If the weather was particularly bad, they would wait
a further week. And if the other party still didn't show after that,
they were to assume they were not joining them. With this sad
realisation they were to push on towards the first Hudson's Bay
Company outpost they could find via Repulse Bay. But long
before that, Fitzjames prayed that they could find something to
shoot or catch along the way.

Regroup

Wilmot and Crampton Bay

IT TOOK JUST TWO DAYS for the ice to set about the ships and hold them fast once more. Though *Erebus* and *Terror* were less than forty miles apart, they were bonded together in the steely clutches of the same ice. Fitzjames and his men set about getting *Prancer* and *Dasher* ready to leave *Erebus* as well as making arrangements for the best possible future that could be expected for her.

On deserting his ship once again, Fitzjames had the heavy chains passed twice around the vessel 'a midships' so that when the ice would eventually nip her so hard that the turpentine would seep out of her timbers, she could relent to the seawater and be sent to the bottom straight and true. Once there, she would be protected from the brutal clutches of the surface's powers that would otherwise conspire to reduce her to matchwood. This was done in the vague hope that she might one day be raised again from the darkest of places between the earth and Hades: the very place that she was named after – Erebus.

Irving Islands

CROZIER HAD MADE SIMILAR ARRANGEMENTS for *Terror* before abandoning her for the second time. He and his thirty-four hands had hauled themselves and their sledges as far as a tiny set of dolostone islands that did nothing more than poke up through the wreckage of candle ice like giant monks' tonsures. Crozier had marked them on his chart as the Irving Islands and whilst there, he had finally relented to putting their dog down.

After the wolf attack, poor Neptune's shoulder wound had festered. He had become pitifully lame. Over the years, Old Nep had become part of the crew in almost every way and he was even good at pulling. On so many occasions the demands to slaughter Neptune had been overwhelming but they could never bring themselves to do it. The dog came to be regarded as a mascot for them all collectively whilst individually, he was everyone's best friend. Even with Graham Gore and his dead people back at Victory Point, Neptune had won the undying respect of the men after he had been prepared to starve rather than resort to living on their dead bodies. In short, Neptune had come to represent the nub of what they hoped remained within themselves: selflessness. Neptune had become the watchdog of their own humanity.

Corporal Firemark had put himself forward for the task because he wanted to ease the evident agony his sergeant was in. But Tozer wouldn't hear of it. As the rest of the sailors caught their breaths and ached, they knew that the sergeant was about to take their dog for the walk that would be his last. Sergeant Tozer clucked his cheek a couple of times and Neptune lifted his heavy head off his front paws as he wagged his tail instinctively; but the dog could sense that something wasn't quite right. Perhaps it was because there would usually be some form of eye contact, but not today. As Neptune's small, chocolaty eyes watched the sergeant walking away from him he was waiting for the next instruction. 'Nep... come on, boy.' The dog stiffly pushed himself up and attempted a trot but all he could achieve was a doleful limp after Tozer who was now leading him towards a couple of huge boulders. Throughout, the men continued chatting as if nothing was happening. As if moaning about cold feet, fantasising about food portions or even coughing could convincingly hide the fact that their hearts were about to break. As the dog and his master disappeared out of view, the chat ran out. Most of the men seemed to brace themselves for the brief whelp after Sergeant Tozer's rifle butt would be brought down smartly onto Neptune's ear. No one could think of anything to say that would block out the sound of their great dog's life being snuffed out, but then, as the sergeant's crunching footsteps halted round the other side of the boulders, PO Armitage started to sing with a voice that had once been fine. Those of the men who were still capable of song, joined in to lend a little forza to the PO's efforts:

Rock of Ages, cleft for me,
Let me hide myself in Thee;
Let the water and the blood,
From Thy wounded side which flowed,
Be of sin the double cure,
Save from wrath and make me pure.

De Haven Island

A proud man is the devil's throne and the idle man, his pillow.

George Swinnock (1627–1673)

Fitzjames and his men found themselves in a frozen archipelago that looked like it had once been spall blown out of the Sherman Inlet like a harpooned whale. This particular 'gutter' was a mile across at its widest and ran diagonally through the Adelaide Peninsula. At the Peninsula's heart lay the Sherman Basin, a relatively sheltered lake some twenty-five miles or so across. Fitzjames would have dearly loved to sail over to her southernmost corner in *Erebus* but, with the water being fresh, the ice hadn't thawed that summer.

He had given his crew thirty days to pull for 160 miles down Sherman in order to converge with Crozier at Lake Franklin. This was a daunting undertaking by any measure, but he had felt somewhat charmed compared to Crozier's lot as he and his men would have to pull an extra forty miles along the coastline of King William and still need to cross the treacherous waterway at Simpson Strait.

From Wilmot and Crampton Bay, *Erebus*'s sailors had to pull themselves over the rotten ice and into the inlet that the nor'easter had packed tightly there. It had been a gruelling struggle to get their boats over the innumerable barricades of pressure ridges, but Fitzjames and his men had covered the fifteen miles from *Erebus* in two days. Ahead of them, a thick-looking weather front that had veered to the S.E. dared them to joust.

As the denser, colder air pushed the lighter air the men could feel the displacement in the form of cold wind – gales of it. Once the tents had gone up on the otherwise empty little island, AB John 'Stickie' Stickland, one of the younger hands from Portsmouth, had become so snow-blind that his swollen eyes had closed like a boxer's so he was treated with a drop or two of laudanum in each eye and left to sleep it off with a damp rag over his face. Before drifting off, he smiled pleasantly as Goodsir tended to him.

'So, do you think there's food in heaven, sir?'

'Heaven?'

'Aye, sir.'

'Scientifically speaking, I'm not too sure about heaven, Stickland. But, er, if there was such a thing, conceptually speaking, I should imagine that there would be ample provisions.'

'And what about hell, sir – would there be food there?'

'Er, again, I'm not so sure about hell either, but if such a place did exist, I think it would probably be safe to assume that there, the damned would be condemned to eternal hunger.'

Stickland grinned. 'So, a little bit like this place then, sir?'

The next morning, the rag remained entirely undisturbed and when Stickie was unable to be roused, the rag was peeled back to reveal no sign of the swelling – just the angelic, smiling face of a lad who had evidently managed to find the only way out of hell.

Once Diggle had drained the blood, Stickie's limbs and head were removed before being swaddled in cloth. These being the more transportable cuts, they would provide the crew with sustenance along the way; even the feet were left in the boots as a means of preservation for them. The offal and ribs were eaten straight away with an almost feverish relish. Dignity had no place here – either for the remains of the deceased or those who were left – and no thought of the person they were eating was given. All they could see was a means of staying alive whilst those who remained knew that this was what would come of them all when it was their time. The only thing that perhaps gave pause for thought was the fact that none of them found the prospect to be dreadful.

Relatively satisfied, and with a gap in the weather before the storm came, Fitzjames had his teams ready to pull further towards their goal and perhaps gain themselves a little distance from what they had just committed – as if physically walking away from their iniquity somehow absolved them.

Just as the men had struck camp, Fitzjames could see some of the hands muttering among each other and could sense something brewing among them. He felt the need to get them back to pulling as quickly as possible in order to distract them from whatever dark thoughts they were now harbouring. The commander carried out a last inspection and chivvied them along. 'Right, boys, let us away.'

Tadman, who had been struggling to lift a little oil cask into the boat, let it drop onto the snow. He turned with back still hunched and fingers still clutching a cask that was no longer held by them. His face belonged to a man at his wits' end.

'Er... Boys? Fackin' *boys*?' The quaking rage in his voice made most of the men stop what they were doing.

'Most of us have enough ink on our skins to rewrite the bleedin' Bible... We got enough hairs on our arses to knit an Afghanistanny rug... and you – you have the brass-necked temerity to call us fackin' boys!'

Fitzjames, having never faced such insubordination in all his life, was at a loss.

'I, er, Tadman, watch your mouth, man!'

To every man's astonishment, Tadman backhanded his captain with a shocking swiftness that no one saw coming – none more so than Fitzjames as he fell backwards onto the ice. Tadman reached into the boat from where he'd been stowing the cask and

produced a long-handled snow knife as he sneered, 'No, sir –
you watch yours!' Pointing the knife with an outstretched arm
as if there was any need to fend off the helpless Fitzjames, he
started to weep. 'There, I've just condemned myself to death. But
at least it'll be a death of my own choosing… anyone gunna join
me, lads?'

There was a voice from the crowd. 'Aye, I'll join you all right,
Tadman – with this…'

Joe withdrew his Bowie knife from its belt. Tadman shook his
head and spat.

'Christ's sake, Blackie – whose side you on?'

'Sides? I thought we were all in this together.'

Tadman held Joe's gaze with the widest grin he could muster
– before Hartnell and Seeley jumped the American. Joe lost his
knife and as he bent to retrieve it, both men swung off him like
dogs on a bear. Tadman put an end to the matter by kicking the
big man in the jaw so hard that he could taste sparks. Before
Joe could find his feet again he felt the cold steel of Tommy's
stolen surgical blade at his jugular as he almost pleaded with him
in a whisper, 'Bloody well leave it, big man, I'm serious.' The
American gave up on his knife and the two Hop Pickers started
wading into him with their boots. Young Davy tried to intervene
but was held back by Goodsir and one or two of the wiser hands.
Tadman sneered at his men's success as he picked up the knife
and admired it, turning to see both sides of the blade as he said,
'There's always gonna be two sides when it comes to surviving,
boy – you just have to make sure you choose the right one.'

After a moment, the dangerous sound of a pistol being cocked
shattered the silence. Pusser Osmer emerged from the crowd
with a service pistol levelled at Tadman's guts.

'Then… you've bloody well chosen the wrong one, Tadman.'

Though the pusser held the weapon shakily, his resolve was
rock steady. Hartnell and Seeley looked to their leader uncertainly for the next move. 'What do we do, Tadders?' Tadman

searched the faces of the rest of the tired, spent men for approval but their cold, impassive faces told him otherwise as he beseeched them to join him. 'Lads?'

The rest of the men seemed to close in on the gang, prompting Tadman to continue pleading, 'Come on, lads! The ice is going to thaw soon, and we can be sailors again… we're not going to make it with this pulling lark… we're better off snuffing it in our ship. Not out here on the bastard ice.'

Some sailors shook their heads grimly and there were calls for the dissenters to give it up. Seeley and Hartnell, seeing the numbers were plainly against them came away from the big Nova Scotian panting like dogs. Tadman sniffed, before letting Joe's knife slip through his fingers and stick into the ice. Fitzjames, getting back on his feet and dusting off the ice and snow, nodded his appreciation to the pusser before taking the pistol from his shaking hands and levelling it at Tadman's forehead.

'Tadman… Able Seaman Tadman, under the Mutiny Act, for conduct prejudicial to good order and discipline whilst at sea, I sentence you. Do you accept my award?'

Tadman sucked his teeth as Fitzjames's right eye lined up perfectly through his iron sights and onto the middle of his own. Seeley and Hartnell were shoved up next to him. The officer repeated himself – this time with an unmistakably final conviction. 'Do you accept my award, Tadman?'

Tadman winced. 'Aye, sir – I accept your award, sir.'

Fitzjames remained unflinching with his pistol aimed. 'Very well, Tadman – start walking.'

Tadman looked around uncertainly. 'Walk? Where to, sir?'

'Well, you have chosen your side and now they are next to you… Why don't you all go to hell?'

Tadman turned to look behind him in the direction of *Erebus*. He grinned again as he turned back at the sailors: his former brothers.

'How does the saying go… misery loves company? Anyone else coming, lads?'

No one responded. Fitzjames wanted to put an end to any further incidents like this for once and for all so he caught the eyes of as many of his men as he could. 'If anyone does feel the need to follow these men, they are completely at liberty to do so, now…' No one moved.

Swiping off his filthy cap, Tadman sounded almost like a child as he said, 'But, sir, what about our allowance, like? What are we gonna do for food?'

'Well, I'm sure you'll be able to work something out among yourselves… perhaps you could draw straws?'

Tadman slid his cap back on and smiled again. 'Good luck, lads – see you when the thaw comes, eh?'

The three men started idly towards *Erebus* as if they were on an evening's mooch along the cobbled docks of Chatham. Fitzjames's men watched Tadman and the last of the Hop Pickers disappear into the loose snow as it swirled with the thickening wind. Without a word, the rest of the men turned back to their traces, slipped on their harnesses and waited for the word to pull.

With Fitzjames as their leader, the sailors may well have had no option but to stay with him, but none of the men could have possibly imagined what their loyalty meant to Commander Fitzjames at that moment.

Cape Herschel

Instruction addressed to Sir John Franklin (cont'd)…

*23. In the event of England becoming involved in
hostilities with any other power during your absence,
you are nevertheless clearly to understand that you
are not on any account to commit any hostile act
whatsoever, the expedition under your orders being
only intended for the purpose of discovery and science,
and it being the practice of all civilized nations to
consider vessels so employed as excluded from the
operations of war; and, confiding in this feeling, we
should trust that you would receive every assistance
from the ships or subjects of any foreign power which
you may fall in with; but special application to that
effect has been made to the respective governments.
Given under our hands, this 5th day of May 1845.*

(signed) Haddington
   G. Cockburn
   W. H. Gage

Sir John Franklin, K. C. H.
Captain of H.M.S. 'Erebus,' at Woolwich,
By command of their Lordships.
(signed) W. A. B. Hamilton

Terror's sledging crews clung to King William's coastline as it trended to the S.E. The men were dead on their feet as they passed the mouth of Washington Bay and as it was late, Crozier decided that they should make camp for the night off the ice. As they shuffled towards Cape Herschel on the far side it was Corporal Firemark who was able to see them ahead. At first, he thought they were reindeer skulking around the rocks. He turned to call his captain but Crozier was already at his shoulder. Extending his telescope as he quickened his step, Crozier scanned the rocks and could see instantly that they were not caribou but people. Of course, the Netsilik had seen them coming from afar like a shuffling trail of sick, coughing dogs and they were very reluctant to meet with what they assumed to be starving white men.

Instead, the Inuit waved their arms in a way to make it clear that the sailors were not welcome and they had withdrawn behind rocks to join their worried women and children who began to wail with fear. Crozier and his men made ready all their available weapons in case of surprise but as they rounded the promontory they could see an already vanquished encampment of *igluk* – by his estimate, enough to house a full dozen families. Feeling compromised, the men of the village had no option but to stand with their bows and their kavivak fishing spears in feeble readiness to protect their kin.

Crozier held up his hand to halt his own men before slowly slipping his shotgun off his shoulder and in a big, obvious gesture, he laid it down upon the ice. Firemark, on seeing this, began to follow suit as his captain calmly and quietly said, 'Corporal... fetch the treasure bag. Tell Sergeant Tozer to do nothing... steady now.'

Crozier, as seemed to be his custom whenever he encountered Inuit, went forward beating his chest slowly and almost chanting as the rest of his men stood about on the ice and caught their breath, '*Kabloonan! Kabloonan teyma Inueet...*'

As he got closer to them, he could see that far from their usual round, healthy outlooks they seemed much diminished. He stopped short by about fifty yards as any step further resulted in the Inuk slowly retreating. And then, the penny dropped. Crozier realised that he and his sailors must have looked terrifying, with their gaunt, bearded masks of starvation that were pierced with wild, baleful eyes. He also understood how they would be suspicious of any hungry strangers in such an awful time of famine – desperate men, capable of desperate acts. Crozier began his chant again, but this time, more softly: *Kabloonan teyma Inueet.*

As Firemark reappeared with the 'treasure', Crozier made another great display of carefully laying out the contents of the bag before him: buttons, beads, combs and any other indispensable knick-knacks – even his own silver spoon. Taking the book of verse from his breast pocket, he unwound the ribbon and laid Sir John's Guelphic Cross down with the rest of the gifts.

As the Inuit men gingerly edged forward with their bows half-drawn, Crozier rubbed his stomach theatrically and said the only words in Inuktitut he knew that referred to any sort of food: '*Took-took?... Neittuke?* Reindeer? ... Seal?'

But as more Inuit emerged from their hiding places and the women hushed their blood-curdling wails, Crozier was appalled to note that they were not much better off than themselves. He noticed an absence of elders, whom he presumed were the first to have fallen onto the ice. He also noticed an absence of dogs – those had probably gone the same way as the elders. Whether it was the wretchedness of leaving behind those loved ones they could no longer feed; or their own terrible pains of hunger; or burning their bridges with their dogs, they all seemed ghostlike and spent.

Soon, the rest of the village materialised to pick the treasure clean and as they did so, none of them took their eyes off the sailors. They too seemed shocked at what they were seeing: the normally strident, over-confident, over-fed Kabloonas reduced to nothing but envelopes of grey skin stretched over shuffling

bones. It wasn't hard for them to understand what the sailors
had been going through in the slightest but instead of pity there
was fear and their own overwhelming sense of preservation. They
had known only too well what desperate men could be driven to
do and, over generations, they had learned from lore what desperate white men had been capable of in the past.

It was Firemark who saw her first. She limped along with
the assistance of a long narwhal horn, which, at its head, had
a yoke that had been carved from the frontal part of the beast's
skull. This she tucked under her left armpit and with her right
arm extended she used it as a counterbalance as she hopped
her leg forward with surprising agility. Aggie scanned the men
desperately for her *anirniq* and when their mutual searches met,
she could barely believe what the ravages of hunger had done
to him. She barely recognised him and had to put a hand to her
mouth for a moment as Firemark ran to her. But then, as they
embraced, mewling could be heard. It came from under the
hood of Aggie's amauti. As Firemark carefully peeled it back, he
revealed within a pouch in the fur, a small child of around eight
months old sucking his tiny little thumb ravenously. Firemark
smoothed his filthy fingers through the baby's already thick
mop of hair and as its cries began to escalate, the corporal could
see that the entire right side of his face bore the same mark of
his own. He hugged them both and wept bittersweet tears that
froze into rime on his beard. Crozier joined them and as he saw
the sleeping *wane*, he put a hand on Firemark's shoulder. 'Oh…
so our tribe increases, Corporal.'

Crozier pulled his mitten off and went to stroke the child,
but then, seeing his own filthy, unsteady hand against the child's
pure skin, thought better of it. The baby began a sort of pitiful,
halting squall. Aggie used Firemark to help her onto the ice and
she took their naked boy out of his pouch, tucking him quickly
inside her parka where he latched onto her breast and began
to suckle desperately. The babe's nostrils flared as he sucked

pointlessly while his clear, sparkling little eyes filled and overran with tears before listlessly whimpering at the absence of milk – only to then start the process all over again. Aggie closed her eyes with the desperation of being unable to feed her own child. Firemark was desolate. He searched Crozier's eyes then shook Aggie's shoulders. 'We must be able to do something for him! God help us… sir – we must help him!'

Crozier seemed utterly lost for a moment or two before trudging back to where their two weapons lay and returning with them – laying them before Firemark and Aggie. 'I need to ask one more thing of you, Firemark… May I ask one more thing of you now?' Firemark looked searchingly into Crozier's pale eyes. Crozier unslung his cartridge bag and fished around for his powder, ball and shot. He buckled it up again and handed it all to Firemark.

'You'll remain here, Corporal – this is your family now. You must do all you can for them, do you understand?'

Firemark's words failed him, so he just nodded as Crozier continued. 'Thank you, lad – God bless you and your family.'

Crozier returned to his men and ordered that camp be made at a respectful distance away from the Inuit. He warned his men to let the Inuit be and briefed them not to entice the poor souls to steal from them by leaving anything unattended. But in the morning they found that the only things that had gone were the Inuit themselves – their footprints leading off landwards, to the east. Frightened by the shocking state of the sailors and confident in the knowledge that neither were in any position to help the other, they had abandoned their camp in the night, taking everything with them but for one thing: a meticulously wrapped seal.

Crozier took advantage of the weather and had his men strike camp themselves before moving off immediately after breakfast. He would have dearly loved to give his people the opportunity of a proper night's rest or two by occupying the relatively warm, comfortable igluk left by the Inuit, but he couldn't afford to waste another day's allowance on being hove-to when they really needed to be making headway.

The men had been particularly quiet during their morning's pull, so at lunch Crozier had insisted that hot chocolate was made for everyone. As was their custom, Dr McDonald and Crozier sat apart from the men. As the doctor tenderly swirled the scant remnants that lay at the bottom of his tinny, he couldn't help but notice that his captain was just staring into his own cup gloomily.

'Everything in order with your cocoa, sir?'

Without looking up from the abyss of his cup Crozier frowned. 'I'm glad they left us.'

'Who, sir?'

'The locals… Reminded me of how uncivilised we've become, you know?'

Not convinced that his cup had quite yielded every drop, McDonald held his tongue out and gave his tinny a little shake. Mercifully, another drop was forthcoming.

Crozier continued, 'Makes me wonder how we'll ever be able to look our families in the eye without thinking about what we've been reduced to here.'

The ship's surgeon lowered his cup and seemed to remember himself a little. 'Ah, yes, conscience – it will kill us all if we let it, don't you think, sir? This is not a civilised place, so we are merely adapting in order to overcome.'

Crozier marvelled at how medics seemed to always have the ability to take everything, regardless of how terrible they may be, so blithely in their stride. Almost as if everything that was happening around them came with the justification and accuracy of seeing everything through the prism of science – as if all life could be somehow filtered through anecdotal evidence, theory, or experimental findings within the pages of *The Lancet* – rather than the intangible, unnecessarily complex spirit of humanity.

McDonald wiped his mouth on his sleeve as he said, 'Survival is nothing to be ashamed of, sir.'

Crozier noticed an upturned 'smile' of chocolate still at the corners of his surgeon's mouth. He took a sip of his own cocoa to hide his own grin.

Gladman Point

THE SNOW AND ICE BLEW into the teeth of *Terror*'s men as they dragged *Dunder* and *Vixen*. The storm had come on so suddenly and ferociously that they had gone too far to turn back but not far enough to make any significant headway. If they stopped now they would perish. Any attempt at taming tentage would be foolhardy in the seventy-knot wind so their only option was to carry on as the Arctic made them run its vicious gauntlet of hail, snow and wind. It was something of a gargantuan victory every time each man was able to move his left foot past his right foot to take another step.

PO Armitage had earned his turn to come off the traces, so he began pushing from the relative lee of the stern. Blinded by both the storm and their own fatigue, the men ahead had been in no position to have witnessed Armitage stumble as they pulled onwards. As he fell onto the ice, he felt nothing but relief for a precious moment. Relief from his burning muscles; his heart pounding against his empty ribs and the tunnel vision that comes with utter exhaustion, hunger, cold and fear.

Though it had only been a brief moment of escape, by the time he came to his senses again, the biting cold soon consumed any benefit and made it not worth the sin.

The men may have moved ahead by what must have been a mere fifty or so strides but as Thomas Armitage squinted through his woollen muffler and silk scarf he could barely open his eyes for the strafing sleet. He started to panic and hollered feebly into the wind, 'Pegsie…! Peglar…! Lads…! Don't leave me…!' But the wind kept his cries exclusively to himself. As he stumbled after them like a blind man at the bottom of the sea, he gauged he would still have been going faster than the men ahead of him as they struggled with their own unreasonable burdens. Something wasn't right. A dread filled his empty stomach. Surely if he kept going into the prevailing snow's direction it would just be a matter of time before he caught up with his shipmates? As the cold consumed him his blood retreated to his core, forsaking his arms and legs. Soon the ability to coordinate either drained away from him as he began to chatter and shiver uncontrollably. But then, a miracle! Up ahead he could just about pick out the silhouette of someone else struggling through the swirling white tumult: another straggler just like him trudging ahead but veering from the wind and the course that they had all been following. As Armitage tried to catch up, he stumbled and fell onto a beach partially exposed by the drifts formed by the squall, and as he did so, the straggler fell with him.

He managed to get to his feet but as he raised his arms in despair, he saw the straggler doing exactly the same through the clearing weather – only the straggler's arms and legs grew monstrously elongated so that they seemingly shackled him to the ice with a thousand sprouting chains. The low sun's diffuse rays shone through the ice crystals that raced through the air so that every contour of the steward's hopeless spectre was projected against a morbidly flickering halo of every hue. Armitage knew it was over. He dropped to the beach again and, once more, his spectre fell with him.

To him the sand felt so comforting, so familiar – relief from the bloody, bloody ice. He began to smile to himself and tried to move his stiffening jaw and sing his gentle, resigned protest to the outrage: *And I would love you all the day, Every night would kiss and play…*

From his breast pocket, Armitage pulled out Peglar's little

book that he had swapped for his own – held in trust on the understanding that if anything happened to either of them, they would be able to pass it on to each man's next-of-kin. Clutching it there in his cold, numb fingers he smiled. He tried to read a little of it for comfort but the wind snatched away some of the loose papers. Suddenly feeling utterly spent, he tucked the book back into his pocket as he lay in the sand and sang himself to sleep. … *If with me you'd fondly stray, over the hills and far away.*

Sergeant Tozer could smell it before he could see the black hulk twenty paces ahead. Unslinging his rifle and pulling the butt into his shoulder he held his free hand up to signal a halt. In turn, the men collapsed quietly onto the ice to take full advantage of any rest and shelter from the now abating storm. A moment or two later, the wind carried the report of the sergeant's rifle as if he had fired the thing next to their ears, but the men were too spent even to flinch.

Some of them speculated in whispers about what it was that had just been shot. One of the carpenters, Tom Honey, hoped it was a whale, whilst Peglar prayed it was a nice big cow. Luke Smith, one of the stokers, tried to swallow some tobacco as he said, 'Maybe he shot another Eskie?'

Lozzer was trying to rub some life back into his legs. 'Nah, bet it's another bleedin' bird… a really, really fackin' tiny one.'

Up ahead, Crozier saw the sergeant hurriedly shuffle into the whiteness before hunching himself in the snow for some sort of protection against the weather as he quickly reloaded. Moments later he took another shot. It seemed like an eternity before Crozier could hear Tozer's west-country lilt carried back by the wind: 'Surr!'

The men slipped their traces and trotted stiffly to join the sergeant. As they did so, the weather thinned so that they could see him setting about the hulk of the musk ox with a venge-ance. He'd already opened the old bull's chest to allow the beast's steaming numbles to cool on the ice. As the others joined, they began at once to flense the ox's pelt as if taking off an overcoat before the freezing cold could set in and make it too stiff to remove. In less than six minutes, the men had gutted, skinned and quartered the beast – just as those from the Palaeolithic Age would have done some 40,000 years ago when they too would have encountered the very same species.

As a full-grown adult, the forlorn-looking beast should have weighed anything up to 800 pounds but like everything else during that cruel summer he had been reduced to nothing but skin, fur and bones to weigh in at half his usual size. Regardless, the musk ox represented a great prize indeed and would give the sailors at least another two-week reprieve.

Leaving no doubts as to the origin of its name, the flesh of an old, out-of-condition musk ox was unsavoury to even the Indigenous people of the North, but for Crozier and his men, it had been as if they had just caught a plump, apple-fed Pegasus that could fly them all away from their agony.

All told, they had come seven and a half miles closer to their objective, reaching the lee of the small bay where the sick bull had been trying to die peacefully. The ground rose to around fifty feet to sufficiently act as a parapet against the storm's assault. Keeping the boats' sides to windward and pinning them to the ice, every hand quickly set about getting camp made for the night. The tents, having been unavoidably stowed wet, were now frozen solid. The men set about them with pick helves in order to cajole them into something that could be unfolded and used as a shelter. As the people toiled with canvas, line and pole, Peglar abandoned his part in the drill by tottering around the ice like a lost sheep as he searched for Armitage. Most of the men guessed fairly quickly what might have happened but as they could still barely see little more than a boat's length in front of them, they understood why Crozier couldn't afford to risk sending any men back to look for him.

In the morning they found the figure of Peglar frozen solid outside his tent. He had been hugging his knees and peering over the top of them in vigil. Staring perpetually outwards – after his greatest friend.

Sherman Inlet

FITZJAMES AND HIS MEN HAD fared little better in the storm as they pulled through the inlet. With its steep sides rising to around 150 feet, the inlet had served as a channel to tongue the wind and snow so that the sailors often had to lean forward with their hands on the ice as they pulled and pushed into the gale's fury.

Relief for the spent men finally came once they had progressed past the School of Whales. The Whales were a little islet group of rocks which put one in mind of a pod of whales that had been caught by a freezing blast and become trapped forever at the entrance to the wide expanse of the thirty-five-mile basin. Once on the other side they would have another sixty-five miles of gruelling overland pulling for Lake Franklin, which Fitzjames estimated would take them at least fifteen days at their current rate.

AB Johnson and Marine Hopcraft, who were walking ahead with their rifles, were the first to approach the giant basin. As they did so, they became aware of a colossal presence – as if the ice was complaining or the wind moaning. The two men unslung their weapons and instinctively made ready their weapons as they strode. As they cleared the headland, they could immediately see the cause of their disturbance: thousands of geese had ill-advisedly settled on the ice. Joe sent Hopcraft back for more guns and shortly Pusser Osmer and three others came forward.

On Osmer's orders, they blazed at the ice and when the entire surface seemed to lift like an exploding, honking, wheeling, flapping white blanket being carried away by the wind, they blazed again. Between them, the little impromptu shooting party managed to reload twice before the birds became a distant blur, cackling away into the lard-coloured sky.

They had brought down just nine birds from twenty thousand. Osmer shook his head at the irony of all those geese: their only tangible means of salvation, there for a fleeting moment but now lost to them. Out of range, one of the winged birds flapped about on the ice in circles, and as it did so, a skinny white fox with oddly green marks around her neck appeared from nowhere. She snatched the goose in her muzzle before trotting off with a nonchalance that reminded the men whose home it actually was. Hopcraft took aim but Osmer pushed the marine's barrel to one side, saying, 'She's out of range, Hopcraft. Save your ball.' Osmer felt like weeping at the fox's better fortune.

Douglas Bay

CROZIER'S TWENTY-NINE MEN HAD TAKEN four days to cover the twenty-three miles from McClintock Bay to Douglas Bay. Their various ox cuts had been wrapped carefully in canvas and, over the ensuing days, each bundle had been reduced in size until finally, as the two boat crews emerged onto the beach at Douglas Bay hacking, wheezing and almost crawling on all fours, they had only two ten-pound bundles remaining.

The aim had been to follow the coastline as it ran to the S.E. as far as the mouth of the Back's River but there the bold line of the cartographer's pen frustratingly ran dry once more. The entire coast to their east was unchartered and assumed to be there but Crozier wanted to be certain about how far the coast actually ran. He could see that it trended away to the east, but he couldn't work out how far his people would have to pull. He dared not prolong their agony by proceeding on the rotting ice which by day had developed a layer of water on it that made pulling almost impossible. The look on Tom Blanky's face alone was enough to assure him that his instincts were correct.

Crozier sent Sergeant Tozer ahead with a telescope to fill in the gaps for them. The sergeant, in turn, called for two volunteers who were encouraged with a slightly bolstered allowance of ox for their troubles: ABs Lawrence and Wentzall haltingly raised their hands or, in Wentzall's case, a thumb and two fingers. As the men, once free of their haulers' shackles, set off they almost seemed to pronk away into the distance like newborn bucks.

The temperature began to rise and with it came the ragged flurries of snow. The consequences made pulling conditions brutal as the fresh snow served to add to the thawing of the ice – protecting it from the colder parts of the days. The new snow also served to obscure where the ice had become rotten in places.

Hauling onshore was even more of a challenge as most of the coastline was rocky or jumbled with candle ice.

Staying two chains offshore on the more reliable, thicker ice was the only viable way to pull but it came at the cost of great exposure to the wind. To make matters worse, four men with badly frostbitten feet made their progress frustratingly difficult, so relay posts had to be established to help drag the men across the ice using the ox's thick pelt. As the men waited for each party to return, they froze, so that their stiffening joints made any restarting an agony.

Both sledges now seemed to take it in shifts to break, but the Honey brothers, as carpenter and blacksmith, had been miraculous in their ability to conjure up usefulness from the most improbable materials. Often working as the men rested, they would still pull as every other man did, but their use of everything they had to hand to keep the sledges moving was ingenious – from using wetted skins stretched along the runners that would turn to ice and reduce friction – to small, jury-rigged sails that could be raised in the rare moments that the wind was favourable, and what the Honeys could do with a length of cord or wire often resembled sorcery.

But there was nothing that could help the men as pulling through the thigh-high drifts was like wading through thick, energy-sapping treacle. Not a day passed when at least one man didn't fall through the rotten ice via a snow-hidden pock – only to be dragged back by his harness, shivering, terrified and angry.

But, as the thawing of the ice presented an entirely new set of perils, the men's thoughts were now beginning to brighten at the prospect of getting into the boats again and doing what they did best: sail with the wind filling their sails and water running along their keel. But if the men rejoiced, it meant Crozier had many more decisions to make and a chessboard of strategies to adapt.

Crozier, feeling that they were pushing their luck out on the ice, ordered the men to move to the shore, and the bay they now found themselves in seemed perfect for their needs whilst they waited for Sergeant Tozer's party to return. They piled snow around their tents for extra warmth and, since the ice looked like it was about to thaw, other preparations were made for them to be there for a possible extended stay. Twice a day Blanky and Crozier would look for a change in the ice and then, after their second day there, they found it as the wind chopped round to the north.

The ice began to break up. At first, it growled and moaned with bleak predictability. Then, with the iceblink skies to the N.W.'s horizon, Thomas Blanky, who with his almost soothsayer-like faculty, had wrinkled his nose without saying a word. Overnight, the wind came on from the N.W. as predicted and the ice began to sway with the swell beneath. As it broke up more it began to pile up and tumble onto itself – often sending breaking waves high above the waterline. Sometimes, the ice floated by as if it was on a fast-moving river as it crammed itself further and further into the basin; and when the leads were open and when the wind came on hard, huge bergy bits would crash around like a fleet of floundering ships ramming into each other with a ferocity that often sent sheep-sized boulders of ice sprawling onto the shore. Even on the two glassy days that they had witnessed in their little bay, the ice outside it continued to cascade into the strait from the south before packing itself so tightly a butter knife could barely be slipped between the fragments. The sailors had no choice but to follow the long coastline round to the east in the huge body of water that lay there.

On their third day in the bay, Sergeant Tozer's party returned – staggering with fatigue and hunger but filled with excitement as they delivered their monumental findings: 'Sir… we're on an island!' To the south, the sergeant had been able to spot a 600-foot bluff called Victoria Headland which marked the extent of a blue-tinged mountain range that continued eastwards as far as the eye could see. Tozer also presented his sketches of the positions of huge jumbles of moving ice; it appeared unlikely that they would be able to sail or row anywhere near the inlet of the Back's River. Instead, they would have to sail the treacherous, ice-strewn strait before landing on the Adelaide Peninsula at Point Ogle and proceed overland from there.

Crozier tugged at his beard as he studied his sergeant's sketch map. He then hurriedly began to apply the observations to his chart as if the information might somehow change or disappear. When he was finished, Crozier shook his head as he noticed that there seemed to be no more blanks left for them to fill: the Northwest Passage, all marked up for the first time. The reality dawned on him that the Passage was a chimera. Even in the freakish years when it was clear, it could still be choked up with whatever the next wind, current or change in temperature decided to bring – whether it was floes or bergy bits or, eventually, pancake ice as a precursor to another winter where the whole cycle would begin all over again. To call this a passage was delusional and its reality was a living network of arteries for a constantly shifting barrier of ice in all of its many guises to pass along: the Northwest Barrier.

The news of King William's Island was another revelation to Crozier – particularly when the likes of James Ross in '30 and George Back in '34 had stated so categorically that it was otherwise. They must have come so close and not spotted it, stopping just short for fear of losing precious days in which the ice could cut them off and detain them for another winter of misery. If they had only probed a little deeper – even by thirty or forty miles or so – they could have marked it on their charts and gone on to claim the discovery of the Passage for themselves. But, at the very least, Ross and Back's caution had allowed them both to live to tell the tale – unlike the precarious situation the Franklin expedition had now found themselves in.

Looking at his chart again, Crozier now appreciated that he needed to head S.bE. for a hundred miles if he was to make Back's River. He quickly determined that they should cross the tempestuous Simpson Strait and touch at Point Ogle. On one hand, this twenty-mile-long sandbar served to fend off the ice for them so that they could land, but on the other, it funnelled the ice down the huge expanse of water that was the Chantrey Inlet and rendered it unnavigable by sea. Chantrey was the very inlet they so badly needed to sail down but the ice was hell-bent on denying them that privilege. If it had been clear they could sail or row straight into the mouth of the river in two, maybe three days.

So, their only option was to touch at Point Ogle. If the sea ice ever cleared from Simpson Strait Rear, they could sail the treacherous fifteen-mile run to the point and then follow the shoreline to the mouth of Back's River. Once there it would be the question of an eighty-mile portage to Lake Franklin and, if they were very lucky, they could perhaps thrash out around five miles a day and be drinking tea with Fitzjames and his men within sixteen days, maybe twenty.

If they were to make the crossing, both boats' stores would have to be left on the beach in order to accommodate sixteen sailors in *Vixen* and seventeen in *Dunder*. Otherwise, the alternative was to ferry the men across and make, by Crozier's reckoning, a total of eight journeys to get all hands and stores across: a very grim, uncertain prospect. Either way, they had come far too far to lose men and boats that would sit heavily in a very fickle sea.

Now with this new appreciation of the topography, all the new variables played out in Crozier's mind as the men slept like babies whenever they were laid up or bantered together as they pulled. Sailors, when required to do so, would fly into any peril unquestioningly when even the hardiest of landsmen would scoff and run. But for matelots, their trust in their superiors was unflinching and total; almost blissful in its ignorance and if, on the rare occasion a sailor might wonder aloud about how some seemingly insuperable feat was to be achieved, they would be airily dismissed with 'that be the captain's business.' Their blind faith was every ship's salvation, but for their leader, the burden of their responsibility constantly weighed heavily on his shoulders and for any leader to show even a moment's lack of resolution, it was to betray a secret: that in reality he usually only knew as much as they did. But that was the captain's business.

Sherman Basin

DUE TO ITS HIGH FRESHWATER content, the ice for Fitzjames's party remained consistently solid. This was good for their heading, as they had no break-up to battle with – just the ice to haul across. The men were in relatively good shape too as the geese had returned to the huge basin the next day so they took another ten of their number for the pot. But with the ice remaining steadfast on the basin and the constant barrage from the hunters, it didn't take the birds long to tweak their migratory route by a few hundred miles.

With no more game to be had and with October just a week away, Fitzjames followed the S.E. line of the basin. Crossing a series of ice-suspended rivers and deltas, he and Joe recced each of them upriver for a few miles in order to establish the direction of their source, discounting any that ran anywhere but from the south or east: towards Back's River. The sheer amount of inlets, rivers and streams that led into the basin were baffling – especially in their wintry guise – but just as Fitzjames was beginning to despair, Joe found one more unassuming frozen rill that snaked off in the right direction. Calling a halt, Fitzjames left the men to get a brew on as he and Joe trudged a mile upstream. Soon after, Fitzjames needed to sit down and check his map… close his eyes for a moment and just think about what on earth to do.

Joe had wandered up ahead and disappeared up another branch of the stream. After a time, Fitzjames managed to compose himself again and follow the big American, praying that he hadn't lost his best man. He couldn't find him – had he taken the wrong branch of the stream? His heart started to race, but after he started breaking into a panicky trot, he was greatly relieved to discover Johnson standing on a high point with the telescope extended. As Fitzjames clambered to join him, he could see the decent-sized river snaking ahead into a deep, wide valley trending to the S.E. for at least twenty miles. By his reckoning, he knew that at the river's head lay Lake Franklin and, thereafter, the Back's River.

Douglas Bay

CROZIER AND BLANKY WOULD WALK to the mouth of the bay to study the ice daily. Hardly a word would be exchanged between the two quiet men but their empathy was total. Crozier had known the ice master since his first expedition with Parry's attempt to reach the North Pole. There was no one he trusted more – perhaps not even James Ross.

Looking out across the Simpson Straits, it was incredible how fast the ice had broken up and shifted. Some days the wind would blow from the south, and the narrow point between themselves and Adelaide Peninsula would be choked with jostling brash ice – then, the next day, the wind would veer to the west, and great fields of ice would slowly hove into view.

On Crozier's chart, it may have been marked as Simpson Straits but, to them, it may as well have been called the River Styx. They would have to wait and be damned to cross it, but in case of any let up in the weather or the ice, Crozier had the boats made ready to be launched at a moment's notice. As they waited, men were sent out to hunt or gather anything they could to burn and, as usual, they would mainly return empty-handed until one day a party managed to drag back some firewood in the form of a spanker boom off some old whaler, prompting Sergeant Tozer to holler as the men struggled past with the twenty-foot-long timber, 'Wassat then, lads – North Pole, is it?'

One of them managed to mutter back, 'If it means we get extra scoff, it can be anything you like, Sarn't.'

Whenever the sea state of their bay would allow, one of the boats would be launched and rods dangled over the gunwales – but fish were few and far between, and certainly not enough to sustain twenty-six men. Some seals were spotted on several occasions, but they remained wisely aloof too. When the boats were launched and he could see the men rowing, Crozier was always amazed at how, whilst on land, his sailors were so enfeebled they could barely lift an oar, but when they were in the boats, they could pull like the devil; their technique allowing the boats to surge forward with every perfectly timed stroke drawn cleanly through the water. Every day when they were on the water, they would get as far as the mouth of the bay and hove-to as they could only watch as the ice floes raced before them like speeding carriages on Piccadilly. This was the limit of their icy pale.

On the beach, McDonald had noted on the sick list that scurvy was setting in with a vengeance again. Their allowance had dwindled down to nothing bar the fish they could catch, or what remained of the dead. Four other hands had gone already and eight men were being treated with the last of the laudanum. It seemed as though everything the men did involved waiting: waiting for the ice, waiting for food, waiting for the dying.

McDonald also noted that a third of the men had lost their minds. Some would sit and cry at nothing, whilst others would rant and rave at everything. 'Old Mac', who had once ruled as Britannia, had been reduced to a wraith just half-whistling to himself all day as he stood nervously on the water's edge, rocking from foot to foot; and Cornelius Hickey walked into the sea after stabbing Reuben Male in the heart five times for stealing his grog (despite the fact that the last of the 4,500 gallons of West Indian rum they had left the Thames with had been finished at Erebus Bay). As for Crozier, he had taken to going for long walks and talking at length to various friends and family members. On one such occasion, he found himself promenading idly along the beach with Sophia Cracroft and as she linked his arm, he found himself pulling away a little as he was ashamed of how scraggy he had become. She just laughed and pulled him closer.

'Don't be silly, Frankie! I'll always love you, no matter what shape you're in. But, you know, you're no use to me here. You must come home to me – and bring these poor wretches with you, my love. You must do you all you can to bring them home. Do you promise me, Frankie?'

He found himself nodding as he incanted, 'Yes, yes… I will. I will do all I can, my darling.'

Then, hysterical shouting from Old Mac diverted Crozier's attention from his apparition of home, back to the colourless reality of their barren prison…

'Monster! Monster!' Old Mac gibbered as he pointed towards the water. Following the direction of the quartermaster's gnarled finger, Crozier could see that a twenty-foot shark had drifted into the bay upside down, her curled pectoral fins lolling around in the current as if languidly applauding her landfall. Some of the men were already running with knives along the beach and into the freezing waves, and in a matter of moments they were dragging her bloated, ragged remains onto the beach. Setting about the corpse with their blades, they had the 400-year-old old gurry shark that had been swimming through the fall of the Byzantine Empire, the rise of the industrial age and the completion of the Great Wall of China reduced to a carcass within minutes.

With the deliverance of the ancient shark, there came a renewed sense of hope. Crozier wanted to give his men one last good feed. He wanted to see the glints back in their eyes and any other signs that could show even just a flicker of their humanity again. And he wanted to see his men energised – perhaps energised enough to slip the boats in the water and row to their friends, whom, he hoped with all his heart, would be waiting for them somewhere on the other side of the water.

Lake Franklin

BETWEEN RIVERS, THE REQUIREMENT HAD been to portage their boats off and on for nineteen miles. Often hip-deep in snow, Fitzjames's men shuttled their depots back and forth all day – only to come back for the boats before doing it all over again, so that for every mile gained going forward there would be the expense of eight miles of jockeying.

To their south, the land rose sharply to around 300 feet. This formed the ranges that held the water before it all soaked through and ran to the rivers and lakes that pockmarked the landscape. To their north, they could see nothing but flat, desert-like tundra – along with the constant dark clouds that marked the Chantrey Inlet and the sea beyond. The land between themselves and the sea was largely floodplain and marsh, punctuated by a million kettle lakes so that from above, the area looked like a giant, muddy sponge.

The river at the bottom of their valley both widened and constricted to form random reaches, branches, bends and lakes with Lake Franklin being the last feature before the Great Fish River ran out into the Chantrey. The lakes had been their only relief as they were a relative breeze to sledge across with a welcome absence of ice ridges to have to push and strain and grunt and sweat over.

Eventually they passed the jagged ice and giant boulders that marked the frigid rapids of Lake Franklin where, at the far side, it was very much hoped they would meet with Crozier and his men.

The thought of this spurred the men on and, as their runners wheezed across the ice, they could often hear unnerving sounds from beneath their feet that jangled their nerves and toyed with their sanity. Someone swore they could hear the sporadic heartbeat of a giant beast and on one occasion Sergeant Tozer had great difficulty convincing everyone to move forward because several of the men had got it into their minds that they could hear ghostly reverberations as if, up ahead, someone was tapping a shilling on a railway track. Even the sound of a sheep's carcass falling off a butcher's hook and clattering onto cobbles was pointed out by a young blacksmith with a vividness that left nothing to their hunger-ravaged imaginations. Their second night on the lake was so still that it brought them an eerie pinging and clunking from somewhere deep below: beguiling whale song one minute, then rude, jarring cracks of a ship's timbers the next. Young Davy Young pulled up closer to Joe and asked with impossibly wide eyes, 'Do you reckon there are whales living under here, Joe?'

Joe smiled. 'I doubt it, kid... if they did, we'd be tripping up over whaling ships, wouldn't we?'

The sounds of lake ice differed greatly from those of sea ice — almost serene compared to the repulsive screeching, howling and whining of a frozen ocean. It was as if one was a beast trying to escape, whilst the other was pleading to be left alone.

Douglas Bay

THEY FILLED THEIR KETTLES WITH the parts of the dead that were best suited for rendering into fat: feet, hands, skin. Using this as fuel, Crozier's people were then able to boil the pissy-smelling shark before they gorged on her for the next two days. For some of the men it was too much too soon so they just fetched her back up again. But, for the majority, surrounded by their brothers, they felt an overwhelming sense of wellbeing and good fortune. They even felt rejuvenated enough to settle some of the bones of their brothers into graves and for those who had managed to keep some of their wits about them they felt sanguine at the prospects of their own bones bleaching next to those of their mates, and for the time being they were genuinely the happiest men barely alive.

The next morning Blanky barged into Crozier's tent. 'Captain, sir! Happen as you'll want to see this…'

As Crozier emerged stiffly from his tent he was greeted with the sight he'd been longing to see for so long: the now familiar jagged barricade across the mouth of the bay had vanished – the ice had been cleared by the keen easterly that was now blasting rain and sleet into his ear.

The boats, having been prepared days earlier with the sledges shipped and the stores lightened considerably, were ready and their few provisions carefully wrapped and stowed. Spare clothing, the second cooker, and anything else that could be considered even the slightest bit luxurious was left in the supernumerary tent well above the waterline.

As Crozier didn't want the fitter men's strokes being put off by the weakest men they were all put in *Dunder* so that they could be towed via a long sounding line by *Vixen*. Just as the boats were being dragged to the water, a worried-looking Dr McDonald palmed his long, red fringe off his forehead as he approached Crozier.

'Sir, um… some of the men don't want to leave – and there are others who just can't.'

'What do you mean, "don't want to leave", Dr McDonald? Do you mean they want to desert?'

'Well, no, sir – what they actually want, sir, is to help.'

'Help?'

Dr McDonald nodded. 'Yes, sir, they want to help you and the others… the able-bodies.'

Crozier dropped his head and studied his dulled sea boot as he muttered, 'I see. Well, they can't, Dr McDonald.'

'Sorry, sir, you mean they can't help?'

'You know exactly what I mean, Dr McDonald: they can't stay.'

'But they think that if they went, they would hold everyone back, sir.'

Crozier shook his head. 'Dr McDonald, belay these thoughts. Please put them out of your mind. We are leaving – all of us, together. Now, is any part of that unclear to you, Doctor?'

Crozier knew that McDonald, as ever, in his flawless logic of triage was absolutely right but as the captain, he found the notion of leaving any man behind appalling. How could he possibly leave any man here, in a savage, barren fiefdom ruled so cruelly, so absolutely, by the climate? But regardless, he appreciated McDonald's sentiments. He knew all too well that the sick were going to be a dreadful encumbrance on the fitter men and that their presence heaped the odds against anyone's survival. As Crozier looked out again to the mouth of the bay he could plainly see that they were at the mercy of the ice that could return at any minute and hold them captive again for as long as it wanted.

McDonald's voice brought Crozier back from his thoughts as if reading Crozier's mind. 'I'm not sure that all of us leaving is a reality anymore, sir. If you take the best men now, at least you will be leaving us with an incredibly kind gesture, sir.'

'Oh, and what would that *gesture* be, Dr McDonald?'

'Hope, sir… you'd be leaving us all with hope.'

Crozier pulled off his cap and mussed what was left of his hair. 'Damn your *hope*, Doctor! It is deeds that get things done – not *hope*… and what do you mean, *us?*'

McDonald looked Crozier, very briefly, in the eye. 'I would obviously have to stay with them, sir.'

'Impossible! Ridiculous notion! Ready your boat, Doctor – underway in ten minutes… Do you understand me?'

'I do, sir… underway in ten minutes.'

Crozier levered his cap back on and turned to walk towards his boat and its crew.

As the men shoved the two boats off into the bay, Crozier looked back and was satisfied to see Dr McDonald, true to his word, consoling the men of *Dunder* – some of whom seemed very reluctant to get in their boat. One by one, they obeyed him like uncertain children. Old Mac, after one last bout of pointing and shouting was tenderly guided onto the boat by a surplus of hands. Crozier, content that all was ready, finally gave the order to stand by oars.

'Give way together!'

Vixen answered well to the men's strokes – despite the additional load of *Dunder* in tow as her crew floundered feebly with their oars. But then, as they approached the mouth of the bay, the load was felt to lighten and Sergeant Tozer as the stroke oarsman looked concerned at what was happening abaft. 'Surr!'

Crozier turned to see that *Dunder's* line had slackened – McDonald had let go the painter. The captain, checking ahead, saw that there was more ice coming in from the south and with it, their only chance of escape would be lost. Looking back again, he could see that *Dunder* was already heading for the beach and, almost in a whisper, he ordered the steersman to keep his heading.

Crozier's tears mingled with the rain as he gave the order to toss oars. As both banks shakily raised the blades of their oars in salute, he had the jib hoisted and let fly in order to pay the highest naval compliment he knew to Dr Sandy McDonald and his people.

Lake Franklin

THE RAIN AND SLEET HAD fallen on Fitzjames's pulling crews for three days before the accident happened. Crossing at the lake's frozen outlet, they had followed Sir George Back's instructions in his 1833–35 narrative of the *Arctic Land Expedition to Find the Mouth of the Great Fish River* to the letter. As they dragged themselves wearily across the frozen lake's outlet, there was clearly something of a frisson among the men as they were just a few miles from the place where they had agreed to meet Crozier. The outlet marked the beginning of the end for George Back's river, and if all went to plan, it would mark the beginning of the end for their journey too.

Marching a hundred yards ahead of his crews, Fitzjames's thoughts were away with the possibility of the Sir John Franklin expedition marching together as one again. Far from out of the woods just yet, at least it felt like they were getting somewhere. Maybe Crozier and his men were already there? Had already caught game or fish for them all to feast upon together? Even the thought of a hot tinny of cocoa made him whimper to himself.

As Fitzjames trudged on, he could hear the grunts and curses of the men behind him as they pulled *Prancer* and *Dasher*. The men were worn ragged, but still, the thought of meeting up again with their brothers buoyed one or two of them into singing another verse of the 'Pully-Hauly Song'. It must have been after quite a few steps before Fitzjames had noticed that the singing had stopped. He turned back to see why the men had gone quiet and they had come to a standstill for some reason. Eager to get off the lake and meet up with Crozier's people, he cursed to himself as he began to stride back towards *Prancer's* crew. 'Jesus wept… what is it now!'

PO Diggle, who was on the lead trace, had called the stop. Joe, a few traces back couldn't see anything. 'What is it, Digger?'

Diggle was now staring at his own feet, crouching as he said with wild staring eyes, 'Dunno – thought I heard something, like…'

One of the men, perhaps drunk on fatigue, started singing again and the usually affable cook screamed, 'Fucking shut up!'

The men were stunned into silence immediately. Then they could all hear it gurgling beneath their feet – hollow clacking of rocks, aerated water, flotsam… all jangled and roaring beneath the ice.

The rotten ice under Diggle's feet gave way. He clawed at the surface briefly before disappearing down the hole. The two tars on the next trace were dragged in after him too. Joe, Young Davy Young and the lads on the next row couldn't get any purchase either so were dragged inextricably towards the hole by their traces. All that the remaining the men and the boat could do was hop and skip as they involuntarily screeched after Diggle. Below, the hysterical PO now found himself suspended just inches above the rushing meltwater as the rest of the men on the trace clung to whatever features of the ice they could grasp, stopping him from being sucked into the seething abyss. *Dasher* went over the edge but miraculously jammed itself in the hole like a toggle, whilst below, Diggle was sucked into the tunnel that was beginning to form Lake Franklin's outlet again. Then one man, clinging on for dear life lost his grip and fell, causing Diggle to disappear further into the tunnel, putting even more strain on all the men's traces. In the midst of all of this turmoil, Joe, who had wrecked his shoulder in the fall, now found himself to be the agonising link between the life of those in the tunnel and the life of the boy on the traces next to him. Some tars from within begged to be pulled out, whilst others begged to be cut loose and let fate take her course.

On the surface, the boat shifted again. *Prancer* and the remaining men whined pitifully along the ice as if a bad dog was being dragged inside for a beating. Osmer and the men pulling on *Dasher* tore themselves out of their harnesses and flew to help. As all hands joined him, they quickly managed to arrest the boat's dreadful progress.

Beneath the ice, Joe cried out in pain as he bore the weight of the three men being sucked into the tunnel on his now shattered shoulder. 'Take my knife, Davy!' Joe motioned towards the knife in his belt. But the boy, horrified at the state of his friend, hesitated. 'Davy! You've got to do this!'

Davy snapped out of his panic and reached over as far as he could stretch. With numb, searching fingers, he grasped the knife. Davy, who looked even smaller with the oversized knife in his hands, hesitated again before Joe calmly nodded his encouragement: 'Cut it, kid!'

Davy, struggling with the knife, hovered it like a sword of Damocles over the trace. 'I can't, Joe… if I do that, I'll lose you!' Davy couldn't resist one last tug at the traces but all he achieved was more cries of pain as Joe's splintered bones stabbed further into his muscle tissue. The four men behind Davy, seeing their salvation in Davy and the knife, were shrieking hysterically at the young lad to cut them loose.

Once more, Joe, still wincing from the pain, tried to smile a little as if to reassure the boy. 'Cut it, son… It'll be all right.'

Davy touched the trace with the razor-like blade. Instantly, Joe and the rest of the men were swept away.

Released, Davy and the other souls were dragged back onto the surface chattering until their jaws blurred – just in time for the ice to shift again and swallow what was left of *Prancer*. Osmer began to weep, 'That's it! That's it! No cook, no provisions and no bloody boat… How in God's name can we go on now?'

Fitzjames was just about to answer when another awful crack rang out from beneath their feet. The purser disappeared into an opening lead. Suddenly everything began to move and quake as the lake ice, weakened by *Prancer*, began to disintegrate. Some men ran for the bank, but it was still some way off as the chasms of more leads began to bar their way as the currents running below broke up the ice. Fragments began to calf, rolling over with their new-found lack of integrity. Those who had jumped or fallen into the freezing water were either crushed by the ice jostling together again, or soon lost consciousness before slipping beneath the seething surface.

Fitzjames managed to keep his balance on a large slab of ice. He spotted Goodsir, who, heavily weighted by his thick, waterlogged coat, was only just able to hurl one arm in front of the other in a desperate effort to swim towards Fitzjames who was holding out his hand for him. By some miracle the two men were able to clasp hands as their icy raft began to move – carrying both men towards the escalating roaring sound of huge monoliths of ice disintegrating against the great boulders that formed the rapids. Peering over his shoulder, Fitzjames could see their progress towards their own fate. He strengthened his grip of Goodsir, but with the added weight of the surgeon and his clothing and the imbalance of their ice raft, he could only hold onto the surgeon as they drifted towards the crystal mist of the rapids.

A serenity came over Goodsir, and Fitzjames could feel the surgeon's grip loosen as he said calmly, 'I, I can't feel anything… I think it'll be fine to let go now, sir.' Fitzjames tried one last time to haul his companion onboard, but it was hopeless. 'I'm so sorry, Goodsir, perhaps we'll meet up at the end of these falls, eh?'

Goodsir smiled as he released his grasp on what remained of his life. As he floated away the last thing the surgeon saw was James Fitzjames get to his feet again and straighten his hat before disappearing over the edge of the rapids. Goodsir, beyond any cold, or hunger, or pain, closed his eyes before disappearing beneath the water that was now flowing back out towards the sea and the Passage.

Simpson Straits, 5 September 1849

LEAVING THE PROTECTION OF THEIR bay, *Vixen* had a short breaking sea that bristled with the jagged teeth of old ice jostling through the currents. Crozier hadn't dared to hoist the main in such a heavily laden boat whilst the ice was ahead of them and the wind was astern. Instead, he counted on his staysail only so that they could react more cautiously in their gibes. With the wind luffing *Vixen's* jib, her sheet was pulled, and the little sail filled. The boat instantly heeled to starboard as she began to run. Taking on an entirely new lease of life, it was as if she was finally freed from her obstinate, lumbering form whilst on a solid surface.

If the sadness of the crew at leaving their people in Douglas Bay was palpable it was swiftly subsumed by a notion of fear and urgency now. The men braced themselves for the shards of ice that now lay ahead of them as it clashed with the waves so that the sea appeared to fizz and boil angrily about them.

The men were soaked through to their skins almost instantly as they used their oars to fend off the chunks of ice that were constantly attempting to batter their craft with each rise and fall of the swell. Crozier, squinting to port, could see the ice choking the sea to the S.W. – along with any chances of their sailing south and into the mouth of the Back's River. With the shocking conditions of the sea and the ice, he took the steering oar himself and sued for the far shore. Over the seven miles of strait he only needed to gybe twice. On their final gybe to starboard they

found themselves running parallel with the long spit of Point
Richardson and the wind served to push the ice up against it so
that they were shielded from the mass of drift ice. As *Vixen* ran
along the leeward shore it was as if the ice had been held back
for them as God had done for Moses and his Israelites and, at
the end, they found a small harbour. Perhaps it was their Ba'al
Zaphon? The place of safety on the other side of their Red Sea
that would lead them to the Promised Land. If not that, then
for Crozier and his people, their landing would mark the start of
another terrible haul along the barren, brutal land once more. It
was a grim prospect, but it was the only one they had.

As the men shivered and cowered low in the boat's thwarts,
Tom Blanky cursed at the spectacle of the ice as it tumbled onto
the beach and piled-up with the enormous pressure from the
south. Finally, and not a moment too soon, the eagle eyes of
the ice master spotted the hidden entrance to a seven-mile-long
inlet. It was protected by an island at its entrance that acted like
a stopper of a bottle. How the hell Blanky spotted that it would
lead to an inlet, Crozier would never know: it was as if his ice
master had a sixth sense for such things.

Port Leopold

INUKSUK: *that which acts in the capacity of a human.* The great ancient inuksuk had stood at Cape Coulman for over 3,000 years. A mere three of those years had passed since Sir John and his men had spotted it whilst they were being sucked down Peel Sound. With fat, chunky blocks for its legs; large, flatter rocks jutting cruciform-like at the shoulders; and huge, improbably counterbalanced chunks of gneiss at the head, the stack of rocks strongly suggested the appearance of a stout, benevolent person waving. Over the millennia for which it had stood, the inuksuk had acted as precisely that for the Netsilik – a comforting sentinel, a sacred monument that marked their home. For any strangers who passed it, they could interpret it as either a welcoming or warning. It all depended on their intentions.

Lieutenant McClintock, Sir James Ross's number two, ordinarily would have marvelled at the ancient cairn, but having just pulled across the ice for nearly 140 miles from *Enterprise* and *Investigator*, he couldn't have cared less.

James Ross, together with his sergeant, had gone ten miles further south to see what lay ahead. Whilst he was away, McClintock and the rest of his men had been tasked with the building of a cairn so big that in the unlikely event of Franklin making any progress through Peel Sound, he would find it impossible to miss. So, using the great rocks of the inuksuk to form a base, McClintock and his men had torn down the pile of 'Eski rubble' and replaced it with their own 'British standard-issue cairn'.

Within it, Ross's people deposited a note that he prayed would shortly be read by their friends:

> *The cylinder which contains this paper was left here by a party detached from Her Majesty's ships Enterprise and Investigator under the command of Captain Sir James C. Ross, Royal Navy, in search of the expedition of Sir John Franklin; and to inform any party that might find it that these ships having wintered at Port Leopold in long 90°W, lat 73°52'N have formed there a depot of provisions for the use of Sir John Franklin's party sufficient for six months; also two very small depots about fifteen miles south of Cape Clarence and twelve miles south of Cape Seppings. The party are now about to return to the ship, which as early as possible in the spring, will push forward to Melville Strait and search the north coast of Barrow Strait; and failing to meet the party they are seeking, will touch at Port Leopold on their way back, and then return to England before the winter shall set in.*
>
> *7th June 1849. James C. Ross. Captain.*

The weather that day was incredibly clear, and Ross could see onwards for what he estimated was another fifty miles or so, but on seeing the rest of Peel Sound so choked with ice to the south, he decided that no one could have possibly made any progress in that direction. So Ross made his current position at Cape Bird his ultimatum and, with bitter disappointment, turned back.

Ross and McClintock's people were back on their ships thirty-eight days later with all twenty-six members needing to be hospitalised. The mainstay of James Ross's searches had been mounted as sledging parties. Per man, their allowance consisted of a pound of biscuit, a pound of meat, a pound of chocolate, half a pint of lemonade and a gill of rum. But despite their comparative banquets, they returned to the ships cold, hungry and sick. In their subsequent reports, Ross's officers would deem their provisions 'insufficient for such labour' even going further to declare that even three times the amount would not suffice. Even the men who remained aboard the ships began to suffer. Three died.

A month later, the same ice that had released *Terror* and *Erebus* that spring had freed *Investigator* and *Enterprise* too.

Despite being provisioned for three years, they nearly ran out of food after only one year and so James Ross had no choice but to call it a day and sail his ships back to London. But before leaving Port Leopold, Ross ordered a house to be built out of his spare timber and spars and left enough provisions for 120 men for six months, including fuel and any other spare necessaries. And high above the waterline he left his fully prepared, fuelled and provisioned steam pinnace – along with a very heavy heart. He had done all he could possibly do to help his dearest friend and the Sir John Franklin expedition. Little did he know, but Ross had managed to get to within 200 miles of what was left of them all. He may as well have been on the moon.

The Cove, Barrow Inlet

AFTER ENTERING BARROW INLET, CROZIER found a cove at the southern end of Point Richardson. It would have been a perfect place to touch were it not for the many hulks of ice that were already mustered like a jagged crystal army defending the cove. Rowing between the ice became futile so the sailors rolled themselves over the gunnels and into the waist-high water so that they could drag *Vixen* through the serried ranks of ice.

Already chattering with cold and exhaustion, they used their oars to lever the ice out of their way and clear a path on the beach. Once clear, the sailors hauled the boat up to the high-water line with what was left of their strength. Every soul, whether through fatigue, cold, fear or regrets for the friends they had left behind, could barely speak.

Crozier, who had shouldered the brunt of the freezing wind was now numb down the entire left side of his body. This made him think that the rest of the men would probably benefit from keeping their blood circulating and their minds distracted, so he had those not engaged in the setting up camp sent off to look for something to eat or burn. With the men put to work, he went forward to see what lay ahead. He clambered up one of the higher hillocks with a fair bit of difficulty, but once at the top, he lensed the rest of inlet which would lead them closer to the mouth of Back's River. On its east bank he saw the high bluffs of Victoria Headland and beyond that he noted even bigger hills trending away towards Repulse Bay. In an attempt to get some circulation going again in his arm he rubbed it vigorously and snarled at the prospect of another night of shivering and worrying about how the hell they were going to make the seventy-five miles or so to Lake Franklin – let alone how they were to proceed to Repulse Bay. Another dark, grey veil of bad weather was coming in again.

By the time he returned to the men, Crozier was quivering with exhaustion. Camp was nearly set up with various cold men shuffling around as they completed their tasks as best they could. At the centre of all the activity, a small fire began to grow as it began to claw at the dampness of its kindling that sailors would randomly add, before sloping off again like children to search for more.

Tugging his mittens off, Crozier rubbed his hands together before producing the oilskin map case from his breast pocket.

Jopson rolled up a small water cask for his captain to sit on. Crozier grunted his appreciation distractedly as he sat down heavily and unfolded his chart. He stared at it without blinking, as if the lines marked on it were about to wriggle and change themselves into something more agreeable to their situation. Without looking up he declared, 'Barrow Inlet…' just as Tom Blanky joined him.

'Beg pardon, sir?'

'This is Barrow Inlet, Tom… George Back named it after John Barrow.'

'Oh, aye, sir? Should I know him, like?'

'No, I suppose not: old feller. Sits behind a desk and collects discoveries.'

'Any good, sir?'

'Eh?'

'His collection, sir – is it any good?'

'Aye, not too shabby – North Pole: magnetic… Antarctica… the source of the Niger and, er… Timbuktu, I think. But do you know what his most prized discovery would have been, Tom?'

Blanky shrugged as he held his hands out to the welcome warmth of the fire.

'Dunno, sir… for us to have got a decent feed out of Diggle?'

Crozier fixed Blanky with his grey, tired eyes. 'Doubt whether the old man would ever be *that* ambitious, Tom.'

Both men returned their gazes to the flames to hide their mirth.

'So, what would Barrow's most prized discovery have been, sir?'

Crozier looked stiffly around him at the bleak expanse of their surroundings. 'This, Tom… us… crossing that strait in that wee boat. We've just completed the life's work of an eighty-year-old civil servant.'

Crozier folded the chart away again. 'So, how does it feel to have conquered the Northwest Passage for Sir John bloody Barrow, Ice Master?'

Blanky smiled to himself as he wiped his eyes with the back of his hand.

'Handsomely rewarding, sir – though, I would have very much liked to have given him the good news myself.'

Sergeant Tozer arrived grunting as he set down a heavy kettle. He came closer to the fire and, as had evidently become the ritual, automatically took his hands out of their mittens to show them to the flames.

'Sir, some of the lads found bits and pieces while they were out on the scrounge.' He swung his thumb over his shoulder towards the kettle that was full of hands and feet. 'Able Seaman Tadman… looking at his tats, like, sir. We brought back everything – such as it is.'

Awful thoughts raced through Crozier's mind. Had Fitzjames's party all landed safely? Why had they left Tadman? He was one of the fitter men on *Erebus* – if he was lost, what hope was there for those who were weaker? Was Fitzjames now heading for Lake Franklin?

The Ice Master interrupted his thoughts as he looked up to the marbled skies. 'Bit of snow coming on, sir.'

Crozier was about to say something, but his head began to swim as the rest of the cold, tired, hungry men shuffled up to the fire like moths hypnotised by the almost viscous orange tongues licking their way around their fuel – fleeting warmth – all that they had left.

Lozzer started to smile to himself. 'Well, lads – it's the end of another thoroughly gripping day, so, with your permission, sir…'

He then made a big show of fishing something out of his inside pocket.

'It's time to splice the main brace, I reckon?'

Using his teeth, he unstoppered a figment of his imagination and spat it onto the fire. He fished an invisible glass from another pocket. Crozier attempted to smile at Lozzer's daftness, but now he felt his face numbing too. At first he put it down to the warmth of the fire. But then, as he rubbed his hands he noticed that his left one had stopped shaking. This would have pleased him had it not felt so strange and tingly. He put his mittens back on and tucked his hands back under their opposing armpits.

Lozzer curled his hand around his imaginary glass and poured himself what looked to be a very large tot of something. He held it to the fire as he squinted to gage its contents before pouring a drop more in so that he was satisfied with the measure. Some of the men looked at each other and shook their heads ruefully. Sergeant Tozer grumbled, 'Oi, Able Seaman Lawrence! What in sweet Mary's name do you think you're doing?' There was a moment or two of uncertainty as the men thought Lozzer was in some sort of trouble. Then the sergeant proffered his own curled hand towards the seaman.

'We ain't watching you drink all that yourself, you jack bastard.'

Lozzer obliged by pouring some of his magic rum for his sergeant. Tozer held it up to his nose and savoured its aroma for a moment or two as he closed his eyes. 'Ah, a drop of Nelson's blood, is it?'

The lads, without missing a beat, immediately proffered all

manner of motley drinking vessels: a stoker was turned away as his glass was dirty, whilst Blanky gave his imaginary vessel a little polish as he winked craftily. 'All right, Lozzer, don't be shy – your mother wasn't.' Then, as everyone was getting ready for the loyal toast, they noticed that Crozier didn't even have a glass. Lozzer shouted his encouragement. 'Come on, sir, you don't want to be left with the sandy dregs, do you?'

Jopson was the first to realise something was wrong and went to assist. Crozier's left arm was stiff and useless – as was his left leg. He tried to say something, but his lips wouldn't part and his eyes blazed wildly in fear. Wentzall laughed and asked how the captain had managed to get such a head start on them before Blanky told him to shut his stupid mouth.

They threw blankets around their captain's shoulders to try and keep him warm. Someone shouted for more wood for the fire only for someone else to say that there wasn't any. Some of the men were so eager to help their captain that they unwound their scarves and mufflers and threw them onto the fire whilst others slid their caps off their heads and tossed them in too. Crozier, with every fibre of his being, managed to slur some words, 'Please, lads – no! Tom, keep them going. You don't need me.' In response, a water keg was smashed and added to the fire.

Blanky looked around the men's faces and could tell what everyone was thinking as their leader jerked and twitched inter-mittently as the clot made its way to his brain. They all knew what apoplexy looked like: and to them, it looked like defeat and liberation all at once. Blanky looked into Crozier's eyes and held his cold, curling, fingers. He smiled with genuine, heartfelt hap-piness as he straightened his captain's cap for him. 'We're staying with you, sir. We've all had enough… isn't that right, lads?' The men roared their answer as if a ship had just appeared on the horizon to liberate them. Tom Blanky stood on a tun and shook his fists as he shouted, 'Burn it all. Burn everything, lads and let's be done with it, eh?'

They were united in what had to be done next. The Honey Brothers set about *Vixen* immediately – kicking out the clinkers from within. The rest of the men ripped out her thwarts, oars, the masts and the sails. Blankets, clothes and furs were thrown onto the fire shortly after. Crozier, unable to either help or stop them, wept silently as he lay within his swaddling of blankets like a helpless, dribbling infant.

As the flames rose, the men's gaunt cheeks flushed with a rare heat that they had done without for far too long. Some even danced. Crozier hugged his blankets tightly as he saw the face of Sophia smiling at him from the other side of the stinging railing of flames – a fleeting illusion of comfort.

So he raised his good, quivering hand in a toast: 'To *us*, brothers… here's not to where we're going… but where we've been.' As the flames danced and crackled around *Vixen*'s carcass, the fire started to spit and hiss as big wet flakes of the new season's snow began to fall. The men returned Crozier's toast. Quietly, proudly, and without any regrets: 'Where we've been.'

Aftermath

Barrow Inlet, Adelaide Peninsula, 29 May 1854

AGLOOKA, MORE OUT OF HABIT than any real purpose, took off his wolf-skin mitten with his teeth, leaving his raw hand free to fumble for his compass. He was also trying to free himself of the urgency to jump to any conclusions – distract himself from all the miserable thoughts that were now beginning to clot in his head. But presently, all he could do was try to have faith in the seemingly indifferent needle of his bloody Kater's compass.

Hindered by the hood of his caribou parka, he flicked it off to let the wind get to the ribbons of his tam o'shanter and long, red whiskers. Aglooka was the name some of the Netsilik people had given Dr John Rae. It meant 'long strides' in their tongue and in John Rae they saw a tall, brusque Kabloona who walked with a sense of urgency wherever he went.

Back in England, the Orcadian with the 'elastic step' was celebrated as one of the finest overland explorers in the world, already mapping thousands of miles of the Arctic coastline for the Empire. Although supremely successful, there were still those at the Admiralty who dismissed his achievements due to his un-British fraternisation with the locals. Nevertheless, the combination of the Scot's legendary stoicism and fastidious cartography made him an indispensable asset. Especially as there were still so many blank spaces that needed to be filled – so much blood mixed with ink in attempting to draw up the Empire's maps and charts. And in so many of those attempts, so many good men had suffered immeasurably there – whether due to poor supplies, inappropriate transport, maps that lied, or, most vitally, their dogged determination not to depend on the wisdom of local 'Arctic Highlanders'.

As Aglooka, Rae had willingly become as close as one could get to being one of *them*: learning their ways to cover great distances quickly and stay alive with relative ease in the harshest, most inhospitable corner of the planet. Truth be told, he felt more at home there with the Inuit as Aglooka than he ever would have been as a Scottish doctor in Queen Victoria's England. There in the High Arctic tundra and polar barrens, life was simple, beautiful and peaceful.

Returning his useless, twitching compass to its pouch and letting his rapidly numbing hand take up sanctuary again within the safety of its mitten, he could see that the squall was now easing. As the weather lifted her swirling white veil, contrasting shapes, shades and contours re-emerged like ghosts returning from some other-worldly jaunt. All around him, the remains of what could only be a wind-torn encampment loomed from out of the whiteness to form a screaming jaw of tattered, canvas teeth. Tents, anchored by their own rings of stone that had, in turn, appeared to have been positioned around an ominous-looking tumulus of drifted snow, gave the overall effect of a canvas henge.

Even with a cursory glance around the camp, it was obvious to see that some attempts had been made to bury the first to go. Judging by the bones they found in the kettles, it dawned on the doctor just how desperate Franklin's men must have been.

After Dr Rae and his party had scraped away at the snow for a while, they began to reveal the charred remains of *Vixen*. As they cleared a wider area around her, they found the bones of more men, around a dozen or so by his reckoning, maybe more. Over the years, the remains had been disturbed, no doubt by various ravenous animals, and as for the kettles, it would be difficult to pin the blame on any animals for what Rae and his companions were now staring at.

It wasn't difficult to recognise the Arctic issue Holland tents and the Navy broad arrows stamped on the cooking utensils. As Dr Rae contemplated the dreadful scene before him, he felt the little boy from the other sledge put his mitten in the palm of his own. Somewhat touched by the tenderness of the moment he looked down at the boy and smiled. The lad didn't look anything like his father – but the port wine birthmark that dominated his right cheek put his heritage beyond doubt.

The sound of footsteps could be heard trotting up behind them… before slowing down as the other man had evidently taken in the dreadful implications of what lay before them. 'I'm so sorry, Corporal,' Dr Rae said, without turning to face his approaching colleague.

Firemark lowered his hood. His face was already streaked with tears. After some time, he said, 'Perhaps it's for the best that they never made it back, sir… Who could ever understand what we went through?' Firemark dropped to his knees and hugged his son as he fought to get the words out. 'That's why they must never know about me, sir.'

Rae looked to windward and his eyes smarted with the cold. 'Aye, you have my word, Corporal.' he said.

Another miserable-looking front was making its way across from the N.W. If Dr Rae's party needed an excuse to leave this awful, wretched place, they now had it. Rae took all the evidence he could carry before setting off for Repulse Bay so that he could begin to try and articulate the horrors that he had found for his report to the Admiralty:

'From the mutilated state of the bodies and the contents of the kettles, it is evident that our wretched Countrymen had been driven to the last dread alternative – cannibalism – as a means of prolonging existence…'

Pelly Bay

RAE HAD DETERMINED THAT THREE more winters had passed since Firemark had joined the Netsilingmiut in Washington Bay. From there they had retreated east where they thought the gulf and the open sea would perhaps give them greater scope for hunting. More of them had fallen as they crossed King William in the cruel, driven snow, but on crossing the sea ice that separated them from Boothia Peninsula they were fortunate enough to encounter just enough ptarmigan there to keep them alive. The corporal's life-taking, lifesaving reach with his long rifle had become a great asset. Eventually crossing the isthmus, they encountered another community who had brought up their dogs in the hope of finding migrating caribou. From there they mounted their qamutiks and returned laden with meat.

They taught the corporal how to sledge with dogs and, in return, he was able to contribute with spoils from his hunting. He found he could often cover as much as a hundred miles a day with their remarkable dogs and would find himself marvelling at how the distance he could comfortably cover was twenty times the amount he was used to whilst hauling.

He was on just such a trip when he came across a party of people from Pelly Bay. They told him that they had been hired as 'Esquimaux assistants' by a Kabloona who had been coming up from Hudson Bay whom they called Aglooka.

Aglooka had been commissioned by the Admiralty to search the west coast of Boothia for Franklin and his men, covering the south as Ross scoured the north. He and his small party had sailed, rowed and pushed their little boats from Repulse Bay, where they found 300 walrus and every other kind of animal possible wallowing on rocks or in the clear, ice-free waters of Hudson Bay. Twenty deer were shot – along with fifty-three brace of ptarmigan, and innumerable salmon and trout caught both in their nets and on their hooks. Up until this point, Dr Rae knew that he was in the much-favoured hunting grounds of the Netsilingmiut, but he had been alarmed by their absence. Finally, having walked and pulled through the cloying snow, Rae's scouts returned with the company of seventeen. They were unusually reluctant to help and were trying to persuade Rae to go away and so misled him as much as possible. He had been puzzled by their behaviour and it only served to pique his interest further. He continued onwards.

Rae saw the *qimmik* approaching and it would have made his jaw drop had he not known how the frigid Arctic air could shatter exposed teeth. His own sledges – of 800-pound boats which had served them so well on the water – were now a dead weight as they sank into the deep snow. But in contrast, the light, nimble dogsled that approached gave the appearance of floating almost magically across the powdery snow. As this strange, almost celestial chariot pulled up, Rae, well-versed in Inuit custom, began beating his chest and hailing in Inuktitut. The driver stepped off his *qimmik* and lowered his hood and saluted. It was Firemark.

'I speak English, sir.'

'Well, I'm Scottish, so I suppose English will have to do.'

As soon as Rae and Firemark approached his village a small crowd gathered to welcome them back and help out with their dogs. Firemark scanned the crowd and eventually, having taken her a little more time to catch up, saw the familiar gyrating, swirling gait of Aguta pushing though the small gathering. As soon as she saw Firemark and their son, she smiled with her wide, white smile. Firemark ran to her and hugged her as tightly as he could. Seeing the boy, his mother pulled down his hood and used her warm palms to rub some warmth back into his fat little cheeks. Rae smiled at the sight of the family and the boy that was an absolute melding of both his parents who were so evidently in love. 'So, Corporal, what have you called the lad?'

Firemark stood up and mussed the boy's hair with pride and said, 'Tiguaak, sir.' Rae's Inuktitut was good, but he wasn't familiar with the name and, sensing the need to translate, the corporal added, 'It means "the adopted child".'

Dr Rae spent two further days with Firemark and his family. At first, he could get very little of the detail from Firemark and, frankly, he wasn't sure that he wanted to. Firemark told nothing of his ship's position and very little of what they did in order to survive, but Rae could see what they must have gone through in Firemark's troubled, constantly welling eyes. The corporal was a man who had known all too well what hell looked like. He knew by dint of the fact that the Scotsman was there with him that his brothers from *Erebus* and *Terror* had not made it – or if they had, it was likely that they would never show themselves to another European again.

Between Rae and Firemark they reiterated that it was best not to mention the corporal or his family when he returned to London. Rae agreed willingly and also decided that it was in no one's interest to press him for any sort of appalling detail. Of course, for the sake of the men's families back home, he thought they did have a right to know the truth and he knew the English Establishment would hate him for it – particularly after they would have to part with a £10,000 reward for a Scotsman's troubles.

As Dr Rae was hurtling back towards Repulse Bay with his Inuit friends, he couldn't help but feel such admiration for these tough, resilient people as their dogs pulled them effortlessly across miles upon miles of ice. Firemark's presence reminded him of how Franklin's people must have fared in contrast by using seamanlike naval techniques: men made to heave at their whale-sized burdens to cover perhaps five miles or so a day if they were lucky. The seemingly impossible was only made possible by the unbreakable spirit and strength of the men hauling. The Royal Navy's insistence on providing a home-from-home, wherever their sailors may find themselves, came with an unbearably heavy burden that would see men of lower ranks dragging everything that was needed for English gentlemen to survive on the ice: from soup, soap and silver spoons – to Bibles, tables and chairs. All to be dragged across the Arctic in sledge-mounted boats weighing tons. Rae thought it ironic how a nation that considered itself the most civilised on earth made its men pull like dogs, whereas a nation they considered savage made dogs pull their men.

Dr Rae's considerable experience made him able to see Kabloonas through the eyes of the Inuit as they watched ridiculous white men clinging to their last vestiges of dignity and culture as they lined up another extension of sovereignty that they felt perfectly entitled to take from those who were already part of the land and the sea.

As for the Inuit, they had been dismissed as savages by Europeans because of their soot-blackened faces and the fact that they were nomads and ate raw fish. This, despite the fact that they had subsisted for millennia in the cruellest environment on Earth and yet, were constantly ready to help any stranger just as willingly as they would their own family. A willingness that even extended to those who arrived in belligerent wooden cities filled with men who were made to pull like dogs.

Before leaving Pelly Bay, Dr Rae purchased all the Western items the Inuit possessed so that he could present it all as unequivocal proof for the Admiralty. These were the items Crozier had gifted to the Washington Bay people: such as monogrammed silver forks, spoons, brass buttons and, most incontrovertibly,

Sir John's gold cross-shaped medal. Out of respect for the dead, Firemark and Rae agreed that they would not admit to going to the last resting place of Franklin's men but would instead say that he found out via 'Esquimaux testimony'. This way he knew that if the news came from them, it would hopefully blur the lines but satisfy the Admiralty enough to stop needlessly sending more men out into the frozen wilds of the Arctic in search of bleaching bones and corroding metal.

Rae had seen all he wanted, including the fact that he'd had to cross an unexpected strait between Boothia and King William's Land. He had shaken his head at the chart he had been following which had been drawn up by the likes of George Back and James Ross and, being 'desirous of being always within rather than of exceeding the limits of truth…' he amended his chart accordingly.

Back's River

NO ONE KNOWS FOR SURE what happened to Fitzjames and his men. A few bones had been found on Montreal Island that had probably been washed up from Lake Franklin and Back's River but there was no evidence of much else. There were reports for years afterwards that some ragged Kabloonas had lived in the woods higher up the Great Fish River, where they reportedly lived on berries, wolves and anything in between. The stories even got as far as the Yellowknives on the Great Slave Lake, who used to frighten their children with tales about the tall white men with sharpened teeth who would eat them if they strayed too far. And throughout the North-Western Territory, any pile of stones that rose higher than a kneecap was torn down by the clamouring hands of those desperate for answers – only to find nothing but schist, gneiss or any other types of metamorphic rock: all common enough to dry the zest of even the most ardent of geologists.

Other than the three men interred on Beechey, the only dated evidence of Franklin's visit had been found in the cairn at Victory Point. The newly promoted Francis McClintock, having searched in vain with James Ross all those years ago, had all his patience and ambition rewarded after being persuaded by Lady Franklin to lead his own expedition to find her husband. One of his young officers, William Hobson, found the note exactly where Crozier's people had left it on 25 April 1848.

Author's Note

TO DATE, OVER FIFTY EXPEDITIONS have been sent out to look for Sir John Franklin and his men, as their pilgrimages, with heads bent, scour thousands of miles of Canada's coastline and waters to pursue a paperchase of relics.

During the middle of the nineteenth century, Admiralty interest in discovery was soon curtailed by the onslaught of the Crimean War. The Victorian extension of the Age of Exploration was properly over. Whether out of disgust, disappointment or boredom, public interest slowly waned too so that subsequent generations of British children grew up to be blissfully unaware of the story of the Sir John Franklin expedition.

But in Canada today, nothing could be further from the truth. The story of Franklin's expedition is alive and well. It has pretty much become lore and is widely accepted by most Canadians as an integral part of their history and their sovereignty of the Canadian Arctic. Taught in schools, (often named after Franklin himself) the tale has even become a cherished part of the Canadian curriculum, and, if pushed or drunk enough, most Canucks can usually be depended on to sing every word of countless ballads and folksongs that 'reach out' for the loss of 'Brave Franklin' or lament poor Lady Jane.

After his own failure to reach out to Franklin and his men, Sir James Clark Ross, one of the finest British explorers ever to set sail, never went to sea again. Instead, he chose to live almost as far away from the ocean as it is possible in England. He purchased an ancient estate in Buckinghamshire and had its park landscaped around a lake with two islands formed in the middle. He called them Erebus and Terror. His note in the cairn at Cape Coulman wouldn't be found by any subsequent searches for another twenty-nine years.

Dr Rae, who with his incredible feats of endurance and leadership – along with his integration with indigenous people was, debatably, the first European to discover the Northwest Passage and live to tell of it. In doing so, he managed to map thousands of miles more than any other man in the Arctic and his record still stands at the time of writing. Rae's achievements would have gained any man who had accomplished even a fraction of what he had a knighthood at the very least, but he evidently forewent that when he delivered the grim news that Sir John's men, members of the Royal Navy, had resorted to cannibalism. The British people, no doubt encouraged by the Admiralty and popular voices such as Charles Dickens', had evidently felt the need to shoot the messenger. His only crime: being right.

As for Sir John Franklin, he was posthumously promoted to Rear Admiral, and Lady Franklin went to great pains (and public expense) to ensure that her husband's efforts have been immortalised in bronze and marble atop many tall plinths around the world. As for Franklin's senior officers, Fitzjames was posthumously promoted to Captain, but, somewhat pointedly, the Admiralty saw fit to let Francis Crozier's rank remain unembellished. And, if there was any remaining ambiguity towards their snubbing of the Ulsterman, in their 1851 commission of a group portrait from Stephen Pearce (*The Arctic Council planning a search for Sir John Franklin*) the likenesses of Franklin, Fitzjames and every man and his dog were sensitively executed for all of posterity to see, but, again, Crozier has been excluded from this painterly backslap. However, not all was lost when it came to commemorating Captain Crozier. The good people of Banbridge put their hands in their pockets and paid for a statue of him in the main square of their lost son's hometown.

The Passage itself would not be traversed for another eighty-one years until Roald Amundsen, the incredibly impressive and innovative Norwegian who had, during the span of a glittering career, twice run circles around mule-like British hubris: the first time in a small herring boat crewed by six men to finally circumnavigate the entire Northwest Passage and the second, to beat the again overly encumbered men under Sir Robert Falcon Scott to the South Pole. For the latter, it is interesting to note that, like Rae, Amundsen also chose to use dogs, rather than men hauling themselves and their burdens of duty to science and the Empire across the ice. It is also interesting to note that the British always preferred to dismiss Amundsen's successes as ungentlemanly because he chose to incorporate his dogs into the planning of his provisions.

Astonishingly, the wrecks of both *Erebus* and *Terror* have now been found. HMS *Erebus* was discovered at the bottom of Wilmot and Crampton Bay on 2 September 2014, whilst HMS *Terror* was found resting at the bottom of her eponymously named bay on 12 September 2016. Both of these incredible discoveries are almost solely down to Canadian and Inuit knowledge, and, having more urgent priorities, the British government quietly gifted *Erebus* and *Terror* to the people of Canada in September 2018 (but with the grubbing legals writing a clause to reserve the rights to any gold that might be found aboard – perhaps in an attempt to recoup some of Frobisher's nuggets in some way?).

As for the Northwest Passage, countries with more proactive military powers now routinely cruise their nuclear submarines silently below the tumult of the ice whilst above it, petrochemical companies prod and probe the area's excellent prospects for oil and gas. As for the Inuit Nations, and indeed the rest of the world, we have little option but to watch all this industry.

In the meantime, the rest of the 'civilised world' burns more and more of those same fossil fuels which, in turn, exponentially exacerbate the problems associated with melting glaciers and sea ice. And though there are still those who deny it, this is to the devastating detriment of our air, our seas, and all the creatures whose lives depend on either. So it appears that we will, in one way or another, eventually conquer the Northwest Passage and the Arctic after all. Though it would seem that any victory there would be entirely pyrrhic.

One thing Franklin's lost expedition could perhaps remind us of is that if there's one thing that is eternally renewable, it is the notion of hope. On 26 September 2019 the new Royal Research Ship *Sir David Attenborough* (complete with its small ancillary boats thoughtfully named *Erebus* and *Terror*) was christened at the Cammell Laird dockyard on the Mersey by their Royal Highnesses the Duke and Duchess of Cambridge. Though it is just the sole replacement for Britain's two survey vessels (the RSS *James Ross* and the RSS *Ernest Shackleton*) its main remit is to monitor the disastrous effects humans are having on our Polar Regions.

But, perhaps more realistically, our hope should no longer rest with big ships bristling with state-of-the-art technology and heroes? Perhaps we should all lay our hopes at the feet of a young woman from Sweden called Greta Thunberg who might finally shame us all into doing something about the richer nations and their unrelenting exploitation of a planet that belongs to us all, equally. And just maybe, as a consequence of listening to voices from unexpected quarters, we will finally be content to leave at least some parts of our beautiful, complex, fragile planet to those who know it best.

A.W., Blackwall, 26 September 2019

Acknowledgements

TO MY FIRST READERS THANK you for not mocking me too badly for my risible first efforts: Barney Wardlaw, Annika Bennett, Tina Clough, Quentin Bennett, David and Kathinka Adams, Pia Laurin, Michael Smith, Greg Henley Price, Rupert Smythe, Richard Dodgeson, Nick McElwee.

My publisher, Toby Hartwell, for giving me my break.

My serene, sleuth-hound editor, Jill Sawyer Phypers.

Paul Belford for proving that you definitely can't judge a book by its excellent cover.

The eagle minds but dove-like benevolence of Karl and Kay Stead.

Margaret Stead – literally, a chip off the old blocks.

Dr Claire Warrior, National Maritime Museum, Greenwich – without your patience and vast knowledge I would have made an utter exhibition of myself.

Dr Anne Keenleyside: a true explorer who worked on a microscopic scale to make a massive difference. Rest in peace.

M.F.D. King for his well-practiced naval vernacular notes (on gash in particular).

Professor Russell A. Potter for his Visions of the North blog – by far the greatest cache for all matters relating to the Sir John Franklin expedition.

Pen Hadow, First to the North Pole, unassisted. His kindness was breathtaking.

Emma Trowell, Stanford's Purveyors of Maps & Travel Guides.

Dr Sarah Evans, Cartographic Collections, Royal Geographic Society.

Dr Katherine Parker, Cartographic Collections, Royal Geographic Society.

Dr Keith Millar, Professor of Medical Psychology, Glasgow University.

Douglas Stenton, Heritage Director, Nunavut.

Mensun Bound, Maritime Archeologist.

Mr Ian Killick, the UK Hydrographic Office.

Ms Frankie Kubicki, Curator, Charles Dickens Museum.

Andrea Tanner, Senior Research Fellow and Archivist, Fortnum & Mason.

Wikipedia – The greatest, most taken for granted start point on earth.

Further Reading

BBC website: https://www.bbc.co.uk/news/av/world-us-canada-49490400

A British Meat Cannery in Moldova, by Constantin Ardeleanu.
https://www.academia.edu/33971164/The_Erebus_the_Terror_and_
the_North_West_Passage_Did_lead_really_poison_Franklins_lost_
expedition?email_work_card=title

Canadian Mysteries: https://www.canadianmysteries.ca/sites/franklin/home/
homeIntro_en.htm

Captain Francis Crozier: The Last Man Standing? Michael Smith (The
Collins Press): https://en-ca.topographic-map.com/

Erebus, the Story of a Ship, Michael Palin, Hutchinson, London

'The Erebus, the Terror and the North-West Passage: Did Lead Really
Poison Franklin's Expedition?' Dr Keith Millar. https://www.academia.
edu/33971164/The_Erebus_the_Terror_and_the_North_West_Passage_
Did_lead_really_poison_Franklins_lost_expedition?email_work_card=title

Russell Potter's Visions of the North: https://visionsnorth.blogspot.com/p/
in-memoriam-william-battersby.html

Royal Museums Greenwich: https://www.rmg.co.uk/
national-maritime-museum

Nautical Charts: http://fishing-app.gpsnauticalcharts.com/